USA TODAY and ⸻ ⸻hor
Janice Lynn has a⸻ ⸻ilt
University and wo⸻ ⸻ily
practice. She lives ⸻ ⸻her
Prince Charming, t⸻ ⸻
Halo and a lot of un⸻ ⸻ bunnies that moved in
after she started her writing career. Readers can visit
Janice via her website at: janicelynn.net.

Sue MacKay lives with her husband in New Zealand's
beautiful Marlborough Sounds, with the water on her
doorstep and the birds and the trees at her back door.
It is the perfect setting to indulge her passions of
entertaining friends by cooking them sumptuous meals,
drinking fabulous wine, going for hill walks or kayaking
around the bay—and, of course, writing stories.

Also by Janice Lynn

A Firefighter in Her Stocking
A Surgeon to Heal Her Heart
Heart Surgeon to Single Dad
Friend, Fling, Forever?
A Nurse to Tame the ER Doc
The Nurse's One Night to Forever

Also by Sue MacKay

The Italian Surgeon's Secret Baby
Redeeming Her Brooding Surgeon
Taking a Chance on the Single Dad
The Nurse's Twin Surprise
A Fling to Steal Her Heart
Reclaiming Her Army Doc Husband

Discover more at millsandboon.co.uk.

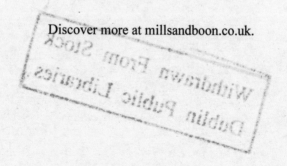

WEEKEND FLING WITH THE SURGEON

JANICE LYNN

THE NURSE'S SECRET

SUE MacKAY

MILLS & BOON

First Published in Great Britain 2020
by Mills & Boon, an imprint of HarperCollins*Publishers*
1 London Bridge Street, London, SE1 9GF

Weekend Fling with the Surgeon © 2020 Janice Lynn

The Nurse's Secret © 2020 Sue MacKay

ISBN: 978-0-263-27981-8

MIX
Paper from
responsible sources
FSC® C007454

This book is produced from independently certified FSC™ paper
to ensure responsible forest management.
For more information visit www.harpercollins.co.uk/green.

Printed and bound in Spain
by CPI, Barcelona

WEEKEND FLING WITH THE SURGEON

JANICE LYNN

MILLS & BOON

To my bestie Kimberly Duffy
for convincing me I needed to visit Seattle.

CHAPTER ONE

DUMPED. HOW COULD Paul have dumped her?

Dr. McKenzie Wilkes stared at the phone message, not quite believing what she was reading.

Not just dumped, but via text. Seriously?

What did it say that Paul had dumped her via a typed message? That she hadn't warranted an in-person kick to the curb?

After more than two years of dating and his promise of undying love, she'd at the minimal deserved a call and explanation, surely? At least Clay, her ex prior to Paul, had broken things off in person rather than through technology.

To be fair, Paul had tried calling the previous evening.

Only she'd not seen the missed call until too late to dial back because she'd been on call at the hospital until six this morning and she'd been swamped. She'd not even seen the notification until long after midnight. Was this what he'd wanted to talk to her about? That he no longer loved her and wanted to end their relationship?

McKenzie bit the inside of her lower lip as she glared at the phone screen. Nope, she was not going to cry. Not going to happen. She had to go inside Seattle Cardiac Clinic for Kids and put on a happy face. How could she not when her patients and their families were dealing with so much more than a broken relationship?

Their sweet little hearts really were broken, physically as well as emotionally. Yet, most of her patients' families had amazing attitudes once the initial shock wore off. Yeah, she had to get her act together and not give in to the urge to go home, crawl into bed, curl into the fetal position and cry until there were no tears left.

Her patients needed her.

McKenzie loved her job as a pediatric cardiologist and advocate for her patients. She often got caught up in work, volunteering to take on extra shifts or canceling plans because one of her patients was in crisis.

She'd thought Paul had understood. Perhaps he hadn't. He worked for an online retailer. His clients didn't die if something went wrong.

McKenzie bit deeper into her lower lip, hoping the physical pain would defer the shattering in her chest.

Paul loved her. Hadn't he told her so hundreds, if not thousands, of times over the past two years? How could he just text that they needed time apart to reevaluate their feelings? That he felt they'd grown apart and had different life views and goals?

Pretty much all her future personal plans were tied up with Paul and the life they'd someday have together. She'd thought they'd be married within the next year or two, would start a family, would grow old together.

Then again, she'd thought the same thing with Clay, hadn't she? He'd ended a seven-year-long relationship that had begun during medical school and ended it when she'd thought they'd be taking that next life step together. Instead, he'd told her he was accepting a residency in Boston and she wasn't invited.

Oh, the pity she'd gotten at home following that breakup. As if dealing with her own inner misery wasn't enough, her mother had just about driven her crazy with date set-ups and poor-you babying.

She'd had to get away. Taking a residency offer in Se-attle had been a godsend in so many ways.

Unfortunately, McKenzie was about to have an emo-tional déjà vu. A bad one. Possibly one worse than the last. In just under a month, she would be traveling to Tennessee for the first time since she'd moved.

For her cousin Reva's wedding with McKenzie as one of the bridesmaids. They'd always planned to be in each other's weddings. McKenzie had even wondered if Paul would use the trip to pop the question himself.

Obviously not.

Why had she hinted to her mother that a proposal might be in her near future? Wasn't that like throwing gasoline on a fire?

Going to Jeremy and Reva's wedding single was not an option. Her mother would feel it her obligation to push every Tom, Dick and Harry at her, all the while offering her looks of pity and conversations about how she'd once again been dumped.

McKenzie's fingers palmed the phone she held as real-ity further sank in. Paul had ended their relationship. He didn't love her anymore, if he ever had.

Sure, he'd never sent her heart into the acrobatics child-hood fairytales had made her think were supposed to hap-pen when she was around her significant other, but she enjoyed his company, their relationship made sense, and she genuinely cared for him. Besides, who believed in those kind of fairy tales, anyway?

Their relationship had been pleasant, comfortable, like warm cocoa on a cold drizzly Seattle night. Paul was de-pendable and made her happy.

She'd loved her cocoa guy. He'd made her feel loved, needed, as if she mattered.

"Hey, Dr. Wilkes," one of her colleagues called, jarring McKenzie to the fact that she was standing frozen to the spot where she'd gotten the text.

"Hi, back," she called, giving a little wave and pretending that her world hadn't just crashed around her as she made her way inside the building and toward her office.

Her hands shook. Thank goodness she was in clinic today and not doing procedures where she had to have super steady hands.

It was more than her hands that shook.

Her entire body trembled.

Paul had dumped her.

Feeling a wave of lightheadedness hit her, McKenzie paused on her way to her office, leaned her forehead against the cold concrete wall, and closed her eyes.

She'd be okay. Even if Paul didn't love her anymore, she'd be fine. Somehow.

Even if she had to go to Reva's wedding and pretend everything was just lovely in her own life despite being single again, she'd survive those looks and conversations behind her back.

Her stomach knotted and sweat burst from her skin.

Oh, how her mother had gone on and on about how she looked forward to meeting Paul, how she couldn't wait to meet the man her daughter loved, planned to marry and start a family with.

Nausea pitched, rising up McKenzie's throat. A fresh wave of clamminess coated her skin.

She was going to throw up.

"Ahem."

At the deep clearing of a throat, McKenzie spun and

almost lost her balance as she came face-to-face with Dr. Ryder Andrews.

Fire spread across her cheeks at the furrowing of his brows.

Ugh. Of all the people in the world to see her on the verge of being physically ill, why, why, why, had it had to be him?

The reality was, Ryder always sent her heart racing, jitters in her veins and a fluttery schoolgirl feel in her stomach. Ugh. She did not like how he made her feel. Even when things had been all flowery and friendly, he'd turned her insides all quivery. Then again, she was a fresh-out-of-residency pediatric cardiologist and he was a highly skilled pediatric heart surgeon.

Of course, she'd been a little in awe. She still was. That was only natural but had always made her feel a tad guilty.

If Paul was warm cocoa that made McKenzie feel warm and cozy inside, Ryder Andrews was 100-proof whiskey, leaving her off balance and fuzzyheaded.

Ryder was not comfortable. He was…concerned.

"Are you okay?"

Tears prickled. Could this day get worse? She just wanted to go home, restart her day. This time, without a dismissive text message and a run-in with her least-friendly coworker.

"Fine," she lied, because no way was she telling Ryder that she'd just been dumped.

He stared at her with his honey-colored eyes, rimmed with thick lashes, that, on the rare occasion their paths crossed, she avoided looking into because she felt as if he saw too much. Like now. Because she'd swear he knew she was lying.

Okay, she had been leaning against the wall and on the

verge of losing her morning's coffee. It didn't take a genius IQ to realize she wasn't on her game.

Of all people to see her moment of weakness, why Ryder?

As brilliant as he was, as great a pediatric cardiothoracic surgeon as he was, McKenzie was positive he didn't like her. She wasn't sure she liked him. When he was around, she felt edgy, as if she was on the verge of saying or doing something stupid. She always seemed to, too. Possibly because she was so self-conscious.

She wasn't one who had to have everyone like her, but Ryder had been friendly in the beginning. He'd smiled and teased her. She'd really liked him. She'd thought they would be good friends. After just a couple of weeks of his being at the hospital, he'd done a complete about-face. He'd never been openly hostile, just went out of his way to avoid her except for when work absolutely demanded they interact.

These days, when their paths did cross, an underlying tension she didn't understand was always present. She couldn't recall having done anything to upset him, had even asked him about it once. He'd denied that anything was wrong but continued to avoid her. She'd started doing the same. Perhaps she was overly sensitive to his attitude change but being around him left her rattled.

Like now.

Looking into those intelligent eyes that probed beneath the surface made her think he already knew she'd been dumped, and he sympathized with Paul for being saddled with her for so long.

"You don't look fine," he unnecessarily pointed out. "Do I need to get you a glass of water or call someone?"

Yep. Her day just kept getting better and better.

"I'll be fine." Which was a more honest answer than her

first one. She would, right? She'd survived her breakup with Clay, and she'd survive Paul ending things.

Because he no longer loved her.

Was she so unlovable that the men in her life always ended up walking away?

"If you'll excuse me," she continued, needing to escape from Ryder's curious gaze before she went full-blown waterworks. "I've got a few things to take care of before I start seeing patients."

Like going to her office and bawling her eyes out.

She walked away before Ryder could say anything more or before she did anything further embarrassing.

Dumped.

Again.

Ugh.

The back of her neck tingling as it often did around Ryder, McKenzie turned, found he stood exactly where she'd left him.

He'd not moved, just stared after her. His brows were drawn together, as if he was deep in thought and not pleasant ones.

Pursing her lips into a tight line, she shot Ryder a look of disgust at his gender, then, head held high, she retreated into her office.

McKenzie closed the door, leaned against it and gave in to the waterworks.

Dr. Ryder Andrews stared at McKenzie's closed office door and felt torn into a thousand directions.

Just walk away, he ordered himself.

She obviously does not want to talk to you about whatever is going on. He sure didn't need to talk to her about whatever was going on.

The less he had to do with Dr. McKenzie Wilkes the better.

Because, when they'd first met, he'd found himself rapidly falling for her. Once he'd discovered she was seriously involved with another man, he'd quickly put a stop to those feelings and avoided her as much as possible to prevent any reoccurrence of his fascination with her.

She'd been upset this morning. Very upset.

When she'd turned from where her head had been pressed against the wall, almost as if for support, her face had been pale, her eyes glassy, her expression almost sallow. As if she were ill.

Walk away, he repeated.

Only, he couldn't not check on her. He was a doctor. She obviously wasn't feeling well. He might do his best to avoid her, but what kind of person ignored when one of his colleagues was sick?

Going to their clinic's break area, he got a glass of water and a pack of crackers. Maybe she hadn't eaten anything that morning and just needed to get a little something in her stomach.

Maybe he was ignoring the obvious, that McKenzie had not been having a hypoglycemic attack in the clinic hallway.

Something more had been wrong than her needing food.

He'd do the right thing. He'd take her the water, make sure she was physically okay, then go back to barely acknowledging her existence.

It's the same as he'd do for any coworker.

Only when he knocked on her closed office door, she didn't respond.

Walk away. Walk away. Walk away.

Why wasn't he walking away and just minding his own business?

"I brought a glass of water and some crackers for you," he told her through the door.

Although he hadn't realized it when they'd met, when he'd looked at her and felt something deep in his gut he'd never felt before, there had always been barriers between them.

No answer.

He knocked again.

Nothing.

He turned to leave. She obviously didn't want to talk to him. He'd done his duty, tried to show common courtesy by getting her a drink and the crackers and she'd not even had the same common courtesy to respond.

What if she hadn't been able to respond?

The question hit him hard, punching him in the gut, and stalling his feet. What if she'd gone into her office and something bad had happened?

She'd looked as if something was really wrong, had been leaning against the wall for support and been pale as a ghost. Had she gone into her office and passed out?

He knocked on the door again. This time brisker and with more urgency.

Nothing.

"McKenzie, open up." Because the more his brain raced, the more he knew he couldn't just walk away without making sure she was all right. He had to know she was okay even if it meant later being accused of overreacting.

Her office door could be locked. If so, he'd break in or get help.

"If you don't answer, I'm coming in to make sure you're not passed out on the floor."

What was Ryder's problem? McKenzie wondered as she lifted her head off her knees and tried to get her blurry eyes to focus on the room around her. He'd barely acknowledged she existed for months and today of all days he felt the need to make sure she wasn't passed out on the floor?

"Go away."

There. She'd answered. He could leave.

"I brought you water and crackers," he repeated.

"You can have them."

Water and crackers weren't going to solve her problems.

"I'm not going away until I make sure you're okay."

Ugh. If he was waiting on her to be okay, he might be there awhile.

She would be okay, she told herself again. Eventually. Hadn't she been after Clay had broken her heart? Sure, it had taken a long time and meeting and falling for Paul, but she had recovered from Clay's blow to her heart.

She had experience in recovering. This time shouldn't take nearly as long to get back on her feet, to make the pain in her chest go away, to not want to burst into tears at every sappy song on the radio.

Yeah, she was a pro at this getting dumped and would be shaking off Paul's wanting time apart. No big deal.

"I'm not leaving, McKenzie. Open up." He knocked on the door again.

Ugh. He was making so much commotion in the hallway he had to be drawing the attention of their colleagues. She could do without everyone there knowing she was Paul's yesterday news.

She stood from where she had been crouched on the floor, wiped her eyes, took a deep breath and told herself she had this. That Ryder was just a man. A gorgeous man who'd probably never been dumped, but, still, just a man.

She didn't bother forcing a smile to her face because she wanted him to know she didn't appreciate his concern. Perhaps she should, but at the moment she just wanted to wallow in her pity a few minutes.

"What is your problem?" she asked as she flung the door open. Okay, so that hadn't been very nice of her, but he was seriously butting into her business and she just wanted to be left alone.

Seeming stunned by her irritation, he held the water and package of crackers out to her. "These are yours."

"Fine. I'll take them." She did just that, taking them from him. "You can go now."

"I… Okay, I will." He studied her face.

McKenzie lifted her chin, almost daring him to say something. Yes, she had been crying. Yes, she knew her eyes were swollen. Yes, it embarrassed her that he was seeing her this way.

"Is there anything I can do?" he surprised her by asking, deflating her false bravado.

"I… No, there's nothing you can do." Nothing anyone could do. Either Paul loved her and wanted to spend the rest of his life with her or he didn't. Embarrassed that Ryder was seeing her when she was so dejected, when she knew her eyes were red rimmed from crying and that she likely had mascara running down her cheeks, she forced a weak smile to her face. "I had a long night on call at the hospital and didn't get much rest. This morning has had a few unexpected things come up." To say the least. "Thank you for the water and crackers."

It was nice of him to get them for her when he hadn't had to. She must have looked really bad for him to have felt the need. If he'd wanted reassurance on that, she doubted she looked any better after her mini-boohoo-fest.

"Truly." She mentally willed the corners of her mouth upward again. "I'll be fine."

With that she closed the door, leaving him on the other side, and her knowing she had to get her act together to make it through the rest of her day.

If Ryder, who didn't even like her, had shown such pity, her friends would be holding an intervention.

She'd wash her face, repair her makeup, and, should anyone ask, she'd blame any remaining puffy redness on her hospital on-call shift. Tonight, in the privacy of her home, she'd give rein to her broken heart.

CHAPTER TWO

A WEEK HAD passed since Paul's decision to rock McKenzie's world. The feeling of being on the verge of constant tears had eased somewhat. Instead, a mounting sense of panic was rapidly taking its place.

In less than two weeks she had to go to Tennessee to be in her cousin's wedding.

Her cousin with the perfect life that her mother went on and on about. That was, when she wasn't going on and on about how much she looked forward to meeting McKenzie's future husband.

Because no matter how many times she'd attempted to tell her mother that she and Paul had broken up, McKenzie hadn't been able to drag the words from the pits of her being.

She didn't want to hear the sorrow, the pity, the disappointment in her mother's voice.

Nor had she been able to tell Reva.

Oh, how she and her cousin had been so close once upon a time. Just for the longest time McKenzie had sensed her cousin's awkwardness with McKenzie's unhappy personal life, her guilt that her own love life seemed to always be so perfect when McKenzie's hadn't. Until McKenzie had started dating Paul, she and Reva had reached the point of barely talking. Only over the past few months as McKenzie had convinced her cousin that, yes, she had her own perfect life in Seattle, had she and her cousin's relationship started getting past the awkwardness that had reared its ugly head when McKenzie had taken the residency in Seattle, despite all her family pushing her to stay in Nashville. Mostly, because they worried about her and wanted to fix her up with blind date after blind date.

No thank you.

Her mother had even gone online trying to find McKenzie dates in Seattle.

Meeting Paul and being able to tell her family to back off had been a godsend. Suddenly the tension between her and her mother had eased, the tension between her and Reva had eased.

Even McKenzie's brother had seemed less worried about her being so far away.

How could she tell them she'd been dumped again?

The pressure to move home would renew, the meddling in her love life—or lack thereof—would start again. You'd think being so far away would keep the damage at a minimum, but McKenzie knew better.

She couldn't go to Tennessee single.

Nor could she cancel out on being in Reva's wedding. If Reva ever found out her reasons for doing so, her cousin's guilt would be tenfold at having the perfect life while poor McKenzie had been dumped yet again.

Getting involved with someone was the last thing McKenzie wanted. Her breakup with Paul was too fresh. Maybe she'd never want to get involved again, but would decide to focus on her career and would dedicate her life to helping heal as many tiny hearts as she could even if she couldn't do a darned thing to repair her emotionally broken one.

McKenzie didn't want to meet anyone, didn't want to

start a new relationship, didn't want the hassle of another heartbreak down the road.

Which explained her rather embarrassing internet search.

She was at the hospital in a small dictation room off the pediatric cardiology unit, waiting on test results on a new admit, and had let desperation take hold during the rare moment of downtime.

She scrolled through her search results for "reputable dating services." Ugh. How could she be so successful in her professional life and so unsuccessful in her personal?

This would cost her a small fortune but would be worth every penny to keep the focus on her cousin's wedding bliss and off McKenzie's latest heartbreak. She'd have to hire someone from Seattle to fly to Tennessee with her, rather than use a Nashville service. She couldn't risk her family bumping into a purchased date and knowing what she'd done. How embarrassing would that be?

Down the road, once they were past Reva's wedding and McKenzie was back in Seattle, she'd tell them the truth.

But to keep everyone happy and her own life a lot less stressful, McKenzie needed a wedding date pronto.

"I'm not sure I want to know."

Oh, flipping pancakes! Ryder!

Face going hot, McKenzie minimized the computer screen and wished she could hide her mortification as easily as she turned to face him.

He leaned against the doorjamb, his brows drawing together, and an odd look on his face. "Did something happen to you and the guy you've been seeing?"

What was he doing there? Okay, so she was at the hospital in the dictation area, but had he forgotten he didn't like her and kept his distance?

Too bad he hadn't avoided her just now.

"You could say that," she admitted, taking a deep breath and not meeting Ryder's intent gaze. Maybe if she didn't look directly at him, he wouldn't see how horrified she was that he'd caught her looking at escort services. Desperate times called for desperate measures.

"I thought you two were long-term." He studied her as if he was trying to solve some great mystery.

McKenzie sighed. He'd already caught her looking at dating agencies, had seen her raccoon-eyed last week. What more could it hurt to admit she'd been dumped? She could hide the truth for only so long before word got out among her coworkers, anyway.

"We were, only now, we're not." She shrugged as if it wasn't a big deal. As if she hadn't spent the last week trying to figure out what it was about her that eventually always drove away the men in her life.

"Good riddance. He wasn't right for you."

McKenzie's jaw dropped at Ryder's unexpected and rather forceful comment. The two men had met only a couple of times and had never had a conversation as far as she knew. Why would Ryder have thought Paul wrong for her?

"Paul is a nice man. I will win him back," she murmured, then blushed when she realized she'd made the claim out loud. Why had she? Yes, she was distraught at the breakup, cared for Paul and had thought they'd marry, but win him back? They'd barely spoken since his devastating text.

"You weren't the one to end the relationship?" Disbelief filled Ryder's voice.

Yeah, right. McKenzie had never been the one to end a relationship. Not ever.

Ryder had straightened from the doorjamb, had moved further into the tiny room.

McKenzie's heart rate sped up and she swallowed as she stared up at him.

She wished she could just disappear. Poof. Be gone.

Ryder gestured to the computer where he'd seen her search results. "Are you planning to try to make him jealous?"

She glanced at the screen, no longer lit with her escort service search. She hadn't, but his thinking that was better than his knowing the truth. "Do you think it would work?"

Maybe if Paul thought she was moving on he'd come to his senses, realize he didn't want to lose her, and they could get back to their normally scheduled lives.

Ryder's dark brow lifted. "Is that really what you're doing? Hiring a date to make your ex jealous?"

Ugh. She sounded pathetic. Would admitting the truth, that she needed a date for her cousin's wedding be more, or less, pathetic?

"It's really none of your business," she reminded him, then blurted out something so crazy she couldn't believe she'd said it. "Unless you'd like to make it your business by being my boyfriend for a weekend?"

Ryder never sought McKenzie out. Never.

But he hadn't been able to get her sad eyes out of his mind no matter how he tried.

Which explained why he'd hung around the hospital despite that he'd just finished checking his last patient consult that evening. Normally, he'd have taken off to make sure his path didn't cross with McKenzie's when he knew she was at the hospital.

Tonight, when he'd spotted her in the dictation room on his way out, he'd been drawn to her, meaning to just walk by and get a glimpse, maybe say hi and assure his mind that she was, indeed, fine as she'd claimed so that maybe, just maybe, her tear-streaked face would quit haunting him.

Not since finding out she was taken had she occupied so much of his mind. Prior to that, he'd thought about her almost constantly.

The past week he'd reverted to doing so again and hadn't liked it.

You knew something had upset her, he reminded himself. Had told himself she'd probably had to give bad news to a family during her hospital shift and that had been what upset her. Lord knew there were times when doing so gutted him enough that he fought tears.

The thought that something personal might have caused her tears had crossed his mind, but he'd dismissed it. Even if McKenzie and her man were having issues, the last thing Ryder wanted was to be a rebound guy.

Been there, done that, had the scars to prove it.

"You want to use me to make your ex jealous?"

"Maybe," she surprised him by admitting. "Are you seeing anyone?"

"No, but—"

"Look," she interrupted. "I'm not hitting on you. Nor do I want to date you," she clarified. Her tone conveyed that she found the idea preposterous. "Not for real. I just need someone to go with me to my cousin's wedding. Someone who won't take things wrong or have any relationship expectations and if Paul gets jealous in the process…" She shrugged.

McKenzie wanted to use him.

"I don't think it fair to invite someone who might get the wrong idea," she continued, perhaps to fill the silence as words failed Ryder.

He liked to think he rolled with the punches, but Mc-

Kenzie asking him to be her pretend boyfriend for a weekend had him speechless.

"I'm not interested in replacing Paul." She took a deep breath. "But going to my cousin's wedding alone isn't a viable option."

The desperation that must have driven her to ask him to go with her kept Ryder from walking away.

Not that he'd say yes.

Her suggestion was ridiculous. Playing McKenzie's pretend boyfriend appealed about as much as the thought of torture.

His gaze narrowed. "When is the wedding?"

"Not this weekend, but next." At his widened eyes, she rushed on, "Short notice, I know."

"You want me to go with you to a wedding next weekend? As a pretend date? No strings attached?"

If not for her serious expression, he'd think she was pranking him.

"Want is such a mild word. I'll gladly repay the favor."

Ryder arched his brow. "You mean when I need someone to pretend to be my girlfriend?"

"Please say yes. I'm desperate." She pointed at the computer screen, reminding him of her escort service search. "Obviously."

"Being a pretend boyfriend for a wedding isn't on my bucket list. Sorry."

Her disappointment had him momentarily reconsidering, then he shook off the notion of saying yes just to ease the desperation in her big green eyes.

Once upon a time he'd have loved the excuse to spend time with her. Fortunately, he'd put that behind him.

Just as he planned to put this conversation behind him.

God, please let Ryder go back to avoiding her, McKenzie

prayed. Because she was absolutely mortified at her blurted plea.

Had aliens taken over her brain? How could she have asked him something so insane?

Desperation really had turned McKenzie's mind to mush.

Ryder didn't even like her, so the very idea of his going with her was ridiculous.

No more ridiculous than hiring an escort service.

She dug her fingertips into her clammy palms.

At least she knew Ryder. He wouldn't get the wrong idea or be some criminal who'd slipped through the company's background checks.

She raked her gaze over his six-foot frame. Chestnut hair, strong nose and cheekbones, honey-colored eyes, dark, thick lashes, full lips framed by deep dimples. Ryder was gorgeous.

She'd thought it the day they met, and that hadn't changed with time.

Of course, Mr. Gorgeous had said no. He avoided her like the plague. Why would he bail her out of an unpleasant situation?

Only why was he still standing in the doorway?

He'd said no. Okay, fine. He should go away and let her get back to her internet search before she was notified regarding her new patient's test results.

"I didn't expect you to say yes." *Shut up, McKenzie.* "I mean, why would you go to Nashville with me?"

He blinked. "You wanted me to go to a wedding with you in Nashville, as in Tennessee?"

Yeah, that was a long way away from Seattle.

Nineteen hundred and seventy-four miles by plane.

Oh, how she knew every long torturous mile of that five-hour flight and how she dreaded every moment.

Just thinking of it had her heart flip-flopping.

Or maybe it was the way Ryder was looking at her that had triggered her cardiac acrobatics.

Perhaps he didn't like flying any more than she did.

"I would have paid your way," she defended, just in case he'd thought she'd meant for him to dig into his own pockets to help her.

He looked insulted and gestured toward her darkened computer screen. "I'm not for hire."

Her face heated. "That's not what I meant. My covering your expenses would only have been fair. You shouldn't have to pay to bail me out of a bad situation."

His expression became pensive. "Is that what this is? A bad situation?"

The worst.

"Spending the weekend with my family will be torture if I go home alone." For so many reasons. "They'll be beside themselves with worry that Paul and I've broken up. The last thing I want is to have everyone focused on my broken heart instead of my cousin's happy day." She sighed. "Plus, I'm in the wedding. I have to go. Yeehaw."

Feeling tears she'd have sworn she didn't have left fill her eyes, McKenzie turned toward the computer. She moved the computer mouse, lighting up the screen again.

"I just want to go home, celebrate my cousin's wedding and enjoy spending time with my family." A tall order, under the best of circumstances and perhaps impossible while trying to forget about her breakup with Paul. "But, no worries, I have a plan."

Not necessarily a great plan, but one that would hopefully suffice to keep her first trip home in eons from being completely ruined.

Maybe it would work.

Were those tears in McKenzie's eyes?

He'd stopped by the dictation room because he'd wanted to assure himself she was okay. Not to cause fresh tears in her beautiful eyes.

Which was what he'd managed to do.

He should have just kept walking, kept with the status quo of going the opposite direction when she was near.

But he hadn't. Now how was he supposed to quit being haunted by memories of her tears when he had another reminder?

When he'd triggered her tears with his prying?

Seeing her upset undid his insides, made him feel as if he'd wronged her by saying no.

McKenzie's breakup with Paul wasn't his problem.

Her trip home wasn't his problem.

So, why were his feet refusing to walk away?

Why was he wondering how difficult it would be to rearrange his hospital and clinic schedules?

"You're sure hiring a date for a weekend away is safe?"

Because he did not like the idea of a hired stranger being with her for an entire weekend.

Without turning to look at him, she shrugged. "It's not something that I've any experience with, but I plan to do my homework prior to finalizing which company and escort I go with."

Ignoring that he still stood there, she pulled out her cell phone and dialed a number from the computer screen.

"Hello? I'd like to make an appointment to possibly hire a date for next weekend." Pause. "Yes, for the entire weekend. If I decide to go with your company, it'll involve being with me around the clock and traveling out-of-state."

Hearing her say the words out loud, hearing the break in her voice, the resigned desperation but determination to proceed with this crazy idea of hers in her tone, left Ryder's insides cold.

He couldn't let her do it.

No way could he walk away and leave her at the mercy of whomever the agency set her up with. What if the guy exploited her vulnerability? Or was a serial killer?

Ryder didn't consider himself any sort of a white knight, but his mother had raised him better than to stand by and watch a woman set herself up to be taken advantage of.

Nope. Not happening.

Walking over to her, heart pounding at what he was about to do, he took the phone from her and disconnected the call.

"Hey!" she fussed, reaching for her phone back. "What did you do that for?"

Hoping he didn't live to regret what he was about to agree to, Ryder handed over her phone. "You're not hiring someone to take you."

Her chin lifted. "Excuse me? I'm a grown woman and can do whatever I choose."

Ryder admired the flash of fire in her green gaze. "Sorry. I should rephrase that."

He took a deep breath, assured himself that he was doing only what any decent person would do, that he had no residual feelings for McKenzie, and that he was completely safe from falling under her spell again because he didn't do rebound relationships.

No getting involved with someone who was already emotionally involved with someone else, whether that was an active relationship, or one recently ended.

Not ever.

He'd go, keep her from possibly risking her safety by hiring a date, pretend to be her boyfriend to keep from spoiling her trip to Tennessee then he'd come home, and they'd go back to ignoring that they even knew each other.

"You don't need to hire anyone—" here went everything "—because I'll go with you to Nashville."

McKenzie couldn't have heard Ryder correctly. Had he really just said he'd go with her?

"I'll need details."

Hands shaking as she gripped the phone, he'd given her back, McKenzie couldn't hide her shock. "You'll go."

"If it means not having to worry about you traveling with a date you know nothing about—" his tone said that she'd been willing to do so was ludicrous "—then, yes, I'll go."

Disbelief filled her.

"Why?" She wasn't sure if she meant why would he worry about her or why would he be willing to go. Both, she decided. She didn't understand his reasons for either.

"Quit looking a gift horse in the mouth, McKenzie." He gave a low laugh, as if this wasn't anything out of the ordinary and she was making a big deal out of nothing. "Just tell me what I need to know so I can get my schedule rearranged."

Because he was going to go with her.

He'd save her face regarding her breakup with Paul, ease any uncertainties her family had regarding her not being happy in Seattle and regarding Reva being the first to marry and McKenzie's suddenly single status. His being there would keep her family from playing pity party and matchmaker.

It could work.

"I'm flying in on Thursday—" saying the word *flying*

had her stomach lurching "—so I can be there for the rehearsal on Friday and whatever else my cousin has planned. If you're sure—" she couldn't believe he was "—then, I'll purchase a ticket for you to fly up on Friday afternoon and to leave after the wedding on Saturday night."

"Is Saturday night when you're coming home?"

She shook her head. "I'm not headed back until Sunday."

Regarding her, Ryder shrugged. "I'll take off a few days, go with you on Thursday, and fly back with you on Sunday evening. I'm overdue a minivacation."

She'd never expected him to say yes, much less rearrange his work hours to accommodate her trip.

"Where will you stay?" She blurted the question without thought, much as she had her initially asking him to go with her. She especially hadn't considered how his next words would turn her insides outward.

"Wherever you are, *girlfriend*."

Girlfriend? McKenzie's eyes widened and her teeth sank into her lower lip. *Hello, crazy heart rhythm*.

Heaven help her.

Her stomach flip-flopped much as it did at the thought of boarding a plane and being trapped inside for hours on end.

His answer shouldn't send her into panic mode.

His intent eyes shouldn't have her heart racing.

But they did. Maybe she hadn't thought this out as well as she should have.

Ryder was an attractive man. Perhaps she shouldn't toy around with dating him, not even when it wasn't real.

"I'm staying at my mom's."

"Fine. I'll stay there. I can sleep on the sofa, if needed." He didn't look concerned. "Unless you think your mother isn't going to like me and will throw me out?"

He was going. Never in a million years would she have thought he'd be who rescued her.

"My mother would like any man who was keeping me from spinsterhood."

It was the truth, but even the pickiest of mothers would leap for joy if their daughter brought home Dr. Ryder Andrews, pediatric cardiothoracic surgeon extraordinaire and gorgeous to boot.

"Spinsterhood?" Ryder's brow arched. "Your breakup with computer guy doesn't catapult you into fear of spinsterhood, surely?"

"You'd think, but try explaining that to my mother."

"If you want me to."

Because he'd be in Tennessee and would meet her mother. Something none of her Seattle friends had ever done, including Paul.

Had she not been so afraid to fly, they'd have gone home to meet her family. Her brother, Mark, had been to Seattle several times and seemed to like Paul well enough. Funny how childhood tragedy could leave one child terrified to board a plane and have another facing his past by becoming a pilot.

"You're really going to Tennessee?" she asked, wanting to make sure she wasn't misinterpreting. "That is what you're saying? You're going to pretend to be my boyfriend for my cousin's wedding weekend, so my family won't start using spinster hashtags when discussing me and I can enjoy my trip home without their pity or matchmaking?"

CHAPTER THREE

Dr. Ryder Andrews didn't think McKenzie had anything to worry about when it came to spinster hashtags.

She was an intelligent, beautiful woman any man would be lucky to spend time with and call his own.

No doubt, when she was ready, she'd soon replace her ex.

But next weekend, she'd be spending with him.

With him playing the role of her pretend boyfriend.

He stared down into the wide green eyes looking up at him, full of hope that he was saying yes. Eyes he'd been avoiding looking into for months because he'd instantly liked McKenzie, been attracted to her, and quickly learned she was taken.

With McKenzie, he'd been tempted to walk down that slippery slope and risk the fallout.

He'd been down that road before, and it hadn't ended well.

That he was tempted to become involved with someone involved with someone else had made him that much more determined to stay away from her as much as possible.

He'd found her eyes enchanting, found looking into them left him unsettled, so he'd stayed away.

Yeah, McKenzie had no worries on growing old alone unless remaining single was what she chose. Not with those killer eyes that flashed with intelligence, lush auburn hair that he'd once thought about running his fingers through more often than he could count when his eyes closed and dreams took over, and a curvy bod that no lab coat or scrubs could conceal. He might have suppressed his fascination with her, but that didn't mean he didn't recognize that McKenzie was a beautiful woman.

If Ryder had to say what he liked best about her, though, his answer would be her intelligence and how she could see outside the box. How, during those first few weeks they'd known each other, their gazes could meet, and he'd know what she was thinking. She'd know what he was thinking. And they'd share a smile. When he'd realized she was off limits, he'd tried to avoid consults on her patients, but when it had been unavoidable, he'd always been impressed.

He'd never met anyone like her, had been disappointed she was already taken, had often had to remind himself to back away and remain aloof so as not to overstep.

He'd asked her once, early on, if she was happy in her relationship. She'd enthusiastically told him she was, that she and Paul were in love and planned to spend the rest of their lives together.

That's when he'd decided to squash his attraction to her.

"I've never been to Nashville," he admitted, knowing she was waiting for him to clarify that he was going. "Maybe we'll get a chance to do a little sightseeing."

"Seriously?" Her forehead scrunched. "You're going with me and will be my pretend boyfriend?"

Rather than see her hire an escort service? Absolutely.

"I'll go with you to your cousin's wedding in Tennessee as your pretend boyfriend."

McKenzie asking Ryder to be her pretend boyfriend had morphed him into the friendly man she'd met initially.

Okay, not quite that friendly, but he at least didn't run in the opposite direction anymore when he spotted her.

Whether at the clinic or at the hospital, he'd smile when their paths crossed, had even stopped to chat when he'd come into the break room and found McKenzie and her nurse there, having coffee while discussing phone calls from patients' parents.

He'd stuck around only long enough to refill his reusable water bottle, but his smile had stuck with her for the remainder of the day.

As long as he was smiling, that meant he hadn't changed his mind, right?

Regardless, his avoidance of her seemed to be a thing of the past.

Such as now with Sawyer Little's case.

McKenzie had been doing her one day a week on call at the hospital when she'd been consulted for the newborn who'd been okay for the first few hours of life but had started having a grayish-blue tinge to her skin—thankfully her mother had noticed and called for the nurse.

The nurse noted a decreased oxygen level and mild dyspnea and contacted the pediatrician. The pediatrician had checked the baby, ordered an oxygen tent and consulted McKenzie as he suspected a cardiac issue in the newborn.

McKenzie was just getting ready to do a crib-side echocardiogram when Ryder had walked into the neonatal cardiac intensive care unit.

Meeting her gaze, his eyes darkened, but then, the corners of his mouth lifted.

Heaven help her, the man had an amazing smile.

That had to be why her breath hitched up a few notches.

An alarm dinged from the next bay over and it took McKenzie a moment to realize it hadn't been a warning bell sounding in her own head.

She really needed to keep Ryder in proper perspective. She was just getting out of her relationship with Paul. The last thing she needed was to confuse Ryder's kindness with the possibility of something more happening between them.

She didn't want anything more to happen between them.

The nurse who was assisting McKenzie with Sawyer glanced up. "That's my other patient. I need to change an intravenous medication bag."

"Go," McKenzie told the woman. Each NICU nurse was assigned two patients, typically. "I'm good and will call out if I need you for anything."

The nurse took off for the next bay. Their unit was designed with an open hallway with each baby in their own semiprivate three-sided bay. The nurse's station was on the opposite side of the hallway and faced the open bays.

Ryder had stopped at the nurses' station and was pulling up a chart on the computer system. He wore dark navy scrubs and she doubted anyone would be surprised if a camera crew walked in and started filming his every move for some medical drama. He looked as if he should be gracing the big screen and tugging on hearts by resolving one medical drama after another.

McKenzie pulled her attention back to the sweet little girl, took warmed gel, tested the temperature on the back of her hand, then applied some to Sawyer's chest.

She ran the conducer over the baby's left ribs, checking the heart chambers, walls, valves and vessels.

She grimaced at what she found.

Sawyer's left ventricle and aorta were too small. There was very little blood flow through the underdeveloped left side of the heart, which explained the faint bluish tinge to the baby's skin despite the oxygen her pediatrician had started.

"You have a minute?" she called over to where Ryder stood fifteen or so feet away.

"Sure." First making a couple of clicks to close out whatever he'd been looking at on the screen, he came into the bay and stood by Sawyer's hospital bed. "Everything okay?"

"Not for this little one. She was born during the night. Mom attempted her first breastfeeding and thought her color looked off. Her pediatrician consulted me. Unfortunately, I'm going to be consulting a pediatric cardiothoracic surgeon and you just happened to be standing nearby."

Ryder glanced down at the almost seven-pound baby with various tubes and monitors attached. McKenzie moved the conducer back over the baby's chest to show Ryder the undersized ventricle and vessel and the lack of blood flow on the left side of Sawyer's heart.

"Hypoplastic left heart syndrome," Ryder said, giving voice to McKenzie's thoughts.

She nodded. "It wasn't picked up on during Mom's ultrasound. She only had one, between four and five months, but the anomaly mustn't have been as prominent as Mom says nothing unusual was mentioned."

McKenzie moved the conducer over to where she could see the ductus arteriosus. The small vessel that connected the aorta to a pulmonary artery was still patent, allowing oxygenated blood to travel from the right ventricle to the aorta. Thank goodness.

If the opening closed, as it normally did within a couple of days, blood wouldn't be able to be pumped to the body.

If blood wasn't being pumped to her body, Sawyer would die.

"Is she on Prostaglandin E1?"

"Not yet," McKenzie answered, knowing they needed to start the substance that the body naturally made to keep the vessel open while in utero, but that the body stopped making at birth. "She'd just started showing symptoms right before I was consulted and you're seeing this as I am."

"Gotcha. I'll get an order for stat Prostaglandin E1 so we can keep that vessel open," Ryder offered, walking over and logging into the bay's computer to type in the order.

The nurse came back into Sawyer's bay and Ryder told her what he'd ordered.

The nurse nodded, then went to carry out the order to start the medication that would, hopefully, prevent Sawyer's ductus arteriosus from closing.

"It's on its way," he assured her, watching as McKenzie still checked the baby with the ultrasound machine.

"Look at the foramen ovale." She pointed out the hole between Sawyer's heart ventricles. "It's patent, but what do you think?"

She let him take the ultrasound conducer so he could run it over the baby's chest to get the views he wanted. He did so, studying what he saw.

"The opening is too small," he yet again verbalized what she'd been thinking.

"She'll need to go to surgery as soon as I can get her on schedule."

"Yes," Ryder agreed. "Her oxygen level is running low enough even with her oxygen mask that you're going to need to put her on a ventilator as well to keep her from getting into trouble."

McKenzie nodded. "Poor little sweetheart has a long road ahead of her."

"Yes, she does, but a road that's smoother than it used to be."

Something in his voice had McKenzie lifting her gaze from the baby to stare at him.

He had an expression she'd never seen on him in the past,

one that hinted his mind had gone somewhere far beyond the pediatric cardiac care unit where they were.

Was he thinking about the research he was involved with?

Ryder belonged to a research team involved in 3D printing of human cardiac tissue research that hoped to eventually be able to use the printed tissue for surgical rebuilding of too-small aortas and to repair other congenital heart anomalies, among other heart repairs.

Not long after they'd met he'd told her the research opportunities had been what led his move to Seattle, that the development of 3D-printed cardiac tissue opened the doorway to great advances and better outcomes of the care they provided their patients, and he'd wanted to be a part of that research.

Was he wishing they were further along so Sawyer could benefit from the research being done at Trevane Technologies?

Or had something else caused the odd look on his face?

"Do you want me to consult one of the other surgeons?"

Seeming to snap out of whatever had momentarily taken hold, he shook his head. "Why would you do that when I'm already familiar with her case?"

"I just thought…" She paused, not sure whether to remind him that prior to a few days before he'd gone out of his way not to share patients with her, that her patients were always assigned to one of his colleagues, but never him. "If you're willing to take on her case, that would be wonderful."

"I'm willing," he assured her as he pulled out his phone and punched in a number. "Oddly enough, I've a Glenn shunt scheduled later this morning on a five-month-old."

McKenzie's brow lifted. Fortunately, they didn't see many hypoplastic left heart syndrome cases, so to diagnose a new one, especially one not picked up on during ultrasound, and Ryder to be doing surgery on another on the same day was indeed a coincidence.

The Glenn shunt was the second phase of the series of surgeries Sawyer would need on her heart. Usually that procedure occurred four to five months after the Norwood, the procedure that would connect the superior vena cava, which brought blood back to the heart from the upper half of the body to the pulmonary arteries to the head and then the lungs to be reoxygenated.

Later, a third surgery called a Fontan procedure would be needed when Sawyer was a toddler. The Fontan would connect her inferior vena cava, which was a big vein that brought the blood from her lower body to her heart, to her pulmonary arteries. Hopefully, at that point, Sawyer would do well and have normal oxygenation of her blood.

Ryder spoke to his nurse practitioner, telling her what he needed so she could handle getting the procedure scheduled. When he finished, he turned back to where McKenzie had told the nurse to gather what she'd need to ventilate the baby.

"I'll make sure Sawyer's Norwood procedure is done prior to our leaving for Nashville. I'll plan to do the surgery but will consult with Dr. Rhea—" another pediatric cardiothoracic surgeon at the hospital "—as he'll be covering my patients while I'm out of town."

"Thank you." She wasn't sure if she meant his taking on Sawyer's case and making sure the baby's surgery happened as soon as possible or if she was thanking him for being willing to shuffle his schedule to go with her to Nashville.

She appreciated both.

"It's my job," he reminded her, seeming almost embarrassed at her gratitude.

It was more than a job. For both of them.

That was one thing they had in common and she could always use as a go-to if they ran out of things to talk about on their trip. They both loved their job, doing what they could to repair tiny hearts, and save lives.

She hoped silence didn't abound because she didn't want to bore Ryder out of his mind.

"Do you want me to go with you to talk to this little one's parents?"

McKenzie's heart squeezed at the thought of what she'd soon be doing. Talking to new parents, explaining what was going on with their precious baby had always been McKenzie's least favorite part of her job.

"Thanks, but I'll tell them what's going on." She wouldn't pass that off on Ryder. She was Sawyer's pediatric cardiologist and needed to meet her mom and dad as they'd be seeing each other many times in the years to come. No doubt Ryder would meet with them soon enough to discuss specifics of the surgery. "Mom was who first picked up on something not being right, so she knows something's up. I'll spend some time explaining the diagnosis and what to expect. You can meet with them later when they've had a bit of time for the reality of what Sawyer faces to sink in."

Because the diagnosis, the stark reality of just how serious the diagnosis was, would put the child's parents into shock—they'd need a little time before they'd be able to process what was happening. It wasn't easy to go from thinking you had a healthy newborn to discovering that without major intervention she'd be dead within a few days.

His gaze met hers. "Do you want to assist?"

Be a part of his team to rebuild Sawyer's aorta? Was that a trick question?

"Absolutely."

"Awesome." His eyes sparkled, conveying he was glad she'd said yes to going into surgery with him.

McKenzie's insides tingled at the way he was looking at her, at the fact he'd just asked her to be a part of his team.

Over the past year, she'd been a part of a few teams he led. Each time, she'd been impressed with his focus and skills as he intricately worked to repair whatever anomaly ailed their tiny patient.

He was such a talented surgeon and always seemed to go above and beyond in the care he provided.

She'd been so excited when he'd first come to work for Seattle Cardiac Clinic for Kids, had hoped to frequently go into surgery with him because of his involvement with several innovative techniques, including his research position. She'd thought about applying for a position on his research team, even.

Those first few weeks, she had been lucky enough to assist with a handful. And what seemed to be only another handful since that time.

Because he'd become almost inaccessible to her, and Dr. Rhea tended to see the majority of her patients.

Maybe she had done something to upset Ryder, she thought for the thousandth time. Whatever, he must have moved past it when she'd asked him to go with her to Nashville. She still couldn't imagine what she'd done, but obviously she had done something as he'd actively avoided her.

Whatever, he wasn't avoiding her anymore and had asked her to assist on Sawyer's Norwood procedure. Plus, he was smiling at her as he hit a button on his phone, making another call to set the wheels into motion to get Sawyer to surgery and to have McKenzie in the operating room with him, along with all the others who would be a part of Sawyer's heart surgery.

Going to surgery with him shouldn't make her so excited, but she'd be lying if she didn't admit that it did. She never wanted any child to be born with defects, but she loved every opportunity to help those who had been.

McKenzie brushed her fingertip gently over the baby's chest and said a quick prayer that everything would go smoothly during this first surgery, and the many more Sawyer would face during her lifetime. Two within her first six months.

It was highly possible that down the road, in addition to all her initial surgeries, that if a heart could be found, Sawyer would need a heart transplant.

If Sawyer survived her first year of life, her odds were good. Unfortunately, the number of babies who didn't survive was still too high.

Ryder's hand covered hers. "You sure you don't want me to go with you?"

Surprised at his touch, at the electricity that shot up her arm, McKenzie met his gaze, marveling at the compassion she saw there, as if he understood all too well the devastation she was about to unleash upon the Littles.

"I… Thank you. That would be wonderful."

Why had Ryder offered to go with her to tell Sawyer's parents their precious baby had hypoplastic left heart syndrome and their lives would never be as they'd thought when they'd arrived at the hospital expecting to bring home a healthy baby?

Typically, by the point he interacted with a baby's parents they already had a good idea of what was going on. The Littles didn't.

But he'd seen the heaviness on McKenzie's heart at the prospect of going to talk to the baby's parents. What was it about her that had him yet again offering to jump to the rescue?

Ryder watched as McKenzie told the baby's upset family why they'd noticed the blue tinge to Sawyer's skin. Seeing how she patiently explained the problems with Sawyer's heart, answering their questions, and even drawing a simple visual of a normal heart and a likeness of Sawyer's, impressed Ryder with her compassion and thoroughness.

It also brought back memories.

Memories that he'd been too young to really understand at the time.

Memories that had changed his life.

Memories he relived every time he went into surgery, knowing his actions and a whole lot of divine intervention determined whether another family would go through what his once had.

"This is Dr. Ryder Andrews. He's a pediatric cardiothoracic surgeon and I consulted with him on your daughter's case. He examined her with me, saw what I saw on the ultrasound of Sawyer's heart. I know this is a lot to take in, but time is of the essence and decisions have to be made.

"I'm going to let him explain his recommendations, and then we'll discuss how you want to proceed."

As McKenzie had, Ryder explained what was needed for Sawyer to survive, he laid out the staggering obstacles that stood in her way, and the different options on tackling those obstacles.

He also gave the less-than-stellar statistics Sawyer faced, even with surgery.

"She'll die if you don't operate? You're sure?"

"Positive. Without a way to get oxygenated blood to her body, she has zero chance of survival. Even with surgery, she might not make it." He referred to the statistics he'd given them with each phase of treatment. "It's up to you on how we proceed. You can choose not to operate if that's what you both want."

"But she'd die!" Sawyer's mother sobbed, triggering her husband to wrap his arms around her.

"With surgery Sawyer faces a lifetime of health challenges, but she does have a good chance of surviving and eventually having a somewhat normal life," McKenzie informed them, reaching over to place her hand on the woman's arm. "The decision is yours. If you need some time alone to discuss it, we can step out for a few minutes."

Sawyer's parents both shook their heads.

"We don't need more time," her father said, hugging his wife tighter.

"Operate," they said simultaneously.

Ryder explained what would happen over the next few days.

Not surprising to him, McKenzie hugged them, assuring she would keep them informed each step along the way.

Ryder shook their hands. As he was getting ready to move away, Sawyer's mother grasped his hand.

Tears ran down her face as her gaze met his. "Please save our baby girl."

Sharp pains stabbed into Ryder's chest. "I'll do my best."

The woman nodded. "Thank you."

"I—I know it's not much, but I do somewhat understand what you're feeling." He took a deep breath. "Over twenty years ago, my sister was born with the same condition Sawyer has." Ryder swallowed back the emotions that hit him when he recalled the turmoil his parents had gone through following Chrissy's birth. The same hell Sawyer's parents faced.

Only Ryder would do everything within his power to make sure Sawyer had a very different outcome from his sister.

"Did she survive?"

Ryder could feel McKenzie's gaze boring into him but didn't look her way. Couldn't look her way.

Wishing he'd kept his past to himself, Ryder kept his focus on the Littles and shook his head. "Technology was very different a quarter of a century ago. Babies with hypoplastic left heart syndrome rarely survived. That isn't the case now. Although there's still a chance Sawyer won't survive, odds are in her favor that she will."

Ryder talked with them for a few more minutes, then he and McKenzie left the obstetrics room Sawyer's mother was still in.

They walked in silence down the hallway to the elevator. Once inside, McKenzie's gaze lifted to his and was full of such emotions it threatened to overflow the elevator car.

"Oh, Ryder," she said with a sigh. "I'm so sorry about your sister."

"Me, too."

"Sometimes our job is so heart wrenching and I wonder why we do this," she mused.

"Not me. I've always known I'd specialize in pediatric cardiology."

Her look was full of empathy. "Because of your sister?"

"Yes," he answered, wishing they weren't having this conversation in an elevator.

Wishing they weren't having this conversation at all.

"Life works in mysterious ways," she murmured. "Your sister's death led you to prevent many more."

She glanced up at him, looked pensive. "Don't take this the wrong way, because I truly am sorry about your sister, but I'm glad you're a pediatric heart surgeon. Very glad."

Ryder nodded. "It's all I've ever wanted to be."

"It's what you were meant to be."

Maybe. He'd never considered any other profession, not even as a small child when friends would say firefighter, police officer, or professional athlete. Ryder had surprised people by saying he was going to be a pediatric cardiothoracic surgeon.

And that's what he'd done.

For Chrissy.

For his parents.

For himself.

A warm hand wrapped around his and gave a gentle squeeze.

Ryder's gaze jerked to McKenzie's green one and what he saw there had him feeling as if the elevator cable had snapped and they were spiraling downward.

Fortunately, he was saved by the elevator coming to a stop and the door sliding open.

He immediately pulled his hand from McKenzie's, resisted the urge to shake away the electricity still zinging up and down his arm.

He needed to be careful.

It would be way too easy to forget she was on the rebound of a broken heart.

CHAPTER FOUR

AN EXHAUSTED RYDER leaned back against the wall in the small doctors' lounge nestled between the men and women's locker rooms. He'd showered, put fresh scrubs on post having been in the operating room with McKenzie and the rest of the multifaceted team that had worked to repair Sawyer's heart over the last seven hours.

He'd been in the operating room for greater than twelve hours on the same procedure in the past when unfortunate complications had arisen, such as bleeding or discovering more anomalies than expected. But typically, an uncomplicated Norwood operation took him around five hours.

Sawyer's had been uncomplicated other than difficulty weaning her off the heart/lung bypass machine. It had taken an extra couple of hours for her little heart to start beating efficiently on its own, but it finally had.

"You okay?"

Ryder's gaze lifted and met McKenzie's green one. Had she come to the lounge looking for him?

He straightened, ran his hand through his hair, then shrugged. "Norwoods are my least favorite surgery to do."

"You and the rest of the team did a great job," she praised, her eyes darkening. "I worried when Sawyer didn't initially respond to being weaned off the life support. I thought we were all going to break out clapping when she finally did."

He'd certainly been clapping in his head. Clapping, jumping for joy, high-fiving his teammates. Sawyer getting off that heart/lung bypass machine as quickly as possible was important.

"You played a huge role in that great job," he reminded her.

Her, the pediatric cardiac anesthesiologist, another pediatric cardiothoracic surgeon, a pediatric intensivist, numerous nurses and surgical technicians—the entire surgical team had done an excellent job.

"Thank you for including me on the team."

Ryder nodded. McKenzie had been on his surgical teams in the past, but she'd never been his first choice of cardiologist. Not that she wasn't excellent at what she did, just that he hadn't wanted the interaction—and his not requesting her in no way hurt her career as Dr. Rhea and another of the pediatric cardiothoracic surgeons preferred her as part of their surgical teams and always requested her first.

Like him, she'd showered and was dressed in fresh scrubs. Her auburn hair was pulled back in a ponytail and a few freckles could be seen across her nose and cheeks. He'd thought it hundreds of times, but McKenzie's ex was a fool.

"You headed home?"

"No, I'm going to check on a few patients, chart, check on Sawyer again, and—" she gave a wry smile "—somewhere during all that, grab something to eat."

"No rest for the wicked," he teased. Teasing her felt good, eased some of the exhaustion cloaking him.

"Speaking of which, you look like you need to crash for a few hours."

He chuckled. Obviously teasing her hadn't eased his

fatigue enough. "Is that a nice way of you telling me I look bad?"

Her cheeks reddened. "That's not what I meant. You just appear tired."

"Like I said, Norwoods aren't my favorite."

"Because of the high mortality rate?"

Not surprised she'd immediately guessed his reason, Ryder nodded. "No doctor wants to go into a procedure that only has an eighty-five percent survival rate."

"Your personal percentage is right at ninety."

He wasn't surprised she knew his stats. All the surgeons at the hospital had above-average percentages and the hospital was proud of that fact. Ryder knew the numbers could be better.

"That's still one out of every ten babies who won't make it to their first birthday." Which gutted him, because that one who didn't make it, that one was someone's Chrissy.

"And nine who will because you reconstructed their heart to where it provides their body with oxygenated blood," McKenzie reminded him, her chin lifting as if to say she'd counter everything he said with something positive. "Sawyer is going to be one of those nine. She's a fighter."

"I hope so." He prayed all his patients survived, even when the odds were stacked against them.

"I'd not really planned to sit down to eat, just to get a yogurt or something since I really do need to check on a few patients." She pinned him with her gaze. "If you planned to head that way, maybe we could walk to the cafeteria together?"

Ryder hesitated. He'd been with McKenzie most of the day, would be with her for an entire weekend. What would walking with her to the cafeteria hurt?

"Sure. I'll walk with you."

"I…" She took a deep breath. "I really appreciate you going with me to Tennessee, Ryder. I know how busy you are and truly if you ever need my help with anything, I've got your back."

Was that why she'd sought him out? To thank him again for agreeing to go with her? He probably shouldn't have for his own peace of mind, but still felt it was the honorable thing to do.

"Knowing I don't have to worry about you getting the wrong idea or having unrealistic expectations from the weekend is such a relief," she rushed on. "That's why I had considered going the hired escort route, so I didn't have the messiness of inviting someone who wouldn't understand that I need the relationship to appear real even though I'm not interested in a real relationship."

Which was good for him to keep in mind. He didn't want a relationship with a woman on the rebound. McKenzie didn't want a real relationship with him. Maybe, despite the fact he found her physically attractive, they could be friends after Tennessee rather than his having to ignore her.

He'd like that, he realized.

Because he liked McKenzie.

Which was exactly why they couldn't be friends after they returned from Tennessee.

What had she done? McKenzie wondered for the thousandth time since she and Ryder had boarded the plane.

She must be crazy to think she could pull this off, to convince her family that she and Paul had broken up, but that she was ecstatic about it as she was now happily dating her colleague, Dr. Ryder Andrews.

No. Big. Deal.

A piece of cake.

Smooshed cake, but cake.

She could do this, could interact with her family all weekend, smile lots, pretend Ryder was the man of her dreams, and that she was over-the-moon happy in their relationship, that she had no remnant feelings for Clay or Paul. Although, she was beginning to wonder what it was about her that made men date her for years, then dump her.

Two men she'd devoted years of her life to and both had ultimately moved on. Was she so unlovable? She hadn't thought so, but if she was the one who kept getting dumped that must mean something.

She'd dated only a few other times. Those had all been short-term relationships and she couldn't recall who had quit talking to whom. Was she batting one hundred per cent dumpage?

Ugh. She should probably do some long, hard thinking on that, figure out what was wrong with her that drove men away. But first things first.

She had to ride in this airplane for nineteen hundred and seventy-four miles from Seattle to Nashville.

Ten million, four hundred and twenty-two thousand, seven-hundred and twenty feet.

Not that she was counting.

Flying terrified her.

They'd not even taken off yet and she was already clamoring to get out of the plane but trying not to let Ryder know he'd gotten himself into more than he'd bargained for.

Would he have still gone had he known she'd probably have multiple panic attacks over flying during their travels?

He'd probably go back to avoiding her the moment they returned to Seattle. Which was sad as she'd really enjoyed the times their paths had crossed the past two weeks.

Taking a deep breath, she told herself she had this, all of this; and in particular, her current situation of being strapped into an airplane seat. She'd flown multiple times in the past and always landed safely, right?

Yes, she'd fought a horrific anxiety monster each time, but she had survived, and she would this flight, too.

Throat tight, she glanced over at where Ryder read something on his phone, hoping that looking at him would distract her from the clawing at her composure.

For now, she'd keep a brave face on and remind herself why she was on the plane.

Yeah, she knew why she was doing this crazy trip to Tennessee.

What she couldn't understand was why Ryder had been willing to adjust his already long hours to work patients in ahead of time so he could easily take off a few days to go with her? Had he needed an excuse to take a break from work that badly?

Right up until they'd boarded the plane, she'd expected him to tell her he'd changed his mind. Why hadn't he?

Had boredom been his reason for saying yes? Perhaps he felt sorry for his dateless colleague and was making her his charity case for the year? Or maybe he'd once had a wedding to go to during a downtime in his life and could relate to how she felt—dumped, dateless and desperate.

Ha. As if.

The man was the department heartthrob and had probably never had a dating downtime his whole life, much less been dumped and desperate.

"Why are you doing this?"

He glanced up from the phone screen. "Reading an article about two-photon polymerization? Because I'm interested in how this technique is being used to achieve scaffolding in 3D printing of human tissue."

McKenzie blinked. That's what he was reading? Not that she was surprised. If ever there had existed a sexy brainiac, Ryder would fit that bill. The looks of a Greek god. A brain that rivaled the nerdiest nerd. She'd always recognized that he was the ultimate package. Only she'd been happy with Paul and hadn't really ever thought about Ryder as anything more than a colleague who'd gone from friendly to avoidance.

Sitting next to him, she noticed. Just as she'd noticed the women eyeing him while they'd waited to board the plane. They'd all looked at her with envy. Ha. If they only knew.

"Isn't that what you're doing in the lab with the laser?" she asked, hoping he'd talk with her to help distract her from their surroundings.

She didn't know a lot of the intricate details, but exciting things were happening at Trevane Technologies in the field of 3D printing human tissue and Ryder headed the clinical aspect of the research in regard to applying it to congenital cardiac diseases.

"Yes, that's one part of what we're doing in the lab," he admitted, tapping his phone. "The article depicts the research a material science institute is doing and what they've achieved using a similar process to bioprinting. Although what we're doing at Trevane is eons ahead in some aspects, their speeds for laying down tissue far exceed anything we've achieved."

"Faster isn't always better," she mused, glancing out the window, then wishing she hadn't. The last of the luggage had been loaded and they'd soon be preparing for takeoff.

"In this case, faster is better. Keeping the printed cells alive is the biggest challenge facing us on creating usable human tissue. If we can successfully print tissue faster, then hopefully we can achieve thicker layers without deoxygenation. Thicker layers means someday being able to 3Dprint vessels, valves, heart chambers or maybe even entire hearts." Passion filled his words. "Can you imagine the implications if we could make a heart for patients needing a transplant rather than having to wait on a donor?"

The thought was mind-boggling, but something that was becoming more and more of a possibility. The research to further develop valve and heart tissue regeneration via bioprinting normally excited her because of what it meant for her patients, for all cardiac patients, and other disease states, too, as the principles carried far greater potential than just with cardiac care.

But, currently, she fought the sensation of panic's hands gripping her throat and squeezing with all their might.

"I'm familiar with Professor Ovikov's work," he continued now that she'd gotten his attention. "We met years ago when 3Dprinting of live tissue was still in its infancy. Brilliant scientist."

Something in the way he said the praise allowed McKenzie to force her blurring gaze away from the window and her mind not to register that the crew had closed the plane door and were moving about the cabin, checking the overhead bins one last time.

And then, they'd take off.

Talk to Ryder. Just carry on a conversation as if nothing monumental was about to happen.

As if she wasn't about to be flung through the air at speeds she was positive humans weren't meant to travel.

"Dr. Ovikov probably says the same about you," she managed to get out despite her mouth deciding to imitate the Sahara. Seriously, how could her tongue be sticking to the roof of her mouth when her palms were sweating like crazy?

Statistics alone said she was safer flying than driving, right? Her brother constantly tossed that out at her when she complained about his chosen career path as a pilot.

"Maybe, but I doubt it," Ryder admitted, staring at her

as if he was starting to pick up on the fact that she wasn't her normal calm, cool, collected self.

Ha. If he only knew how far from the dedicated pediatric cardiologist she felt.

"Our research overlaps and we have similar goals," he continued, his honey-colored eyes darkening as he studied her.

Just keep talking. Distraction was the best way through this. They'd soon be in the air. Then she'd settle down a little. She didn't like any part of flying but takeoffs and landings were always the worst. Always.

Ryder probably already regretted agreeing to do this wedding weekend. The last thing she needed was to freak out on him before they were even out of Seattle.

His gaze had narrowed.

Yeah, he was definitely on to her.

She swallowed, fought to keep her tone steady, and forced a smile to her slowly numbing face. "Is that a nice way of saying he's your competition for upcoming grants?"

See, she sounded semi-normal. Her voice had broken only a little.

"She," Ryder corrected, his expression saying he'd caught that tiny vocal glitch. "Dr. Anna Ovikov."

Something in the way he said *she* truly distracted McKenzie from the plane as she wondered just what his relationship had been with said "she."

Professional or something more?

She mentally scolded herself.

Look at her. Getting all curious about a pretend boyfriend.

"That's fine. Go ahead. Read her research. Just don't forget why you're here," she reminded him, digging her fingers into the airplane seat to the point she was surprised her nails didn't break.

"How could I forget," he teased, the corner of his mouth lifting even though his eyes were still dark with concern. "It's not every day I play a coworker's pretend boyfriend."

"Shh," McKenzie scolded, looking around to see if any of the other passengers had heard what he'd said. Across the aisle from him sat a teenaged boy wearing earbuds with his eyes closed. His mother was engrossed in a book. Neither was paying the least bit of attention to her and Ryder. "You can't say such things. You never know who's listening. You have to stay in role at all times this weekend."

His brow lifted. "You're sure just telling your family the truth wouldn't be easier?"

"Positive." For so many reasons. "You don't know my mother."

She would be all aflutter trying to make sure McKenzie was really okay with the wedding, would be devastated that McKenzie had been dumped again, especially right before Reva and Jeremy's wedding. She'd feel obligated to do something, anything, to make McKenzie feel better. Which would make her feel only worse. She didn't want her mother setting her up on blind dates or throwing men at her all weekend.

And then, there was Reva.

Beautiful Reva who was always the belle of the ball but had always felt guilty if McKenzie hadn't been included. Reva always included her. Her cousin would have major guilt at her own happiness if McKenzie was suffering from heartbreak.

Everyone would be worried about her, wanting her to move home so they could help nurse her broken heart. They'd never leave her alone.

She'd just have to prove to them that she was happy, didn't need their interference or pity.

Ryder was that proof.

"But I will know your mother soon."

Which almost made her as nervous as the thought of the plane taking off.

"Yes, you will." Swallowing, she dug her fingertips deeper into the seat as she held Ryder's gaze. "Just make sure you act as if you really are my boyfriend. Please. It's important my family believes you're crazy about me."

If they thought her happy, they wouldn't worry. Not worrying meant not meddling.

He didn't look concerned. "Shouldn't be a problem."

The air in the plane was so thin. Any moment she expected her knuckles to break through the clenched skin of her fingers.

"Because you're certifiable for agreeing to this?"

He grinned. "Something like that."

She was struck again by just how handsome he was. Not that she hadn't always known, just she'd categorized him in her mind to where she'd never thought of him as more than just that—a really hot guy she worked with, who made her uncomfortable with his overabundance of pheromones, and who hadn't liked her.

With his going above and beyond this weekend, with how his smile made things better, she'd never be able to relegate him to two-dimensional again.

He should smile more right now. She needed him to make things better.

She forced herself to take a deep breath, then another. "Truly, I appreciate you doing this."

Even if he'd come only as an excuse to look up an old girlfriend.

"I expect you to return the favor someday."

"By going to a wedding with you as your pretend girlfriend?" Odds were he'd never need her to do any such thing and they both knew it.

"Something like that."

"We've been cleared for takeoff," the captain said over the intercom speaker.

"Oh!" McKenzie gasped and grabbed hold of Ryder's arm. Talking with him, she'd kept that they'd taxied away from the hangar and out onto the airstrip at bay.

They were literally preparing for takeoff.

As in about to leave the ground and zoom through the air as if gravity wasn't a thing to be concerned about.

McKenzie worried about gravity. A lot.

"You okay?"

"Do I look okay?" she bit out, knowing her fingers were digging into his arm but not able to pry them loose. Something about holding onto him made her feel safer.

"Not particularly."

She closed her eyes, knowing any moment the plane was going to start moving again. When it did it wasn't going to slow down for a long, long time.

Five hours. That's all. Just five hours, then she'd be in Nashville and back on the ground.

Help, her mind screamed. Get her off the plane. Pronto. She couldn't do this.

She had to. She'd done it before and landed just fine. She'd do it again. For Reva and the rest of her family.

But, oh, how she wanted to get off the plane.

"McKenzie?"

"Mmm?" she managed, wondering just how thick her throat had swelled because getting air in and out was impossible.

Why couldn't she have just told them all that she couldn't get off work? She hadn't really had to go to Reva's wedding? Her cousin could have gotten a different bridesmaid, could have had her big day without having McKenzie there.

"Open your eyes."

Her mind registered that Ryder had leaned closer, but she didn't do as he'd ordered. Ordered because that's what his words had been, a command.

"McKenzie." His tone was softer, coaxing even, this time. "Open your eyes."

She did so, meeting his gaze, and forcing herself not to look away.

"You're afraid of flying?"

"What gave you that idea?" she ground out between clenched teeth.

He grinned, then surprised her by prying her fingers from their death grip on his arm and lacing their hands. "You forgot to tell me you were afraid of flying."

She hadn't forgotten. She'd just hoped she'd be able to hide her fear. She hadn't flown in over two years and had hoped her phobia wouldn't rear its ugly head to the point she wouldn't be able to control it. Wasn't that what the tablet she'd taken was supposed to help with?

"Too bad I didn't forget to make my flight."

Ryder had the audacity to laugh. "Now, now. You wouldn't want to miss your cousin's wedding."

"Fifty percent of marriages end in divorce," she spouted, thinking her hand would soon be so clammy it would slip right out of his hold. "I should just take my chances that this won't last, and she'll think me brilliant for not wasting my time."

"Such a cynic," Ryder mused, studying her so intently that for a moment his looking at her rivaled her aviophobia.

"A realist." The plane started moving, building momentum as it sped down the runway. Unfortunately, McKenzie's stomach stayed behind. "Oh, God."

"Praying is good."

If McKenzie wasn't sure she was about to die, she'd scold Ryder for making fun of her.

Only her heart was beating as if it thought it had to power the engine to lift the plane off the ground and was doing its best to meet the burgeoning demand.

Five hours.

Five hours she'd be stuck inside this plane thirty or so thousand feet in the air, defying gravity.

Hopefully defying gravity.

She sucked in a breath.

Or more like she tried to suck in a breath, but nothing happened. No air filled her lungs. Just more and more panic taking over as her stomach was lost somewhere on the airstrip.

She couldn't breathe, felt increasing light-headedness.

She was going to die from lack of oxygen on a 747 Jumbo Jet.

Her mind started going hazy as her lungs refused to adjust to accommodate her body's need for oxygen.

"Help," she squeaked out, trying to convey to Ryder that she was a goner.

Not sure what he could do, what anyone could do at this point as they barreled down the runway, she let go of his hand and went for her seatbelt, thinking maybe if she loosened it from where it constricted around her waist, she'd be able to get in a breath.

It didn't make sense that the strap at her waist prevented air from entering her lungs, but she fumbled with the latch, planning to free herself, and do who knew what?

Ryder's hand covered hers before she could work the latch loose.

Still, her insides shook as panic threatened to implode within her.

She couldn't do this.

McKenzie lifted her gaze, planning to tell him as much.

She stared straight into honey-brown eyes that were close, closer than they'd ever been, and they stared back.

Eyes that momentarily stole her breath even further, sparking a new plethora of emotions deep inside her.

They searched hers, seeing everything within her, she was sure, knowing she was wondering what it would feel like to lose herself in those eyes while kissing him.

His lips were even closer. As close as they could possibly be as they covered her own in a kiss.

She should pull back.

She should slap him or do something, right?

Wasn't she supposed to be clamoring for freedom from the plane? For oxygen?

Only oxygen didn't seem so important with Ryder's mouth covering hers, coaxing her to return his kiss as his gaze stayed locked with hers.

She hadn't planned to kiss him, but her lips were doing just that. How could they not when he was so irresistible?

Good grief. She was kissing her pretend boyfriend.

Who she'd thought didn't like her.

He must, though. Otherwise, he wouldn't have agreed to this crazy wedding trip.

Or be kissing her, right?

Whether she wanted to give a response or not, his lips were firm against hers, delighted by her reaction.

McKenzie reacted. Oh, how her insides were reacting to Ryder's mouth on hers.

If she'd ever wondered, which she hadn't, not even in her wildest dreams, now she knew.

Dr. Ryder Andrews was excellent at mouth-to-mouth resuscitation.

CHAPTER FIVE

Ryder had witnessed only a few panic attacks during his lifetime, but he'd seen the alarm in McKenzie's eyes moments before they'd squeezed shut, had watched her frantic movements, and knew he had to do something to defuse the situation.

He hadn't planned on kissing her.

He'd meant to take her hand into his and offer reassurance. Instead, when her lips had started moving toward him, he'd instinctively pressed his lips to them.

Bold, perhaps wrong, but the terror on her face had disappeared almost instantly, replaced with surprise. Any moment he expected a new wave of panic to fill her eyes when she registered that they were kissing.

Panic was filling him that they were kissing.

Because his automatic reaction of wanting to soothe her, to stop her anxiety, might destroy everything.

Fortunately, the fear didn't return in those gorgeous green eyes.

Instead, her gaze darkened with curiosity. Soft, pliable lips willingly met his.

Which might explain the mounting panic in his own gut.

What was he doing kissing McKenzie?

She was using him for the weekend. He knew upfront that he was nothing more than a means to an end.

Kissing her before they'd taken off the ground might not have been his smoothest move.

Because she was kissing him back and that edgy sensation in his stomach wasn't because the plane had lifted off and was ascending at a rapid rate.

He was miles high in ways that had nothing to do with leaving the ground.

He and McKenzie were kissing.

Holding her gaze, his grip on her hand eased, cupping her face instead as he explored the recesses of her pliant mouth, thrilling as she continued to kiss him.

When he pulled away, he stared into her hazy eyes, and waited to see what she'd say. Would she think he'd taken advantage of her near panic attack?

She inhaled a deep breath and stunned him by saying, "Someone should market that."

Not even close to what he'd expected her to say about their kiss.

She took a quick glance out the window, then nervously back toward him. "I didn't even notice when the plane lifted off the ground. That's amazing. Thank you so much!"

"You're welcome?" Ryder blinked, not quite sure how to take her gratitude. McKenzie kissing him back had sucker punched him, leaving his head in the same state she'd been in as the plane had started taxiing—a panicked mess.

Kissing her was dangerous when he had no intention of having a real relationship with her.

She still looked a little addled, but not as she'd been before.

"But I'm not sure how that particular technique could be marketed without a whole lot of backlash."

She took a few deep breaths, but her color remained good. "You're probably right, but I still say you should go for it."

Which is what he'd done. Gone for it and kissed McKenzie.

"Sorry," he said and meant it. "I shouldn't have done that."

"Are you kidding me?" Her brows veed and she waved away his apology as if the kiss had been no big deal. "You saved me from succumbing to the panic behemoth that grips me at takeoff. Yet something else I owe you for, which I don't like, but thank you for saving me on this, too."

She acted as if the kiss hadn't meant anything.

Ryder wasn't sure if he was grateful or offended that she'd dismissed their kiss so readily.

Offended.

Definitely offended.

His insides were shattered at the electricity their kiss had sparked to life, and she was being flippant about their kiss.

Which was good as he shouldn't have kissed a woman who was vulnerable over having just gotten out of a long-term relationship. You'd think his having mentioned Anna would have been enough to have had him keeping his mouth to himself.

"Now, can you do that for the next five hours until we land?"

Ryder blinked. He couldn't have heard McKenzie correctly.

Before he could respond, she laughed. "I'm kidding, of course, and am mostly just rambling on to distract myself from the fact that we're in the air. I detest flying."

Under different circumstances, Ryder wouldn't have minded kissing her for the next five hours. Circumstances that didn't involve him being the rebound guy.

McKenzie might need a distraction from her fear of flying, but he needed a distraction from their kiss. He'd ponder at how well they fit together and what he was going to do about it later, when he wasn't sitting beside her, when the sweet taste of her lips didn't linger, when she wasn't look-ing at him as if she really did want him to kiss her again.

She settled back into her seat, closed her eyes, and took several deep, measured breaths that told him she wasn't as over her anxiety as she let on.

Either that, or his kiss had shaken her more than she'd said. His guess was on the flight being the cause, though.

"Have you always been afraid to fly, McKenzie?"

She grimaced and didn't open her eyes as she said, "Since I was six."

Six. That was specific, but it wasn't so much her words as how the color had drained from her face that had him curious.

"What happened when you were six?"

Would Ryder understand if McKenzie said she didn't want to talk about the reasons why she hated flying?

Because she never, ever, ever talked about why.

Which made her next words surprise her as much as they must have him.

"My dad died in a plane crash."

Eyes squeezed tightly shut, she felt Ryder's movement in the seat next to her, wasn't surprised when his hand cov-ered hers again. Strong, warm, talented hands that repaired his patients' hearts.

If only he could repair all the broken things about hers.

"I'm sorry, McKenzie."

"Me, too," she whispered, keeping her eyes closed as if that could somehow block out that she'd told him what she'd never told Paul.

Why was that?

She'd planned to marry Paul. Ryder was just a colleague who was pretending to be her boyfriend for a weekend wed-ding. No. Big. Deal.

Only his kiss had been a big deal.

Sure, the flip-flops her belly had done were likely the result of the plane lifting off the ground and nothing to do with his kiss. But Ryder had done what she'd have argued was impossible. He'd distracted her through takeoff.

She might make him a permanent travel accessory.

"What happened?"

She let out a slow breath, trying to push some of her sorrow out along with the air. His was a natural question, just not one she wanted to answer at any time, much less while ascending to thirty thousand feet.

"I suppose now is the worst possible time for me to ask, eh?" He made a noise that was somewhere between a sigh and a groan. "I really am sorry, McKenzie."

"It was a long time ago." Although that day, the aftermath, was heavily imprinted upon her mind to where she could relive the tragedy daily in vivid detail if she'd allow herself to. She didn't.

She certainly wouldn't allow the memories to take hold while on a plane.

"He was a pilot." Hello! Where had that admission come from? What was she doing? She did not want to talk about this.

Opening her eyes, she glanced toward Ryder, saw the empathy and interest in his gaze, and heard herself tell him things she didn't normally say out loud.

Normally?

She never said them out loud.

Never. Ever. Ever. Not to anyone.

"Dad owned a small plane and gave flight lessons." Once upon a time she'd loved to fly. She'd been too young to know any better. "He thought he was invincible." She paused, swallowed the lump in her throat. "He wasn't."

Ryder's thumb brushed over her hand in a soothing caress. "You were six?"

More aware of his touch than she should be, especially given their conversation, she nodded. "My brother was ten."

Ryder's brow lifted. "You have a brother?"

Despite the waterworks threatening to spill from her eyes, she laughed at the surprise in Ryder's voice. "When I claim him."

"You've never mentioned a brother."

"There are a lot of things I've never mentioned to you," she reminded him. "We're work colleagues. Why would I tell you about my personal life?"

Ryder's silence felt heavy between them.

"That may have been true in the past," he finally said. "But now I'm your pretend boyfriend so you should spend the next five hours filling me in on what I need to know for us to pull this off."

"I've been thinking about that," she admitted, her mind racing through all the things she'd dwelled on since he'd agreed to go with her to Tennessee. "We should stick to the truth."

"You've changed your mind about our pretending to date each other?"

Was that excitement she saw on his face? Maybe he really did regret the fiasco he found himself in.

"No, not about that," she shook her head, "although I understand if you want out."

"I don't want out," he assured her. "This is way more interesting than my previous weekend plans."

Which made her wonder just what his weekend plans had been? What had he been willing to give up so that he could go with her to a wedding celebrating people he'd never heard of until a few days ago?

"Good." She sighed her relief. "My family knew I was

dating Paul, that he and I had been together for years. They expected us to eventually marry." They could still marry if they got a second chance. "They'll be shocked we broke up." McKenzie was shocked they'd broken up. "They won't question that you and I are a recent development. As such, we won't be expected to know everything about each other."

"True, but there are some things, as a couple, that we should know," he pointed out.

Curious, she asked, "Such as?"

"What's your favorite color?"

"Blue," she answered without hesitation, frowning at him. "Boring question."

He ignored her jab. "Why blue?"

"Because it's the color of the sky."

"This coming from a girl who's afraid to fly."

"Woman," she corrected. "Woman who is afraid to fly. There's no shame in my fear. Lots of people prefer keeping their feet on the ground and I have a good reason for my dislike."

"Agreed." After a moment, he added, "Green."

She cut her gaze toward him.

"Because it's the color of new beginnings."

As in this weekend? she wondered, then frowned at her thought. This wasn't a new beginning.

"And because it's the color of your eyes."

The color of her… McKenzie's breath caught, and her stomach clenched much as it had when he'd kissed her.

Pulling her hand from his, she frowned. "You don't need to lay it on so thick. I'd prefer believable to syrupy sweet with saccharine drizzled on top."

"Nothing thick about saying I like the color of your eyes when I do like the color of your eyes." He settled back into his seat and pulled up the article he'd been en-grossed in earlier.

She stared at him, not quite sure what to think, espe-cially when he added, "You have great eyes, McKenzie."

McKenzie swiped at something tickling her nose. As she did so, noises penetrated the hazy world of sleep she dwelt in, stirring her to wakefulness.

She opened her eyes, realized she was pressed up against Ryder's strong shoulder, and that there was a drool spot on his shirt.

Her drool.

Yikes.

She sat up, pretended a poise she didn't possess as she got her bearings and wiped her mouth.

She was sitting next to Ryder in a plane speeding to-ward Nashville.

Only there were no clouds out the window.

Just lights and other planes breaking up the darkness.

They'd landed!

She glanced at the time on her fitness watch. Good grief. She'd slept through most of the flight and the landing.

How had that happened?

She was glad she'd slept through it.

Only she winced at the tiny damp spot on Ryder's sleeve.

Realizing he was watching her, she grimaced. "Please tell me I didn't snore."

One corner of his mouth lifted. "Only a little."

She couldn't tell if he was teasing or if she truly had. She didn't suppose it mattered with a pretend boyfriend.

It wasn't as if she was trying to impress him.

Only he was a coworker, quite gorgeous, and thought

she had great eyes, so it wasn't wrong to want to not totally embarrass herself.

She couldn't believe she'd fallen asleep.

Then again, she'd not slept well since prior to her breakup with Paul. Still, never would she have dreamed she could sleep on a plane.

She gave Ryder a look of gratitude. "Thank you."

"For?"

"Making that the best flight I've ever been on."

Having Ryder beside her had to be how she'd relaxed enough to doze off. Which was odd since he didn't relax her. Far from it.

She'd never felt so far out of her comfort zone as when he'd kissed her. Only…

"By boring you to sleep?" His tone was teasing.

"By helping me unwind enough that I could sleep. Big difference."

Seeming to like her answer, he nodded. "You do look calmer."

Wondering if that was his subtle way of telling her that her makeup was mussed and her hair wild, she stretched to pull her bag out from beneath the seat in front of her.

When she'd retrieved her compact, she glanced in the tiny mirror.

Rather than the mess she expected, her mascara had miraculously stayed on her lashes and wasn't all down her cheeks other than faint smudges she quickly wiped away.

Digging in her bag, she found a lipstick tube.

"No need for that," Ryder assured her, watching her. "You look beautiful."

"Thanks." His compliment warmed her insides, but she put her lipstick on anyway. She'd need all the armor she could muster prior to facing her mother and the rest of the crew.

Too bad lipstick didn't come in chainmail.

Who'd have thought Ryder's calm, cool and collected pediatric cardiologist colleague was terrified to fly, albeit, she certainly had good reason?

Or that she'd be nervous as a kitten about seeing her family?

Or maybe it was her family meeting him that had her so on edge?

"Is someone meeting us?"

She shook her head. "My brother offered, but I wanted us to have our own transportation. I arranged for a rental car."

"In case we need to make a quick escape?" he teased, hoping to elicit a smile, even if just a small one.

She didn't, just nodded. "Exactly."

Which made him wonder about McKenzie's relationship with her family. She'd considered hiring an escort service to keep from making the trip home alone. Just what kind of pressure had her family put on her in the past?

"Surely they aren't that bad?"

Shaking her head, McKenzie sighed. "They're not bad, just think it's within their right to meddle in my life. Always have and likely always will try to."

"Is that why you moved across the country? To get away from them?"

"Of course not." But she hesitated long enough that he wasn't sure she bought her answer any more than he did. "But my mother did once sign me up for a speed round dating service night. And then there was the time she contacted local churches to find out if they had programs for singles to meet."

"Seriously?"

McKenzie nodded. "Oh, yeah. Mama has no problem with meddling in my life even from half the country away."

"Is that why you ended up in Seattle?" he wondered out loud.

"I visited Seattle with a group of friends while in med school and fell in love with Pike Place Market and just everything about the city." Her appreciation for the city sparked to life in her eyes. "I applied for residency there, got it, fell further in love with the city, and when I was offered a permanent position at Seattle Cardiac Clinic for Kids, I stayed. How about you?"

"Similar story in some ways. I'm originally from Atlanta, went to medical school in Birmingham, did a cardiology, then a surgery residency in Pittsburgh, then took the positions with Trevane and Seattle Cardiac Clinic for Kids."

Ryder stood, stretched out his six-foot-plus frame as best as he could in the plane aisle, before grabbing their carry-on bags from the overhead bin.

She stood, double-checked their seats to make sure they hadn't left anything, then took her bag from him. "Thanks."

Once inside Nashville Airport, they made a pit stop, then went to the lower level where McKenzie had made arrangements to pick up a rental car.

"Nice," Ryder teased when the clerk handed over the keys to a minivan.

"This isn't what I purchased," McKenzie argued, but to no avail.

Ryder didn't mind, but McKenzie had the clerk checking again to make sure there wasn't another option.

He'd stowed their bags in the back of the minivan.

"I'm driving since I know where I'm going," she informed him, climbing into the driver's seat.

They made a quick late-night fast-food run, but otherwise it was only a twenty-minute drive from the airport. The closer they got to McKenzie's family's house, the tenser she got.

The house was a moderate-size old-style ranch.

"Be prepared for anything," McKenzie warned as they got their luggage out of the van. "It wouldn't surprise me if they were all here and jumped out at us when we walk in. Aunt Myrtle may or may not be dressed if that happens."

Ryder's curiosity was piqued, but the only person who'd waited on them was McKenzie's mother. They'd not made it up to the porch when the front door flung open and the petite woman hurried out to wrap her arms around McKenzie.

"Hello, Mama," McKenzie whispered just loud enough he could hear. "I've missed you, too."

"Let me look at you," her mother exclaimed, pulling back and eyeing McKenzie in the porch light.

"Don't you dare comment on how I've grown," McKenzie warned, but was smiling and glassy-eyed.

Ryder could see that despite the fact McKenzie lived so far away, there was no shortage of love between the two women.

"Grown? Ha, you look as if I need to put some meat on you. You're nothing but skin and bones," her mother countered, which Ryder found interesting as McKenzie's mother was a tiny thing herself. "This must be your new guy."

"Mama, this is Dr. Ryder Andrews." She gave him a here goes everything look. "Ryder, this is my mother, Roberta Wilkes."

Ryder smiled at the petite woman with dark eyes and hair. Although he could see the resemblance between McKenzie and her mother in bone structure and body build, McKenzie must have gotten her coloring from her father.

He stuck out his hand. "Nice to meet you."

McKenzie's mother clasped his hand between hers, then

dropped his hand and gave him the biggest hug he'd ever had. "We are so glad to finally meet you."

McKenzie sighed. "Mom, you make it sound as if I've been hiding him away. Ryder and I haven't been dating that long. Just a few weeks."

Roberta gave her daughter a pert look. "Long enough that you brought him home to Reva's wedding."

"There is that. Sorry, Ryder." She turned to her mother. "It's late, Mama. We have a busy few days ahead of us, and we're worn out. Can you let us know where we're sleeping?"

Their rooms ended up being McKenzie's room. As in singular.

"Your cousin Jeffrey and his wife and kids are in your brother's old room. Your brother won't be in until tomorrow and says he'll take the sofa."

"I can take the sofa," Ryder offered despite knowing his six-foot frame wouldn't comfortably fit. It was the right thing to do and he had to halt the panic rising in McKenzie's eyes.

"That isn't necessary," Roberta assured him, looking quite proud of herself. "I'm a modern woman."

"You were a modern woman before women were modern," McKenzie said under her breath, but Ryder heard.

Perhaps her mother had, too, as she gave McKenzie a stern look before smiling at Ryder. "You'll have to excuse my daughter. Flying addles her mind a little."

CHAPTER SIX

NOT IN A million years had McKenzie ever envisioned that she'd someday be standing in her childhood bedroom with Dr. Ryder Andrews, with him pretending to be her boyfriend.

One just never knew where life was going to take them.

Most women would be arguing to get Ryder into their bedroom. Here McKenzie was trying to figure a way to keep him out and coming up short for a feasible reason that wouldn't raise her family's suspicions.

"Sorry, Mom," she sighed. "I'm exhausted and like I said, we have a big few days. I want to hit the sack if that's okay. It's been a long day and flight."

They both knew how traumatizing boarding the plane and the five-hour flight was for her.

Or that it usually was.

She still couldn't believe she'd fallen asleep on Ryder's shoulder and missed almost the entire flight and all of the landing.

Best. Flight. Ever.

Her mother leaned in and gave another big squeeze, as if she knew where McKenzie's thoughts had gone. "No worries. I'm so glad you're home."

"Me, too," she said and meant it. It had been too long since she'd been home, but Seattle was a long way from

Nashville for someone terrified of flying. It wasn't as if she could just hop in her car and go home for a quick visit.

But she could have come home for a visit, a voice nagged. Could have and should have.

Maybe, just maybe her flight back to Seattle would be as smooth as the flight to Nashville and she could put to rest some of her flying fears. Doubtful, but the flight there hadn't been nearly as bad as expected. Thanks to Ryder.

Her mother gave him a sly look. "And don't even think you're sleeping on my sofa, young man. I won't have it."

McKenzie shrugged. "I'll take the sofa."

Both her mother and Ryder launched into arguments of why that wasn't happening. Fatigue washed over her. It really had been a long day and she was exhausted.

"I told you I'm a modern woman." Her mother pointed Ryder in the direction of McKenzie's old room.

He looked toward her for guidance.

Too tired to care what he thought, she told him, "You may as well follow me."

Once her mother had given them both another round of hugs and closed the door behind her as she left the small bedroom, McKenzie's shoulders sagged. She sank onto the edge of the full-sized bed to stare at the man who hadn't moved from the spot near the door. Was he thinking of making a run for it yet?

She wouldn't blame him.

"I'm sorry."

"For what?"

"That. This." She stretched her arm out to indicate the room where he was trapped sleeping with her. "I'll take the floor and you can have the bed."

"Quit stealing my lines."

"You're doing me a favor. I should be the one to take the floor."

He shook his head. "Not happening."

She gave him a tired smile. "Thank you, Ryder. Just know I appreciate you being here."

His smile filled her with warmth.

"You're welcome, McKenzie. It's been interesting."

No doubt. From her fear of flying to drooling on his shoulder to meeting her mother, he hadn't seemed bored or shown the slightest irritation, just patience and a kindness that surprised her. Although, she wasn't sure why as she'd witnessed the same traits demonstrated with how he treated his patients.

"You want the bathroom first?" she offered, pointing to a door on the opposite side of the room. "It's a Jack and Jill, which means my cousin Jeff, his wife and kids are on the other side so watch the noise. Hopefully, they haven't left it too messy, but check the lid just in case. They have a four-year-old son."

Ryder chuckled. "Brings me back to my college dorm days. You sure you want me to go first?"

She nodded and watched as he grabbed his shaving kit bag from his suitcase, along with pajama bottoms and a T-shirt, before he headed into the bathroom.

Once the door closed, she fell back against her bed and stared at a spot on the ceiling.

Truth was Ryder had been a much better travel companion that she'd expected. Probably better than Paul would have been.

Paul would have complained about her drooling on his trendy clothes and leaving him to entertain himself during the flight.

Ryder had been…nice.

Nice? Calling his kiss nice seemed almost an insult. The man could kiss.

No wonder she'd done just fine during takeoff. His kiss

had sent her mind soaring before the plane had ever left the ground.

Which confused her. Less than a month ago she'd hoped to someday marry Paul and spend her life with him. How was it Ryder's kiss had electrified her, left her wanting more?

She shouldn't want Ryder to kiss her. Shouldn't be thinking about his kiss. He'd kissed her only to stop her panic attack. She'd kissed him only because she'd been panicked.

Knowing she was going to pass out if she didn't get out of the bed, she forced herself up and began unpacking her suitcase and storing the items into her closet. She paused to smile at some of the things her mother still had hanging as if they were waiting on McKenzie to come home to wear them after all these years. A jacket with a basketball emblem emblazoned on the sleeve had her reaching out to touch the well-worn material.

Good grief, her prom dress even hung in there. Why would her mother keep that? Even if McKenzie had wanted to wear the dress, she wouldn't be able to shimmy that tiny dress up past her hips, much less zip the thing.

When Ryder had finished in the bathroom and came back into McKenzie's room, she'd finished unpacking her suitcase and was pushing the bag into her closet.

Glancing over to where he walked toward his suitcase, her gaze collided with bare feet.

She gulped.

She'd never been a foot person, quite the opposite, but Ryder's feet were sexy. Her gaze rose higher, taking in his flannel pajama bottoms that somehow managed to look like they belonged in an ad, over his Seattle sport team T-shirt that looked soft, well-worn and accentuated his waist and shoulders.

She should have just stopped right there and looked

away, but she didn't. Instead, her eyes moved onward to pause at his lips.

His lips that had kissed her on the plane.

Kissed her quite thoroughly. Her lips tingled at the memory. All of her tingled at the memory.

Tingly pleasure swept over her. Then, realizing she was gawking at him, heat flooded her face.

Get your mind away from that kiss, she ordered herself. Thinking about kissing Ryder when he was in her bedroom was not okay.

None of this was real.

Her gaze caught his honey-colored one.

Oh, yeah, he knew she'd been checking him out. Her face burned. He was here as a favor. What was wrong with her that she was looking at Ryder as if…as if this was real?

He was hot and outdid any teenaged fantasies she'd ever dreamed up in this room. Or anywhere else. Just wow.

And not where her mind should have gone about a pretend boyfriend.

Seeing Ryder at the hospital and clinic and acknowledging that he was drop-dead gorgeous was one thing. Having him in her bedroom and perusing him in a completely sexual way was quite another.

She needed to get her head on straight. No doubt her reaction was just extreme travel weariness and her intense emotions to flying including gratitude for his distraction.

She straightened from where she'd been kneeling, putting the suitcase in her closet, and pasted a smile on her still-flaming face as if she hadn't been looking at him as if he were chocolate dipped and she were a chocoholic ready to binge.

Ryder dropped his toiletries bag on top of his suitcase, then turned toward McKenzie. His lips twitching, he arched a brow. "All unpacked?"

She stood just a few feet away—anywhere in the room was only a few feet away.

"Um, yeah. You're welcome to hang anything you want to in my closet." Her cheeks flushing, she immediately averted her eyes.

McKenzie had never looked at him the way she currently was.

As if she was seeing him as a man. A desirable man.

Okay, maybe during their kiss, but he wasn't sure because she'd been so focused on the plane ride and had acted so no-big-deal afterward.

But in that moment their eyes met, hers had glowed as if she liked what she saw. A lot.

Ryder felt his own cheeks flush, knew he needed to get his thoughts back under control because nothing could happen physically between them.

Not tonight or at any point that weekend.

McKenzie was vulnerable, on the rebound. Ryder refused to be a rebound fling.

"I…um…" She paused, gave him a tentative smile that set warning bells off in his head. "I'm going to brush my teeth and change into my pajamas. Take my bed, please."

Take her bed, please? McKenzie thought, mortified as she washed her face and went through the motions of getting ready to go to sleep.

With Ryder in her bed.

Ryder whom she'd worked with for months and who she'd always agreed with her coworkers was easy on the eyes. But McKenzie had never really seen him. Because Ryder had always made her nervous when he was around, she'd never let herself fully take in just how sexy he was.

Had she known that if she'd let herself, she could have fallen into fantasizing about him, so she'd kept blinders

on to avoid a guilty conscience since she'd been commit-
ted to Paul?

Ryder was hot.

Scorching.

Glancing at herself in the bathroom mirror one last time,
she frowned at the haggardness of her features.

Yeah, Ryder looked fab after hours of travel. She just
looked tuckered out.

Fine. Despite her sudden acute awareness of his overabundance of maleness, they weren't really dating. He was
her pretend boyfriend and they weren't about to do anything except make a trip to night-night land.

Even if part of her wished this was real, that she and
Ryder were embarking on a real relationship, that the sexual
tension she felt was more than just her sudden awakening
to his overabundance of testosterone.

When she tiptoed back into her room, closing and locking the adjoining bathroom door, she came to a halt.

"You're not in my bed," she accused, frowning at where
he'd made a pallet of sorts on the floor with a fuzzy blanket
he'd pulled from the foot of her bed. He had one of her old
throw pillows tucked beneath his head. It wasn't much of
a pallet and there wasn't an extra blanket for him to cover
up with unless he took the comforter.

"You take the bed."

"Ryder," she began, feeling guilty that he was at her feet.

"There is no way I'm sleeping in your bed and making
you take the floor."

McKenzie eyed where he lay on the floor, then her full-
size bed, and came to a quick decision. "Fine. We'll both
sleep in the bed."

She'd keep her fantasies and her hands to herself.

His eyes danced. "You must have liked our kiss better
than I thought."

Cheeks heating, McKenzie tossed a throw pillow at him. "For that I should leave you on the floor."

Sitting up to catch the pillow, he chuckled. "You definitely should."

Something in the way he said his words, or maybe it was the way he was looking at her, shot a burst of feminine awareness through McKenzie.

"I'm not sure I'd trust myself if I was in that bed with you." Her breath caught. "You wouldn't hurt me."

She knew he wouldn't. Not even for a second did she believe otherwise.

"Never, but I'm a healthy man with normal sexual urges and you're a beautiful woman." His grin was a bit lopsided, but then his face took on a more serious expression. "Trust me, it's better if I stay on the floor."

McKenzie's heart raced at his words, at what he was saying. If they both slept in the bed he thought they might have sex. She didn't sleep around. But, the way her body was reacting to the thought of having sex with Ryder, she knew he was right.

"It's not as if I wouldn't stop you if you were doing something I didn't want you to be doing." Good grief. She'd practically just told him that she wasn't opposed to their having sex.

Staring at him on the floor, she wondered what it would be like to have sex with Ryder. To kiss him with abandon? To be kissed by him, her lips, her neck, her breasts? To press her body next to his, skin to skin, nothing between them as they moved in pleasure?

Tingles ran up and down her spine. Tingles all over her.

Any moment she was going to throw back the covers and invite him to join her there.

"True, but you're very tempting."

"Are you saying you want me?" How she found the nerve

to ask, she wasn't sure, just that the question spilled from her lips. Her gaze remained locked with his as she waited for his answer.

Looking way too sexy for a man sitting on a makeshift bed on the floor, he hesitated only a moment. "I'm not saying I don't. But I won't have sex with you this weekend, McKenzie. You're just out of a long relationship, this is pretend and neither of us want it to be real."

He's wrong, she thought. She did want it to be real. Real enough that he climbed into her bed and... McKenzie's cheeks heated.

Or maybe it was the visions that danced through her head at his "normal sexual urges."

Goodness, he must give off some major pheromones because she so didn't think like this. This looking at a man and wanting him to give in to his "normal sexual urges" and touch her.

Especially a man she barely knew.

And worked with.

And who always made her jumpy.

Maybe because he was a sexy beast and she just hadn't added up that it was the sexual vibes he gave off that made her uneasy. Sex was good, but not something she'd ever dwelt upon.

The heat in Ryder's eyes said he didn't feel the same.

Sex mattered in Ryder's world.

Looking at him, sex mattered in McKenzie's world, too.

Realizing he was probably giving up a highly sexed weekend to accompany her, McKenzie made a mental note to buy him a bottle of his favorite wine when they got back to Seattle.

Because as flustered as he had her hormones and mind, he was right. They shouldn't have sex.

But she wanted to.

And that knowledge blew her mind.

Trying to clear her head, she stared at him, wondering how she could have ever been around him and not registered how charming his grin was.

"You're right. Neither of us want a real relationship and won't be having sex this weekend." She climbed into her bed, pulled the comforter free, and tossed it on the floor, leaving only the sheet to cover herself. With as heated as she currently felt, that should be plenty. "Now you have something to cuddle with."

From the floor, he chuckled, the sound of which continued to warm her insides all toasty in ways she really didn't like. Pretend boyfriends were not supposed to make their pretend girlfriends feel toasty.

"Night, McKenzie."

Lying in her bed from her teenaged years with Ryder lying on her floor seemed surreal, but no more so than the fact he'd kissed her on the plane. Or that she'd looked at him and had a visual flash of having sex with him.

"Goodnight," she whispered, closing her eyes and thinking her mind might be racing too much to sleep.

And that if sleep did come, she prayed it wouldn't be filled with dreams of the man on the floor next to her bed.

"Sweet dreams."

"Stop that," she ordered without opening her eyes.

"What?" he asked, all innocent, as if he hadn't just read her thoughts again.

"Talking when I'm trying to sleep."

He laughed and McKenzie's mouth curved upward as sleep took hold with the sweetest dreams filling her mind.

Someone was in the shower, singing.

The thought hit McKenzie as she rolled over in bed and let her arm flop over the side.

When her hand came into contact with warm flesh, her eyes flew open at the same time as she jerked her hand away.

Where she was, who she was with, whose warm flesh that had been, registered instantly.

"Good morning to you, too." The man she'd just hit chuckled from the floor.

Glancing at Ryder over the edge of the bed, she wrinkled her nose. "Morning."

"Sounds as if someone's having a good morning," he mused, stretching his arms up over his head, pulling his T-shirt tight over his chest and abs.

McKenzie squeezed her eyes shut and fell back against her bed. This was a new day and she wasn't letting her mind go to where it had been as she'd drifted off to sleep.

Ha. She was pretty sure her mind had been in an orgasmic sexual dreamworld with Ryder all night.

"Sounds like my cousin Jeff." If anything could get her mind off sex it was thoughts of her cousin Jeff.

"You have a big family?"

"Big enough." Which really wasn't much of an answer, she realized. "My dad and mother both had a sister apiece, so I've a few cousins and extended family. Most live around here, but a few of us have escaped."

"You seemed happy to see your mother."

"I was. I am," she corrected. "It's been a long time since I've been home. I guess you figured that out last night."

"Because you don't like flying?"

"Among other things."

"I want to ask…"

"But you're not going to because you know I'm not going to answer," she cut in, sitting up on the side of the bed. "Is it really morning? Because I just want to sleep a few more hours."

"Makes sense since we're in a different time zone."

"Quit being all logical."

"Fine." He grinned. "I'll be illogical."

"Ha. I think you covered that when you agreed to come with me this weekend."

He shrugged. "It's not been bad so far."

"Besides the near panic attack and having to sleep on the floor," she teased, appreciating his comment that it hadn't been bad more than she should.

"Besides those things," he agreed, still grinning as he let his gaze run over her.

Self-conscious of her first-thing-in-the-morning appearance when he looked so amazing with his sleep-tousled hair and quick smile, McKenzie frowned. "What?"

"Just taking in the real McKenzie."

"As opposed to the fake McKenzie you normally see?" Normally he didn't spend much time looking at her, period.

"Not fake," he said with way more consideration than the early morning warranted. "Just always well put together."

She half-smiled at her current state of morning hair, no makeup, and morning-after-travel eyes. "Ha. That's definitely not how anyone would describe me this morning."

"If you're fishing for a compliment, I'll take the bait. You're beautiful."

She hadn't been, but his compliment pleased her.

"Thank you." And then she didn't know what to say as the silence stretched between them, so she got out of bed. "It's possible Jeff will use all the hot water while he gives his full rendition of the greatest eighties," she warned. "I'm going to make some coffee. You want a cup?"

He shook his head. "Never touch the stuff."

Halfway to the door, McKenzie paused to look at him in horror. "Say what?"

He laughed. "That stuff you guzzle by the gallon," he wrinkled his nose, "I never drink it."

He'd noticed she drank coffee?

"I knew there had to be something wrong with you," she mused.

His lips twitched. "If my distaste of coffee is the worst thing you discover about me this weekend then we did good."

"Are there worse things to discover than not liking coffee? Is that even possible?"

He shrugged. "That depends on how much you like coffee."

"Let's just say it flows freely through my veins."

From the bathroom, they heard the connecting door to the other bedroom open and close.

"He's out! I'm headed in there before someone else does!" And with that she scooped up her shower bag and the clothes she'd set out the night before and disappeared into the bathroom.

Ryder stared at the cup of coffee Roberta had put in front of him and wondered if he'd have to down the stuff to keep from offending her. He really didn't like coffee, but apparently McKenzie's family drank it like their lives depended on it.

"So, tell me about your relationship with my daughter."

Roberta clearly wasn't one to waste time. She leaned back in the chair next to his and sipped on her coffee.

"I imagine it's much as McKenzie has told you. We work together, have been seeing each other a few weeks, and she invited me to come with her this weekend."

"She's never brought anyone home before," Roberta pointed out.

"I wouldn't read too much into that as she told me it has been several years since she's been able to come home."

Roberta snorted. "Since she's chosen to come home."

"Flying with her, I'd say it's more than a choice that's kept her away. She told me about her father," he defended. Although he didn't fully understand McKenzie's reasons for staying away, he suspected her fear of flying topped the list.

Roberta looked surprised. "She told you about Phillip?"

Nodding, Ryder picked up the coffee to have something to do with his hands while facing her scrutiny.

"I can't believe she told you about Phillip," she continued. "She never talks about her father. I sent her to several therapists and she still wouldn't talk about what had happened. Why did she tell you?"

Probably because she'd been on the verge of hyperventilating and he'd been in the next seat over.

"Mom, stop grilling Ryder."

"Afraid he can't take it?" a slightly balding man asked as he came into the room, two kids on his heels.

"Jeff!" McKenzie threw her arms around the man who picked her up and spun her around.

When he put her down, McKenzie was laughing.

"Good to see you, cuz. 'Bout time you came to your senses and came home."

"Just for the weekend. No way am I staying long enough for you to be a pain in my butt the way you were most of my life."

"Nothing you didn't deserve," he assured her. "Nashville has babies with bad hearts, too, you know?"

"I know." Her voice was low and held a sad tone when she answered, but then she stooped down to the little girl literally hanging onto her cousin's leg. "Speaking of babies, you sure have grown since I saw you last," she told the child who just stared at her with big eyes. "How old are you now? Twenty?"

Grinning a bit shyly, the girl shook her head and held up three fingers.

"Three?" McKenzie looked impressed. "That's getting big way too fast, if you ask me."

The little boy who was a spitting image of his father only with a thick shock of blond hair stepped forward and held up a handful of fingers. "I'm four."

"Closest thing I've got to grandchildren," Roberta complained in a half whisper meant to be heard by all. "I don't think this girl here is ever going to give me a grandchild of my own. Although," her mother's gaze ran up and down Ryder, "I may be closer than I'd thought to some beautiful grandbabies."

Her face going pink, McKenzie shook her head. "I've no rush to procreate. Besides, I'm sure that brother of mine is giving his best efforts to produce a grandchild."

"If you ask me, he should forget marriage and keep playing the field as long as he can," Jeff interjected, giving Ryder a nudge on the shoulder. "Right, buddy?"

Ryder was one hundred percent sure he'd been led down a rabbit hole where there were no safe answers. The women eyeing him warned he'd best not agree, and his man card was in serious jeopardy with McKenzie's cousin if he didn't at least make a manly grunt.

McKenzie rescued him by noticing what he was holding. "Hey! I thought you said you didn't like coffee."

Everyone in the room glanced at his still-full cup.

"I don't," he admitted. "But I've never had Tennessee coffee, so who knows?"

McKenzie's mother's house was apparently the wedding meeting place headquarters. Ryder was introduced to family members of various ages.

"He's a hunk," Julianna, her cousin Jeff's wife, told McKenzie in a whisper not meant to be overheard, but that Ryder had. "No wonder you preferred him over the computer guy."

"There was nothing wrong with Paul," McKenzie defended, obviously not wanting her family to think poorly of the man she'd spent two years in a relationship with.

"Then why isn't he here with you?"

"Things just…" She glanced toward Ryder, saw he was watching her with interest, then blushing, looked back toward her friend. "We just didn't work out."

"And now you're dating a hottie coworker and brought him to Tennessee to meet your family?"

"That sums it up," McKenzie agreed with a smile Ryder could tell was fake. "I'm dating my hottie coworker and brought him home to meet all of you. Whatever was I thinking?"

Julianna laughed, then shot another glance toward Ryder who pretended as if he had no clue what they were discussing.

"Well, if you ask me," she said, waggling her brows, "this one's a keeper."

"Maybe." McKenzie sent another apologetic look toward Ryder. "It's too early in our relationship to be having this conversation as we've just begun to date, right, Ryder?"

"Oh, I don't know," he teased, not paying heed to her look of warning. "I've always believed that when you meet the right person time doesn't really matter so much."

Several gazes zeroed in on him. "Is McKenzie the right person?"

There was a chemistry between them he'd immediately felt, but she wasn't the woman for him. He knew better. But he'd promised to impress her family with pretending to be crazy about her, so pretend he would.

"Only thing I can find wrong with her is her predilection for coffee more than me, but other than that, she feels right."

CHAPTER SEVEN

"Sorry about that," McKenzie apologized the moment she was alone with Ryder. Awkward didn't begin to cover how she'd felt about her family putting him on the spot, or herself for that matter. "My family can't fathom that I'm happy without being married."

Not that she didn't want to marry someday, but she really was happy.

"I take it your brother is still single, too?"

"Not for lack of trying. He's been married twice. His job is hard on relationships."

"I still can't believe he's a pilot."

She nodded. "I can't stand the thought of him going up in those planes, but he loves it. As much as Dad did or maybe even more. Mama doesn't say much, but it has to bother her, too."

"But not as much as it bothers you?"

"Why do you say that?"

"Because that's why you don't live here. Because you can't stand knowing when he's in the air."

McKenzie didn't answer. She hadn't really thought about Mark's flying playing into her reasons for not living in Nashville.

"I shouldn't have said that." Ryder reached for her hand

and gave a gentle squeeze. "What do I know? I've not even met your brother."

"You're right. You haven't." But he'd seen through her better than she'd seen through herself, because she acknowledged that he was partially right. She hadn't liked being home and knowing when Mark was in the air. Her brother swore he only felt alive in the air. McKenzie felt terrified at just the thought.

But foremost, medicine had led her to Seattle. Clay had just dumped her to head to Boston. She hadn't wanted to stay in Nashville, had seen the residency in Seattle as an opportunity to discover who she was.

She'd met Paul and been dumped again.

She pulled her hand free and walked across the room, stared at the random items on her dresser top prior to turning back to face Ryder.

"His first wife swore if he'd loved her half as much as he'd loved flying they wouldn't have fallen apart."

"Interesting at how you both dealt with your father's death so differently."

"Isn't it, though? Mark was older, had more time flying with Dad. Whereas I had nightmares for years where I was in that plane with him when it crashed." Sweat prickled her skin at the memory. Forcing it away, she sighed. "Look, I hate to abandon you to a few hours of hanging out with Jeff and his kids, but we ladies are supposed to meet the others at the bridal shop this morning to pick up my dress. Let's hope it fits."

His gaze skimmed over her figure. "Here's hoping. You sure you don't want me to go with you?"

"To a bridal shop?"

"Might be better hanging with you than whatever I'll end up doing with Jeff."

"Possibly." There was no telling what Reva's older

brother would have Ryder doing. "I really do appreciate you coming with me this weekend."

"No problem." Ryder watched McKenzie reach for her purse off the dresser. "And, McKenzie?"

She turned toward him.

"I'm sorry about your dad."

"Thank you. It was a long time ago."

But not so long ago that it didn't impact her present.

He stood. "I'll walk you to the car."

"There's no need."

"Sure, there is," he assured her. "Your mother will wonder about us if I don't."

"Oh, I guess you're right."

When they reached her mother's car, Roberta got into the driver's seat. Julianna was already in the back seat next to Casey in a child's safety seat.

Ryder opened the passenger door for McKenzie. "Bye, honey. Have fun."

Glaring at him while she climbed into the car, McKenzie's nose crinkled with displeasure at his use of a pet name. "No name calling, remember? I've told you I prefer you to use my name."

"I'll keep that in mind. Have a great time with your mother." He fought chuckling as he leaned forward and pressed a quick kiss on the side of her mouth. One not meant to be full of passion, but not so quick as to just be a peck, either.

"I…uh, thank you. I will." Obviously flustered by his kiss, she gave him a hesitant look. "You're sure you're going to be okay with Jeff while we're gone?"

Although he shouldn't be, he was pleased that his kiss had thrown her off-kilter. "I'll be fine."

Mostly, he believed he told the truth.

* * *

"So, tell me about this hot new boyfriend none of us have heard anything about."

McKenzie blinked at her cousin Reva.

They'd barely been at the bridal shop ten minutes. She supposed she should be grateful the question hadn't been the first thing out of Reva's mouth.

Not that her mother hadn't grilled her about Ryder the entire drive into town before dropping her and Julianna off at the dress shop, then heading on to Reva's mother's house to help with whatever Aunt Jane needed.

Then again, it could be worse.

Reva and her family could be grilling her about Paul and not believing her when she said he was ancient history.

"This weekend is about your love life, not mine," she reminded her cousin, eyeing her reflection in the mirror. Although a little snug around the bosom, the bridesmaid dress fit perfectly otherwise.

Reva laughed. "So, true, and I don't mind at all being the center of attention."

Just as well as her beautiful cousin had always held that honor, even in high school. Men had always thrown themselves at her, had done all they could to hold her attention, and it had always been Reva who'd bored with her relationships and ended them.

"But my love life is old news around here," Reva insisted, fanning her face as the seamstress made a last-minute adjustment to her wedding dress. She'd lost weight and wanted the bodice tightened a smidge. "Tell us about yours."

"Not much to tell," she admitted, still going with the truth as much as possible. "Ryder and I work together and have just recently started dating."

Reva's brow arched. "Yet you invited him to come home with you?"

"Of course, I brought him." She hoped she inflected her tone with just the right amount of "duh." "If you were dating a gorgeous pediatric cardiothoracic surgeon, wouldn't you have invited him?"

"If I were dating that man, I'd never leave home," Julianna spoke up from where she fiddled with tying a ribbon on Casey's head in a big bow. "I almost ditched you gals so I could stay at Aunt Roberta's just to drool over him."

McKenzie suppressed a giggle. She'd have to tell Ryder as he'd likely get a kick out of the comment.

"It says a lot about how he feels for you that he was willing to fly across the country to come to a wedding," Reva insisted, keeping her arms held up so the seamstress could work. "Most men hate weddings."

"Ryder isn't most men." So true. Just look at what she'd put him through so far and he'd not uttered one word of complaint.

Instead, he'd been…wonderful.

"It's serious, then?"

If only.

Now where had that come from?

Getting involved with Ryder for real was not what she needed. Hadn't the past taught her anything? Did she really want to get involved with him just so he could dump her down the line, too?

Sensing every woman in the bridal shop's eyes focused on her, including little Casey's, McKenzie hesitated. If she said yes, her family really would be pushing her and Ryder down the aisle. If she said no, then they'd either think she was crazy or that Ryder wasn't that interested.

"It's too early to say." She didn't meet any of their curious gazes as she went back to looking at herself in the mirror. "Do you think we should let the bust out just a little?"

The shop keeper gave a horrified look from where she worked on Reva's dress. "Absolutely not. It's a perfect fit. You want it a little snug to hold everything in place."

There was that. McKenzie stifled a smile as the conversation turned back to the wedding.

That is, until after she was out of the bridesmaid dress and back into her own clothes and Reva tackled her.

"I'm so glad you're here. I've missed you so much." Reva pulled her in for a hug. "And don't even think you've been gone so long that I didn't recognize what you did earlier. Some time before I say I do tomorrow, you and I are going to have a big talk about your new guy. I can't wait to meet him tonight."

McKenzie hugged her cousin. "I've missed you, too."

She had. They'd been so close.

She could blame no one but herself that they no longer were, as she'd been the one to stay away.

Because she couldn't stand the thought of being in an airplane? True, but had that been the main reason she'd not come home?

Was it possible she'd been a tad jealous of her cousin? That she'd jumped at the residency in Seattle to step out of her beautiful cousin's shadow and the pity her family had been dishing out over McKenzie's breakup with Clay?

"I wish you'd gotten to come home for my bridesmaid party last weekend." Reva giggled at the memory. "We had so much fun peddling around Nashville."

"Getting drunk on a bicycle bar isn't necessarily my idea of a good time." Realizing she sounded condescending, she added, "You know I never liked riding a bicycle."

"Come on." One of the bridesmaids hurried them. "If we

don't get a move on, we're going to be late for our manis and pedis."

McKenzie glanced at her nails. Her cousin had a flair for gorgeous nails and was always posting a pic on social media of some fantastic manicure with elaborate designs. McKenzie did well to keep hers trimmed and had thought she'd done great with the French manicure she'd taken time for earlier that week. She cared nothing about having her nails redone, but this weekend wasn't about her. So she smiled and went with the flow.

In the middle of their morning of pampering, everyone chitchatted about the wedding, about where Reva thought they'd go on their honeymoon as her husband-to-be had kept it a surprise.

On cue, a courier arrived and presented Reva with a jeweler's box.

"Oh, my goodness!" Reva exclaimed, reading the card out loud, then pulling out a gorgeous diamond bracelet.

"He's so romantic," one of the bridesmaids cooed.

"You're so lucky," another said.

Reva was lucky. Lucky in love. Lucky in life. Always had been. Not once had her cousin ever been dumped.

Reva was wonderful. Why would any man dump her?

Was McKenzie that unwonderful that every man dumped her?

McKenzie bit into her lower lip, chiding herself for the green she'd just felt rush through her veins. She was happy for her cousin. Ecstatic. Just that it would have been nice to have had a little of that lucky at love along the way herself.

They were served champagne and strawberries. McKenzie rarely drank but emptied her glass during her pedicure.

By the time they went to meet the guys for a late lunch at Reva's mother's, McKenzie couldn't decide if she was starved or tipsy. Or both.

"Cooking for everyone on the day before your wedding was a lot for Aunt Jane to take on."

Reva laughed as they piled into the prearranged limo that would take her cousin wherever she needed to go that day.

"She loves it, and you know it. She's been looking forward to this day my whole life."

"As have you," McKenzie reminded her. "I can recall many a time you played dress-up with curtain sheers as your pretend veil."

"Ha. We had fun, didn't we?"

Yes and no. Reva had always been the bride during their play. Never McKenzie. Perhaps that had been a sign of things to come?

"I should have borrowed some of Mom's old curtains for tomorrow, eh?" Reva giggled.

"I seriously doubt that," McKenzie mused, having seen her cousin in the gorgeous dress at the bridal shop.

"Maybe she'll pull them out for you to use," Reva teased.

Wondering at her own botched relationships, McKenzie snorted. "I have no need for curtain sheers or a wedding veil."

"Who knows? Maybe this hot doc, as Aunt Roberta called him, will be the one to change your mind and finally get you to the altar."

Which was what she'd wanted her family to think. That Ryder was crazy about her and she wasn't alone in Seattle.

She arched a brow. "Mom called Ryder a hot doc?"

Reva nodded. "As did Julianna. She said she almost fainted when she walked in on him in the bathroom this morning."

McKenzie grimaced. "That sounds much worse than what it was. Ryder was completely dressed and had just finished brushing his teeth. It wasn't as if she caught him in his skivvies."

"Whatever it was, he flustered her enough she texted to tell me. She said his chest and abs were perfection."

"Yeah, well, compared to your brother, most men's abs would be considered perfection," McKenzie teased. "But Ryder is hot."

She'd have said so a month ago, but just how much so hadn't registered.

Or if it had, she'd just not paid any attention because of Paul and thinking her future was all neatly tied up.

How wrong she'd been.

Ryder, Jeff and a couple of kids paused from tossing the football back and forth on Jeff's mother's front lawn to watch the ladies pile out of the limousine.

"Hello, Hot Doc," McKenzie greeted him.

Ryder's brow lifted. He was even more surprised when she wrapped her arms around his neck and kissed him.

A kiss that was meant for the benefit of their avid audience, one of whom let out a wolf whistle.

Not a problem. Ryder kissed her as if he'd been longing to do so his whole life.

Maybe he had.

When she pulled back, smiled up at him with eyes that were a bit glassy, he grinned down at her.

"Miss me much?"

"Bunches. Couldn't you tell?"

He leaned in so the others couldn't hear. "How much champagne have you had?"

"Not nearly enough," she answered, smiling at him as if she thought he was the greatest thing ever.

He knew it was pretend, but her look was getting to him. Did she ever realize what she was doing? That she was on the rebound and that messed with her emotions? Made her more vulnerable?

"But I did have a couple glasses of champagne while getting my nails done."

She held her fingers out for his inspection.

Knowing they were still the center of attention, that all the women had paused on their way into the house to watch them instead, Ryder took her hand in his and lifted it to his mouth, placing a kiss on each fingertip.

"You're good," McKenzie praised, a bit breathy.

"I'm just getting started."

Which was the truth. For whatever reason McKenzie felt the need to be part of a couple in front of her family and wanted him to act crazy about her.

Kissing her, looking into her eyes, did make him crazy. He was playing a dangerous game. One where he was liable to get burned if he wasn't careful.

Because he wanted McKenzie and feeling her desire during their kiss, as she looked up at him, was playing havoc with his resolve to protect himself.

"I can't wait to see how you finish."

Havoc.

"Are you flirting with me, McKenzie?"

Her cheeks flushed. "Is that not okay?"

The vulnerability in her question about undid him, about made him forget his need to protect himself and instead dive headfirst into wiping away all her self-doubts. He'd like to get a hold of Paul and every other man who'd ever hurt her.

"Okay, that's enough of that," Reva interrupted them, having obviously been ignored for as long as she was willing. "Introduce me to your fellow, Kenz."

McKenzie's cousin was a beautiful woman and had a smile that drew a person in. But Ryder's gaze quickly returned to McKenzie, saw that she was watching him closely for his reaction to her cousin.

"I've heard a lot about you today, Dr. Andrews," the bride-to-be claimed, her smile genuine, as was the hug she surprised him with. "We're all glad you're here."

When Ryder's gaze cut back to McKenzie's she was no longer smiling, or even looking at him. Instead, she seemed bored with the conversation, and mumbled something about finding lunch.

From the lush trees along the edge of where the wedding would take place, Ryder watched the groom and his men line up in front of the wooden archway that would be further decorated with fresh flowers prior to the wedding the following day.

The women, including McKenzie, were to the back of the garden area set up to seat around two hundred people. The trees lining the area provided natural shade and a sense of privacy from the outside world.

A wedding coordinator with a clipboard was instructing and positioning everyone in the wedding party where she wanted them to stand during the ceremony.

Reva was getting married at an old plantation house that had been converted into a wedding venue. The sprawling white farmhouse with its white columns in front and wraparound porch were impressive, but it truly was the scenery around the house and rustic-looking barn that had been built as a reception hall that made the place. Rolling green hills dotted with sprawling oaks, the bluest sky he could recall ever seeing, flowers of all varieties, and a flowing stream that ran along one side of the property.

"Now, ladies," the wedding coordinator continued snapping orders. "I want you hidden back behind these terraces until after the music starts tomorrow."

She put each bridesmaid where she wanted them, had them pretend to hold their bouquets. Then, at designated points in the song, she sent each woman toward the podium where the groom and his men waited.

McKenzie was the second bridesmaid out from where the bride would take her place after all six women had made their way to the front.

McKenzie never looked toward Ryder during her jaunt down the aisle. She just stepped up front to where the wedding coordinator had told her to go, stood holding her pretend bouquet, and kept her gaze trained toward where the other bridesmaids came down the aisle one by one until it was time for Reva to make her grand entrance.

It might be only a rehearsed ceremony, but McKenzie's cousin's appearance garnered everyone's attention, including her groom's, as if she were truly making her grand entrance.

Ryder hadn't met Jeremy yet as the groom and his groomsmen had spent the day on their own adventures. The smile on his face was genuine, as was the love in his gaze when it landed on his bride.

McKenzie was also smiling, but something was off. Ryder wasn't sure it was something anyone else would pick up on, but the way she held her body, the way her smile didn't reach her eyes tugged at everything in him, making him want to go wrap her in his arms and promise to make right whatever was bothering her.

He wouldn't be doing that. At least, not for real.

The couple ran through a mock ceremony with the wedding coordinator stopping them time and again to redirect anything not exactly as she and the couple had previously discussed. When they'd finished and the last of the wedding party had exited the area, she clapped her hands and the handful of people sitting in the pews followed suit.

"Now, this time, we'll run through without interruptions," the coordinator instructed. "If you mess up, just keep going as if this is the real deal. No stopping. Pronto."

The petite woman might have been a drill sergeant in a previous life.

As everyone was resuming their previous places, Ryder moved to one of the pews near the front. Several family members and friends of the wedding party sat in the area, chatting while they waited for the rehearsal to begin again.

"You must be McKenzie's Dr. Andrews."

Ryder glanced up at the man who slid into the pew next to him and nodded.

The man stuck out his hand. "I'm McKenzie's big brother, Mark."

Ryder shook the man's hand. "Ryder."

"I grilled her on you over the phone, but she didn't have a lot to say. Just that I'd like you. She said that about the last guy, too."

"You planning to grill me now to see if you have better luck?" Ryder guessed.

The man gave him a stare down that belonged on a certified interrogator. "It's a big brother's job to look out for his little sister. For the record, she was wrong. I didn't like the last guy."

"Fair enough, and to be honest, I wasn't crazy about him, either," Ryder admitted, earning a quick snort from McKenzie's brother. "What do you want to know?"

"How long have you been seeing my sister?"

"A few weeks."

"Yet she brought you to Tennessee to meet her family? That seems fast."

"Bringing me here may be why she's with me at all," he admitted, sticking with the truth. "I got the distinct impression coming alone wasn't an option she was willing to accept."

Her brother studied him. "You might be right. My mom worries about her."

"As does her brother?"

"Yeah, he does, too, although she's seemed happy enough when I've visited Seattle."

"You get out to see her often?"

"A few times a year. Enough to have my opinions on the guy you replaced. Good riddance."

Ryder waited for him to say more.

"I'm glad she finally saw the light."

Ryder wouldn't correct his assumption that McKenzie had ended the relationship. He'd made the same mistake.

"All of which worked to my advantage," Ryder acknowledged. "If she'd been happy with the last guy I wouldn't be in Tennessee."

"True that."

Both men turned to watch McKenzie slowly make her way up the aisle to the front. When she passed them, her gaze met Ryder's, lingered a moment, then lit on her brother and she grinned.

Ryder almost thought she was going to bail on the wedding procession so she could fling herself at her brother, putting to rest any notion that the two weren't close.

The wedding party went through another mock ceremony, without the bride and groom saying actual vows, then exited as they would the following day.

Ryder wasn't surprised when McKenzie came barreling toward them and flung her arms around her brother.

"Mark! I didn't know you were here."

"Hey, squirt. Miss me much?"

"How embarrassing?" She wrinkled her nose. "Do. Not. Call. Me. That."

He laughed. "Outgrown your nickname?"

"That has never been my nickname. Only you have ever used it and I've always hated it."

Ryder watched the interplay between siblings and could see the closeness that as an only child he'd never experienced. Would he and Chrissy have shared such a bond if she'd lived? He'd have done anything for the chance to know.

Turning her big green eyes toward him, McKenzie smiled and unlike earlier, her smile was real. "Ryder, let me introduce you to the bane of my childhood and for the record if you ever call me squirt, you're history."

Her brother arched a brow. "That sounds painful on a lot of different levels."

"Having you for a brother was painful." But McKenzie was laughing as she said it.

The wedding coordinator clapped her hands and called for everyone to head toward the rehearsal dinner hall.

"As that woman is the bane of my present," McKenzie sighed. "She is so organizing."

"It's her job. Dealing with bridezillas day after day, no doubt she has to be," Mark suggested.

"Reva isn't a bridezilla."

On cue, their cousin burst into tears and sat down on one of the pews.

Mark gestured to their cousin. "You sure?"

"Positive, but that's my calling card to go check on her." She gave her brother a hug, then turned to walk away, and as if an afterthought, turned back, stood on her tiptoes, and kissed the corner of Ryder's mouth.

That was twice she'd kissed him. Once had been for the benefit of the women watching her greet them. That one must have been for her brother because Ryder wasn't sure anyone else had been paying them the slightest heed.

He wasn't complaining. This pretend boyfriend gig came with amazing perks.

Their eyes met, held.

"Sorry you keep getting abandoned."

"You can make it up to me later," he teased.

Her eyes widened with surprise, then after a nervous look toward her brother, she slowly smiled. "We'll see."

Both men watched her rush over to the bride-to-be and kneel next to her, along with the groom and two other bridesmaids.

"That was interesting," Mark mused.

"Your cousin having prewedding nerves?"

"My sister having pre-you nerves," Mark clarified. "Despite the fact my mother threw you in the same bedroom, you've not had sex, have you?"

Leaning back a little, Ryder eyed the man. "With all due respect, whether I have or haven't had sex with McKenzie really isn't your business."

Mark laughed and play punched Ryder's shoulder with a little more zest than just for fun but not meant to truly inflict much pain. More of a warning shot.

"For the record," he cautioned. "Everything to do with McKenzie is my business. I wouldn't take kindly to anyone hurting her."

Admiring McKenzie's brother for his protectiveness of her, Ryder nodded. "Noted, but I don't foresee that being a problem."

After this weekend of pretense, they'd likely go back to rarely seeing each other.

"Also, for the record," Mark continued, his eyes glittering as if he was about to impart great knowledge, "that wasn't boredom flashing in my sister's eyes just then."

Ryder's heart pounded harder than usual at her brother's

observation. She was just acting, keeping up the pretense, he tried to tell himself, but didn't believe.

Which meant he needed to be all the more diligent in keeping their boundaries in place when they were alone.

He watched as she wiped a tear from her cousin's now-smiling face. Within seconds, bride and groom were hugging and McKenzie was shooing everyone still there to leave.

"Come on. Let's go find some of this overpriced food," Mark told him as McKenzie rejoined them, giving them curious looks as if wanting to know what they'd been discussing.

"Sounds good." Ryder placed a possessive hand on McKenzie's lower back as they headed in the direction the others had gone. "I'm starved."

He'd meant for food and not McKenzie, right? But the smile she was giving him had him wondering if he was just fooling himself, if he'd just been fooling himself from the beginning, that he could spend a weekend with McKenzie and it all be pretend.

CHAPTER EIGHT

McKenzie HADN'T THOUGHT about how much Ryder would have to be alone due to her duties as part of the wedding party.

Now, for instance, she was seated at the wedding party table rather than next to him for the rehearsal dinner.

Fortunately—or unfortunately—her brother had taken it upon himself to keep Ryder entertained.

Or perhaps her brother was entertaining himself at her expense.

Certainly, Mark had taken great pleasure in torturing her throughout their childhood and teen years.

She also knew her big brother would feel it his obligation to thoroughly interrogate Ryder and no doubt already had. What was Ryder telling him?

Or worse, what was Mark telling Ryder?

She shot them a worried glance.

Both men looked relaxed, deep in conversation, and to be enjoying the moment. Mark threw his head back with laughter at something Ryder said.

Interesting. Mark and Paul had gotten along okay enough when Mark had flown into Seattle and they'd all gone to dinner. But she couldn't recall them ever sharing any laugh-out-loud moments. She'd always thought they mostly tolerated each other for her sake.

"Reva's not the only lucky woman here tonight."

Surprised at the comment, McKenzie glanced toward Callie.

Yes, she was lucky Ryder had agreed to this pretense. She almost felt guilty that he had and was being subjected to her family's questioning, guilty that she was using him to stave off pity and perhaps to curb her jealousy at her cousin's good fortune.

Ugh. She hated that seeing Reva had brought a jealousy to surface that she'd not acknowledged she'd had.

"Is he as good in bed as he is to look at?"

McKenzie's gaze went back to Callie. Her high school friend watched Ryder with hungry eyes, probably the way McKenzie had been looking at him that morning when he'd stepped back into her room after his shower.

Yeah, that just-showered look that morning had been outright sexy.

Very sexy.

As had their kiss in Aunt Jane's front yard. Why had she felt the need to lay that one on him? For show in front of her cousin and the other women to say, hey, Reva's not the only lucky one? If so, how petty of her. But maybe Ryder had been right in thinking the champagne had played a role. Had it given her just enough gumption to kiss him that way, not for show, but because she'd wanted to kiss him and doing so in front of her cousin and the bridesmaids had given her the perfect excuse?

McKenzie swallowed, then, remembering Callie waited for an answer, shrugged. "I don't know," she admitted. "We've only been seeing each other a few weeks."

Callie's perfectly drawn-on brow lifted. "Girl, what are you waiting on? I saw that kiss earlier. Hot. Hot. Hot. If that man was within my hands' reach, I'd know everything about that body of his and he'd definitely know every inch of mine."

Um, yeah, that put a few images in McKenzie's head. Images of exploring Ryder's body, of his exploring hers.

Images that should not be in her head.

Because he was a pretend boyfriend, not a real one. Only more and more she hated the pretense, wished Ryder really wanted her, that everything about this weekend was real.

"Leave her alone," Reva ordered, leaning over toward them from where she sat on the other side of Callie. "McKenzie's just getting out of a long relationship. It makes sense that she'd be hesitant to move too quickly even with a man as wonderful seeming as Ryder."

Reva's quick defense shot guilt through her. Reva had always dragged McKenzie along to all the popular places, had always defended her to anyone who said the slightest negative thing. Her cousin was a much better person than she was and deserved to be happy.

And so did she.

McKenzie's gaze shifted back to Ryder. Was there even a chance of their pretense growing into something real?

She'd have to be dead inside not to react to his overabundance of testosterone.

Not to notice how her body came alive when they kissed or even when he smiled at her.

Perhaps that's why she'd gone for the kiss at Aunt Jane's, because she'd needed the surge of energy his kiss shot through her.

What would he say if she told him she found him attractive, both physically and as a person?

Callie gestured toward where Ryder sat and gave a wistful sigh. "Like I said, lucky you. That man there is the perfect solution to forgetting every other man who ever walked the face of the planet."

All three women looked toward Ryder. He must have sensed their gazes on him as he glanced their way, gave McKenzie a slight look of question, then winked.

"Lord help me," Callie said, fanning her face. "If you decide you don't want him, send him my way. I've not just gotten out of a long relationship and have no reservations about letting him rock my world."

McKenzie fought the urge to fan her own face. Ryder's wink did funny things to her insides. Like make them get all warm and squishy.

Warm?

That was like calling a volcanic eruption a lit match.

"I'd mention your brother," Callie continued, "but we both know that would never work since he's gone so much. I'd get lonely and end up making us both miserable."

Had her mother gotten lonely before her father's death? McKenzie hadn't really thought about what her parents' lives were like before her father died. She'd known her mother had gone through numerous relationships. Had she been trying to curb loneliness? Or had Roberta been lonely long before due to the often out-of-town nature of her father's work?

"Is Ryder going with us after we leave here?" Reva asked. "Lunch was fun, but I hope to get a chance to get to know him while y'all are here and tomorrow is going to be busy."

"Just a little busy. It's kind of your big day." McKenzie smiled at her cousin. "But on Ryder, I honestly haven't had a chance to ask him about tonight."

"I feel guilty I monopolized you all day." Reva's painted lips pouted a little. "Then again, Ryder gets you all the time and this is the first time I've seen you in a couple of years so it's only right he has to share."

Point taken. McKenzie would do better on coming home for visits.

Especially now that she knew she could get through a flight without going into full panic attack mode.

"But, seriously, you've done your bridesmaid duty. Go eat your dessert with your guy and Mark," Reva insisted, having caught McKenzie watching the two men talking and laughing together again.

"Sorry." She glanced toward Reva. "You're sure?"

Reva nodded. "Absolutely. We'll catch up when this is over when we're out on the town."

"But we can't stay out too late on the night before your big day," McKenzie reminded her. She wasn't tired at all, but knew she'd feel the time difference come morning.

"We won't. But going out dancing for a couple of hours will be fun. Besides," the bride assured her, "it's not like I'll sleep if I try going to bed early. Not when I'm so wound up."

Probably not, McKenzie admitted, appreciating Reva's okay to leave the bridal party table to go to Ryder and Mark.

"Care if I join you two for dessert?"

"You get kicked out of the wedding party already?" Ryder teased, pulling a chair over for her to sit next to him.

"I think they were worried about leaving you two alone too long and agreed I should come see what was so funny."

Her brother's eyes twinkled. "I've been telling him about that time you ran through the house naked at Christmas."

"Ah, the infamous naked at Christmas story." McKenzie scowled at her grinning brother. "I was two."

"I might have left that detail out," he admitted, not looking a bit remorseful.

"Ignore ninety-nine percent of what he tells you." McKenzie turned to Ryder. "Are you okay with going to the Wild Horse Saloon? Reva wants the whole gang together for one night of fun on the town, even if for just a couple of hours."

Ryder's eyes lit with surprise, but he nodded. "What's a trip to Nashville without a visit to a honky-tonk?"

"Do you line dance?"

Ryder shook his head. "Is it a deal breaker if I say no?"

"Not really," she admitted. Paul had been a lovely dancer, but they'd danced only when attending social events that just happened to have dancing.

"Is Callie still single?" Mark asked. "I noticed her looking this way several times."

"I think so." After all, she had been drooling over Ryder. "But it wasn't you she was looking at."

Mark's gaze met hers and he grinned. "That jealousy I hear in your voice? Afraid she's going to move in on your man?"

"No," she assured him, her chin lifting in defiance of his claim. "Why would I be jealous?"

Why indeed? Because her brother knew her too well and had called her out on it. Right or wrong, she was jealous at the thought of Callie making advances on Ryder.

Ryder reached out to take her hand. "You know, I'm not interested in anyone but you," he added, lifting her hand to his lips and pressing a kiss to her fingertips.

Although she knew the gesture was just for show, electricity shot through her as she stared into his eyes.

Electricity and a desire so strong for his words to be real that her knees weakened. Pretend boyfriend Ryder was better than any real boyfriend she'd ever had.

If only he really was her boyfriend and had meant what he'd said.

He didn't, but she was thankful he was here, that his generosity had given her a peaceful visit home.

She rewarded him with a smile, then, giving in to whatever that volcano-like warmth inside her was, she leaned in, meaning to press a kiss to his mouth.

"McKenzie!"

Pausing mid-pucker, she glanced toward the direction she'd heard her name called from.

Across the room, an elderly man was lying on the floor with several people huddled over him. Jeremy's uncle Daniel!

McKenzie and Ryder rushed over to where he lay. "What happened?"

"We're not sure. One minute he was talking and the next he went pale, then collapsed to the floor."

Jeremy's uncle and aunt had come over to her soon after they'd arrived and given her a big hug, asking her about her life in Seattle, and saying how proud they were of her and her accomplishments. Now, the sweet man in his early sixties was unconscious.

"He's breathing, but shallow," Ryder told her from where they stooped over him.

They loosened his shirt buttons and Ryder bent to listen to his chest.

"His heartbeat is bradycardic."

"Pulses are faint, thready," she added, her finger against the unconscious man's left radial artery.

"Is he okay?" someone asked as McKenzie continued to press her finger against the man's wrist.

"We're not sure," she admitted, propping his feet up onto a nearby chair to increase blood flow to his heart. "Has he ever blacked out before? Any known health problems?"

She was used to dealing with kids but had done multiple adult rotations during her residency. Some things were basic medicine. This was one of them.

"Diabetes, high blood pressure, high cholesterol," an

older woman began spouting out. His wife looked as if she might collapse herself any moment.

"He had a stent placed in his right coronary artery a few years back but has done well since that time. I don't recall him ever having passed out, not even before his stent."

Had the stent placed in one of the main arteries supplying his heart with oxygenated blood become blocked again?

"Grab my purse," she ordered Callie, for the sole reason she was the first person McKenzie made eye contact with when she glanced up. She had a resuscitation mouth guard in her bag that she carried with her at all times.

Just in case.

She motioned for her brother to help Jeremy's aunt sit down as McKenzie dialed 911. Regardless of why Uncle Daniel had passed out, he needed a full medical workup as his risk factors were high. They needed to get an ambulance on the way STAT.

"Do you have his blood sugar meter with you?"

It was unlikely the man's sugar had bottomed out since they'd just eaten, but anything was possible.

Ryder had leaned down and was pressing his ear against the man's chest to listen to his heart sounds.

"I have one in my purse," someone else said, grabbing her bag and dumping the contents onto a nearby table so she could quickly hand over a clear bag that held a glucometer, a tube of test strips, some lancets and a few disposable gloves.

"Daniel," she said to the unconscious man just in case he could hear her. "I'm going to check your blood sugar. In just a minute you're going to feel a stick in your finger."

With her cell phone held between her shoulder and her ear, McKenzie reported his status to the dispatcher while she slipped on a glove, pulled the protective cover off one of the lancets and poked the tip of the man's finger. Taking one of the test strips, she pressed the edge to the drop of blood.

Within seconds, the machine flashed with the reading.

"Two hundred and sixty-one." Much too high, but not the cause of the man's syncope.

What worried McKenzie the most was his lack of response to her sticking him with the needle. He'd barely made a sound at what should have triggered a pain response.

Her gaze met Ryder's and she knew he was thinking the same thing.

The dispatcher said he had an ambulance on its way and McKenzie handed her phone to someone else to talk to the man so she could focus on the patient.

"Mr. Carter?" Ryder shook the man, trying to get a response. "Can you hear me? I need you to open your eyes."

Nothing.

Ryder rubbed his knuckles across the man's sternum with good force which should have elicited a grimace.

McKenzie wasn't surprised when it didn't since he'd failed to react to the lancet.

She placed her finger over his radial pulse again and couldn't find it.

"Ryder," she said firmly to get his attention, not wanting to alarm everyone crowding around them, but becoming alarmed herself. She moved her fingers to his carotid, searching for a beat in case she'd just missed it, but knowing she hadn't.

Reading her mind, Ryder bent his ear to the man's chest again.

"Mr. Carter?" he repeated, shaking the man vigorously. Nothing.

He checked Daniel's airway, then muttered a low curse

as he pressed his hands over the man's chest and began doing compressions.

Thankful she'd sent Callie to retrieve her purse, McKenzie grabbed the mouthguard, ripped off the plastic covering and gave two breaths.

Ryder counted out loud and McKenzie gave the two person CPR recommended two breaths to his every fifteen compressions.

In between breaths, she checked for a carotid pulse, for any sign he'd resumed breathing.

Nothing.

She and Ryder worked together, keeping the rapid lifesaving rhythm going in hopes of reminding Daniel's body of what it should be doing.

After the fourth set of delivered breaths, her own breath caught.

"There's a pulse! Faint, but it's there," she excitedly told Ryder, relief coursing through her entire being.

"Thank God," someone in the crowd said, reminding McKenzie that they had an audience surrounding them. As she and Ryder had worked, she'd completely forgotten where they were. Everything had faded away except for her and Ryder and their efforts to save the man's life.

McKenzie was thankful, too, for the pulse, but knew they were far from out of the woods. Ryder continued to do the compressions, and as McKenzie bent to give her two breaths, the man finally took one on his own. She waited to see if he was going to take another, didn't like how much time passed and went ahead and delivered two more.

"I hear the ambulance sirens," someone unnecessarily said as the distant wail couldn't be missed.

Now, that was something McKenzie was also thankful for. Daniel needed medical attention fast as she was almost positive he'd had a myocardial infarction.

They continued to assist the man's basic vital functions while they waited on the ambulance to arrive. Time seemed to drag but it couldn't have been more than a minute or two in reality.

As his breathing and pulse were sporadic at best, neither she nor Ryder stopped their cardiopulmonary resuscitation efforts.

Just as the emergency sirens came to a halt outside the building, Daniel opened his eyes.

They were blurred, staring up in dazed confusion. McKenzie wasn't sure they were registering much, if anything, but, oh, how she rejoiced at seeing the flicker of movement quickly followed by his taking a deep gasp of air on his own trailed by another.

"Oh, honey." His wife could apparently no longer stay back in her nearby chair and knelt next to him, leaning over, tearful as she continued to talk almost incoherently. "Love you…so scared…please don't…"

McKenzie could make out only part of her words they were so muffled with tears, and she felt moisture pricking at her own eyes. How much the woman loved her husband, how scared she was, poured from her shaking body.

McKenzie dealt with a lot of sad things in pediatric cardiology but hadn't dealt with an acute heart attack adult patient since residency. It was unlikely that Ryder had either. He seemed to be taking it all in his stride.

McKenzie stayed crouched next to the man, closely monitoring his vitals. Ryder stood to make room for the emergency medical workers to rush to the patient's side. He began filling them in with who he and McKenzie were and what had happened while the crew completed a quick assessment of their own.

"Daniel, it's McKenzie Wilkes. I'm Reva's cousin and a doctor. We're at Jeremy and Reva's wedding rehearsal dinner," she told him to help ground him to where he was and hopefully help keep him calm. "You passed out and we called for an ambulance. The paramedics are here now. They're going to take you to the hospital to be checked further to find out why you lost consciousness."

"I'm okay," the man mumbled low, garnering everyone's attention at his whispered words and weak attempt at sitting up. "Just my chest feels heavy. Sharp pain."

As if to confirm his words his hands went to his chest.

"Don't try talking," one of the paramedics advised, covering his mouth with an oxygen mask.

Quickly, they had an intravenous line in, and he was being rolled to the ambulance on a wheeled stretcher.

Jeremy's aunt and a couple of other family members stayed close to the stretcher, planning to drive to the hospital. McKenzie and Ryder moved along with the stretcher as well, available in the unlikely case they were needed further, but far enough back as to not be in the way.

Most of the guests followed the procession, watching as Daniel was loaded into the ambulance and as it noisily took off with two cars of family members on its tail. Slowly, the guests began returning to inside the rehearsal dinner venue.

Once they were inside, everyone looked around at each other in an anticlimactic way of not knowing what to do next, their over joyous celebrating from earlier having taken a nosedive at Daniel's scary episode. Did they all just pack up and go to the hospital? Or did they proceed with the rehearsal dinner and afterward plans as if nothing had happened to keep from spoiling Jeremy and Reva's rehearsal?

Apparently knowing everyone would look to the bride for guidance, Reva took a deep breath.

Pride filled McKenzie as her cousin spoke.

"Anyone who wants to go on to the hospital, please do. No worries about us. As long as Uncle Daniel is okay, we'll be fine." She smiled at the crowd. "We'll finish here, pack up the leftover food and send it back to Aunt Roberta's house for anyone staying or visiting there to munch on over the weekend. Then, we'll check on Uncle Daniel before we decide whether or not to cancel the rest of our plans."

"Not our wedding plans," Jeremy quickly clarified, shooting his bride-to-be a concerned look. "Regardless of what happens, those plans are noncancelable because I'm marrying you tomorrow."

He lifted her hand to his lips and pressed a kiss there.

A collective sigh resounded across the room, McKenzie's included. Another ping of jealousy also hit her.

Had Paul ever looked at her that way? She wondered. With such love shining in his eyes?

If so, he hadn't for some time.

She'd been so caught up with her career that she hadn't noticed. Or maybe, she hadn't wanted to notice that Paul was no longer enamored of her.

Nor had she noticed that she hadn't been head over heels in love with him. She'd cared deeply for him, had been content with the life she'd believed they'd have together, but had she been with Paul to appease her worried family and fallen into habit rather than love?

When she got back to Seattle, she was going to find more balance in her life. Hadn't she moved to Seattle because she'd loved walking along the pier? Loved feeling the wind in her face and the sea breeze filling her soul? Because she loved just meandering through Pike Place Market people watching and browsing the goods? And always she'd left with a huge bouquet that made her smile each time she saw it in her house? How long since fresh flowers had adorned her kitchen table?

That balance might not include Ryder or any man, but

McKenzie planned to make a few changes, including making time to come back to Tennessee at least annually.

Ryder held out his hand toward her, leading her away from where the crowd lingered, discussing what had happened and how calm Reva was about the ordeal.

Glancing toward Ryder, McKenzie's breath caught as it seemed to have started always doing when he came into view. Truly, he literally took her breath away.

Was it just him and his supersized pheromones that made her so aware of how much a man he was, how much a woman she was?

"Are you okay?"

McKenzie blinked at Ryder. "Yes, thank you," she told him and meant it. She really was. Better than she'd felt in weeks. "How did it take me so long to notice what a good man you are?"

Probably because he'd avoided her, and his overt masculinity had made her uncomfortable when patient care required they interact.

"Good question and one I often ask myself. Let's just be glad you finally noticed."

No doubt his words were for their observers' benefit, as were his next actions. He leaned down and pressed a quick kiss to her lips.

Which left her confused. Had she purposely not acknowledged her attraction to Ryder due to her relationship with Paul? Because the uncomfortableness she always felt she now knew to be sexual tension.

She'd be lying if she didn't admit to feeling electrified at where his lips had pressed against hers. And disappointed the kiss hadn't been more than a swift peck.

Because McKenzie wanted to kiss Ryder. For real.

She wanted to do lots of things with Ryder. For real.

CHAPTER NINE

"Vine to the right and hold. Right foot step to the right," the dance instructor said via her headset microphone to be heard over the country music playing in the background of the iconic Nashville honky-tonk on Second Avenue.

Jeremy's uncle had indeed had a heart attack with a blockage in the right coronary artery. Upon arrival at the emergency room, he'd immediately been taken to the heart catheterization lab and had the blockage stented. He was stable, in the cardiac care unit for the night, and doing well with several family members waiting for their brief visit that would be allowed every two hours for a few minutes each.

After going back and forth about whether or not to cancel their original plans, the wedding party and their dates had headed to downtown Nashville at Jeremy and Reva's insistence. As they'd wrapped up the rehearsal dinner so early it was barely eight o'clock when they arrived at the hopping venue on Second Avenue.

Luckily, they caught a group leaving and grabbed their vacated table up near the bar. Part of their crew, all guys, were still there, having a beer, and claiming to be holding the table. Ryder, Jeremy and a single brave groomsman had accompanied the women to the dance floor. Ryder wouldn't have minded staying with the guys at the table, but he had to admit, he was enjoying listening to McKenzie sing along with the country song's lyrics while she went through the motions being given by the dance instructor.

She was a good dancer and kept rhythm perfectly with the directions. He suspected she'd already known the dance prior to their fifteen-minute lesson. But her laughter was contagious, and she seemed to be truly relaxed for the first time since they'd arrived.

He could hold his own on a dance floor during a slow song, was passable during faster dances, but he'd been telling the truth when he implied that he wasn't much of a line dancer.

McKenzie had insisted he join her on the dance floor for the class that was just starting as their group arrived and he hadn't had the heart to disappoint her.

Fortunately, he quickly picked up the dance with only a few missteps.

Like now when he went left when he should have gone right, leading to McKenzie bumping into him when he stepped into her dance space.

Which had happened only because he'd been watching her smiling face rather than paying attention to what he was doing.

"Oops!" Laughing, she grabbed hold of his arm to steady herself. Her palm was warm against his skin.

Warm? Warm didn't scorch straight through every layer and singe a man's insides. McKenzie's touch did that, quickening his pulse more than moving to the music had.

He usually tamped down his attraction to her, but they were in a public place. What could it hurt? After all, they were a pretend couple. A little heat sparking between them would add to the show they were putting on for her family.

"Sorry." He grinned down at her although he wasn't sure he was sorry as her fingers lingered on his arm.

"No worries." Rather than let go, she slowly let her fingertips graze over his skin in a light caress.

Shivers ran down Ryder's spine.

What would it feel like if McKenzie ran her fingers that way over his chest? Over his abdomen? If while doing so she looked at him with the light shining so brightly in her big green eyes? If those eyes darkened with desire?

They would. Ryder saw the sexual energy in her eyes when she looked at him. It had always been there, lurking beneath the surface, tormenting him with the knowledge she'd belonged to another.

McKenzie was no longer in her relationship. She looked at him with passion in her eyes.

But Ryder knew all about a woman on the rebound, about how they could project their feelings, how a rebound fling often soothed a deflated ego.

Ryder swallowed the knot forming in his throat.

If anything happened between him and McKenzie, she'd be using him.

The last time a woman had used him he'd been left with a gaping hole in his chest. He refused to go through that again.

But in this moment, dancing with McKenzie, feeling the energy of her laughter, of her sexual energy, remembering anything other than the fact he wanted her seemed impossible.

Oblivious to his thoughts, she leaned toward him and spoke up so he'd hear her over the music. "You're doing great."

Well, he had been until she smiled, her eyes flashing with another spark of feminine awareness, and his feet took on a mind of their own. He stepped into her dance space rather than out of it, again.

Her lips formed an O, then she laughed but kept going

through the steps as instructed by the woman moving around the dance floor, giving pointers.

When Ryder bumped into McKenzie a third time, he shrugged as if he didn't know how it had happened.

"Hey, are you doing that on purpose?" She gave a suspicious look, but her eyes were dancing with delight.

Doing his best to maintain a facade of innocence, he asked, "Would I do that?"

Keeping in step, she arched a brow. "Two weeks ago, I'd have said no. That you'd have done anything to move away from me rather than closer. Now…"

She was right. He had avoided her. Because she'd been seriously involved with another man and when he was around her, he'd wanted to toss aside his common sense and make her his. He might have even been successful, but he didn't go after women who had boyfriends. Or women who were on the rebound from a man they'd planned to marry.

He'd learned that lesson with Anna and wouldn't make the same mistake twice.

His gaze met McKenzie's. She looked at him as if she wanted to strip his clothes off and explore every inch of him.

Was it for show because her friends and family were there?

"Now?" he prompted, wanting to hear what she had to say, to see if she'd flirt back, even if only a little, as he rocked his hips forward and held, then shifted to the left, then rocked to the right, keeping time with the music.

"Now?" Her eyes twinkled. "I'm sure you would."

He laughed. "You might be right."

"Might be?" Her gaze was still locked with his.

"You sure you're a beginner?" Reva called from the opposite side of McKenzie, interrupting their banter. "Because you're picking that up awfully fast."

"Hello?" McKenzie play scowled at her cousin. "Did you not just see him almost knock me down half a dozen times?"

Smiling, Reva shook her head and called, "I must have missed that."

Ryder winked conspiratorially at the bride-to-be who was enjoying herself despite the medical drama at her rehearsal dinner. Probably because her husband's uncle was expected to fully recover and might even be released from the hospital the following day so long as nothing unexpected happened between now and then.

"Okay, now, ladies and gentlemen," the dance instructor said. "From the beginning. Let's go."

The music started over and they went through the motions to the decades-old hit about an achy broken heart. They danced and Ryder kept his body in his dance space, rather than invading McKenzie's, although the temptation to bump her just for another touch was strong.

When the song ended, he was glad he had stayed focused on the dance, because, eyes sparkling, mouth curved in a big smile, she wrapped her arms around him in a hug and squeezed.

"That was amazing. You were amazing!"

Her arms around him was amazing. So amazing Ryder felt his resolve melting. In its place was happiness that he was relaxed, away from work, dancing with a beautiful woman who was flirting with him as if she planned other dances, more primal, in her mind.

"Never say you can't line dance again," she warned.

"Pretty sure being able to follow step-by-step instructions doesn't qualify me to say that I can line dance," he pointed out, wondering what she'd say if he just held her in the hug forever?

Her body felt that good.

Like he wanted to hold her body against his for a very long time. Ryder fought to keep his lower half from reacting in an embarrassing way.

Around them, everyone clapped and thanked the instructor. Eyes locked, he and McKenzie parted and did the same.

The band took the stage again and launched into a slow song. Next to them, Jeremy pulled Reva to him.

McKenzie's gaze lowered and she started walking off the dance floor.

"I don't think so," Ryder said, reaching for her hand even as he acknowledged slow dancing with her would do nothing to stop the erection threatening to make itself present. "If I had to line dance then you don't get to run away when I get an opportunity to show off that I don't really have two left feet despite recent evidence to the contrary."

"You're sure?" she asked, looking as if she wanted to stay, but was hesitant, in case he didn't really want to slow dance and she didn't want to force him to stay.

He wanted to hold McKenzie in his arms.

Any excuse would do.

"Positive." He pulled her to him and put his hands at her lower back, holding her close as they began to sway to the country love ballad.

McKenzie's head rested just beneath his chin as they moved in perfect harmony to the song Ryder had never heard before but would never hear again without thinking of McKenzie and this moment.

Without remembering her light flowery smell and warm body next to his wreaking all kinds of havoc with his internal circuitry.

Holding her like this had him wondering what it would have been like had McKenzie been single when he'd arrived in Seattle. What if Paul had never been in the picture? What if he'd never had to tamp down the way she burned his insides and instead could have let her set him on fire over and over.

Her fingers toyed with the hair at his nape. "Thank you, Ryder."

"For not stepping on your toes?" Her fingers in his hair was making his feet happy enough to walk on air.

"That," she agreed, brushing her thumb slowly across the back of his neck, "and everything else. For coming with me this weekend, for being so great at the rehearsal dinner, for saving Jeremy's uncle's life."

"That was a partnered effort," he reminded her, pressing his palm into the curve of her lower back to keep her close. Her body next to his felt good. "You played just as big a role in saving his life as I did."

"Thanks, but I don't think so. You were wonderful. Jeremy's family all think you're a hero. My family, too. Which is great, only…"

"Only?" he prompted.

Her gaze lifted to his and she searched his eyes, making him wonder just how much of his thoughts she'd read, especially when she answered his question.

"None of it is real."

They weren't real, McKenzie reminded herself for the dozenth time in the past five minutes.

Literally, she kept reminding herself, because it was easy to forget they were pretending when Ryder smiled at her with a certain look in his eyes.

Ryder wasn't her boyfriend.

Despite her reminder that had been for herself as much as for Ryder, he was smiling.

Why wouldn't he be? It didn't matter to him that they weren't real, that the sexual tension building between them on the dance floor was a byproduct of proximity, pretense and young, healthy bodies rather than something more.

Her family all bought that they were a real couple.

Only rather than being happy at how well her plan was working, she laid her head back against his shoulder and moved to the music with him in slow, rhythmic movements and fought sighing.

Because they were doing such a good job pretending that they were convincing her, too.

She liked how he held her, firmly against him, but not too tightly.

Being in Ryder's arms, having him hold her next to him, feeling his warm breath against the top of her head, was an experience unlike anything she recalled.

She couldn't remember having her ear pressed against Paul's chest, listening to his heartbeat, or perhaps feeling it against her cheek more than actually hearing the resounding *lub-dub* over the twangy love song, and being so aware of each beat. Of being aware of the strength of the chest she leaned against. Of being so in sync with that rhythm and becoming mesmerized by the tune it played.

Of being so aware of the spicy male scent surrounding her and flashing her back to when he'd stepped into her bedroom fresh from his shower that morning and filling the room with him—his scent, his presence.

Of how her thighs had clenched, her heart had quickened, her throat had tightened.

The song ended and another started, its beat a little faster than the previous song. She and Ryder didn't pull apart, just kept moving to the music.

She closed her eyes.

This feels right.

Only it was make-believe.

Ryder's lips brushed against the top of her head, softly,

but she'd definitely felt the caress. Opening her eyes, she caught Reva and Jeremy watching them. Smiling big, her cousin gave a thumbs-up sign.

Down the road, many years from now, she'd tell Reva the truth. Her cousin would understand why she'd wanted Ryder with her. No one wanted to come home for a wedding single, dejected and at her meddling family's mercy.

She might even admit to the green tinging her blood at how Reva's life was so wonderful and to the guilt she felt at her jealousy.

Glancing over at where Jeremy and Reva were hugged up on the dance floor still, her cousin laughing at something he'd said, McKenzie's chest squeezed. That's what she wanted. Someone to love her and laugh with her and want to spend their life with her.

Was that such an impossible want?

"What are you thinking?"

She lifted her head from Ryder's strong chest to look at him. "Nothing, why?"

"You got tense. Everything okay?"

The man was too observant.

Still, McKenzie had no real regrets on bringing Ryder with her. To have come alone would have thrown an ugly wrench into McKenzie's entire visit.

Because of him, this weekend had been fun, exciting and full of self-discovery.

"Just thinking how nice this is, spending unpressured time with my family, getting to know you, dancing with you," she admitted.

"It is nice, but don't forget none of this is real."

No chance of that happening.

"It would be nice if it were, though."

He stiffened against her and she realized they'd stopped

dancing, were standing close, and to the casual observer probably just looked to be talking.

Obviously, her last comment had raised his hackles.

Embarrassed that she'd let herself get caught up in the heated emotions being with him caused, she forced a smile in his general direction.

No worries, Ryder. I know this is only pretense to you.

That's all it had been to her, too. Initially.

Now, she wasn't so sure, which was obviously making him uncomfortable.

She'd save him from having to stress that they weren't real and never would be.

"Now, no more serious talk. Let's have some fun."

Just after eleven Ryder and McKenzie were back at her mother's house. Her cousin Jeff and his family had already called it a night, as had her mother. All the lights were off except the front porch and a couple of night lights.

Mark was still out with the others, saying not to wait up on him as he'd likely find more comfortable sleeping arrangements than the sofa.

Ryder let McKenzie use the bathroom first, wandering around her childhood room to check out the boy band posters adorning her walls. He could just imagine her and Reva blasting the music and singing along at the top of their lungs.

Seeing how close they were, he wondered again why had she chosen to move so far away from her family?

With him, his parents were super successful single children of small families and, with Chrissy's death, he was an only child. There were no big gatherings at holidays or chaotic shared bathrooms. Next to McKenzie's family, his home life seemed quite dull.

He picked up a framed photo off her dresser. McKenzie held a volleyball and Reva was in a cheerleader out-fit. They were hugged up like the best of friends, much as they'd been embracing on the dance floor.

When the connecting bathroom door opened, McKenzie had changed into shorts that were barely visible beneath an oversized T-shirt.

His breath caught at the sight of her shapely legs, brushed-out long hair and freshly washed face. She was beautiful.

Brilliant and beautiful.

Sexy as hell.

"Your turn," she offered, unaware of the lust she was unleashing in his body while she hung her dress back onto a hanger in her closet. When she turned, realized he'd been looking at the photo of her and Reva, something flashed in her eyes that struck him as odd.

Then realization hit.

He felt such a fool. How had it taken him so long to fig-ure out the truth?

Then again, he'd been blinded by his own attraction to McKenzie, blinded by her recent breakup with Paul.

Paul had been a rebound relationship.

Ryder set the photo frame back on the dresser. "I like to think I'm pretty astute, but I completely missed what was going on here."

"Oh?" Her gaze lifted to his much as a doe's caught in a headlight.

"I assumed it was something that had happened between you and your family that had you moving to Seattle, but then you all seemed so close that I'd decided I was wrong."

"I never said anything happened to cause me to move to Seattle other than that I fell in love with the city," she reminded him, placing her fists on her hips as she re-garded him.

"But," he continued as if she hadn't said anything, "it was you and Reva who had a falling out."

"You're crazy," she accused, but looked away as she busied herself straightening the clothes in her closet. "My cousin and I did not have a falling out."

"I knew you were stressed about coming home, but I got that a wedding is a little more pressure to not be single. Now, it all makes sense. What happened between you and your cousin?"

"Nothing happened."

He wanted her to tell him the truth, rather than him having to pry it from her.

Frustrated, he said, "Something happened. Otherwise I don't think you'd have moved quite so far."

McKenzie didn't meet his eyes. "You're drawing wrong conclusions, Ryder."

"Am I?" His brow lifted, then he shook his head. "I don't think so, but I'll let you think you're deceiving me the way you're deceiving yourself if you really believe that."

She rolled her eyes. "You barely know me, haven't even been in this house twenty-four hours. So, don't you go psychoanalyzing me, Ryder."

"Then you and Jeremy were never a thing? Because my guess is he's what came between you and your cousin."

McKenzie burst out laughing. "Jeremy and I were never a thing. I knew him in school, of course, but he, and every other guy, was crazy about Reva. How could they not be? She's wonderful."

"Then who came between you?"

"No one," she repeated. "I—I was involved with someone during my senior year of high school and into college, but Reva never dated him."

"Did she want to?"

"Not to my knowledge. Clay didn't break up with me

because of Reva, Ryder. He left me to take a residency in Boston and I took one in Seattle. End of story."

"How long were you together?"

"What does that matter?" She took a deep breath. "Seven years."

All this time he'd thought it was Paul who was his greatest competition, Paul who he had to worry about being a rebound guy from. Was it actually someone he'd never heard her mention?

"Not that it's any of your business, but Clay and I dated for seven years. We planned to both go to Seattle." She gave a wry snort. "I didn't even know he'd applied for a residency in Boston. My family worried about me going so far away when I was upset about the breakup and wouldn't know a soul. They didn't understand that going to Seattle rescued me from their pity."

"Loving you and wanting to help you through a breakup isn't the same thing as pity."

"How would you know, Ryder? I seriously doubt that anyone pities you. Do you want to know what my biggest issue is since coming home? That I'm freaking jealous of my cousin's happiness. Don't get me wrong. I'm glad she's marrying Jeremy, but what is wrong with me that I can't have a good relationship, too?"

She was standing close to him, glaring up at him with eyes that flashed with anger and hurt.

He didn't want to fight with her and searched for the right words to answer her questions.

Her questions that cut to his very core.

But she wasn't finished, and perhaps hadn't even wanted answers to her questions, but was just shooting words out at him like emotional arrows meant to pierce deep.

"Good for you on figuring out that not only was I dumped by Paul, but also by a man I'd given seven years of my life to thinking we'd someday marry, too." Another self-deriding snort flared from her nostrils. "Obviously, I'm very dumpable."

"You're not very dumpable."

"Right." Seeming to deflate, she gestured toward the bathroom. "Don't you need to change before bed?"

"You mean floor?"

Her gaze narrowed. "I'll gladly take the floor."

"No." He regretted his stupid quip. "I don't want you taking the floor."

She didn't answer, just stood waiting for him to go to the bathroom with her chin lifted.

Which gutted him.

What he wanted more than anything was to wrap his arms around McKenzie and wipe the exhausted, dejected look off her face.

"I'm sorry."

Her chin hiked up a few more notches. "I don't want or need your pity. I'm fine."

Gathering his pajama pants, Ryder crossed the room to the bathroom door, paused a moment as he racked his brain for something to defuse the tension between them.

The last thing he wanted was to upset McKenzie, although he seemed to be doing a good job of doing just that.

"I really am sorry I jumped to conclusions, McKenzie. I wish you'd told me everything. It would have made things make sense."

"No doubt, you're right," she surprised him by saying. "I doubt you've ever been dumped, so how could you possibly understand that I might not have wanted to admit to just how dumpable I am?"

He understood more than she thought. He'd been dumped, had his heart broken and probably even been the recipient of some of that pity she'd mentioned.

"Neither of them deserved you."

"Just go get ready for bed," she ordered, no longer meeting his gaze. "We've got a long day in front of us tomorrow."

When Ryder had finished in the bathroom, he wasn't surprised to see her curled up on the floor, pretending to be asleep.

Fine, let her pretend.

He'd just pretend like he believed her and put her faking it butt up into the bed. Walking over to the bed, he pulled back the covers, as if he was about to climb in, then squatted beside her and slipped his arms beneath her.

"What are you doing?" she squealed as he lifted her from the floor.

"Tucking you in, Sleeping Beauty."

"Put me down." She wiggled in his arms.

"Planning to," he assured her, setting her onto the bed, then pulling the covers over her body while she stared up at him a bit slack-jawed. "Goodnight, McKenzie. Sleep tight."

She glared at him as if he represented everything wrong in her life.

Maybe he did since she was using him as a shield against having to face those things.

Reaching over, he turned the lamp light out, then took a deep breath.

He'd had to kill the light.

Because looking down at her, her eyes flashing green fire, her lips pursed in anger, his every instinct had been to kiss her.

To kiss her until she was breathless, and her anger burst into flames of desire.

To kiss her until she forgot about Clay.

And Paul.

Any every other man she'd ever cared about.

Ryder wanted to kiss her until she couldn't think about anyone other than him.

His instinct wanted that kiss, wanted all those things, but he wouldn't do any of those things.

The last thing he or McKenzie needed was another rebound relationship destined to end in disaster.

Lying down on the floor, he listened to her breathing go from loud, exaggerated huffs to calmer, even breaths, but he knew she wasn't asleep.

What would she say if he reached up and took her hand into his? Would she smack it away? Or would she let him hold her hand the way he wanted to hold her?

"I have been dumped."

Silence met his admission.

"I mentioned her to you on the plane. She and I were in Pittsburgh together. I knew she was just coming out of a bad relationship, but I got caught up in a whirlwind romance with her."

Why was he telling her about Anna?

"I was crazy about her. When I started sensing her pulling away, I became more desperate to change her mind." Pain slashed at his chest at the memories of how he'd been used. "Seems she'd started talking to her ex again. They were sleeping together, but she worried about ending things with me because of our research." He paused, took a deep breath. "She resented that she felt she couldn't end things with me and finally she admitted she'd only used me to get back at her ex."

Ryder curled his fingers into his palms, pressing the tips deep into his flesh as he continued. "I was angry at her for not being honest with me. I hated myself for being so stupid and allowing myself to be used, and swore I'd never make that mistake again."

He uncurled his fingers, let out a slow breath. "So,

when you accuse me of not knowing what it feels like to be dumped, you're wrong. I know all too well."

McKenzie lay perfectly still in the bed, but he knew she'd heard ever word he'd said, that she was processing his admission.

"For whatever it's worth, they were fools for letting you go."

Silence met him, and he wondered if she'd say anything at all.

Then she softly said, "Seems the world is full of fools."

The pain in her admission punched him. McKenzie was so much more than both men. Ryder couldn't understand why either would have let her go.

"You're better off without them." His words seemed blasé even to him. Just something people said when someone ended a relationship. But his words were true. If the men hadn't cherished McKenzie, had been willing to let her go, she was better off without them. "Surely you recognize that?"

"As you're better off without Anna?"

Had he said Anna's name out loud? Ryder knew he hadn't. But then, one of the things he'd always admired about McKenzie was her sharp mind.

"I am," he acknowledged. He was. Although he hadn't seen it at the time, Anna hadn't been the right woman for him.

Ryder waited for McKenzie to respond, but despite the fact she lay awake for a long time, she never said anything more.

Just lay in her bed, her breathing even, but not to where he thought her asleep.

Which meant what?

He'd done nothing wrong. She'd dragged him into this

wedding weekend. He'd had every right to ask about Reva, to think a man had come between her cousin and her.

McKenzie bringing him to Tennessee might have been the best thing for everyone involved. He could see that now.

Everyone, that is, except Ryder, as the last thing he needed was to be a rebound guy, again.

CHAPTER TEN

MCKENZIE HAD LAIN awake a long time and once she'd fallen asleep had passed out to oblivion to everything around her.

She'd not heard Ryder get up, get a shower and leave the room, but he wasn't on the floor.

Panic hit.

Had he had enough of this crazy situation and left?

The thought that he might be gone made her head light. *Please don't let him have left.* For so many reasons, she wanted Ryder with her in Tennessee.

Not the least of which was how happy she felt when he was near. How aware she'd become of her body when near him.

He'd been doing her a favor and she hadn't given him all the facts.

He'd been used in the past. Yet, he was essentially allowing McKenzie to do the same, to use him to pretend everything in her life was wonderful when it wasn't.

Why had he agreed to come with her to Seattle?

Thanks to his having blocked her out after those first few weeks he'd been in Seattle, they barely knew each other.

Yet, truth be known, Ryder knew more about her than any person in Seattle, including Paul.

She owed Ryder an apology. He'd had every right to ask

about her life since she'd dragged him right smack dab in the middle of it.

She'd gotten so angry at him the night before, but in truth, she'd been angry at herself, ashamed of herself, and perhaps having a bit of a pity party for herself, which she detested.

Please let Ryder forgive me.

Getting out of bed, she paused long enough to go in the bathroom to brush her teeth, then went searching for him, wandering into the kitchen where she found her mother, Aunt Myrtle, Julianna, and a few cousins spread out around the kitchen.

Ryder wasn't there!

Her heart sank, her mind racing ahead to returning to Seattle to find him, to talk to him, to make him listen.

"Good morning," her mother greeted from the sink where she washed dishes.

"Morning," McKenzie said back, heading straight for the coffee pot. She needed coffee. Then she'd figure out her next move.

"Coffee's fresh," Julianna assured her from where she lorded over her three-year-old, trying to make Casey eat. "And dark."

"Perfect."

"Your fellow is out in the garage helping Mark and Jeff figure out what's wrong with my car," Aunt Myrtle informed her, not looking up from her crossword puzzle.

Ryder was still there? He hadn't left? Thank God!

The emotions flooding her that he hadn't left had her grabbing hold of the countertop, sending a happy tremble down her spine.

"I wondered where he was," she said to no one in particular, just needing to let some of the joy inside her escape.

"They all went out there right after Myrtle arrived and

complained about the noises her engine was making," her mother said, rinsing a mug and placing it onto a towel.

Did Ryder know anything about working on cars? Did her brother and cousin, for that matter?

What did it matter so long as Ryder was still there?

"What's wrong with your car, Aunt Myrtle?" McKenzie asked as she poured a steaming cup of coffee, then added just the right amount of cream and sugar.

"If I knew, I wouldn't need them to figure that out."

Julianna glanced up from where she fed her youngest, her gaze meeting McKenzie's. Both women suppressed a smile at their quirky great-aunt.

"Hope they get it figured out. I've a pinochle game next week I'd hate to miss."

McKenzie leaned back against the countertop, sipping her coffee, taking in the commotion around the kitchen. Home. The sights, the smells, the feeling. She was home.

"You want me to help with the dishes, Mama?"

"No, thanks, honey. I'm about finished." Her mother placed a cup in a drainer, then dried her hands on a dish-towel.

At that moment, Ryder, Mark and Jeff came into the house. All of their hands covered in grease, and they were talking and laughing among themselves.

McKenzie's breath hung in her throat at seeing Ryder, at hearing his voice, his laughter. Thank goodness she'd not had coffee in her mouth, or she'd have possibly choked.

Oh, Ryder, I'm so sorry about last night.

Not that he could read her mind, or had even looked her way, but she willed him to know how sorry she was and to forgive her.

"Mark!" her mother squealed when her son moved to-ward her as if he was going to give her a hug.

"Don't touch a thing!" Jeff's wife added.

"Y'all don't look ready to go to a wedding," Aunt Myrtle said matter-of-factly from where she frowned at them over the top of her newspaper.

"Dibs on the bathroom," Jeff called, heading down the hallway.

Mark walked over to the kitchen sink, picked up the dishwashing detergent and squirted a big glob in his hand.

"Mom, I'm going to scrub up, then hop in your shower."

"Don't you go making a mess in my bathroom," she warned.

While all the commotion was going on, McKenzie had kept her gaze pinned on Ryder. Had held tightly onto her coffee mug because her hands shook.

Because she could tell he was avoiding looking at her, as if he didn't know what to expect when he did.

When their gazes met, her chest fluttered, reminding her she owed him an apology for the night before.

For involving him in this whole mess.

"I'm sorry," she mouthed, giving a small smile as a peace offering.

From where he continued to stand just inside the doorway, he half-smiled back.

Oh, heavens. Everything was going to be okay. He hadn't left. He'd smiled back. She'd get a chance to tell him all the things she'd thought of while lying in her bed the night before.

She'd get a chance to tell him that when he smiled he cleared the clouds from her world and made her feel as if she were lifting her face into the sunshine.

She'd get a chance to tell him she didn't understand all the things going on inside her, but one thing was glaringly clear. There was nothing pretend about the way her heart contracted because of him, nothing pretend about how seeing him set her libido ablaze, nothing pretend about how she'd trusted him with her deepest secrets the night before.

She put her coffee mug down and gestured to the sink. "Let me help you get clean before my ride to the venue gets here."

His gaze not leaving hers, Ryder stepped up next to McKenzie and held his hands over the recently drained sink.

McKenzie picked up the grease-cutting detergent and squirted some in his palms, turned on the water, and checked to make sure she had the temperature correct. She watched as he rubbed his hands together, scrubbing around his nails, rinsing, then holding his hands out for another round of detergent.

McKenzie obliged, but rather than watch him, this time, she took his hand and a dishcloth and began wiping at the remaining dark spots.

Why was her heart racing at washing his hands? This was ridiculous. But no more so than how the slightest brush of her fingers against his sent shivers over her skin.

Ryder's gaze lifted to hers in surprise, but he didn't say anything, just let her clean his hands.

His strong, talented hands that were capable of saving lives.

Hands that felt good in her own.

Hands she wanted holding hers, touching her, caressing her.

Afraid to look up for fear of what she'd see in his eyes, McKenzie dropped the cloth into the sink, pulled his hands beneath the running water to wash away the suds, and lingered there as the warm water flowed over their hands.

Knowing she needed to convey something of what she was feeling, she laced her fingers with his and held on tight.

Water rinsed over their hands much longer than necessary before McKenzie reluctantly turned to grab a dry cloth.

Ryder turned off the faucet and shook the excess water from his hands. McKenzie wrapped his hands in the towel, patting him dry.

"Thank you."

"You're welcome." Could he see everything bursting within her?

Needing to be sure he knew how much she appreciated him, how sorry she was for how defensive she'd been, she lifted Ryder's hand to her lips and pressed a kiss there.

If he'd looked surprised at her washing his hands, he looked stunned at the kiss. Regardless, he quickly masked it.

"You must have slept well."

"Eventually. I had a lot on my mind," she admitted, going back to massaging his hand with the towel. "You?"

"Same."

Her gaze met his. She sucked in a soft breath, then squeezed his hand. "Sorry if I kept you awake."

He hesitated only a second, then said, "You really need to do something about that snoring."

Her brows V'd as relief filled her at his teasing. "I don't snore."

"Sure, you do. It's quite adorable." He laughed, then pulled her to him, whispering in her ear. "We have a very attentive audience."

Which she had completely forgotten.

Because all she'd been thinking was how happy she was that he was there.

She forced a smile. "Keep up the good pretense."

McKenzie hadn't seen Ryder since she'd left her mother's house. She had spent the remainder of the morning with the rest of the bridesmaids being painted, powdered, curled, sprayed and beautified to the point McKenzie's eyes threatened to cross.

Still, she had to admit the bridesmaids all looked beautiful in their peacock-blue dresses and updos. As should be, none of them compared to her stunning cousin, though.

Reva made a beautiful bride who'd rival any magazine cover.

She'd chosen a slightly off-white form-fitting lace dress with a creamy ribbon at her waist. The neckline hinted at her cleavage but didn't reveal any secrets.

They'd had hundreds of photos taken around the venue, outside. Individual photos. Photos with the bride. Photos with the groom. Photos with the groomsmen. None of the bride and groom together though as they'd gone with the tradition of the groom not seeing the bride on the wedding day prior to her walking down the aisle to him.

Then it was time for the wedding.

"Thank you for being here."

Surprisingly, McKenzie hadn't felt a bit green all day. Probably because she'd been too distracted by thoughts of Ryder and wanting to strangle him that he'd thought she was pretending.

There had been nothing pretend about how she'd felt seeing him walk into her mother's kitchen, how she'd felt holding his hands while she washed them.

She liked him. Crazy that admitting that she liked her pretend boyfriend made her happy, but it did.

It also made her crazy.

Ryder had been used in the past, had been hurt.

Smiling at Reva, hoping her cousin was always as happy as she was at that moment, McKenzie hugged her. "I love you, Reva. I wouldn't have missed your wedding for the world."

She meant it, too. She was grateful for her cousin's wedding, for it forcing her home, for it forcing her to evaluate a lot of things about her life and choices.

For pushing her into convincing Ryder to come to Tennessee.

No matter what happened, she was grateful she'd gotten to know him, gotten to experience how it felt to kiss him.

If those had been his pretend kisses, she could only imagine what his real ones were like.

"Don't make me cry," Reva ordered, air-kissing McKenzie's cheek.

The music hit the note where McKenzie was to come out. She made her way, keeping her smile bright for the ever-present photographer.

Trying to keep the appropriate pace and not fall on her face, she walked down the aisle.

Her gaze sought where she knew Ryder would be sitting, spotted him, and she smiled.

A smile that came automatically and naturally.

A smile that came from deep inside.

A smile he returned and that even though it might be for show truly made her feel better.

Despite his having put on a good show that morning for anyone who might be looking their way, she couldn't help but wonder if that was all he'd been doing.

What if, unlike her, he hadn't started to have real feelings? Real desires?

Callie joined her in the wedding lineup, then the music changed to what every moment of the day had been building up to. Every wedding guest stood, turned to look toward where the bride would soon appear.

And then Reva was there.

McKenzie's heart filled with pride at her beautiful cousin's obvious love and happiness as she made her way down the aisle to her waiting groom.

The wedding ceremony went perfectly, with the groom soon kissing his bride.

McKenzie was paired with a groomsman, and arms linked, they walked back down the aisle with the photographer snapping away as they did.

They posed for photos that included the bride and groom, then were soon dismissed while the photographer took shots of just the bride and groom.

Once inside the reception hall, McKenzie immediately sought Ryder.

"Looking for someone?"

"Oh!" She spun at his voice, almost losing balance as she stared into his honey eyes.

"Sorry." He grabbed her elbow, steadying her. "I didn't mean to startle you."

"Were you waiting on me?"

"Something like that."

He must have been, otherwise, he wouldn't have been so close to the door because she'd barely made it inside the reception hall.

Just looking at him filled her with such jitters, with such a need to talk to him, away from the crowd.

"I—I don't want to stay here, Ryder."

His brow lifted. "You want to go back to Seattle?"

"Yes, but that's not what I mean." She grabbed his hand and pulled him toward the door she'd just come through. "I need some fresh air."

"Even though you just came from outdoors?"

"Work with me here," she ordered as she took off in the opposite direction of where the bride and groom were still snapping shots.

She walked until she came to a gazebo that was laced

with deep red knock-out roses. Inside the gazebo was a bench and just beyond it was a small gurgling creek.

"Wow," she breathed. "Beautiful."

"Yes."

McKenzie turned toward him. He'd been looking at her and not the gorgeous scenery.

"I'm sorry about last night, Ryder. I wanted to tell you this morning, but I overslept and then we were never alone and… I should have told you about Clay."

"You could have told me."

She nodded. "I should have. Only…"

"Go on," he repeated.

"Only, you are a gorgeous, successful man. What sane woman wants to tell you she wasn't worth hanging on to by any man she's ever dated?"

"You don't believe that, do you?"

She shrugged. "Not really."

"Wherein lies the problem. Have you ever considered that there were other reasons why your relationships don't work out?"

McKenzie took a deep breath, stared out at the pond. "It really is beautiful here, isn't it?"

"Is that how you deal with things you don't want to deal with? Change the subject?"

"You want me to go into the details of my breakup with Clay? Or give you all the details of my breakup with Paul?"

"It's not on the top of the list of conversations I'd like to have with you, but if it would help you to talk about it, I'm game."

Why was she getting upset with him again? She'd spent the entire day planning to let him know how much she regretted their disagreement the night before.

She winced. "I don't want to talk about any man but

you, Ryder. I want to talk about us, about what's happening between us."

His lips pressed to a thin line.

"Don't confuse this weekend with something real, McKenzie. You're on the rebound and that makes everything feel more intense."

She opened her mouth to correct him, but he pulled her to him, silencing her just as she realized someone was nearing the gazebo.

"Is everything okay?"

Reva! McKenzie should have known the photographer would want photos at the gazebo and creek.

Rather than answer her cousin with words, because words failed her, McKenzie placed her hands against Ryder's cheeks, stood on tiptoes and kissed him.

Because if she couldn't tell him with words how she was feeling, maybe she could show him.

It's for show, Ryder reminded himself.

That was the only reason McKenzie was kissing him. Because her cousin, Jeremy and the photographer had walked up on their discussion, and true to everything about this weekend for McKenzie, she didn't want there to be the slightest dark cloud on her cousin's big day.

Ryder should care that he was being used, should pull away. He did care.

But this was what he'd agreed to.

For all intents and purposes, he had agreed to be used.

So, he kissed McKenzie back as if he believed she was kissing him because she wanted to kiss him rather than to reassure their audience who might have picked up on their tension.

He kissed her as if the sweetness with which she caressed his face was a true lover's touch.

"Ahem," the photographer interrupted.

Ryder's gaze locked with McKenzie's, he waited for her to pull away from him. Slowly, she did so, her eyes hazy, her lips plump from their kiss, as she turned toward her cousin.

"Oh, sorry. We just needed a few minutes to ourselves. You know how it is." With that, McKenzie grabbed his hand. "We'll get out of the way."

CHAPTER ELEVEN

"THAT KISS, THOUGH!" Reva cooed later when the wedding party was seated at the front of the reception hall. "I thought smoke was going to start coming out of your ears any moment when we walked up on you at the gazebo."

Fighting rising heat in her face, McKenzie smiled at her cousin. "Ryder is a good kisser."

"Have you slept with him yet?" Callie asked.

McKenzie didn't answer.

"Girl, what are you waiting for? You're sleeping in the same room. Please tell me you're not making him sleep on the floor." Callie fanned her face. "That man is hot."

Ryder was hot. He was also not really hers. Kenzie had never slept around, had only ever been with two men. She couldn't just sleep with Ryder because of his close proximity. She needed more than that to give her body to a man.

"I imagine no one makes Ryder Andrews do anything he doesn't want to do," McKenzie answered, glancing over at where Ryder sat with her brother. The two of them seemed to have truly hit it off and were once again deep in conversation.

"He seems a great guy, Kenz," Reva pointed out. "I hope it's not too long before we're celebrating your big day."

McKenzie almost choked on the bite she'd just taken.

"Let's get through your wedding day before we start

planning mine." Which might not have been the right thing to say as Reva's eyes widened with delight.

"I knew it."

McKenzie got through her wedding obligations and was grateful when the wedding party were freed from their duties so they could mingle among the other guests.

"Okay, I need all the single ladies," the wedding coordinator announced. "Come on, girls. It's time for the bouquet tossing."

McKenzie reluctantly joined the other single women. Reva met her gaze, winked, then turned to toss the bouquet. Rather than join the scurrying to catch the flowers, McKenzie stepped back, happily letting Callie snatch the bouquet.

When she rejoined Ryder and Mark, the two men shook their heads.

"I'm disappointed. You should have had that bouquet."

"I didn't want that bouquet," she pointed out.

"Okay, gentlemen, it's your turn," the coordinator announced. "Gather up front."

"You don't have to go up there," she told Ryder.

"Sure, I do," he countered, standing, then bending to give her a quick obligatory peck on the lips. "Wish me luck."

Knowing several of the guests around them, including her brother, could hear everything being said, McKenzie smiled. "Go get 'em, Tiger."

When Ryder caught the garter, he held it up like a prized trophy, looked McKenzie's way, and waggled his brows. The crowd loved it and let out cheers.

McKenzie's face burned, but she kept her smile in place.

"Looks like you finally have one wanting to stick around," Aunt Myrtle said from a table over. Her voice was loud and carried to where half the guests in attendance had to have heard, Ryder included. McKenzie blushed.

"Look what I got for you," he bragged, twirling the garter on his finger.

"Hate to break it to you, but perhaps you didn't notice during the bouquet toss, I don't want that."

Grinning, he leaned in close and whispered, "Sure, you do. Everyone here will be busy talking about my catching this rather than you missing the bouquet that practically dropped into your arms. You can thank me later."

That's why he'd caught the garter? Because he was still trying to help her save face?

She'd never met anyone like him. He had no reason to help her, and yet, he was determined to do everything he could to make her look good.

She wanted to hug him. For real.

"Now, congratulate your man."

McKenzie's brows started V'ing together, then she recalled they really were the second most-watched couple at the wedding.

"Congratulations, Ryder." She smiled beatifically, leaned close to his ear and whispered, "You planning to wear that for me later tonight?"

If she'd been trying to leave Ryder speechless, good job.

Because, although he could think of dozens of responses to her comment, he couldn't form the words to say a single one.

Because his brain kept getting stuck on the fact that she'd been flirting with him.

For real.

Self-preservation demanded Ryder keep his guard up.

Because staying away from McKenzie once they were back in Seattle was going to be more difficult.

He'd do it, though.

The wedding couple's first dance was announced, then

the groom danced with his mother, and the bride her father. Then everyone was invited out onto the dance floor.

Knowing he'd keep his promise to her for the rest of the weekend, that keeping that promise was his motivation for wanting to take her out on the dance floor, Ryder stood, held out his hand. "How about it, McKenzie? You up for a foot-stomping two nights in a row?"

Hesitating only a moment, McKenzie placed her hand into his. "I'm not worried. I'll just be sure not to stand next to you during any line dances, and I should be fine."

Perhaps McKenzie had drunk too much of the free-flowing champagne. Perhaps it was how Ryder was putting on such a great show of being enamored with her that even she was convinced.

Perhaps it was how her body melded against his during the slow songs and how their eyes held each other's during fast ones as their bodies moved to the music.

Perhaps it was like he implied and the attraction she felt was simple genetically embedded chemistry that a gorgeous, intelligent man was near and she was DNA coded to respond.

She didn't believe so, but what did she know? She'd gotten things all wrong in her past relationships.

What made her think she'd do any better in a fake one?

Regardless of the reasons why, her body was responding.

To every look, every touch, every whispered comment, every laugh at something she said, every gentle kiss he bestowed on her hair while he held her close and they swayed to Reva's playlist.

Each song was like another round of foreplay, building tension within her, wearing down her reasons why she shouldn't invite Ryder into her bed that night.

It had been a while since she'd had sex.

But she didn't recall ever wanting it quite as badly as she did at the moment.

So badly that she was ready to ditch the wedding, take Ryder home and do all the things to him that her family and friends thought she should already have done.

"What are you thinking?"

McKenzie lifted her gaze to Ryder's. What would he say if she told him she was thinking about how much she'd like to strip his clothes off him and find out if he was as good in bed as she suspected he was?

Would he accuse her of not knowing what she was feeling? Of just being on the rebound and so not capable of rational discernment of her emotions?

"That Reva's wedding went well."

As if he knew that hadn't been what she was thinking, Ryder's brow arched. "Any regrets on coming this weekend?"

"None." She hadn't. Would she say the same if she failed to act on her attraction to Ryder? Would she forever wonder what would have happened if she'd told him she didn't want him to sleep on the floor? That she wanted him in bed, with her, but not to sleep?

Later that night, Kenzie was still wondering the same thing when she finished in the bathroom, came back into her bedroom, and saw Ryder lying on his pallet on the floor.

She paused by the door, hesitant, wondering which she'd regret more: climbing into her bed and falling asleep alone or inviting him into her bed and not sleeping at all?

Having no doubt heard her enter the room and wondering why she'd stopped just inside the door, he opened his eyes.

His beautiful honey-colored eyes that seemed to glow in the soft lamplight.

McKenzie swallowed.

She wanted to have sex with Ryder.

How crazy was that when she knew they weren't really a couple, when she knew that when they returned to Seattle tomorrow evening the pretense would be over and it was all too possible that he'd go back to avoiding her?

They were in the here and now.

In the here and now, Ryder was with her, was lying on her bedroom floor looking at her with those magnificent eyes. It might just be the convenience of proximity that caused the flash of heat, but she saw the lust burning in his gaze that she suspected flickered in her own.

But he didn't say anything, didn't even move, just watched as she crossed the room to stand next to the bed.

He wouldn't say anything, would let her climb into her bed and lie there wishing he was with her.

She couldn't do it.

Her whole life she'd settled when it came to relationships, to sex, to the men in her life.

Tonight, she wasn't settling.

She wanted Ryder, wanted the warmth of his touch, the heat of his kisses, the burn that spread inside her at anticipation of what she was about to do.

Rather than climb into her bed, or even to invite him to join her there, in case he said no, McKenzie knelt, straddled Ryder, her hips positioned perfectly over his as she leaned forward to press her lips to his.

Sexual tension had been building between them all night. All weekend. Longer.

But Ryder hadn't expected McKenzie to act on what was blazing between them.

He'd thought as long as he didn't say anything, she'd get in her bed and go to sleep. Tomorrow they'd go back to Seattle, then he'd make sure their paths didn't cross for long enough for him to get his attraction to her back under control.

Because it was out of control.

Or maybe he'd fallen asleep and was dreaming, and her hair didn't really cascade around him as she explored his mouth with hunger that matched his.

Whatever, he thrust his fingers through the silken tresses and pulled her to him, deepening their kiss.

She shifted above him, and he had to close his eyes to keep from lifting his hips to push into where she straddled his body.

He wanted to strip away their clothes, the thin blanket covering him, and thrust into her for real.

The deeper, the better.

Under different circumstances, he'd roll, pin her beneath him, and take control of what was happening.

He should stop her. Should remind her she was on the rebound. Should remind himself she was on the rebound.

"We should stop. Your emotions are high from the wedding. You'll regret this in the morning," he warned.

"You're wrong," she corrected, shifting her bottom over him. "This has nothing to do with the wedding and everything to do with you. I want this. I want you."

"McKenzie," he groaned. He wanted to do the right thing. For her. For him. He should stop her.

Then again, maybe this was what the entire weekend had been building up to. What had been building since they'd met.

Whatever the case, Ryder didn't stop her.

Couldn't stop her.

Instead, he used every ounce of willpower to let McKenzie lead, for her to dictate what happened every step of the way, no matter where that took them.

Whatever happened between them would be of her doing, her choice.

He'd wanted her from the beginning. Had only been fooling himself that he was over his fascination with her during the time he'd been avoiding her. He hadn't been over a thing.

Which was why he'd not been able to walk away when she'd needed him to go with her. No way would he have let her spend the weekend with a hired escort.

Perhaps he was no better, but he'd never intentionally hurt her. Had always tried to do the opposite, hence his staying away from her when she'd been with her ex for fear he'd act on his feelings for her, that he'd seduce her into something she didn't want.

He'd been seduced from the moment he'd met her and had instantly wanted her.

Now, she was above him, her hot center pressed over where he ached as she kissed him into oblivious pleasure.

He was oblivious. To all reason. To logic. To common sense. To everything except McKenzie.

When she moved against him, Ryder couldn't keep his hands off her any longer and skimmed them over her back, tracing her spine, cupping her sweet bottom gliding against him.

"Touch me," she moaned. "Please, Ryder, touch me. I need you to."

He planned to touch. Every last inch of her.

Excitement filled him as he slid his hands beneath her T-shirt and pulled the material over her head, revealing her bare chest beneath.

Her bare chest that had him arching upward to wrap his mouth around a pink tip.

Her thighs clenched at his waist as he gave a gentle suck, then he moved to the matching peak.

She leaned forward, supporting her upper half by placing a hand to each side of his head, giving him easy access to the treasures he'd uncovered.

He suckled, teased, licked and nipped until, moaning, she arched, then sat up enough to support her weight on her knees to each side of his hips. Her hands tugged on his T-shirt. Ryder raised his upper half from the floor, making removal of his shirt easier.

"You have a beautiful body," she praised, running her hands over his shoulders, then down his chest to mere inches away from where her lower half met his.

"As do you," he assured her, reaching for her breasts again. "As do you."

They kissed, touched, grinded against each other, until both were desperate for remaining clothing barriers to be gone.

McKenzie moved off him, and he helped strip away her pajama shorts and underwear.

When he reached for the waistband of his pajama bottoms, she covered his hand with hers.

Please don't stop me, he thought, at the same time as he had no doubt he'd do just that if it was what she said she wanted.

"I don't have protection," she said instead, disappointment shining in her eyes.

Relief filled him.

"I do. In my wallet."

Mixed emotions crossed her face. "Of course, you do."

He paused in reaching for where he'd left his wallet on her nightstand. "Did you want me to say I didn't have protection? We don't have to do this if it's not what you want," he reminded her.

They shouldn't do this. Deep down he knew that. He

also knew it would take a stronger man than him to deny
McKenzie if she wanted to make love with him.

"I do want this, so very much, only…" She closed her
eyes. "It makes sense you'd have protection. I'm glad you
have protection, and yet…well, I guess it makes me aware
of how much more experienced you are than me."

Ryder snorted with a bit of irony. Once upon a time
he'd had an active sex life, but not since moving to Seattle.
Quite the opposite. Sex for the sake of sex had quit appeal-
ing years before.

"It might surprise you how long it's been since I've had
sex."

For months, he'd wanted only one woman and she'd belonged to another man.

Tonight, she belonged to him.

Her body.

Her mind.

Her heart?

Self-conscious that she was naked and had stopped him
prior to his removing his pajama bottoms, McKenzie nodded, although she wasn't sure if she was agreeing with
his comment that how long it had been since he'd had sex
would surprise her or if she was nodding her agreement
with the thought that he should be naked, too.

Had it really been that long for him?

Did it matter? She wanted him. He wanted her—for the
moment, at least.

For now, that was enough.

Rather than say anything more, she finished the job he'd
started, pulling his pajama bottoms and underwear off in
one movement with the help of his lifting his hips.

Her breath caught at the true magnificence of his body.
She visually traced down his shoulders, his chiseled chest,

down his abs to where a trail of hair pointed to pleasure. Just wow.

Her gaze lifted to his. "You're sure you're really a heart surgeon and not a professional athlete?"

She'd thought he looked the part of a television doctor in the past. Seeing him naked reinforced her thoughts that his body was made to be admired.

She admired. Oh, how she admired.

His brow lifted. "Who better to take care of their body than someone educated on the benefits of exercise and proper diet?"

"True." Not that McKenzie hadn't enjoyed every bite of the cake and goodies served at the wedding—she had. "But I don't know of any real-life doctor who looks like you."

"I'm not the only one who works out."

"You're the only one who makes my fingers want to do this." She traced her finger over his chest, down his abs and happy trail in the pattern her eyes had previously taken.

Ryder sucked in air, his stomach muscles tightening. McKenzie thrilled at his reaction to her touch, that there was no denying that he wanted her.

Yet when she went to touch him where he strained toward her, he grabbed her hand, stopping her.

"Not yet. If you touch me there, I'll have to have you soon thereafter."

McKenzie's thighs clenched at the prospect, her whole body tingling. "Isn't that the idea?"

He shook his head. "My idea is to touch and kiss every inch of you first."

His words set off explosions in her head, in the pit of her belly, at her very core. She always had thought him a smart man. They'd go with his idea. Most definitely. Because she wanted him touching her, kissing her.

Every inch of her wanted to be claimed by him.

"Oh. Okay."

"Yeah, oh. Okay." His words were half-teasing, but his eyes glittered in ways she'd never seen him look at her. In ways she'd never seen any man look at her.

Pure male power and possessiveness. She was his and he planned to claim his prize. Her.

McKenzie saw stars. Lots and lots of stars.

Which was pretty amazing since she lay on her bedroom floor, gasping for air, basking in the glow of having had really great sex, the best sex of her life.

The best sex of anyone's life.

Had to be.

And that was with them trying to keep quiet so as not to wake anyone else in the house.

McKenzie had wanted to scream out in pleasure several times, and almost had with her last orgasm, but Ryder had caught her cry with his mouth as he'd toppled over the edge with her.

The man was incredible.

Pure and simple.

His intelligence, his kindness, his body that moved with hers in a primal rhythm she'd never danced before, one of pure, orgasmic pleasure.

She'd done a better job with picking out a fake boyfriend than she ever had picking out a real one.

"That was better than I thought it would be."

McKenzie's happy haze dissipated. Still breathing hard, her heart hammering against her ribcage, she rolled over to look at him. "Did you think I'd be bad?"

Chuckling, he rolled onto his side, too, and faced her. "I thought you'd be wonderful, and you were. More so than I'd thought possible."

"Nice save."

"The truth." He cupped her face. "You were there. There was nothing mediocre about what we just shared."

"You're very good," she admitted.

"As are you."

He'd certainly made her feel good, made her feel sexy, as if he'd read and aced the manual to her body because he knew every trick to eliciting a response.

And, although she was still breathless from what they'd just done, she put her hand against his chest, felt his heart, still beating as erratically as hers, and took comfort that she wasn't alone in what she'd just experienced.

And because she could, she leaned over and kissed where she'd touched.

"McKenzie, I don't think you should—"

"Shh…" she whispered. "I know it's too soon. That's okay. I just want to touch you. Slower this time."

Because she wanted to make as many memories as possible before the sun rose and their time in Tennessee ended.

As with the previous morning, Ryder beat her out of bed. Literally bed for them both as at some point during the night, they'd moved from his pallet to her bed and she'd slept next to him.

Not necessarily cuddled against him, but his arm had been around her when she'd dozed off into exhausted, but happy sleep.

She'd missed that arm when she'd awakened, missed the man she'd hoped to wake next to and even, perhaps, kiss good morning, too.

She supposed it was no wonder she'd slept late. There hadn't been a lot of sleeping going on during the night and she suspected it had been almost morning when they'd moved to her bed.

That she'd enjoyed the night so much frightened her.

She was just out of her relationship with Paul less than a month ago. She'd asked Ryder to come with her because she hadn't wanted to jump into a new relationship and had never dreamed she'd become so emotionally entangled with him.

Had never dreamed they'd have done the things they'd done last night.

She needed to be careful. Ryder was a great guy, a phenomenal lover, but that didn't mean he'd want anything more than this weekend with her.

Did she want more than this weekend?

That hadn't been her goal when inviting Ryder. Quite the opposite. She'd planned to return to Seattle, take time to enjoy the city, enjoy life and her amazing career, to take some time for herself, no boyfriend required.

Which left her where this morning?

McKenzie wanted coffee but opted for a shower and full face of makeup prior to making her way to the kitchen.

"Morning," her mother, Mark and her cousin's family greeted.

But McKenzie's eyes zeroed in on one person. One person who had mumbled a good morning, too, but who had barely glanced her way. Was he as confused about how they should act this morning as she was? Trying to figure out what last night had meant? Or if it had meant anything at all other than that they were physically compatible?

Very physically compatible.

How did one act the morning after the most amazing sex of her life which just happened to be with a pretend boyfriend and her family was there to watch her every move?

No wonder he couldn't look at her.

"You slept late this morning."

Leave it to her brother to point that out.

"I'm still on Seattle time." True, although it had nothing to do with her being the last one to rise.

"I can't believe you're already leaving," her mother sighed. "I don't want you to go."

"Me, either," she admitted. "But I love my life in Seattle." She really did. "You should come visit."

"I will," her brother commented and was the only one to do so.

McKenzie understood that. She was petrified of flying but forced herself to do so on occasion. Roberta hadn't flown since her husband died. McKenzie doubted her mother ever would, again.

She walked over to her mother, kissed the top of her head. "I'll come home again soon, Mama. Maybe at Christmas if I can arrange my schedule to be off work for a few days."

"That would be wonderful." Her mother patted McKenzie's arm, then reached out and placed her hand over Ryder's forearm and did the same. "You're invited, too, of course."

Ryder, who'd been watching the interplay while still avoiding making eye contact with McKenzie, gave her mom a half-smile. "Thanks. I'd like that. I've enjoyed my first visit."

His only visit? How crazy that his doing what she wanted, pretending to be her boyfriend, left her unable to know how to take anything he did or said when her family was around. Would he really like to come back or had he just said that?

Ugh. McKenzie's brain hurt. She had no one to blame but herself. But the smiles on everyone's faces all weekend, the lack of worrying about how heartbroken she'd been when she moved to Seattle and no new worries over Paul having done the same just over a month ago had been worth it.

Odd, it seemed a lifetime ago since she'd been involved

with Paul, planning to spend the rest of her life with him, and yet it really hadn't been that long ago.

McKenzie got her coffee, joined the others at the table, and pretended that she wasn't hyperaware of Ryder being next to her.

She'd not had awkward mornings-after with Clay or Paul. At least, not that she recalled. Then again, she'd not had incredible nights with them, either. Just… She glanced toward Ryder, willing him to look up and smile at her, anything, just some sign that things were going to be okay. That when this was all said and done, they'd at least be friends.

McKenzie never got her smile.

The morning passed quickly with lots of family stopping by to say their goodbyes.

No one commented on the tension between her and Ryder. It seemed impossible that they couldn't have picked up on it, and she wondered if they knew what they'd been up to during the night.

They'd kept the noise down. At least, she thought so. The reality was, she'd been so caught up in Ryder, she really didn't know how much noise they'd made.

Regardless of what her family knew or didn't know, they'd given lots of heartfelt goodbyes, well-wishes and pleas to come visit again soon.

McKenzie would.

Hopefully she'd make it home at Christmas or the week after Christmas.

By the time they were in the rental van on their way toward Nashville Airport, McKenzie was an emotional mess. From saying goodbye to her family, to knowing she was about to board a plane, to not knowing how Ryder really felt about what had happened between them.

She gripped the steering wheel tighter than necessary, cast a glance toward where he fiddled with his phone.

"Thank you for coming with me, Ryder."

He looked her way. "Sure thing."

"My family loved you. The trip couldn't have been any more wonderful. I really do owe you."

"I'm glad it all worked out."

Maybe they would have progressed to beyond pleasantries, but Ryder's phone rang.

McKenzie could tell the call was from someone at the hospital. When that call finished, he made another, checking on a patient. Was he purposely avoiding talking with her?

Was he worried she'd read too much into the night before? Afraid she was going to expect more from him?

Did he not realize the thought of diving into another relationship scared her almost as much as flying?

She sighed.

He'd given her what he'd agreed to, gone above and beyond. What had she expected? For him to date her a few years, then dump her?

Much better if they had their one night and left it at that.

Only the thought that they'd go back to how things were before didn't feel right. She didn't want that. She wanted… She didn't know what she wanted, but not for them to go back to completely avoiding each other.

They had an hour to kill at the airport, found seats near their terminal, but were surrounded by other passengers waiting on their flight, precluding any real conversation.

Ryder wandered off, came back with a book, and started reading.

Yep. That was a sure sign he didn't plan on them talking on the plane. Maybe he thought there was nothing more to say and wasn't suffering from the same mental tug-of-war that she was. And not just the one with flying anxiety and logic that she'd be fine.

Ugh. She dug into her bag, pulled out a prescription bottle and took her anxiolytic tablet. Maybe she wouldn't fall asleep on him this time. If she did, well, at least she wouldn't have to sit in five hours of uneasy silence.

If she made it through the flight.

She'd done so well up to this point, not having a single panic attack while checking into the airport. Possibly because she was so distracted by the man next to her.

Think happy thoughts, she told herself over and over.

Unfortunately, her most recent happy thoughts all seemed to star Ryder.

After they boarded the plane, got settled into their seats, Ryder turned to her, his gaze full of concern. "You doing okay?"

Emotions hitting her that he'd finally looked at her, really looked at her, that his eyes revealed he wasn't indifferent, she nodded. "I think so."

"Good."

But when the plane started moving, making its way toward the runway, McKenzie changed her mind, wondering if she was going to come out of her skin.

Breathing was difficult. Sweating not so much so.

Don't do this, she ordered herself. She was fine. This was ridiculous.

Only sitting in the seat was becoming more and more challenging.

"You got this," Ryder assured her, taking her hand. "Just take a deep breath and let it out slowly. You can do this."

It was the first he'd touched her since they'd fallen asleep next to each other after a whole lot of touching and she almost cried out at the burn of his skin against hers.

McKenzie's poor nervous system must have been on overload at the onslaught of sensations holding his hand added to her already hyped-up, under-attack neurons.

She stared at their entwined hands, tried to form words to ask him where they went from this weekend. That conversation would distract her from where she was, that she was about to fly.

Then again, his answers could trigger anxiety of its own.

The thought of not seeing him, spending time with him, hurt, but the thought of continuing what they'd started would cause pain unlike any she'd ever known.

"Your family is great, McKenzie."

She knew what he was doing and appreciated his wanting to help her through the next few minutes. Then again, he could just want to save himself a whole lot of embarrassment if she gave in to her desire to claw her way out of the plane.

"I liked them."

"They liked you, too." Understatement of the century. "Nothing would please my mother more than if you were my real boyfriend."

Ack. Had she really just said that? What was she trying to do? Pour gasoline on the fire and see just how hot her anxiety could burn?

McKenzie glanced up just in time to see Ryder's dark eyes. She really should have just kept her mouth shut the entire flight home. Maybe that would be best for the rest of the flight before she said all kinds of other crazy things.

Things like that because of him what could have been the worst weekend of her life had actually been one of the best.

Things like that last night had exceeded anything she'd ever known and had set the bar so high that the thought of never reaching that pinnacle again was almost enough to make her cry.

Things like that if she didn't know she'd only end up

dumped down the road, she might want to pursue a real relationship with him.

But she did know. History had taught her well.

The pilot announced for the crew to prepare for take-off. McKenzie automatically dug her fingers into her seat and braced herself.

She very seriously doubted that Ryder planned to kiss her through today's takeoff.

No doubt he was eager to be back in Seattle, away from her and their pretend relationship.

Last night hadn't been pretend.

Don't be silly, McKenzie, she scolded herself.

Last night had been nothing more than sex. Good sex. Amazing, blow-her-mind sex. But sex was probably always that way for Ryder.

As the plane taxied down the runway, McKenzie's stomach tightened, as did her grip. Ryder must have felt sorry for her, because he squeezed her hand.

She focused on where his hand covered hers and remarkably, her rising panic waned some. It didn't disappear, but did ease enough that she settled back, closed her eyes, and let the events of the past weekend play out through her mind.

No matter what, she was glad Ryder had come to Tennessee with her, that she'd come home to be in Reva's wedding and to visit with her family.

Her only regret was that she'd waited until her last night in Tennessee to have sex with Ryder.

With that thought, she squeezed her eyes shut, gritted her teeth, and forced each breath in and out as the plane sped up and lifted off the ground.

There had been no kiss this time.

Nor were there any false hopes regarding anything between them being real.

CHAPTER TWELVE

RYDER SLUNG MCKENZIE'S bag strap over his shoulder, along with his own. "That it?"

Releasing the handle on her suitcase that he'd gotten off the baggage carousel, she nodded. "Yes, thank you. I can carry that, so you don't have to."

"Not a problem. I've got it." Mostly because he wanted to walk her to her car.

Hell, he wanted to bring her to his apartment and make love to her in the privacy of his bed.

But he wouldn't.

Whether she'd had sex with him out of an emotional post-wedding high, or just because he'd been convenient, or just that she'd decided to act on the physical chemistry between them, the reality was, less than a month ago she'd planned to spend her life with another man.

He'd learned his lesson well enough in the past and wouldn't be making that mistake again. He might have been her pretend boyfriend, but he wouldn't be McKenzie's rebound guy.

He should have stopped her the night before, because he could no longer look at her without having flashbacks of her above him, moving sensuously and rocking his world.

Yes, he'd always felt desire when he saw her. But now he knew—knew and wanted more.

Only he didn't.

He and McKenzie had had a great weekend together. A weekend that was so much more than he'd ever expected to have with her. It was enough.

It had to be.

He wouldn't have McKenzie be the next Anna in his life.

They reached her car and he loaded the luggage into the trunk, then turned to face her.

"Um, thanks for going with me." She toyed with her key fob. "For everything, really."

"You're welcome."

"I…um…well, I guess I'll be going." She turned to get into the car, then paused, turned back to him, stood on her tiptoes and pressed a quick kiss to the corner of his mouth. "I'm not sure why you agreed to this weekend, Ryder, but you certainly saved me a lot of heartache. Thank you."

He hoped he hadn't caused a lot of heartache for himself in the process.

"You're welcome." How banal.

She eyed him a bit nervously. "So, where do we go from here?"

He stared into her green eyes and wondered what it was she wanted him to say. "A real relationship between us wouldn't work."

Statistics said they'd fail. Rebound relationships rarely even made it beyond the six months' mark.

She gave him a wry smile, as if she'd known that was what he'd say and didn't disagree. "I'll admit our pretend relationship was pretty fab, though."

True. It had been. Enough so that the thought of not seeing her, not holding her or kissing her again seemed impossible.

"So." She let out an exaggerated breath. "Is this where we just walk away and go back to the way things were?"

"Yes." It's what they should do.

"Do you really think we can do that? After, well, you know?" she asked, still fiddling with her key fob.

"No, I guess not."

"Me, either." She seemed relieved at his answer. "But I hope we can still be friends. I really do appreciate everything you did." She hesitated, as if she considered saying more.

He didn't want her gratitude.

What he wanted… Hell, if he knew.

He'd be grateful he had this weekend to know her better, to get such an up-close glimpse at the woman who'd captured his imagination. A pretend weekend relationship would be enough.

"Goodbye, McKenzie."

Her eyes widened a bit in shock, then she nodded, mumbled a goodbye of her own.

Just as he started to lean down to kiss the corner of her mouth, she stuck out her hand. His gaze dropped to it.

All pretense was gone. They were back to reality. It's what he'd crazily agreed to, what she'd always wanted.

Ryder shook her hand, wondering if that would be the last time they'd ever touch.

Wondering what she'd do if he pulled her close and kissed her.

Which would be stupid since he knew this was goodbye.

She pulled her hand free, searched his eyes for a brief second, then climbed into her car.

Rather than head toward where he'd parked, Ryder watched McKenzie drive away, wondering at how he could already miss her when she'd never really been his to miss.

Ryder was back to avoiding her.

Three weeks had passed since their trip to Tennessee.

McKenzie shouldn't care that she knew he put effort into making sure their paths crossed as little as possible.

She should appreciate his efforts as it prevented awkward encounters and second thoughts on whether she should have let him walk away so easily.

Nothing about being away from him felt easy and she didn't appreciate his avoidance.

Like now. She'd been on call at the hospital all night, had just gotten paged to check on a neonate in the NICU, and there he'd been, larger than life, and making her heart pound so hard it had to be creating shockwaves on the plethora of cardiac monitors in the unit.

When she'd spotted him her smile had been automatic. Even the tiniest glimpse of him made her insides light up. But that light had dimmed almost as fast as it appeared. As rather than return her smile, he'd given a nod of acknowledgment, then turned away.

Which hurt.

How could he just turn away as if they hadn't had the most amazing sex on her bedroom floor, twice, before climbing up into her bed and holding each other long into the night?

As if they hadn't shared looks and kisses an entire weekend?

As if... Ugh. She had to stop.

Ryder had done her a favor. Had pretended to be her boyfriend. He'd never promised, or even alluded to wanting, anything more.

Anything more scared her. One weekend as Ryder's pretend girlfriend had turned her world upside down. What if they got involved for real, how would she cope when he walked away?

Clay and Paul's walking away had hurt, but she'd sur-

vived. With the impact Ryder had had on her psyche, she
wasn't so sure she could handle being dumped by him.

Which was enough to keep her from reaching out to him
and telling him how much she missed him.

McKenzie's phone buzzed from her scrub pocket. She
glanced at the message and her heart squeezed for more
than one reason.

Whether either of them wanted to or not, she and Ryder
would soon be forced to interact.

Sawyer Little was in respiratory distress and on her way
to the hospital via ambulance.

McKenzie met the paramedics wheeling Sawyer into the
emergency department. She'd wanted to be right there when
the baby arrived.

As had Ryder.

Working beside him added a new level to the intensity of
the moment, to the stress of Sawyer's heart possibly failing.

Testing immediately began.

Nurses carried out orders as McKenzie and Ryder gave
them.

"Please don't let her be in heart failure," McKenzie whispered softly as she ran the ultrasound conducer over the
baby's chest. "Please. Please. Please."

The surgical sites looked good. The rebuilt aorta had
good blood flow via the surgically connected proximal pulmonary artery. The pulmonary veins had increased pressure, which happened sometimes, but that shouldn't have
put the baby into respiratory distress. However, the fluid
built up in the baby's lungs could, and had.

Pneumonia? Or her heart's inability to efficiently pump
fluid and the fluid had backed up into Sawyer's lungs, filling the tiny air sacs and preventing oxygen exchange?

Sawyer needed to go back on life support stat to take

the workload off her heart and clear out the fluid, if it was cardiac in nature.

If infectious in nature, well, they'd deal with that, too.

"The surgical site looks patent," Ryder commented. "Her blood is being oxygenated. I don't see any evidence of a clot or failure of the repairs."

McKenzie agreed. "It's possibly pneumonia."

Ryder nodded. "I hope not, but not uncommon after being on a ventilator for several days. It could have been slowly worsening since her hospital discharge."

McKenzie ordered blood cultures and labs, determined to quickly get to the root of whatever was causing Sawyer's problems.

The baby's life depended on it.

"I'm going to suction her," Ryder said.

They continued to examine the baby, working, prodding and poking.

Tubes seemed to be coming from every aspect of the baby's body.

"I still don't find any evidence of a clot, but her rhythm is jumpy."

"I'm ordering an inotropic," she told him, then did so.

Ryder glanced toward a nurse and gave a verbal order for additional medications.

"Ryder!" McKenzie couldn't hold her cry in when Sawyer's rhythm took a drastic drop.

But he was already responding, giving the baby a nudge.

Knowing time was of the essence, McKenzie pushed medication into the IV port, then got her intubated.

McKenzie and Ryder stayed with the baby over the next two hours, working with her almost nonstop to insure the tiny heart didn't succumb to the strain of the excess fluid and ensuing shock.

Once the baby was stable, they transferred her to the

neonatal intensive care unit. Kenzie and Ryder stayed close during the transfer.

"I can stay with her," Ryder offered as they headed toward the unit.

McKenzie shot him an *Are you crazy?* look. "I'm not leaving, if that's what you're getting at."

"You've been here all night."

He knew her on-call schedule? She supposed knowing would make it easier for him to avoid coming around.

"I'm fine." Mostly, she was. She'd caught a few hours' sleep here and there during the long night.

"I'll be here, anyway, McKenzie. It seems crazy for you to stay past your on-call time when I know you're tired."

Don't read anything into his concern. It wasn't personal. He was just being nice.

Perhaps she was tired, or just cranky, but she didn't want his nice.

Her chin lifted. "I'm staying."

Ryder's gaze narrowed and he studied her, then seemed to accept he couldn't change her mind. "I get that, just hate that you're doing so unnecessarily."

She frowned. "And I get that you'd rather I not stay so you don't have to be around me, but tough luck. Sawyer is my patient, and I'm staying."

At her comment, Ryder winced ever so slightly, but didn't deny her claim.

There wasn't a need when they both knew what she said was true.

Too bad being here with him, even under duress and when she really should be feeling tired, had her feeling more alive than she'd been in…three weeks.

McKenzie should have gone home, Ryder thought for the dozenth time. Why had she had to be so stubborn? What had she been trying to prove?

Instead, she'd set up watch in Sawyer's bay, determined to be close if anything changed on the baby's status while they waited on test results.

Once Sawyer was settled into the NICU bay and her heart rhythm and oxygen saturation, lower than normal even with supplementation and breathing assistance, stabilized, Ryder had gone to check on another patient, the patient he'd actually come to the hospital to check, but had gotten side-tracked from by Sawyer's arrival.

Coming back to the infant's bay, he'd not been surprised to find McKenzie in a chair, half-asleep, but ready to jump into action at the first sounding of a vital sign change alarm.

She didn't open her eyes at his entering the room, but her breathing pattern changed, so he knew she wasn't asleep.

She knew he was there and was choosing not to have to interact with him. Her accusation earlier hit him. He did avoid her. How could he not when being near her made him want to forget common sense and lessons hard learned?

Surely, she agreed avoidance was for the best or she wouldn't be pretending to be asleep.

He checked Sawyer, eyeing every one of the dozen monitors keeping tabs on the baby.

Just as he was turning to leave the bay, McKenzie's phone went off. When she answered, he could tell it was the lab.

He waited, wanting to know what the test results were.

When she hung up the phone, she turned her lovely, concern-filled green eyes his way.

"Sawyer's white blood cell count is twenty-seven thousand."

Ryder winced. Her numbers should be under ten thousand.

"The fluid is from pneumonia," he said unnecessarily.

McKenzie nodded. "The lab is sending off the sputum sample you suctioned, but it'll be a few days before we know for sure. I'm ordering additional RNA viral testing, then I'll go talk to Sawyer's parents."

"I'll stay here while you're with them."

She started to argue. He could see the denial on the tip of her tongue, but she stopped herself, nodding instead. "I plan to okay the Littles to come back here with her for a while, to give them some time with her."

She didn't say *just in case*, but he heard the unspoken words.

"They'll appreciate the time with her."

McKenzie nodded, glancing toward the baby with so many wires and tubes attached that she seemed almost unreal.

"They have to be terrified that she's in distress," McKenzie said, so softly Ryder barely heard her.

Ryder imagined any parent would be. Even without the current situation, Sawyer's parents had a long, stressful road ahead of them due to the baby's congenital heart defects and any number of complications that could occur.

That likely would occur from time to time.

McKenzie knew that, but her heartfelt whisper didn't surprise him. McKenzie had a big heart, one that loved her job and her patients.

His reaching for her hand was automatic. He regretted it the moment her surprised gaze jerked to his.

The moment her cool-to-the-touch skin still managed to shoot fire to his core that spread through his whole being, reminding him of how it had been with McKenzie.

How he'd been with her.

"Ryder, I…" She paused, pulled her hand away. "I've got to go speak with Sawyer's parents."

With that, McKenzie left, but it wasn't long until she returned to the bay with the Littles. Ryder's heart went out to the young couple who couldn't take their eyes off their baby and all the attached tubes and wires. They'd seen worse after her heart repair, but no doubt the image was still intimidating.

"Let's give them a few minutes," he suggested, taking McKenzie's elbow, ignoring that he was yet again touching her, and guiding her from the bay. There were several nurses at the nurses' station, and Ryder just kept walking.

See why he couldn't be near her? His hand was still on her elbow.

When they reached the elevator, Kenzie pulled her elbow from his grasp. "Where are we going?"

"To the cafeteria. When's the last time you ate something?"

She gave him a blank look.

"That's what I thought. Even though it's essentially a waiting game to see if Sawyer responds to the medication we're giving her, I imagine you're planning to stay close tonight."

McKenzie nodded.

"Let's get something in you so you don't get run down and end up picking up a bug yourself."

For a moment he thought she was going to tell him that whether or not she got run down wasn't any of his business, but instead, she sighed. "I wouldn't mind a cup of coffee."

Despite the tension between them, he couldn't help grinning.

"What?"

"You and your coffee."

"Just because you don't like it doesn't mean it's not amazing stuff."

"Apparently."

When they arrived at the mostly empty hospital cafeteria, they went through the line, each purchasing a few items before they sat down at a table together.

"How is your family?"

"Good. They've asked about you."

Ryder looked at her in surprise. Not that her family had asked about him, but that she was telling him.

"I told Mark the truth. He was livid I'd felt the need to bring a pretend boyfriend home, but admitted he also understood why I had, and, on second thought, he thought it brilliant."

"Your brother is a good guy." He'd truly liked the pilot.

"Most days." McKenzie sighed. "He said the same thing about you."

"That I was a good guy?"

Pulling the top off a yogurt cup, she nodded. "He said you had to be a good guy to agree to be my pretend boyfriend."

"It wasn't so bad."

"But not that good, either?"

Ryder met her gaze. Was she talking sex? Because she'd been there, knew sex between them had been beyond good.

She glanced down. "Sorry. I shouldn't have asked that."

Let it go, he ordered himself, but couldn't. "I'm curious. Why shouldn't you have asked?"

She took a deep breath. "Because, in spite of everything that happened, you're back to avoiding me."

There was that. That she sounded hurt gutted him. He didn't want to hurt her. Not ever.

"Things are complicated," he admitted, searching for the right words and not sure it was possible to find them.

"If we hadn't had sex, would you feel differently?"

Sex with McKenzie had been life-altering, but it wasn't the sex he missed most. Yes, he wanted her, to kiss her and make love to her sweet body over and over.

But it was her smile, her wit, the way when her gaze

met his he knew what she was thinking, the way when she laughed his insides filled with joy, that he missed most.

Which made him a fool. He'd have sworn he'd learned his lesson with Anna and would never let his emotions get caught in a rebound relationship again.

How wrong he'd been.

"No, McKenzie," he admitted, giving a humorless snort at the irony of the situation. Had he really thought he could be her pretend boyfriend without ramifications? "If we'd not had sex, I'd feel the same."

Which was the unfortunate truth.

CHAPTER THIRTEEN

MCKENZIE STAYED AT the hospital that night.

Sawyer remained stable on life support but showed no sign of improvement. They were keeping her lightly sedated to decrease tissue oxygen demand and to make tolerating the ventilation easier, so the baby hadn't regained consciousness.

Not that she necessarily would have anyway.

Sawyer's parents had also stayed at the hospital all night. McKenzie liked the couple, watched them a bit enviously as they comforted each other at the depth of their daughter's illness.

Had Ryder's parents once sat in a hospital room watching over their ill daughter, knowing only a miracle would keep them from losing her? A miracle that hadn't come.

No. No. No. She wasn't going to think of him.

Nothing about the man made sense.

She just needed to stay away from him.

She was on her way out to the parking garage when her phone dinged. For one crazy moment she wondered if it was Ryder. If he'd had second thoughts and realized sex between them had changed everything.

You're crazy, girl. Sex doesn't change things for guys. Not outside romantic movies.

Besides, she didn't want to be hurt again. Three strikes

and you were out, right? Clay and Paul had already done their numbers on her heart. She wouldn't give Ryder the chance.

Once inside her car, she pulled out her phone, expecting to see a message from the hospital or even Reva as they'd texted and called several times.

What she hadn't expected was to see a text from Paul.

"I've missed you."

Hello. McKenzie's eyes widened at Paul's admission. She took a sip of her wine because she didn't know what to say.

What she couldn't say was that she'd missed him.

Ryder on the other hand…nope, she wasn't going there.

"I was hoping you'd say you'd missed me too," he said, giving a nervous laugh. "Maybe just a little?"

McKenzie was saved by the waiter bringing their meals and her making a pretense of being starved as she dug into her sweet potato.

McKenzie wrapped her lips around her fork and eyed her ex. He truly was a handsome man. A good man.

But her heart didn't do somersaults when she looked at him.

Not like… Ugh, there she went again.

"I made a mistake, McKenzie. I'm not sure what I was thinking breaking things off. I think I just hoped our being apart for a while would make you ready for us to begin the next phase of our lives."

That got her attention.

"What next phase of our lives?"

"Marriage, kids, you know."

"That's a cop-out, Paul. We'd discussed marriage."

"Always in the terms of way off in the future. I'd been

trying to pin you down on wedding plans for months and you kept putting me off."

She didn't recall any major discussions about getting married, just vague ones about someday. She'd been good with someday as she'd not been ready to slow down on her workload.

"There was no rush," she admitted.

"Don't you think there should have been? That you should have been excited about being my wife?"

McKenzie opened her mouth to deny his claim. She had been...or had she?

She'd started dating Paul after her mother's signing her up for that speed dating event. Had she fallen into their relationship for convenience? Continued seeing him because he was a good man—comfortable?

"You never let yourself fully get onboard with our relationship, and I always felt it," he continued. "I always wondered if it was that other guy, the one before me, but I can't help but wonder if he didn't run into the same wall I did. That you refuse to let yourself love."

That was a joke. She loved. She'd loved Clay. She'd loved Paul. She'd loved Ryder. They'd all been the ones to leave.

She'd loved Ryder? That one had her pausing. She hadn't loved Ryder. She'd...

Her gaze met Paul's.

A whole lot of realizations swamped her. Realizations that she had cared deeply for Clay, for the man sitting across from her, but she hadn't been in love with either.

But she had been in love.

Was in love.

With a man as emotionally inaccessible as...as she'd been to the man she was dining with.

And yet...

"I—I'm sorry, Paul." She folded her napkin. "You're a

good man, but if tonight is about us getting back together, it's not going to happen."

Just being content, comfortable in a relationship, was overrated, and not something she'd ever settle for again.

McKenzie strolled through Pike Place Market, stopping at one vendor's booth, then another, pausing to watch workers toss a purchased fish, then meandering over to her favorite coffee shop to buy a cup of pick-me-up.

Coffee soon finished, she stopped at a booth, bought a gorgeous bouquet.

It was only a few short blocks to her condo, but rather than go straight home, McKenzie headed down to the pier, traveling past a couple of cruise ships as she headed in the direction of the aquarium. She enjoyed each step, breathing in the seaside air, embracing the wind against her face.

She truly loved this city. Eventually, it was possible she'd move back to Nashville, but other than her family being so far away, her life was in Seattle.

McKenzie paused when she came to the pier, walked out onto the decking, and wondered if she'd see any seals.

Leaning against the railing, she watched a fishing boat in the distance, listened to seagulls calling, the sounds of the city behind her, sounds of the harbor before her.

Having the day off work was nice but meant zero chance of bumping into Ryder.

She closed her eyes, breathed in the sea air.

She planned to talk to him. To tell him everything in her heart.

Ryder was worth taking a chance that he'd tell her he didn't want a relationship. Worth risking having her heart shattered down the line if he was willing to give them a chance.

Ryder was worth facing her fears, worth risking heart-break, worth being dumped a third time.

McKenzie's heartbeat sped up and she gripped her bouquet tighter as she stared out over the water.

Was Ryder at the hospital? Home? Somewhere else?

He didn't live that far away. She could walk the few blocks but seeing him was too imperative to go on a wild goose chase.

Taking her phone from her pocket, she dialed his number.

When he answered, her heart soared.

"You've heard the good news?"

The good news was that he'd answered his phone. Hearing his voice set endorphins off that had her smiling despite how nervous she was to have called him.

"Sawyer's white blood cell count is nine thousand." Excitement filled his voice at the baby's normal lab value. "I took her off the vent and she's holding her own."

"Oh, wow!" she said, getting distracted by what he'd said. "That is good news." All her patients were special, but Sawyer was more so, probably because of the connection with Ryder. "You're at the hospital?"

"I was until about an hour ago," he told her. "I came home to grab a shower and something to eat. I'll probably head back that way later this evening."

He was home.

McKenzie began walking in the direction of his apartment.

"That's great about Sawyer," she said, clutching her flowers in one hand and her phone to her ear with the other. "I know the Littles must be ecstatic."

"They are. Hopefully, if Sawyer continues to improve, she can go home in a few days."

"I'll swing by to check on her when I'm at the hospital tomorrow, and to say hi to the Littles."

"Sounds good." Silence then. "Is everything okay?"

"I've been at Pike Place," she told him, not wanting him to end the call. Not when hearing his voice motivated her feet to move faster. "For once, there's not a cloud in sight and the sunshine is absolutely gorgeous. I'd say, everything is wonderful."

At least, she hoped it would soon be.

A little confused by McKenzie's call, Ryder hung up his phone and put it on his bathroom counter.

She'd caught him just after he'd gotten out of the shower. He'd been standing there, towel-dried hair, towel around waist, talking to her as if they were old friends.

He blamed his excitement over Sawyer's improvement.

But he could just as easily have blamed his excitement on hearing McKenzie's voice.

Ryder finished drying off, went to his bedroom and pulled out a pair of sweats to go for a run.

Running cleared his head.

After talking with McKenzie, his head needed clearing. He missed her.

Despite his still damp hair, he pulled a T-shirt over his head, then grabbed socks and shoes.

Just as he was tying his tennis shoes, his door buzzer rang.

"It's me, McKenzie."

Ryder's hands shook. McKenzie was outside his apartment building, wanting to be let inside.

"That's not a good idea."

"Ryder, I'm not going anywhere until we talk. Let me in."

"By the hair on your chinny-chin-chin?" Because her

threatening to huff and puff and blow away his best intentions wouldn't surprise him. She had the power.

"There's no hair on my chin," she countered, sounding so indignant he grinned in spite of his inner turmoil.

"The code is seven, seven, six, seven." Immediately, he regretted giving her access to get into the building.

They didn't need to be in his apartment. Alone. He couldn't be trusted to keep a straight mind.

Only when she knocked and he opened the door, meaning to go outside the apartment and suggest they go for a walk, she smiled so brilliantly at him he forgot everything, including how to breathe.

"Hello, Ryder," she said as she stepped around him and into his living area. "Nice place."

Closing his apartment door, he turned, blinked at where she was taking in his home. "What are you doing here?"

She gave a lopsided smile. "I'd think that obvious. I came to talk to you."

"We just talked on the phone." Noticing what she was holding, his forehead scrunched. "Nice flowers. Are they for me?"

She glanced down at the multicolored bouquet, then laughed. "That would be fitting under the circumstances. Here."

She held them out toward him, but Ryder didn't move to take them. "What circumstances? Why are you at my apartment, McKenzie?"

"You aren't going to make this easy, are you?" She took a deep breath. "Ryder Andrews, I'm crazy about you, miss you like mad and am here to ask you an important question."

She really had gone mad.

"Will you be my boyfriend this weekend? Only, this time, for real?"

* * *

Okay, so not what McKenzie had planned. At all. She'd thought she had everything straight on what she'd say, but then she'd seen him, and all she'd really wanted to do was throw her arms around him and tell him how much she'd missed him.

"McKenzie," he began, looking torn. "You know how I feel."

"Actually, I don't know how you feel," she interrupted, waving the flowers at him. "What I know is that because you got hurt in your relationship with Anna, you're unwilling to have a real relationship with me."

"Give me those," he said, taking the flowers from her. "You're making me uncomfortable."

"Good."

"Uncomfortable is good?"

He looked so confused McKenzie almost laughed.

"Absolutely."

"You've lost me."

But she hadn't. She could see it in his gorgeous eyes, in the way that they followed her every move. She really did make him uncomfortable in the most wonderful way possible.

"Don't you see, Ryder? If I made you comfortable, none of this would matter. You wouldn't be torn about your feelings for me. The past wouldn't matter in connection to me and you wouldn't have felt the need to avoid me." A light clicked. "That's always why you've avoided me. Because I'm uncomfortable."

The truth bubbled inside her. How could she not have realized?

"None of this comfortable/uncomfortable stuff matters, McKenzie. I'm not willing to have a relationship with you."

"We already have a relationship. One that started when

we met and got put on hold until I asked you to go away
with me."

"As your pretend boyfriend."

"The only thing pretend about that weekend was what
we were telling ourselves. Everyone saw the truth, but us."

"What truth would that be?"

"That we're meant for each other."

Ryder closed his eyes and groaned. "You're here to tor-
ment me, aren't you?"

His words caused her a moment of doubt, but then she
reminded herself that he was using what happened with
Anna in an attempt to shut her out.

"Possibly. I had dinner with Paul last night. He wanted
to get back together."

Ryder's expression darkened. "Then why are you here?
With flowers?"

She moved closer to him. "I don't want to get back together with Paul. Or Clay."

The last time Ryder had bared his heart hadn't ended well.

Because the woman he'd been baring his soul to had
been in love with another man.

"This isn't easy for me, either, you know?" McKenzie
jabbed her finger against his chest. Would she keep doing
so if she realized how each touch sent shockwaves of awareness through him?

"I've been dumped by every serious relationship I've
ever been in," she continued. "Someday, you may do the
same, but I've realized that someday might not ever come
and wouldn't that be a beautiful thing if it didn't?"

Meaning he might not ever dump her.

"I wouldn't."

She stared up into his eyes. "Deep down I believe that,
Ryder. It's why I'm here. Because, not so long ago, I thought

three strikes and I was out, but in reality it's third time is the charm."

This should be easy. McKenzie was here, baring her soul to him. But old hurts cut deep.

"You can't be sure this isn't just a rebound reaction."

McKenzie laughed and shook her head. "I'm not on the rebound from Paul."

"How can you be so sure?"

"Because I was never in love with Paul. You're not the only one hiding behind walls. Part of me is terrified of being in a relationship with you because the stakes are high. I've seen what that can do to a person. I saw what it did to my mama when my daddy died."

He captured her finger poking into his chest, held it close to his heart.

"I think it's why I stayed in relationships that weren't right for me," she continued. "Because I knew that even though it would sting if they ended, which they did, it wouldn't shatter my world."

"Is that why you're here? To start another relationship that isn't right for you?"

She shook her head. "For the first time in my life, the right man is in my life. Only he isn't in my life, and that's why I'm here."

How did he explain this to her? Make her understand all the things running through his mind, through his heart?

"I have been crazy about you from the moment we met," he admitted. "Do you know how it feels to want someone so much and to know you'll never have her? That's how I felt about you right up until the day you asked me to be your pretend boyfriend."

"I didn't know. I thought you didn't like me, that I'd done something to upset you."

He snorted. "You weren't supposed to know. I didn't

want you or anyone to know how I felt. And, the only thing you did to upset me was be in a serious relationship with Paul."

"You never let on that you wanted me."

"Nor would I have had he not made the mistake of breaking things off. I'd been there, done that and planned to never get involved with another woman who was on the rebound or seriously involved with someone. Not easy when it came to you, but I managed by keeping my distance. I didn't want to like you."

"But you did anyway." She smiled as she said it, flattening her hand against his chest, covering his heart.

"Obviously."

"Not from where I was standing. I couldn't believe when you said you'd go with me to Tennessee."

"I couldn't stand the thought of you hiring an escort and possibly being taken advantage of."

"Because you thought I was on the rebound?"

"Yes."

"I am on the rebound." She stared him straight in the eyes. "From a relationship with my pretend boyfriend who stole my real heart. It's his for the taking. All he has to do is say yes."

McKenzie waited to see how Ryder would respond. Did he want her heart? Want her?

What she'd seen in his eyes had made her think he did, but she needed to hear him say the words. Needed to know he wouldn't push her away.

"I love you, McKenzie."

Not *yes*, but she'd take those words, would take them and cherish them.

"Tell me again," she said, wrapping her arms around his neck. "Tell me over and over."

"I plan to." He kissed her, long and hard and with a possession like she'd never felt. Because she'd never been loved the way Ryder loved her. She'd never let him go, knew without doubt he'd never let her go again.

"Every day for the rest of our lives, McKenzie, I'll do more than tell you. I'll show you."

And he did.

* * * * *

THE NURSE'S SECRET

SUE MacKAY

MILLS & BOON

This one is for my editor, Julia Williams.
Her patience and insight
have been a lifesaver at times this past year.
Thanks very much, Julia.

PROLOGUE

'LEAVE YOUR BROKEN heart at home and go and do what you're good at and used to enjoy more than anything. Dance the night away. Have some fun, sweetheart.'

Her dad had had a point, Stacey Wainwright admitted as she gazed at the heaving dance floor in front of her. It seemed as though all the medical staff from the London General Hospital were here at the Doctors and Nurses Ball—except of course that wasn't possible, with some having to cover the night shifts.

Since she'd never worked there she wasn't known here, except by the two friends she'd come with, both nurses, but she could still enjoy herself. *If* she let go of the handbrake that had been holding her back over the past year.

It was twelve months since the day she'd been stood up—not at the altar but in her parents' lounge, where she'd been putting the finishing touches to her wedding dress for the big event in four days' time. Her heart hadn't recovered, and neither was it likely to start without her making an effort to get out and do the things she'd used to love.

It didn't come easily since, for the first time ever, she had to do all those things, like dancing, *alone*. So she hadn't bothered.

'Let's rock and roll!' Ada all but leapt onto the dance floor in the beautifully decorated hotel conference room.

'You coming, Stacey?' she asked, with a warning that she'd better be.

It was time to get out and about, Ada had said when mentally twisting Stacey's arm up her back last week to convince her to join them here.

'In a minute.' She needed to get a little more of her delicious cocktail on board to build up the Dutch courage needed for her to let loose. Once she'd loved nothing better than a good party, but nowadays she was out of practice.

Watching her friends making moves nearly in time to the music, without any hesitation, she chuckled. 'Here I was, worrying I wouldn't be able to keep up, but I'll be fine.'

'You into dancing? As in really into it? I've got two left feet, but what the heck? I enjoy myself anyway.' Katie grinned as she poked her cheek with her straw.

She'd only met Katie an hour ago and liked her already. 'I used to do a lot of it.'

Stacey sighed. She'd better get started on having this fun and letting her hair down. Show some resilience. If any man wanted more than a dance or a drink with her, she'd cope. Just say no. She'd only known one man completely, and they'd been best friends most of their lives before their friendship had turned to love. And then Angus had said he didn't want her any more, didn't love her as much as he'd thought, and felt she was still a friend, though no longer the love of his life. He'd snapped his fingers and broken her heart.

Stop thinking about him. He doesn't belong here.

'Is there a dance every year?'

'I think so. I came last year soon after I began working at London General. It was a masked dance party, but the masks didn't last long. I remember two absolutely hammered registrars removed more than their face attire. They weren't exactly studs.' Katie laughed.

'It's usually the ones who aren't who put it all out there.'

'True. You got a man in your life?'

'Afraid not.' If she had he'd be here with her, wouldn't he? Then again, she couldn't guarantee that any more. The man she'd loved with all her being hadn't been there for their wedding. 'I'm taking some solo time at the moment.'

Katie glanced at her with shared sympathy in her eyes. 'You and me both. Don't know why a good man is so hard to find. Or I'm very picky. My last one was a hunk but had the attention span of a gnat when it came to our relationship.'

'I'm sorry to hear that,' Stacey said.

'It's all right. I'm better off without him, though I could do with a replacement soon. What happened with you and your last man?'

Only man. 'We had different ideas about the future.' He'd wanted to spend it with a woman he'd met four weeks before the wedding. After another deep swallow of her drink, Stacey stood up. 'Come on. Let's join the others.' Before the questions became too intense, before she let the past interfere with the present. This was not the night for spilling to someone she barely knew how her one and only boyfriend had had a change of heart.

'About time, you two,' Ada shouted above the music. 'This is fantastic.'

Stacey felt the music grip her, and instantly her feet were moving in time as though they had a mind of their own. Her hips swayed as she raised her arms and went with the rhythm. Closing her eyes, she let the liberating sensations brought on by the music take over. Should've done this ages ago. It *was* fun. *And* relaxing. Surrounded by people intent on having a great night, she was finally having a blast.

Opening her eyes, she stared around at the sea of bodies crowding the floor, all the females glammed up in chic dresses. Her blue and green long strapless dress was complemented by blue nearly sheer leggings and a green bow in her long hair and had all come from the charity shop, the price tag being the decider on what she'd wear. It didn't look half-bad, and the amazing make-up job her friend had done made her feel awesome for the first time in a year. Made her feel light-hearted and free of the past—if only for a few hours.

'Can I have the pleasure?' A deep-voiced, stunning-looking man stood before her.

She smiled. 'Sure, as long as you're not expecting anything too boring.'

'After watching you, I can't imagine you being boring.' Reaching for her hand, he led her deeper into the pulsating crowd.

He'd been watching her dance? She scoped the man before her. His white open-necked shirt was a perfect fit, a tantalising V giving a hint of a broad chest, while his tailored navy-blue trousers enhanced slim hips. Quite the picture, Stacey thought, swallowing hard. He had a strong jawline and an alluring mouth, those full lips giving her ideas she hadn't had in a long time. His eyes, direct and amused, were intriguing, like there was a load of sensuality shining out at *her*. Talk about itemising a guy, but, yeah, she sighed, she liked what she saw. Wanted to know more about him. Was this what waking up was all about? Like a sudden bang on the head? Or was she overreacting as a consequence of only ever dating Angus? If this was what having fun meant she might need to go carefully, not leap in and make a disastrous mistake.

Or I could try relaxing and having that fun I intended when I left home.

Relaxing came easily when she absorbed the music. Her hips swayed, her feet doing their own thing with no worries about being in time. Dancing was in her blood, something she'd done from the day she'd put on the pretty pink dancing shoes Santa had given her when she'd been three. Looking up into the eyes of her partner, she gasped. He was watching her with a smile and warmth in his gaze. Her stomach tightened, and she tripped.

Instantly he caught her, held her long enough for her to get her balance, then dropped his hand.

'Th-thanks.' A gentleman, and gorgeous. Glancing around at the other men on the dance floor, she had to acknowledge he wasn't the only good-looking guy in the room. But…deep breath…he pushed some of her buttons when no one else did or had. Again, she was probably over-reacting. *Relax.* Strange how quickly the tension slipped away, and her body continued moving effortlessly in time to the music.

'Come on.' Reaching for her hand, he raised their arms high and with his other hand on her waist, he gently pushed her into a twirl. Next she was being tipped backwards so her hair fell in a long line towards the floor. She spun upright and did another twirl, coming back to face him. 'I'm enjoying this.'

Suddenly Stacey laughed, letting the music and her partner take her on a ride of sensual movement. At least it seemed sensual to her. Another glance at her partner and her breath stuttered in her lungs. He looked as relaxed as she felt. He also looked a little bit surprised. Was he not used to having fun with a stranger, either?

That beautiful mouth spread into a crooked grin. Which set her heart racing.

'You're done this before,' he said.

'Once or twice.' Why *had* she stopped? She didn't need Angus to go dancing. There were plenty of nightclubs near where she lived with her family, and plenty of friends to go with. As of now there must not be any backing out when someone suggested a night on the town. She couldn't use her family commitments as an excuse since her father was over his depression from losing a foot and well on track with studying for an accounting degree. 'I've danced most of my life in one style or another.'

'But nothing boring.' His grin widened.

'You're on to it. You're not so bad yourself.' Flirting? Wow, old Stacey was returning in a rush. No, she hadn't flirted before, never had the need. Angus had always been there like an extra limb.

'Glad you noticed.'

How could she not? Those long, muscular legs moved slickly in time to the music. His hand when he held hers was strong and warm. And made her palm hot and tingly with a sensation she'd long given up on ever feeling again. Except this seemed sharper, more tingly. Guess when a drought broke the ensuing result would feel stronger.

The guy had her hand again, and his other hand splayed on her lower back pressed gently for her to twirl. Once more she was tipped back, then pulled upright and spun around, first one way, then the other.

'That's awesome.' A smile broke across her face as she studied the man holding her. Not once had she felt awkward or worried about taking a tumble. He knew what he was doing and held her just right. He knew what he was doing? What was he doing, apart from dancing with her? Seducing her? If he was, she didn't care. This was why she was here, to enjoy herself, and if things got out of line she would walk back to the table and have another drink before re-joining Ada and co on the dance floor.

The music halted. The sudden quiet was awful. She wasn't ready to stop. Stacey stepped closer to her partner, not wanting him to disappear on her just yet.

A member of the band stood up with a microphone. 'I know this is different to what we've been playing, but it can be fun, if not hilarious. You're such a boisterous crowd that we're going to play a Cha-Cha. Even if you don't know how to deal with that, just leap around in time to the music and you'll be fine.'

Stacey grinned. 'I can Cha-cha. I even quite like it.'

'Me, too,' murmured her dance partner. 'We're good to go.'

Locking her eyes on him, she tried to banish her surprise. He was staying around for more dances with her? Why wouldn't he? She hadn't squashed his toes or made a fool of herself. This was what being single at a party was all about. Getting amongst it, with a good-looking man to boot—who did delicious things to her insides. Perhaps she should look for a duller partner before she lost all common sense. Brilliant idea, if she wasn't intent on at last getting over Angus, and now she was having so much fun moving on, it was suddenly imperative to keep going. The time had come to stop looking back and asking, 'What if?'. This man was hot and fun, so she needed to make the most of him and step outside her comfort zone, which frankly had got boring. 'We are?'

'Yes, unless you've got other plans?'

More laughter bubbled up her throat and across her tongue, obliterating her hesitation. 'Nope, none at all other than enjoying myself.'

'Then bring it on.'

The crowd on the floor was thinning as the band struck up. 'Hope we're not the only ones left out here,' she said.

'We'll give them a show if we are.' Her partner laughed. 'Just relax and follow my lead.'

Taking his hand, she breathed deeply and smelt excitement in the air. And tripped before they'd gone more than

two steps. 'Damn,' she muttered. 'That won't happen again.'
Concentrate on dancing, not sniffing his scent. Or feeling
that warm hand holding hers. Or the way his leg pushed
against hers as they raised their legs in unison. The more
she immersed herself in the heat surrounding them the
more she forgot to focus on where to put her feet, and the
better their dancing became.

'You're a natural.' The man's mouth was close to her ear.

Her mouth dried. Settle, girl. He only meant dancing,
nothing else. 'Sure am.' She leaned back to look at him. Everything about him was magnificent, wonderful. Abruptly
she turned her head, afraid her face was giving too much
away.

He spun her around in a circle as they danced. 'What's
your name?'

So he wasn't about to stop dancing and say thanks, it's
been a pleasure, and walk off the floor. 'Anastasia.' She
gave her full name, something she usually only did when
filling in legal documentation. About to retract it and say
the shortened version, she hesitated.

'It suits you.'

Anastasia it was, then. 'How does a name suit a person?'

'You're fun and happy, as is your name.'

*Okay, everyone, listen up. As of now my name is Anas-
tasia, not Stacey.*

But she couldn't help being honest. 'I'm not always fun
and happy.' Silly woman. Should've kept that to herself.

'No?' Disappointment blinked out at her from those mesmerising eyes, but his lips quirked as though he was holding back a laugh. 'Guess that makes you normal, then.'

'Afraid so.'

Take that however you wish.

Surely he'd be going in search of someone else to dance
with now? Hopefully not when she'd made up her mind to

let loose a little—with him. Damn, but she was hopeless at this. Should she grab his hand tightly so he couldn't get away? Yeah, right. Then he'd really be running. So what happened next? More dancing? A drink? Mix and mingle? Talk about being out of practice. 'What are you known by?'

'Noah.'

Odd that they only exchanged first names, but it might be best. All fun, and no tomorrow. Who needed to get caught up in too much talk and a lot less fun? Not her, not tonight. Her pulse rate dipped. What if she wanted to see him again? Getting ahead of herself? Sure she was. Enjoying the moment, finding her feet in this dating game, and *having some fun* was the only way to go. She was fizzing on the inside as the beat in her wrists sped up again. Getting on with the dancing and fun and stop thinking beyond now took over.

Stacey's feet moved, her body swayed, and they were away, her hand in her partner's as they swung their legs high, then he had her in his arms, tipping her back further than before, and she was raising her leg beyond high. Around them others were trying to do the same with mixed levels of success, and some on the sidelines were clapping. At them? Who knew? She wasn't stopping to find out. This was amazing. She could do it all night. She grinned at her partner and continued dancing, rolling her hips and lifting her feet.

When the band finally stopped for a break, Stacey's lungs were working overtime, making her chest rise and fall rapidly. 'I need a drink after that,' she managed between sharp breaths. So much for dancing like a mad thing all night. She was whacked, and thrilled at letting go all the restraints she'd known for the past year. Why hadn't she done this sooner?

'What would you like?' Noah asked, also gasping.

'A mojito, please, Noah.' It did make a difference, knowing his name. They were no longer complete strangers.

'Come on, let's get to the bar before I pass out from lack of liquid.' He took her elbow and led her through the crowd as the DJ put on a song, this one a little quieter and slower. At the bar, he pulled out a stool and continued holding her elbow until she was seated.

Once their drinks were in front of them Stacey thought everything would become awkward. They didn't know each other. Forget awkward, she decided. 'I haven't had so much fun in a long time,' she told him honestly.

'I'd have thought you went dancing every Friday night the way you handled that.'

'Been busy with other things,' she said, adjusting the truth a little, then hurried to change the subject away from her. 'What about you? Do a lot of nightclubbing?'

'Can't say I do. Like you, it's finding the time.'

'Which…' She stopped. No, don't spoil the night getting to know personal details. The anonymity of it all gave her the freedom of being herself, being able to dance and have a drink and not think about overstepping the mark. Of finding who she really was now she was unattached. There might be a totally different person lurking inside, a stronger, more entertaining woman—one who was thinking too much when she should be focusing on now.

'No questions?' he asked with a smile. 'That's a good idea. We're having a great time with no comebacks. Shall we take our drinks out into the foyer? It might be a little cooler there. And quieter.' He spoke close to her ear.

She stifled a gasp as his breath grazed her skin, sending a ripple of heat to places that hadn't been warm for a long time. When she nodded, he took her elbow to help her off the stool. Definitely a gentleman as well as a hunk. Would she bump into him around the hospital she worked at over the coming days? What would his reaction to her be then? Or hers to him in the light of day and work? There'd been no sign of him during the previous two weeks, or she'd passed him and not noticed his looks. Huh? How likely was that when they instantly turned her into a hot mess?

Relax...go with the fun aspect. He's not hurting you, quite the opposite.

With her glass in one hand, she let him lead her out of the room. This was the way to having a great time.

'Forget quieter.' Stacey laughed, and she was doing a lot of that tonight. The band had come on again, now even louder, and more people were making their way out here. Sipping her drink, she looked around, a big smile on her face. What a night. She wanted to pinch herself.

They stood in companionable silence, cooling down as their drinks disappeared—probably too quickly for someone out of practice, but, hey, she was getting back on her feet, right? Then Noah took her in his arms and began dancing around the edge of the foyer, easily avoiding those standing in groups, talking. As he reached a far corner he paused and gazed down into her eyes. Forget companionable. Butterflies flapped wildly in her stomach. Her skin heated.

'Thank you for a wonderful evening.'

Stacey blinked. 'No, thank *you*.' The heat in her body began dissipating. Was this the end? He'd go one way, she the other? She wasn't ready to say goodnight.

'Thank us. I was dragged here by a friend who I haven't seen most of the night. I'd intended sneaking away early, then along came this amazing dancing lady.'

Phew. That sounded positive, didn't it? 'Is that a chat-up line?' she gasped, unable to believe she'd asked that.

The corner of his mouth lifted as he smiled. 'It wasn't meant to be.'

Damn. If ever the moment to continue moving on from the past was going to happen, surely this was it? Another deep breath. Give it a go. What was there to lose? 'Do you think you could kiss me?'

'Are you a mind-reader?' He bent his head and brushed his mouth across hers.

'Absolutely.' See? It wasn't so difficult to take the enjoyment another step. She inhaled, smelt spice, and man. Oh, yes, man. This man. Hot, strong, pulse-racing scent. Her mouth opened under his, and somehow her breasts were up against his chest and her feet lifting onto their toes. And she was kissing him back. Kissing Noah, a man she'd only met hours ago. And loving it. Loving the sensations zapping through her body, touching her stomach, her toes, her breasts, her centre. All on a kiss.

Splayed hands rested on her hips. Then that delicious mouth pulled back. Serious grey eyes filled with sparks of heat locked on her. Desire? For her? 'Anastasia?'

She nodded slowly. 'Noah.'

'I've got a room upstairs.' He grimaced. 'That sounds corny. But I've been here for three nights as I've packed up my house. I'm heading away tomorrow.'

So she could continue to let her hair down, have that fun she craved, and go home knowing she wouldn't bump into him at the hospital and be embarrassed if it didn't work out. She slipped her hand into his before she could overthink what she was doing. To hell with the past and the future. She'd seize the moment and make the most of what was on offer. 'Yes, please.' Ouch. What did someone say in this situation? She'd never faced it before. How naïve could she be? It was definitely time to get out there and learn a thing or two.

The lift was empty and seemed to fly to Noah's floor. Within moments they were inside his room, kissing as though their lives depended on it. Hot strokes from his tongue turned her to jelly. Had her holding on to him tight, pressing her body to his. Made her crave to be taken. Here. Now. His hand slipped between them to cradle her breast, his finger tweaking the peak, sending bolts of desire slicing through her straight to her point of need. 'Noah,' she growled against his mouth.

Lifting her into his arms, he carried her to the turned-down bed and laid her on it. He stood upright to pull his shirt over his head, exposing the broad, muscular chest she'd imagined. Then he was taking off his trousers. His erection burst free of his underwear and Stacey groaned with need. She wanted him, all the way, now.

'Slowly,' Noah murmured against her ear as he lay down and reached for her, removing her clothes tantalisingly slowly. His hands were magic on her hot skin. His tongue a tease as he tasted her neck, shoulder, first one breast, then the other.

She swallowed a scream, pushing her breasts up closer to that source of wonder. Her hands were working his backside, kneading and stroking, kneading, stroking. Then she reached for him, wrapped her fingers around his hot, throbbing need and rubbed him.

'Anastasia. Wait.' He groped in his trouser pocket, removed his wallet and tugged out a condom packet.

Anastasia. It was like another version of herself. A version who wasn't waiting for her past to catch up and move forward, a version who was moving ahead, making the most of what she had and not wishing for what was gone. Touching Noah, his back, those chest muscles rippling under her fingertips, his flat stomach, and beyond.

Then he was above her, touching, bringing her to a climax like no other, and she was bucking under him. Taking him in and losing herself in a wave of desire and longing and heat.

As he joined her in their release she had one sane thought. *I've done it. I'm free.*

When the alarm went off at five thirty in the morning she slipped out of bed before Noah had opened his eyes and ducked into the bathroom for a quick shower. At some stage during the night he'd mentioned having to leave for the airport by six, and she didn't want to hang around, dragging out the last moments with this amazing man.

Dressed, feeling a sight without make-up, she headed through the room to the door, where she paused for one more look at the man who'd given her so much without realising it. 'Noah? Thank you.'

He turned from digging clothes out of his case. 'Whatever for?'

'Helping me get on with my life.'

'You're welcome.' His smile was a gem, and one she'd take with her throughout whatever lay ahead.

CHAPTER ONE

Three years later...

'WELCOME BACK TO the madhouse,' Liz said as Stacey Wainwright stepped into the nurses' office on the surgical ward where she was head nurse.

'Thanks for nothing.' It had been hard, packing her lunch and heading out the door, leaving her daughter behind with Dad after two weeks spending time being with Holly, playing, walking in the park, reading stories. 'I'll get over it,' she told the other nurse.

'And that's not this job you're talking about,' Liz answered with sympathy in her eyes. 'I don't know how you do it.'

Neither did Stacey sometimes. If it weren't for her parents, especially her father, being the daytime carers she'd probably have found some other way to stay solvent and be with Holly, but it wouldn't have been easy. 'I manage. So does Holly. She adores her granddad.'

'Who spoils her rotten.'

'Funny, that. He never spoilt me or Toby.' Her brother took pleasure in teasing Holly about that, even when she was too young to understand.

'Grandparents' rights, eh?' Liz tapped the computer screen. 'Let's get this done so I can go get some breakfast before sleeping the day away. It was hectic in here last night. Two new admissions, both with post-trauma surgery after a multiple pile-up in the Rotherhithe Tunnel. I've got individual care on each, but they shouldn't deteriorate unless the unexpected happens, which we know often does.'

Liz continued going through the patient list. 'This one.' She pointed to the last name on the list. 'Jonathon Black. Keep an eye on him. He had his pancreas removed thirty-six hours ago because of cancer. Early this morning he complained of increased pain and his temperature's spiking. Joel upped his antibiotics in case there's an infection developing.'

Stacey studied the notes on the screen. 'Joel wasn't too concerned?' If the duty registrar was okay with these results then so should she be, yet unease was rising, and she knew not to ignore that.

'He suggested a CBC, but I haven't had time to take blood.'

'I'll see to it.' Nothing like a normal white-cell count to counteract the sense of an out-of-control infection coming into play. 'Anything else I need to know? Apart from who's getting married, divorced, having another baby?' She grinned. She'd missed everyone while she'd been away. They were a tight-knit group on the ward, and outside work.

'Come on. We were expecting you to come back with some gossip about what you've been up to and who you've been seeing.'

'Get out of here. I'm going to see Mr Black.'

I'm not telling you about the guy I went on a date with.

There'd be no end to the quizzing. Anyway, while she liked Matthew she wasn't overly enamoured and wouldn't be following up. The few times she'd dated over the years since *that* night with Noah in an effort to keep moving on had only made her regret more than ever not getting his contact details.

Not only because of Holly either, but because there was no denying the intense longing to see him again she couldn't douse no matter how hard she tried. He'd got to her in unexpected ways, like being kind and gentle, exciting and sexy. Of course there was a lot to learn about him, and she wanted to more than she could believe, even after all this time.

That one night when she'd danced like she'd never quite done before, or since, had totally distracted her from the past and made her happy beyond belief. It had been out of this world, as had the man she'd danced and made love with.

Talk about a life-changer. Holly was the result, and she wouldn't alter a thing, other than find the man and tell him he was a father. So far, her endless search had come up blank. It was hard with only a first name to go on. The world was full of Noahs, apparently. He'd got away and her disappointment was huge. There'd been a connection she'd not expected, and she wanted to follow up. Sigh.

'Hey, Stacey?' Liz called. 'There's a new surgeon on the ward. He started a week ago, so I haven't met him since I've been on nights and he hasn't been called in. He's Jonathon Black's surgeon. Mr Kennedy. Quite something, apparently. And I'm not talking about him as a surgeon.' She grinned.

Stacey waved a hand over her shoulder. 'Thanks, Liz. I'll give him your phone number when I see him.' A laugh followed her down the ward as she went to see Mr Black.

She'd meet the surgeon soon enough. In the meantime she had a job to do. 'Hello, Jonathon. I'm Stacey Wainwright, the head nurse on this ward. I've just returned from leave and have been getting up to speed with your details.'

'I heard you were due back today.' His face was red and puffy around eyes filled with pain.

Stepping across to read the monitor showing his BP, heart rhythm and temperature, she said, 'I hear you're uncomfortable and that your temperature has risen. What about pain in the region of your surgery? Has that quietened down since the op?' Despite the notes on the computer, she liked to ask patients about their symptoms, in case any details were left out.

'It's hurting more than ever. The pills I've been given haven't helped.'

'Do you mind showing me where this pain is exactly?' Stacey lifted the sheet to pull up the hospital gown he still wore for ease of access and keeping pressure off the wound a pyjama bottoms waistband might cause.

'All around here.' Without touching his abdomen, he indicated an area forward of where his pancreas would've been situated.

'Not up here?' She lightly touched the surgical wound.

'That hurts, but the deep pain is away from there.'

Add in the thirty-eight-point-five-degree temperature, the deep red shade in his face and upper body, and there was definitely something more than an infection of the internal wound going on. Or so her gut told her. 'I'm going to take a blood sample and send it to the lab. Then I'll call your surgeon and inform him what's going on.' She'd also put Jonathon's breakfast on hold for now. If he had to go back to Theatre he didn't need food in his belly. 'We'll get this sorted for you.'

'Thank you, Nurse. I am worried that something else is happening.'

'Try to relax. I know, easily said. Please don't accept food or anything to drink.'

He nodded. 'I understand.'

'Show me again where it hurts the most.' When he indicated the same spot, where the appendix was, she asked,

'On a score of one to ten, ten being the highest, what would you say the pain is?'

'Eight.'

'Right. I'll get the blood-test kit.' On the way she stopped at the office and asked for Mr Kennedy's speed-dial number. She had a sinking feeling that whatever was causing Jonathon's distress was rapidly becoming urgent.

'Mr Kennedy.'

Her brow furrowed at the sudden voice on the other end of the line. Shaking away an odd sensation she couldn't explain, she said briskly, 'I'm Stacey Wainwright, head nurse on Surgical. I think you need to see Jonathon Black. He has severe pain and an increased temperature. I'm about to take an EDTA specimen.' She filled in the details.

'It's likely an infection of the wound, possibly internal. I'll be up in a few minutes.'

'Thank you. I have a feeling it's something else. Appendicitis, even peritonitis.'

'I'll investigate all possibilities when I get there.' The phone went dead.

Fair enough. He was the doctor. She the nurse. In the past she'd met doctors who put nurses down, but she'd never been able to keep her thoughts to herself when she believed there was something happening with a patient that hadn't been considered. He hadn't had time to consider anything, hadn't observed his patient this morning, and she was about to meet him. She hoped Mr Kennedy wasn't going to be the kind of doctor to give a rebuke for putting her opinion out there.

She shivered. That sense she'd missed something when he'd first answered her call returned. Like she knew him, but as far as she could recall she hadn't worked with any doctor of that name. Guess she'd know soon enough.

With the blood-test kit in hand, she returned to her patient. 'Jonathon, let's get this done. Your surgeon will be here to see you shortly.'

'You don't muck around, do you?' His smile was tight with pain but there was also relief in his voice.

'I try not to.' She pushed up the sleeve of the gown and put the tourniquet in place before wiping an area above his vein with antiseptic fluid. 'One sharp scratch.' The needle slid in, and the tube began filling. She decided to take a tube to be spun for serum as well in case the surgeon asked for biochemistry tests. It would save time and discomfort for Jonathon if she didn't have to come back for another sample. 'There, done.' Snapping off the tourniquet, she withdrew the syringe and began labelling the tubes.

'Didn't feel a thing.'

Probably because he was focused on the pain from his abdomen. He looked worse than he had minutes ago. If his appendix was playing up then she'd bet her lunch it was now in an advanced state and would need urgent surgery. Slipping the tubes into a plastic bag, she stood at the end of the bed and said, 'I'll get this taken to the lab, then I'll be back.' Hopefully by then the surgeon would be here, and she could relax.

The door to the room darkened. 'Good morning, Jonathon. I hear you're having more pain than you should be.'

The bag containing the blood sample slid from her fingers onto the bed. The blood in her body dived south, leaving her head dizzy. Her mouth dried. Her stomach roiled. Noah?

Jonathon looked beyond her. 'Mr Kennedy—am I glad to see you. Though Stacey's been very helpful, hasn't doubted that I'm telling the truth about increased pain.'

Mr Kennedy. Phew. She could relax, put her head back on straight, make her stomach behave. It wasn't Noah. Why would he be Noah? The same sensations that had excited her that night three years ago when she had been with him were winding through her, tightening her in places, softening her in others. What were the odds? For one, because he'd been at the hospital ball she'd presumed he worked in the medical world, yet she could've been wrong. And if she'd been right there were numerous hospitals in London, and a darned sight more out in the world. Looking online was an unsolvable nightmare, like asking where was the best place to go for ice cream. She hadn't seen his friend at the ball at all so couldn't track him down, and the hotel Noah had been staying at had refused to give out his name. No, it wasn't Noah. Couldn't be. Though she wanted to find him for Holly's sake. *And mine.* She'd believed she'd be ready if the chance came up. Got that wrong. She was anything but ready.

With a deep breath, she turned around. 'Hello, Mr...'

Noah stood before her. Looking as stunning as last time she'd seen him. More so. Her memories hadn't lied. That good-looking face with the strong jawline and wide mouth was exactly as she recalled. His suit enhanced his broad shoulders and the wide chest that led down to slim hips and muscular thighs. Oh, man, could she remember those. On a deep breath, she looked up into familiar grey eyes. Yes. Deep grey like these ones. The only difference was the shock radiating out at her.

Gripping the bed end to keep from face-planting on the floor, she stared at Noah. Yes, Noah. No one else. The man who'd helped her get on with life by being exciting, and kind, and tender, and fun. The man who'd hung around in her head ever since, teasing her about the feelings she had for someone she'd known for less than a day. Warm feelings of longing that were making themselves known right now. He'd also been a part of what had unexpectedly thrown her into turmoil and given her the greatest gift ever. Holly. Her daughter. *Their* daughter.

Stacey's knees buckled and her ribs hit the end of the bed. Fighting to stay upright, she held on tight and closed her eyes to focus. It couldn't be him. But it was. Finally she'd found Noah. Ironic, because today she hadn't been looking for him. Worse, he was as attractive as she remembered, which was odd, because she'd never thought she'd feel this way again after Angus had jilted her. *He'd* been the love of her life.

Yet Noah had excited her very differently, had her wondering if her love for Angus had been all she'd thought. Now, three years on, she'd accepted that her one-night fling with Noah was always going to have been more exciting than the man she'd known all her life. She'd tried to move on from Noah and that night. One night was a lot to hang hopes and dreams on, but impossible to forget with Holly a constant reminder.

Then there were those memories of respect and gentleness, of giving herself to him. Here he was, standing a metre away, and she knew she'd been wrong to think she could forget him. He was special. He had pressed all her buttons. Staring at him now, her throat dried even as her knees started tightening to keep her upright. 'Noah,' she squeaked.

He gasped, 'Anastasia?'

Strike me down. Noah stared at the apparition at the end of his patient's bed. After all this time the woman who'd given him one night to remember, to *never* forget, was standing in front of him, looking as stunned as he felt. 'Anastasia? As in Stacey Wainwright?'

Her nod was abrupt. 'Yes. Noah, as in Mr Kennedy,

surgeon, I presume.' There was the faintest twitch at one corner of her exquisite mouth.

A mouth he'd kissed deeply and longed for again and again over the years when he'd been so far away from London, at the bottom of the world. A mouth that had done wondrous things to his body. Then he surprised himself by chuckling. They'd talked like that the first and only time they'd been together, each on the same track as the other, like they were kindred souls. There was a thumping going on behind his ribs, as though he was happy to bump into Anastasia again. Which he was, but so happy he felt a new world was opening up before him?

He'd often wondered what had happened to the woman with an easy sense of fun and eyes that sparkled with merriment. The first woman he'd felt anything for since Christine, the ex who'd let him down big time.

He breathed deep. Yes, there it was. That citrus tang hung in the air between them. A scent he'd taken with him as he'd crawled out of bed the next morning and hurriedly prepared to get to Heathrow and eventually New Zealand in an attempt to get away from his father's family and have time for himself. He'd joined his cousin from his mother's side, shared an apartment and worked in the same hospital while getting a wealth of experience in general surgery.

Anastasia had gone with him in his head, often tempting him to return home and hunt her down. He hadn't, because he was cautious about giving his heart to anyone again. Yet deep down he did want to find a woman to trust his heart with, to love unconditionally—if only he could let go of his hang-ups from the past.

He'd dated on and off, and no other woman had been a patch on this special lady he'd had so much genuine fun with three years ago. She'd raised hope he might be able to find the love he'd spent a lifetime looking for. She'd become an itch under his skin, a constant irritation. Now here she was, beautiful, and very real. 'We meet again.'

Her eyes were wide, and those yellow and green flecks in the deep brown shade were shining. That thick, dark blonde hair was tied back in a ponytail falling down her back as straight as it had been when he'd swung her around on the dance floor. Her hair had been loose then, silk running between his fingers. His muscles tightened at the memory. And another of her mouth on his skin as she whispered hot, sweet nothings. Now, her voice was cooler, like she was fighting with this sudden reunion. 'We do. And we'd better get on with why we're here.'

His patient. On the phone she'd suggested Jonathon might have appendicitis, and he'd wondered if she was right. For once, he didn't want to be here, looking into a patient's details and making arrangements for whatever was required. No, he wanted to snatch Anastasia—to hell with Stacey—to him, wind his arms around her and hold on tight. He didn't want her to go away. He'd longed to find her, and here she was.

Now what? Walk away while he could? Because something said it would get harder to do the longer he hung around, that if a deeper relationship with Anastasia failed he'd be more heartbroken than when Christine had done her number on him. Anastasia was special, but that didn't mean she'd be good for him. Did he truly want to keep avoiding risking his heart or did he want that love he'd always longed for since his parents had died? Was he going to risk all to find out? How could he not? She'd be almost impossible to walk away from this time, and they'd only just met again.

'Noah?' She leaned close, watching him with a warning in her eyes.

Of course. Forget what *he* wanted. He *was* at work and

Jonathon was waiting for him to gather his scattered brain cells and be of some use. But, hell, after all this time wondering about the woman he'd spent a beautiful night with, he'd bumped into her, and he just couldn't let it go. Not even briefly. 'Talk later over coffee,' he told her, hauling back his shoulders and stepping up to the bed. 'Jonathon, I hear you're suffering more pain than when I saw you yesterday, and that your temperature has risen.'

'Yes, I started feeling the pain around lunchtime yesterday but thought it was all to do with the operation. Only the pain kept increasing, despite the drugs I was given, and now it's unbearable.'

'I'll take a look.' Anastasia had already closed the curtains around them and disappeared just when he needed her as a nurse, and not a wonderful memory. Flicking the curtain aside, he headed for the door, only to pause as she came towards him.

'I've sent a haematology specimen to the lab as ordered by Joel. I also took a biochemistry blood in case you required more tests.'

She was onto it. 'I can't argue with that.' Relieved she hadn't dashed away to put space between them and send in another nurse, he struggled to keep on the subject of Jonathon's problem. 'You think this is more than the original site becoming infected?'

Her eyes widened as she stared at him. Obviously not used to a doctor asking her opinion. 'The pain Jonathon's having is eight out of ten, and where he indicates it's coming from isn't where you operated.'

He had no doubt she had an idea what the problem was. 'Let's take a look.' He turned back into the cramped space around the bed. 'Jonathon, can you show me where this pain is.'

Anastasia helped their patient expose his abdomen, then she stood aside.

Noah tried not to breathe too deeply to avoid that scent that said *Anastasia*, and got on with what he was good at. As his fingers probed Jonathon's abdomen he felt the man tense. 'There? Or here?'

'The second place. The other hurts but when you touch the second one, it's like a knife going in.'

Which was what was probably going to happen soon. 'I'll wait to see what your white-cell count is but I suspect it's going to be high.'

The man looked at him blankly, shaking his head. 'Meaning?'

'White cells fight infections and to do that they rapidly increase in number. Unfortunately, the result will be the same if there's an infection where I removed your pancreas. But going with where the pain is, I believe…' He paused and looked across to Anastasia. 'I think you've got acute appendicitis, which means the appendix has to be removed.'

Her mouth twitched. But she remained silent.

Damn, how he remembered that twitch. It had wound him up so much, had him touching her again and again. He really knew so little about her, but it seemed he knew what mattered. He'd like to change that, add to his memories. True? Yes, damn it, it was.

'More surgery?' Jonathon's shaky question broke the spell.

Concentrate on the patient. 'Yes, Jonathon. I know you won't be keen but there's no choice. If we're right—' Anastasia's eyebrows rose. 'If *we're* right, that appendix has to come out as soon as possible or you'll become dangerously ill.'

'This doesn't have anything to do with the first operation, does it?'

Fortunately not. Noah shook his head. 'The pancreas and appendix are two separate organs. This is a completely new problem, and bad timing. Or you could say good timing because we're onto it, and you don't have to wait for surgery.'

'Whatever. You're the boss.' Jonathon shrank back into his pillow.

Anastasia quickly fixed his robe in place and tucked the bed cover over the worried man. 'You'll be fine. Mr Kennedy did a great job of that pancreas, so this next op will be just as good.'

How did she even begin to know that? A scar told an observer very little, except maybe he could be a tailor if he ever wanted to change careers. Looking at her, she smiled softly at him, and tenderness sneaked into Noah's tense muscles at the thought she'd believe he was a capable surgeon even if until a few minutes ago she hadn't even known what his specialty was.

He liked being accepted in a positive way without having to explain himself, and Stacey had just done that. His shoulders loosened some more. It didn't happen often. In fact, he'd struggled most of his life since he was ten to be good enough at anything, especially where his uncle was concerned.

Apparently he had his mother's genes, and those were wrong for the Kennedy family. His mother had enjoyed life immensely, had been a loving person who'd seen the best in everyone and not the bad. According to Uncle Robert, she'd led his father away from his role in life by being too outgoing and bringing all sorts of people into their circle, instead of toeing the line and behaving properly. When Robert had disapproved of Christine, it had been more of the same complaints, except for once he'd got it right about her being a greedy woman who'd wanted nothing more than Noah's wealth.

Noah glanced at the nurse helping his patient. She had a similar zest for life to his mother. Being proper would definitely be anathema to her, if he'd read her correctly that night. He'd swear he had. 'Can you let me know the moment those lab results come in? And get a CPR on the bio sample.'

'Sure.' A smile lit up her face. 'Where will I find you?'

As in she didn't want to lose him again? Not yet, she couldn't. Not until they'd had a coffee together, at least. He laughed at that idea. Unbelievable, but sitting down with a coffee would be fine. Talking, catching up on the last three years—make that all the years because they knew so little about each other—held an allure that he had to follow up on. And therefore a reason not to spend time together away from this ward, and getting caught up in her loveliness. He downplayed the hidden message he thought might be in her question. 'Call my hospital number. I'll be waiting to hear from you,' he said professionally, trying not to imagine kissing her again.

The smile slipped off that delightful mouth. 'Right.'

He left the room without a backward glance because if he looked back, he'd stay talking when he had a surgical list to get through, one that had been increased with Jonathon Black now needing an appendectomy. Not a doubt. No ignoring that scent that was Anastasia either. Or the way his step was lighter than usual as he made his way down the ward to the lift. At least the citrus didn't follow him. Though memories of a shapely figure, gentle hands, soft skin, incredibly sexy moves on the dance floor, and in that darkened hotel room did.

Anastasia, Stacey, worked here where he'd been contracted as a general surgeon at the same time as picking up a partnership in a private practice along the road. He'd found her, and could admit to certain feelings that he'd been trying to deny. Now that particular riddle was finally solved, he didn't have a clue what to do next. Take a chance? Or back off? So typical in his world of relationships. After Christine he never intended getting caught up in another one—they hurt too much when they fell apart. Yet while his encounter with Anastasia had only involved hours it felt as though a lot more of him had got caught up with her. He was afraid to try for love again, even if Anastasia had left her mark on him. They had seemed to click the two times they'd been together, like they just knew each other even when they didn't. Not in an expansive way yet. He sighed.

The lift pinged and he stepped inside amongst other staff. Did he really intend staying single for the rest of his life? Not having a family to love and cherish like his parents had him until they'd been abruptly taken? He didn't believe he was loveable. His relatives hadn't come anywhere close when it came to loving him. They hadn't loved him at all, and still didn't.

Then there was Christine. He hoped Anastasia was the polar opposite. Not every woman was a money-hungry ice queen. Christine had fooled him into thinking otherwise simply because he'd been desperate to find a happy, loving environment like his life had started in. Not every woman was Christine. She came from a poor background and had a lifelong dream of marrying money.

But how did he know Anastasia wouldn't be the same? She might be just as good at putting up a façade. Get a grip. At that dance she'd smiled wholeheartedly at him and made him feel warm and special. In the morning she'd turned down his offer of a taxi home. Then again, anyone with half a brain could've sounded genuine, especially to him after the greatest sex he'd had in a long time.

Ping. He made to step off, hesitated and looked at the floor indicator. Great. He'd gone up rather than down, and the lift had more floors to go before returning to the theatre level. Stepping back, he found a corner and leaned back against the cold wall.

It had been one night in paradise. No questions, no hang-ups, no expectations. He'd been himself, a rare event, resulting in a fantastic time. Since then he'd often wondered who the woman he'd made love to the night of the dance was... Where she worked...if she was a doctor or a nurse...did she work at London General—which, according to his friend when he asked, she didn't—and did she ever think of him?

Now he had the answers to most of those questions, he needed to find out more. The way she'd already tipped him sideways worried the hell out of him. Temptation in a nurse's uniform. If he ever found the love he'd been seeking for so long, would he always be waiting for the axe to fall?

His parents had been the best mum and dad out there, loving him unconditionally, making him feel wanted, needed. He'd loved them back just as much, though naturally he'd pushed every button they'd had and some. He'd had a happy family life—until that fateful night when he'd been ten years old.

He'd been staying with his best friend down the road in Bloomsbury when the doorbell had rung. It had been so loud and shrill in the quiet evening that he'd felt a chill up his back. He'd never been able to explain why he'd known something wasn't right and that it involved him. Uncle Robert had been standing on the doorstep, and the news had been grim.

His parents were dead, killed in a car accident, and from then on he was to live with his uncle and aunt and cousins. It was a lie because within three months he'd been sent to boarding school, and had only gone back to the house for those school holidays when he hadn't gone to his friend's home. Since that day he'd been searching for love like that

that had been stolen from him, but he'd always been afraid
that if he found it, it would once again be whipped away.

Yet he'd fallen for Christine and married her. In the beginning she'd been friendly, and keen to have two children,
though he'd learned after the wedding that making love was
only for ovulation days. Oh, and the fortune he'd inherited
from his father was necessary to keep her happy, and the
London house equally important. It hadn't taken long to
realise that the deep, abiding love his parents had had and
which he'd been looking for wasn't happening with Christine so he'd filed for divorce. Thanks to the pre-nup he still
had most of his inheritance. Letting his father down on that
aspect would've decimated him. But neither had he been
miserly, making sure Christine didn't go without.

Ping. 'What floor do you want?' a young woman asked.

'Two, thanks.' Better let her press the button. That way
he might arrive where he needed to be.

Not where he wanted to be. Which was in a café with
coffees on the table between him and Anastasia. If she even
liked coffee. He'd better start calling her Stacey, in front of
staff at least. That'd keep everyone else away from trying
to guess what their relationship was about. It might also
help him remain grounded and not rushing into something
he might later regret.

To think he'd woken that morning fully expecting a normal, chaotic day in Theatre and on the ward, dealing with
other people's problems, and getting up to speed with the
staff and this hospital and how different it was to work in
London compared to Auckland, where everyone was more
relaxed with each other, and he'd enjoyed getting to know
his cousin from his mother's side. It had been tempting to
stay but the sense of unfinished business back in London
had nagged.

Anastasia had also always popped into his head at those

moments, and many others. Already there'd been days he'd regretted returning home, but responsibilities had called in the form of his uncle and aunt, and he wasn't one to neglect duty. Even when it involved people who'd neglected him. So here he was, and he'd make the most of the situation.

His thoughts returned to Anastasia. Her ready smile and sparkling eyes, her deep, genuine laughter full of happiness. Her hourglass figure, and those dance moves.

His gut clenched, his heart flipped, and a sigh trickled over his lips. Should've stayed in Auckland. It would've been easier, safer, and a whole lot more boring now that he'd found Anastasia again.

CHAPTER TWO

STACEY HELPED JONATHON into a clean gown. 'The porter will be here shortly to take you down to Theatre. Mr Kennedy has put you first on his list and is waiting for you.'

He'd prioritised Jonathon when she'd called with the lab results, said he'd already decided he was going to operate because something was seriously wrong, and he believed it was appendicitis. And he'd acknowledged Anastasia's opinion. Yep. They did have an unexplainable link between them.

Just listening to that deep gravelly voice gave her the shivers in the nicest, warmest way possible, and reminded her of what lay ahead before she could even consider anything else. He was the father of her daughter. That would be a game changer. Whether he liked her or not. Whether he wanted to spend time with her, or never see her again other than on the ward.

Another thought stopped her in her tracks. What if he turned against her when she told him about Holly? Got nasty and said she was lying? All very well being able to prove his parenthood, but that didn't mean he'd remain friendly. She might have to apply for a new position. She loved this job, was so proud of being head nurse, and changing jobs would hurt like hell.

So don't even consider it. Stand your ground. You've done nothing wrong.

'The doc doesn't muck around, does he?' her patient said.

'It appears that way.' Was Noah like that in all his endeavours, or just with patients requiring urgent care? How would he take her news? It'd knock him for sure. But how would he react? She doubted he'd procrastinate. He'd taken her into the centre of the dance floor the moment she'd said yes to dancing with him, and when she'd asked him to kiss her he hadn't hesitated. A man who knew his own mind. Another point in his favour was that he hadn't been pushy or demanding when they'd made love. He'd been considerate and gentle. Yes, and hot and wonderful. She flapped a hand in front of her face. 'It's warm in here.'

'Can't say I'm noticing,' Jonathon commented.

'That's probably nerves. I'll get you a blanket. Oh, hi, Jim. Jonathon, your porter's here.'

Dashing to the storeroom, she got a blanket, and after wrapping Jonathon up snug she went to check on one of the women who'd been involved in the pile-up last night. 'How's she doing, Ada?'

The nurse looking after Patsy Miller was reading the cardiac monitor attached to her patient. 'She nodded off after I administered some morphine. She has a history of arrhythmia and was operated on for a perforated bowel last night. Her obs are good, though I'm watching that heart monitor like a hawk.'

'Good. Let me know if anything changes.' She headed back to the hub to look at the notes on Mrs Miller. Noah was her surgeon, which meant he'd been working during the night, and didn't look at all tired this morning. It also meant another reason for him to possibly visit the ward later. No avoiding him. *I don't want to.* But there was the

Holly issue. He had to be told sooner rather than later, or when he heard about Holly, he'd think she'd been holding out on him for her own reasons.

Damn it, she liked the man, or what little she knew of him. Liked? Okay, he'd been fun, caring, sexy as all be it, and prepared to stop what they'd started if she'd had a change of heart. He'd insisted on paying for a taxi for her, though he hadn't won that one. She more than liked him, way more. She froze on the spot. What if he was married? Already had a family of his own? Why hadn't she thought of that before? Because she'd hoped they might have more in common than one night. Not thinking about that until she'd seen him again.

Whatever the answers to her questions, he was Holly's father, and didn't know it. He had to be told. Next move— hers.

She'd do it ASAP. She needed to ask Noah to have that coffee he'd mentioned. Forget time to come to terms with him being back in her life. But though it was all very well knowing and believing in what was the right thing to do, it was a totally different prospect now the time was here to follow through. Keeping Holly a secret had never been on the agenda. Still wasn't. Except she felt awkward about walking up to him and saying, 'Hey, have I got news for you.' So, ask him to meet after work.

'Want a coffee?' Jason leaned over the counter, inter- rupting her chain of thought.

Not with you, or anyone other than Noah. Deep breath. 'Sure do. I'll be along in a minute.' Stacey glanced at her watch and was surprised to see nearly an hour had passed while she'd been doing the 'paperwork'. Noah would've finished operating on Jonathon Black. Unless there was more to the man's pain than they'd believed.

The phone by her elbow rang. 'Surgical ward, Stacey speaking.'

'Anastasia. Sorry, Stacey, it's Noah. I thought you'd like to know your summation of Black's condition was correct, though it'd gone further and turned into peritonitis.'

Coming from him in that deep, gravelly voice, she liked it when he said 'Anastasia'. He made it sound special, theirs from that wonderful night they'd shared. Except everyone would want to know why he did. She huffed out a breath. 'You got it in time. Are there any side-effects at the pancreatic site?'

'We need to be vigilant over infection. I've prescribed stronger, intravenous antibiotics to start immediately.'

This was good. They were surgeon and nurse, discussing a patient, not two people catching up after a long time with only hot memories—and a child—between them.

Don't forget where this has to go—Holly.

A quiver started up in her hands. 'I'll make sure everyone knows the situation.'

'Anastasia, how do you feel about catching up with me away from here?'

Excited. Nervous. Scared. Happy. No, not happy with Holly in the middle of everything. But it had to be done. *Ta-da, ta-da*, went her heart. Why couldn't her life run smoothly so she could shout, *Yes, I'd love to, and by the way...*

'I'd love to.'

She had to, didn't she? If nothing else, she had to suss him out as her daughter's father. Forewarned was forearmed, or so they said. Just because she found him attractive and desirable, it didn't mean he was perfect. Certainly didn't endorse him as a parent, though even in the short time she'd spent with him she'd swear he'd be a good father. Maybe she was biased. After one night in his bed?

Well, his kindness, gentle touches and readiness to follow her lead did say a lot about a man. But there was no delaying telling him the truth.

A low chuckle came through the phone, making her smile. 'You haven't changed a bit.'

Oh, yes, I have. Because of you, I got over Angus. Though I'm still wary of trusting a man with my heart again. Also, because of you, I'm a mum with the most adorable little girl imaginable.

'Call me when you have a spare moment.' The phone banged hard as she put it back on its holder.

Closing her eyes, she pictured Holly on the swing in the park yesterday, giggling as the hem of her pink, frilly skirt blew up under her chin. Holly, her darling girl. Noah had to love her. Had to. No option, or she didn't know what she'd do. As long as he didn't try to take Holly away from her. He wouldn't. But compared to her family, he'd be well off. He was a medical specialist so might think he could provide a better life for their daughter. He'd have the battle of all battles if he tried that on. But she was getting ahead of herself.

He knew nothing about what had gone on in her life after they had parted that morning in his hotel room. She wanted to take her time learning more about his lifestyle and him, before exposing herself and Holly, but she didn't have that right. She could only trust her gut instinct—Noah Kennedy would do the right thing by them all. Fingers crossed.

'I gave up waiting.' Jason plonked a full mug in front of her and pulled out the other seat at the counter.

'Sorry, you know how it is. Mr Black's had an appendectomy and will be back on the ward later this morning. We need to keep a close eye on him for developing infection at the original operation site, and make sure it's not ramping up this latest problem.'

'Poor guy. He'll be sore for a while.' Jason munched on a biscuit. 'So what do you think of our new surgeon?'

My lips are sealed.

'So far I like him.' She spluttered into her coffee. 'He seems to know what he's doing,' she said, trying for a smile but suspecting it came off as a grimace.

'Guess that means he'll be too busy for his ward round today.'

She shook her head. 'No mention of it.' She needed to know if Noah was going to turn up so as not to get taken by surprise and look out of her depth. Ward rounds were a piece of cake, all part of her duty, but Noah suddenly appearing in front of her was not. 'How much have you had to do with him?'

Jason shrugged. 'Much the same as with any of them. He's an okay guy, though. Not arrogant and willingly shows concern for his patients. They all seem to think he's the best.'

He's the best.

That Stacey understood. Jason had described the man she'd met, without the patients. He had been the best for her when it came to dancing and making love. And sharing jokes and laughter. And changing her life. The phone rang again, and she left Jason to deal with the caller. Her work inbox was full of non-urgent messages that had to be dealt with sooner rather than later, because the inward flow never stopped and only caused her a headache if she ignored them. Staying on top of everything was the only way to work in this busy environment that she loved being a part of.

It'd been her ambition to become a nurse since she'd been a child and played with her grandmother's nursing badge. Once she'd even dressed up in a white uniform and cap like Gran used to wear as matron and had gone off to the fancy-dress party at school, proud as punch to sport the treasured badge. That badge had become hers when Gran had died, and was still in her jewellery box, polished and shining.

'Have you got a free moment, Anastasia?'

Her head jerked up and her gaze met Noah's full on. 'Yes, I have.' A glance at the wall clock showed midday. Past lunchtime for her. Where had the morning gone? Out with those blasted emails, no doubt. Rising from her seat, she rubbed her lower back, which was aching from sitting so long hunched over the keyboard when she wasn't talking to various nurses about their patients. 'I hear Jonathon's a lot more comfortable than he was first thing this morning.'

'I'm pleased to hear it. Now, is there somewhere we can talk? I don't have long with Theatre beckoning.'

'Who do you want to see first?'

Noah looked down at her, his mouth doing that one-sided smile thing. 'You.'

'This isn't a ward round?' He was still watching her, and that smile was still happening. Her insides softened. He was gorgeous.

'Not at all.'

Of course he only did those twice a week. 'Oh.'

'Don't tell me you're stumped for words. I don't believe it.' He grinned.

She couldn't help laughing. He had a way of talking to her that made her feel good about herself. 'You'd better.'

'The staff kitchen? It's close and time's short.'

The poky room where they made coffee and ate sandwiches at a speed that gave them indigestion? Her heart dipped. Not much going to happen in there, especially if anyone else was there. There'd be no space to breathe in air. 'Sure.' She led the way, aware of Noah behind her every step.

Despite the tight knots in her neck and shoulders she felt

good. Hope fought with the Holly knots in her stomach. If she and Noah could get along this easily after a very brief history then the future could be bright. Not for them as a couple or anything so deep and meaningful, but so they could share parenting. Actually, that made her nervous. She wasn't ready to give up any of what she had with her daughter, while she wanted so much more with Holly's father for herself.

He touched her shoulder lightly. 'Where have you gone?'

She shivered. His touch sent sparks in all directions. Beware. This man saw too much for her liking. 'I'm right here, ready to hear why Mr Kennedy wants to talk to me privately.' And to talk about themselves, learn more about him, let him know where she came from in terms of family, and what Angus had done to her. Because she would tell him all that, and then he might understand why she'd been so willing to have fun that night they'd inadvertently made a baby. The night when she'd woken up from the apathy Angus had left her with, when her heart had come alive. Still was if the thumping going on was anything to go by. Noah Kennedy did that to her as easily as he'd kissed her. Heat trickled into her cheeks as a wave of longing rolled through her.

'Guess that's my cue to get a wriggle on.' He was watching her too closely, but at least his smile remained. 'I can't believe I've finally caught up with you. It's wonderful.'

Again he'd got to her, softening the tension holding her tight. On again, off again. He was wonderful, and had her dreaming of them being together, close and personal. Nothing like her usual calm disposition.

Show him that and only that side of yourself.

'We could dance around the room.'

Without hesitation, he reached for her, took her hand and one step. 'I'm on if you are.' His smile lightened his face, and lifted her spirits higher. 'You're just as I remember.' He blinked.

Laughter bubbled up her throat as she pulled away. 'That would so not be a good look if anyone walked in. They're already wondering why I'm Anastasia to you.' So was Stacey. It had been a bit awkward when Jason and Liz had commented. She hadn't realised they'd been within hearing distance when she'd talked to Noah earlier, but she should've known. There were no secrets amongst staff on the wards. People were always popping up all over the show, doing their jobs and homing in on background conversations.

Noah nudged the door closed, shutting them into the airless space before tugging her close. 'I once met this amazing Anastasia who loved to dance, among other things, and if I change her name to Stacey that night will fracture.'

She stumbled, ducked away from his hand when he reached to catch her. 'You what?' His memories were that good? This was nuts. They'd had a blast, sure, and she'd been hooked for life, but did *he* really feel it had been so good he didn't want to forget it either?

'How soon can we catch up? I want to talk with you, see you, hold…' He stuttered to a stop, blinking furiously.

Had he made a mistake, saying that? Her shoulders slumped. Of course he had. But it did seem she rattled him as much as he did her. Something else they had in common, along with understanding each other without explanation. She took the bull by the horns, laid her hand on his arm, breathed deeply, and said, 'Coffee after work tomorrow?'

'Not a mojito?'

Knowing where those led, she shook her head. 'No.' She relaxed enough to grin, though gulping would've been easier. His face wore a teasing expression, but his eyes held a perplexed element to his mirth. It wound her tighter, while heating her blood. This man was a puzzle. She enjoyed puzzles, especially hot, friendly, fun puzzles.

'I'll be finished around six. That work for you?'

'Yes, perfect.' Hopefully her parents would understand and babysit. Today she needed to get home.

To hold my girl and reassure myself I'm about to do the right thing.

'Done. Where's home these days?'

'Same place.' Had she told him last time? 'Harlow.'

The door swung wide and Jason strolled in. 'All right if I grab some lunch?' he asked Stacey.

'Go ahead. We've finished in here.' Ignoring the way Noah lifted one eyebrow in her direction, she headed out. 'Phone me here where to meet you,' she said quietly.

'No problem.' His devastating smile set sparks flicking right down to her toes and all places in between.

By three o'clock and shift handover she couldn't wait to get out of the place, away from constantly looking over her shoulder to see if Noah might've popped onto the ward, even though it was impossible since he was in Theatre all afternoon.

She couldn't believe her luck when there were seats available on the train home. She wouldn't have to swing from the ceiling handles while thinking about the day she'd just had. Sinking down on the seat, she tipped her head back and closed her eyes. Noah was back in her life, this time for a lot longer than one night.

Memories slammed into Stacey. His laugh was her favourite. It made her toes curl and her heart soften when she'd believed that would be impossible. There were the hot, sexy images as they'd danced. Even hotter and sexier ones in that hotel room. Hardly solid proof that he was a good man, the sort of man to be a wonderful father. While gut instinct said he would be, how reliable was that? She could be deluding herself because she was attracted to him. So much relied on her getting this right. So, so much.

Holly's giggling face leapt into her mind, shoving Noah aside. Her little girl, the love of her life.

I promise with all my heart to love and care for you, to do whatever it takes to make you happy and safe, to be the best mother I possibly can be.

The first words she'd spoken to Holly when the midwife had placed her in her arms after the birth. Now she had to tell Noah about his daughter. Yes, she did. All part of the promise to Holly. The sooner the better; get it over and done with. If he really was the man her tingling nerves said he was, then all would be fine. If she found he wasn't, then what? It was highly unlikely and, regardless, he was still Holly's father.

For three years she'd continued checking with friends at other hospitals, and especially those at London General, if they'd heard of him, and come up with *nada*. Every time it'd saddened her, made her think she might never again know the man who'd brought her alive the way he'd done that night. And that Holly would never know her dad.

Now he'd turned up she wasn't quite as prepared as she'd expected to be. Holly should be her main, and only, consideration. She had to be certain her girl would be safe and loved by her father. She would tell him tomorrow night.

Leaping off the train at her stop, she all but ran home, and burst in through the front door. 'Holly! Mummy's home.' Dumping her bag on the floor, she raced through the house, barely able to breathe for the need to hold her girl blocking her throat.

'We're in my office,' her father called.

'Holly, love, where are you?' She shot through the door and scooped her baby into her arms and held her close, brushing kisses over her head. 'Oh, my girl, Mummy loves you so much.'

Holly wriggled and pushed at her mother.

'Sorry, am I holding you too tight?' Stacey loosened her grip but didn't put her down.

At his desk, her father was watching them with a question in his eyes.

She looked away, returned to gazing at her precious girl, who was wriggling harder.

'You want to get down?'

Holly nodded. 'Please, Mummy.'

'Okay.' It was hard letting her go, as though this was a warning of how it might be in the future. Weekends with Daddy, weekdays and nights with Mummy. No way. She couldn't give up any time with her daughter. Her eyes watered as she set Holly on her feet and didn't let go of her arm for a moment too long.

Holly bounced away, leaving her mum's heart cracking.

Her dad stood up and came across the room. 'You've found him?'

'Noah, Dad. His name's Noah.' Her father knew her too well. As long as he didn't see her excitement and bewilderment and start asking unanswerable questions.

'That's a yes, then. I'm glad you're sticking up for him like that. It's a good sign. Where did you bump into him?'

'He's now working at London Riverside. On the surgical ward. He never worked at London General, only went to their ball for his friend's sake.' Her body was shaking, releasing some of the tension that had been growing all day. 'He started while I was on holiday. Who'd have thought after all the trouble I've gone to trying to track him down?'

'You've talked?'

Her head dipped in acknowledgement. 'About patients, about us knowing each other briefly. He calls me Anastasia.' Her voice rose. 'No one calls me that.' But it'd been the only name he knew for her. 'I like it,' she admitted. Then she looked to her father, as she had often in her life, because he'd been her rock whenever things turned to custard. 'Dad, what am I going to do?'

Reaching for her, he wrapped her in a familiar hug. 'You already know the answer to that. You'd have told him years ago if you'd been able to. It's not as if you didn't want to contact him.'

Stepping out of her dad's arms, she sat on the edge of his desk. 'I haven't found out where he's been yet, but when I do I'll brain him for not telling me his full name and phone number at the time.' Finally she began relaxing. 'It's going to be all right.' It had to be. Her gaze swooped over Holly, and her heart clenched with love. 'It will be.' Just who she was reassuring she wasn't sure, but she had to believe it or everything would become a nightmare.

Noah let himself into his house and dropped the keys on the oak side table before heading to the sitting room and a large glass of whisky. What a day. Standing at the French doors leading out onto a patio, he stared blindly at the garden beyond. Anastasia had fallen back into his life. Just as easily as leaves being blown off the trees outside.

Sipping his drink, he tried to empty his head of images of Anastasia. Or Stacey Wainwright. Either version of her name was as pretty as she was beautiful. To him she was Anastasia, and always would be, which suggested he wanted a lot more contact with her now they'd met again. Contact, or something stronger? Deeper?

Could he be overreacting to this stunning woman who came with memories he hadn't managed to delete? Memories that kept him awake some nights, tightening his belly, heating his skin. They'd never faded, not a bit. They'd given him a better reason to return to London than bailing Robert out of the financial debacle he'd got into, even if he hadn't known if he'd find her. She might've even been the reason behind his feeling of missing something important if he continued to stay away.

Yet now Anastasia had resurfaced he was afraid. She might be attractive and funny and delightful, but that wasn't enough incentive to risk his heart. Just because he felt excited at seeing her again, it didn't make her the woman for him. What with moving back into his London house, organising and attending meetings to resolve Robert's financial crisis, as well as taking on the positions as head general surgeon at London Riverside and the private practice, it made sense that his brain was miles behind with what had happened today.

Strange how the years in New Zealand hadn't dampened his need to follow up on that special night he and Anastasia had shared. Her dance moves still turned him on while lying sleepless in the night. His memory drew up more pictures of the woman who'd been so generous with herself and taken all he'd offered with pleasure. Her slim neck had been pale during a London winter with no sun. That thick, dark blonde hair spread across the pillows had tantalised with its silky smoothness. She was a stunner. Then and now. And always smiling. That hadn't changed much either, unless she was with a patient who needed consoling as he'd observed with Jonathon Black.

Why hadn't he taken her phone number? Right now he wanted to hear her voice with its suppressed laughter or full-on happiness. Like the citrus scent, her voice had followed him to the other end of the world to pop into his mind at unexpected moments and fill him with that longing for love he'd known most of his life.

Love. Something he'd had little experience of since his

parents had died. At first he'd believed his uncle and aunt would automatically love him, and when they hadn't he'd felt he was somehow lacking. He'd tried harder to please them, only to be sent away to boarding school, where he slaved his guts out to get top grades so they'd come to love him.

When he'd met Christine he'd felt a glimmer of hope, and when they'd married the glimmer had become a beacon. It had never bothered him that she didn't come from money. He'd wanted to share everything he had, especially his heart. But she didn't love him, not in the way he'd anticipated. It was his bank account that had drawn her to him, and she'd made a fool of him with her promises of love. He'd rushed into marriage, wanting to be with someone he believed loved him back, to be a part of their life, to share raising a family in a loving environment such as he'd known for the first ten years of his life. Christine was finally out of his life for ever, and he didn't regret that at all. But he was wiser, warier, and not prepared to try again and come up against a cold heart hidden behind sweet lies.

So, Anastasia. Their encounter had only involved moments on the ward, yet it felt as though a lot more of him had got caught up with her. Which he didn't need. Wrong. He did need what she might have to offer, if it was genuine, and how was he to know that? To trust his own judgement when he'd failed abysmally last time?

Need was one thing, and it was debatable whether he did need her, or if this was unsatisfied lust. But what about want? Did he want her? Impossible to know after such a short time together. Forget his body's reaction to her today. Just because those feelings of tenderness and longing and heat were the same as last time, they didn't make this a ticket to wholehearted love on both sides.

For all he knew, she might be married, or in a relationship.

What about her shock when she'd turned and seen him? He recognised it for exactly what he'd felt at that moment. Total disbelief, and something like excitement. And, yes, the happiness had been in her face too. They got each other, even after three years. So, now what?

The phone rang. Noah stared at the name on the screen with distaste. The man who'd often said that if his father hadn't married his mother then Dad would still be alive.

'Robert.'

'Noah, you didn't come up to here yesterday as promised. I've been trying to get hold of you all day.'

He hadn't agreed to go, let alone promised. 'I was busy at the hospital.' And talking to interior decorators about making his house a home again after the mess his uncle's sons had left it in. So much for the idea it would be better to have the house in use while he'd been in New Zealand. The refurbishing was going to take months and cost a small fortune.

'Your aunt would like to see you.'

Funny how that was the case now that Robert's many millions had dwindled to a few. 'I'm busy this coming weekend so I'll come the following Saturday if that suits.'

'It'll have to, I suppose. We'll expect you at twelve for lunch.' Click. Gone. Classic Robert, who he no longer called uncle. That was a term for someone he cared about and who cared about him for more than a massive top-up of his bank accounts.

Maybe he should run away with Anastasia and have some fun, like his mother apparently had with his dad. Except running away hadn't been the case. That was Robert's perspective because he lived a 'proper' life amongst snobbish, wealthy folk. His dad hadn't given up his medical career or his home; he'd merely shared everything he'd had with the woman he'd adored. Noah sighed and sipped his whisky. It wouldn't hurt to apply the brakes and take things one day at a time. But it would be hard with his body craving Anastasia. Damn it, for all he knew, she might be hungry for money and happy to do anything it took to get it, including fool him into believing she meant everything she said.

Getting a little carried away here.

But that was what saving his heart had him doing, despite the caution he should be applying. Though if Anastasia truly had a happy, loving approach to life and could share that with him, he might be more than prepared to take a gamble.

CHAPTER THREE

STACEY GOT TO the hospital early and headed for the cafeteria. 'Toast and tea, please,' she said to the young guy behind the counter.

'I'll bring it over when it's ready.'

'You're a star.' Tiredness dragged at her feet. Most of the night had been spent tossing and turning and wondering how she was going to broach the subject of Holly with Noah. At five, she'd thrown the blanket aside and gone into her daughter's bedroom and stood staring down at the little body of magic. How she'd managed to produce such a gorgeous child was beyond her.

From the day Holly had been born Stacy had been head over heels in love with her, and nothing had changed. Not because she'd had to give up her newly found independence and single life, not because she had to rely on her mum and dad to look after Holly while she went to work and added money to the household. Not because she was so tired at times that she could barely stand up. All of those things and more were worth it just to have her girl in her life.

Sitting down, she checked her phone in case her mum had tried to get hold of her. Nothing. She could relax. Though with Noah back in the picture it wasn't that straightforward. Her reaction to him yesterday had been over the top. Yet she'd loved the excitement pouring into her. He'd rocked her boat the first time they'd met, and yesterday he'd gone and done the same all over again. She could admit to never feeling like that about Angus but, then, they'd been so familiar with each other it probably hadn't been possible.

'Here you go.' Her toast and mug of tea appeared on the table before her.

'Thanks.' A sense of familiarity struck her, warmth and excitement winding her tight and fizzing in her veins. Her skin prickled. Glancing around, she found Noah Kennedy watching from a table across the room with a thoughtful expression darkening his eyes. A shiver rippled through her. She stared at him; really looked at him. Not as a lover, or as Holly's father, but as a man she barely knew yet yearned for in every way imaginable. There weren't enough answers to all her questions in his steady gaze, yet still she believed in him, and wanted more.

Noah got up, mug in one hand, a plate in the other, and came across. 'Mind if I join you?'

'Of course not.'

Far from it. She'd put difficult subjects on hold for now and spend time enjoying his company. Who knew what she might learn? Or she could just spill the beans and see where that went. In here? With someone she knew likely to pop in at any moment? Maybe not.

'You're in early.'

'There wasn't a lot in my pantry and, anyway, hanging around waiting for the toast to burn is a waste of time.'

'You wouldn't think to turn the knob down a little?'

'Knew I should've asked someone how to fix my problem.'

'Where do you live?'

'Bloomsbury.'

No way. Her stomach dropped hard. He was having her on. But looking at him she knew he wasn't. Gulp. 'Nice.'

Very nice, if you were into that sort of lifestyle, and she doubted she'd ever be. She was comfortable with little money and a small, crowded house filled with those she loved.

Watching her intently, he said, 'It has its uses, like being close to everything I enjoy about this city, for one.'

'I suppose you don't need a monthly train pass.' She smiled. What did it matter where he lived? Unless he wanted to use that as leverage to gain more access to Holly than she was prepared to give. Her skin prickled. Holly. Caution rose as reality sank in. She really knew very little about this man. Her palms moistened. Was it enough? It had to be. Holly existed. No changing that.

'Trains are the easiest way to get around. No parking worries.' He was still appraising her.

'Is there a problem about something?' May as well be direct.

'Not at all.' The appraisal continued, then he leaned back in his chair with a wry smile. 'Sorry. I'm still getting used to the fact we've met up again.'

She wasn't about to admit to the same thoughts. 'Have you been in London for the last three years?'

'No, I left for Auckland the morning we woke up in my hotel room. I went for a year and stayed three. I hated leaving.'

'Then why did you?'

'Other responsibilities in England.' He turned to look across the room, effectively shutting down the brief conversation.

She studied that strong jawline, the sharp, see-everything eyes that were the colour of burnished steel; the wide chest.

He turned back. 'Now *you're* staring.'

'I am.' And liking what she saw. Her phone vibrated.

Mum. She picked it up and tapped the text icon. 'Sorry, need to get this.'

Morning, sweetheart. You left early. Hope you got some sleep and didn't spend all night worrying about Noah. Holly's devouring Rice Crispies, with more on the floor than in her mouth.

Smiling internally at the mess she could envisage, Stacey sent a smiley face and set her phone down to eat some toast. Sensing Noah was watching her again, she looked up. Sure enough, his gaze was fixed on her. Her grin slipped. 'Yes?'

'Can I have your phone number?'

Reality check. It was great he wanted to get in touch with her. She couldn't wait to spend time with him away from here. Telling him about Holly wasn't the issue. She'd decided tonight was the night for that, but—and it was a big one—she just wasn't ready to lose Noah before she'd really found him, as in knowing him better and letting the passion she felt for him have its head. She was smitten with him, and that was hard to let go of so soon. He'd woken her up, and she'd never gone back to sleep, always hoping he'd return one day. Now he had, and there was a lot on the line.

'Anastasia?' He tapped her hand, lingering over the last touch. 'You don't want to give me your number?'

Shaking her head, she said, 'Of course I do.' She rattled it off and he put it into his contact list, trying to ignore how his finger felt on her skin—hot and tempting.

'I'm messaging you so you've got mine.'

Ping.

Glad to catch up with you.

Deep breath.

Same:

It was true. No matter what lay ahead. Unable to stop herself, she leant forward and touched his fingers, squeezed them lightly.

Noah glanced at his phone, smiled, and stood up, saying, 'See you tonight.' He strode away, totally relaxed. A surgeon with a busy day ahead. A man who touched her like no other and had her smiling even when she was freaking out about Holly. He'd got under her skin and woken her up to new possibilities of love.

It had happened so fast it made it hard to believe it was real, and for the intervening years she'd tried to make herself believe she'd overreacted to an off-the-scale night. But from the moment they'd bumped into each other yesterday there was no denying she felt warm and excited about the possibilities. She wanted to be with Noah, to really get to know him, while feeling she already did. Was *this* love?

Liz waved from beside the counter and held up a mug. 'Want another?' she mouthed.

Stacey nodded, before surreptitiously running a finger beneath her eyes to remove unexpected moisture before Liz came across and noticed. Love and Noah in the same sentence tickled her insides and had her heart beating wildly. Caution was needed here. Lots of it.

'I see you were enjoying Noah Kennedy's company.' Liz sat down in the seat he'd vacated.

Enjoying? Absolutely. 'It's always good to get to know our specialists a little, don't you think?' Put it back on Liz and hopefully she'd drop the subject.

'You're not fooling me, Stacey. I saw you go all bug-eyed when he was on the ward yesterday.'

'Must've had something in my eye.' She grinned. What the heck. 'Only reacting as I've been told all the females have since he started.' At least that showed she hadn't got it wrong when it came to Noah's sexy looks.

'Why does he call you Anastasia?'

She'd prepared for this during the night. 'It's my full name, and when we met once years ago, I was sometimes using it.' Once, and only with Noah, but that was for her to know. 'Stacey's a whole lot easier to spell,' she said with a laugh. 'Or so I've been told.'

Liz chuckled. 'Fair enough. So you've met him before and yet you didn't appear to recognise his name. Interesting.'

'It was a brief encounter. You know how those go. Hi, I'm Anastasia. You're...?'

'Where'd you meet?'

'At a dance. He'd come with a friend and didn't know anyone else. We ended up dancing together most of the night.'

'You didn't hang onto him?'

Time to stop this. 'Nope. I had other things going on at the time.' Now drop it. 'Let's go see what we've got this morning.' She stood up.

'Sit down. There's twenty-five minutes before we're due on the ward.'

Sinking down, Stacey gulped coffee and pretended nothing was out of the ordinary with this conversation until it was time to leave.

An hour after signing on, a patient was brought up from Theatre who'd been taken out by a car on a crossing.

'Miles Canton, thirty-one years of age, fractured femur and hip, four fractured ribs, pneumothorax to left lung and perforated large colon.' The orthopaedic surgeon, Ian Blackwell, had accompanied his patient to the ward. 'He's a competitive cyclist so his fitness will help recovery.'

Stacey nodded, then her breath got stuck in her throat as Noah came up behind Ian. 'Problem in Theatre?' she gasped, unable to stop the thrill cascading through her.

Noah shook his head. 'We're waiting for Theatre to be cleaned up and readied so figured I'd fill you in on the details I had to do with in Miles's case. I've put a tube into the chest cavity. The lung is starting to move. The colon injury was straightforward but nil by mouth until otherwise advised.'

'Of course.' Stacey nodded. 'Liz, I want you with Mr Canton. One on one for today and we'll assess the situation before handover.' Two different and complex sets of surgery on top of each other would have knocked the man around, despite his physical condition. 'There're only two other patients in room three at the moment so put him there so he can sleep.' Fingers crossed.

'Thanks, Stacey. That'll be best.' Noah gave her an appreciative smile.

A smile that sent her heart rate into overdrive. She had it bad. She was only doing her job and yet felt as though he'd complimented her. 'Right, Liz, you're good to go with Mr Canton?'

'On my way.'

Inadvertently she glanced at Noah and saw him watching her with a hint of laughter in his eyes. What was that about? 'Noah?'

'I'd like to see Gloria while I've got a spare moment.' He hustled her along the ward without another word. Thankfully he had enough nous not to take her elbow, and yet she felt as though he'd been about to. That really would have sent everyone's eyebrows halfway up their foreheads. 'How is she this morning?'

'Her wound is healing well, the pain's dropping, though

she understands some of the reason is the continuous dosage of morphine. She's chomping at the bit to go home.'

'I'll change the pain relief medication. From what I heard from Joel yesterday, I'm happy to discharge her.' Noah breezed into the room and all conversation amongst the patients stopped as the women looked at him. 'Morning, Gloria. I hear you're packed and waiting for my signature.' He strode up to her bed.

Stacey resisted winking at the other women and flicked the curtains around them. It was so tempting to be unprofessional because she totally understood their drooling expressions. But she was head nurse and did not want to risk a black mark against her name.

Gloria smiled and looked to Stacey for support. 'Why hang around here when I've got my family waiting for me at home?'

'Is this family going to look after you? Cook your dinner? Make your bed, and generally run around for you?' Noah asked.

'My husband will.'

'Or else?'

'Exactly. He knows when he's onto a winner.'

'I know the consequences if I don't obey she who should be listened to.' The curtain flicked open briefly as Gloria's husband, dressed in a business suit, joined them. 'Morning, Mr Kennedy. Darling.' He dropped a kiss on Gloria's cheek.

'I'm glad you're here, Darryl,' Noah said. 'I'm sending Gloria home, but we need to discuss future treatment.'

'There's always a reality check.' Darryl pulled a chair up to the side of the bed and took his wife's hand in his.

'All right if I sit on the end of the bed?' Noah asked. 'I don't like towering over people when we're talking.'

'Fine.' Gloria's face had lost some colour. Knowing what

lay ahead would be daunting, and she'd probably tried to forget all about it for a while.

Stacey filled a plastic cup with water and handed it to her, received a grateful nod.

'First we have to get the site where I removed your breast completely healed. Only then will we start you on chemo. The treatment is exhausting, and it takes its toll on your body, so best to start in as good a condition as possible.'

'How long are we talking?' Darryl asked.

'Six weeks is optimal.' Noah gave them time to think about this, then continued. 'After you've finished chemo we give you a break before starting radiation which is far less distressing. Though I warn you it'll still make you tired.'

Gloria gripped Darryl's hand. 'I do remember the details from when we first came to see you ten days ago, but this is real. Like it's started and isn't over by a long way.'

Stacey looked away from the anguish in the couple's faces. Cancer was a bitch. No other word for it.

Noah was nodding in agreement. 'Most patients say much the same. You're focusing on one day at a time, one treatment at a time. You've had your mastectomy and your body's responding well. Soon we'll move on to the next phase.'

We. He was with them all the way. As they said their goodbyes and headed out of the room, Stacey's heart expanded for this caring man. He really was special. In more ways than one. Could he be a great dad? She believed so. Could he be a great partner? Someone she could trust with her heart? What? She gasped. She'd been thinking how she wanted more from him than just the role of Holly's father. But it was early days. She wasn't falling in love with him. But she'd had strong feelings for him right from that night they'd made love.

'Stacey? You all right?' Noah asked, looking at her as though there was no one else.

Gulp.

'Yes, just…'

Think of something. Quick.

She coughed against her arm. 'I've got a tickle in my throat.'

And I'm lying on a beach in Hawaii, Noah thought.

Something had disturbed Anastasia's usually calm attitude. What'd they been talking about? Gloria's upcoming treatment. Nothing there that he could see to upset Anastasia. 'Are you sure you're okay?' he asked as they walked towards the hub of the ward.

'Like I said, a tickle in my throat.' She was looking anywhere but at him.

Noah breathed deeply. It seemed Stacey could be hiding something but now was not the time to try and find out what. Of course it might not concern him but that gut instinct that came into play around her was knocking hard again, this time negatively. As though he couldn't quite accept Anastasia was nothing like Christine. Or was he trying to find Christine inside her so he could protect himself from getting too involved? Glancing at his watch, he said far more calmly than his heart beat suggested possible, 'I'll drop in on Jonathon while I'm here.'

'Sure.'

They went into Jonathon's room and greeted the patient. 'Morning, Jonathon. I see you're improving fast now we've got that appendix out of the way.'

'I feel better. Has the infection gone?'

'It takes a bit longer than that. The antibiotics are doing their job and I'll be able to lower the dosage within twenty-four hours if this progress keeps up.' He continued asking and answering questions, noting Anastasia was busy avoiding him while being right across the bed and jotting down things he said that were important to their patient's file.

But when they left Jonathon, she murmured, 'Thanks for calling me Stacey on the ward. Most of the time anyway.'

Could that be what was bothering her? That much? All using her full name said to anyone was that they'd known each other before he'd started here. It wasn't enough for her to gasp and lose colour in her cheeks. No, definitely something else was going on, and it involved him, he'd swear, because they were always in sync. Which didn't make sense considering how little they'd had to do with each other. He was probably being paranoid. 'Still on for catching up after work today?'

'Yes, absolutely,' she said quietly. Where had cheerful Anastasia gone?

'I could try to get away sooner since you finish at three. Or you could do what all women I know do when they've got time to kill. Go shopping.' He was beginning to enjoy winding her up.

'Guess you don't know me, then.'

'I'm trying to but you're putting up road blocks.' How much did he want to push this? Hadn't he decided he had a heart to protect? Yes, and he'd also recognised the need he felt when around her had to be looked into further.

Anastasia stopped. Worry darkened her eyes, whitened her lips. 'Noah.' She looked around, then back at him. 'There's a lot you don't know about me.'

'Are you married?' Why hadn't he asked before? Because if she was, he was out of here, no matter what he felt. There wasn't a ring on her finger, but some staff left them at home during working hours.

'No,' she snapped, flicking a look his way he couldn't interpret.

Not married, but maybe not single either? He took another glance, and saw her eyes were narrower and she was entirely focused on the wall behind him.

'What keeps you busy apart from work?' Now he'd started, he wanted to ask more.

'Family.'

She'd shut down. Why? It had been three years since they'd had that time together, and anything could've happened. Where was the harm in asking? He had to look out for himself. She wouldn't have been hanging around all that time on the off chance they'd meet up again. Especially since amazing sex and great dancing were hardly recommendations for a long-term relationship, though he could think of a lot worse. Of course she'd have found a man, but mightn't have reached the stage they were calling it a relationship. It wasn't as though she was unattractive or undesirable, or unfriendly.

There was a strange sensation in the bottom of his gut; like sadness, or was it disappointment? Couldn't be. Now he'd caught up with Anastasia excitement tingled continuously throughout him, like he had something to look forward to. Something warm and caring, not cold and filled with greed.

Okay, admit it. He did want to spend time with Anastasia. Hope for something more with her kept rattling around inside. Not just another one-night stand. He wanted her in his arms, touching her, kissing her. Danger warnings flashed in his head. He could be falling for her, and how would he ever know if he got it right this time? What if she did turn out to be another Christine? Out to get a man who had money to support her and give her a life of luxury, and by chance he fitted the bill? 'You don't live alone?'

After a deep breath, she continued more calmly. 'At the moment I'm living with my parents and brother. Dad had a truck accident and lost a foot a few years back. Since

then he's qualified as an accountant and is slowly building up a clientele, but there's not a lot of income coming
in. My brother's at university, and Mum works as a recep-
tionist at the local medical centre. I'm supporting them as
much as I can.'

Kind and generous as well as fun and exciting. And
not well off financially. Yet the tightness in his shoulders
backed down after her straight answer. It was hard to hear
any falsehood in her voice. 'So no shopping.' Strange how
he could smile quite easily now. There was no man in her
life. He leaned closer, his gaze fixed on her mouth. Then
he jerked upright. What was wrong with him? This was a
ward. Stepping back, he hauled in air.

'I get in my fair share, believe me.' She was laughing
again, apparently unaware of his reaction to her. Also,
surprising how quickly she could restore her good mood.
'There are some great charity shops in our district.'

'You're a recycling fan.'

'Who isn't?'

'When it comes to clothes, you're looking at the ultimate
waster of clothes.' Then he went back to her family. 'Your
father's accident must've been a hell of a shock for you all.'

'It was, but he's tough, and is truly happy doing what
he is. He and my brother attend the same university, and
there's always something they're competing over.'

'Your brother's doing a BScs too?'

'Heck no. That would be too much to handle. Toby's
doing science.' Pride filled her voice, and her face.

'You love them.'

'Of course I do. And Mum. She's the backbone of our
family, keeps us all on track.'

So simple. Naturally she loved them. No doubts. As
he hadn't had any with his parents. His phone vibrated.
'You're very lucky.'

'I reckon. I'd better get back to work.'

'I'll see you later.' With that she headed away.

So they would have time to sit down together and catch up. On what? They only had dancing and sex between them. Yes, but he wanted a whole lot more. He knew that now. He wasn't going to walk away—yet. He had to decide how far to take this, and if he wanted to try again to find happiness. In a very short time, Anastasia had done this to him. Tipped his world on its head.

The phone stopped vibrating. Damn. He'd been distracted. Not good. Unprofessional. Tapping 'return', he waited to find out who needed him.

'Noah, it's Angela. Theatre's ready.'

'On my way.' Time to focus completely and utterly on what he was here for.

As he waited impatiently for the lift, he watched Anastasia talking to Jason. The more he learned about Anastasia, the more his interest grew to find out even more. He was attracted to her. And not only physically. Her smiles blinded him. Her laughter lifted his spirits. Her gentleness and care with patients touched him. She was not a Christine, nowhere near close. She was a giver, not a taker. Yet he couldn't just let go of his hang-ups and dive into a relationship. The past held him back.

What if he never found the kind of all-encompassing love he hoped for? He couldn't settle for second best. That much he did know. Everything else was up in the air. Except that Anastasia turned him on in a flash. She also brought a lightness to his heart he hadn't known before. She seemed to understand him without knowing him. She was special. She looked out for her family, shared their pain and happiness.

But was she worth the risk? Would she hurt him? Everyone in a relationship got hurt at some time or other. It went with living together. But deep, long-term hurt was his biggest fear. He'd survived it when his parents had died, though how, he had no idea, except pure grit, which for a ten-year-old seemed abnormal. It probably came from having no one to stick up for him.

Robert certainly hadn't wanted to hear him cry or talk about how he missed Mum and Dad. His aunt had told him it was natural to feel those things but good people never talked about them. And then there was Christine. He had tried to talk to her about his past and how he'd felt. She hadn't said anything like his uncle and aunt. No, she hadn't said a word at all. Had just asked if he'd finished and picked up her book to continue reading. The Ice Queen.

He should've seen the warning signs then, but he'd been desperate to love and be loved. Before they were married she'd always managed to avoid that conversation, and he'd let her, not wanting to sound like a man who couldn't cope with life. Afterwards he'd wanted to tell her so there were no secrets between them. What a success that had been, but at least he'd finally admitted where he stood with her and had started divorce proceedings not long after. Better alone than ignored.

Anastasia tensed suddenly, as though sensing him watching her. Again on the same page.

He stepped into the lift now open before him and went down to work. That was the cure for most things that ailed him. Work meant getting involved with other people's problems, medical issues. Some were straightforward and had a good ending, some were not. Those were hard to deal with, and often went home with him, waking him in the middle of the night, when he'd think if only he could do more to save these people.

He did all he could, and more, but it would never be enough. Early in his training days he'd learnt to hold himself aloof from others' misery, not to get involved beyond the facts, but he didn't always follow his own rules. Partly because it was impossible, partly because it made him feel he was turning into Robert if he did.

Being around Anastasia might be the best thing to happen. Might turn him around and return him to being more like his mum, as he had been when he'd been little. Hard to imagine being that happy-go-lucky person again. Worth trying for, though. Being happy. Cheerful. Looking forward rather than over his shoulder at the past. Loving someone more than life itself. Even if it meant risking his heart.

Something to think about over the coming weeks. First, he'd meet Anastasia after work.

He laughed out loud as he stood in the lift full of staff. 'Great day, isn't it?' he asked in general, and had to bite his tongue at the ensuing silence.

So he was going mad. Bring it on. It felt far better than the serious life he knew all too well.

CHAPTER FOUR

'I'M AT CONNOR'S CAFÉ.'

Stacey grinned as she did an about-face and strode back the way she'd come to the café she'd passed only minutes earlier. She couldn't wait to see him. So much for common sense. But for sure, she was not losing control with Noah this time. There was too much at stake. Though she couldn't fault her actions last time. She'd had a fantastic night, which had resulted in Holly arriving into her life. Excitement filled her at the thought of being with Noah away from work, however briefly.

'You're looking lovely,' said the man dominating most of her thoughts when she walked up to him at a table tucked into the back of the noisy café where people were eating early dinners. Bending close, he kissed her on both cheeks. 'How are you?'

Worried, nervous, excited. Mostly wound tight with longing. She smiled. 'Happy.' Unless—until—everything came tumbling down around her red-tipped feet. Leaning in close, to feel that lithe body against hers. The need to get even closer overtook everything else. Rising on her toes, she locked eyes with Noah and touched her lips to his. Just like three years ago, her inhibitions were blinded around Noah.

Noah kissed her back, this time longer and deeper, sending her world spinning. Finally he pulled away, leaving her hungry for more of him. 'Your happy disposition is contagious.' His smile was wry. He took her hand and held out a chair with the other. 'Coffee's coming. I also ordered a platter of cheeses and crackers to fill the gap.'

'Thanks. I'm a bit peckish.'

'Me too, and dinner's a way off as I've got a patient to check up on later. He haemorrhaged excessively during surgery.'

Fair enough. She didn't have long to talk to him then. 'Never good. What were you operating on?'

Noah shook his head. 'We're not at work now.'

Nice one. More excitement touched her.

Quieten down, girl.

'Fair enough.'

So what would they talk about? Holly. That was why she'd come. That, and to be with Noah.

'Do you ever think about that night?' Surprise flitted through his expression, as though he couldn't believe he'd asked.

Well, Noah, neither can I.

It was up front and had her wondering where this was going. Another one-night stand? Did she even want that? The moment she'd seen him on the ward she'd felt all those same exciting sensations she'd felt back then, and something more. A connection that really couldn't be explained other than it felt right.

The coffees and nibbles arrived.

When the waitress had gone Stacey told Noah truthfully, 'Yes, I have. Often.'

The surprise lightened. 'Me, too,' he admitted. Then, 'As you were leaving, you said thank you for helping you get on with your life. What was that about?'

Looking into those grey eyes, she found genuine interest, and it gave her a sense of having found a man she could tell her all to. Starting with the truth about her past. 'A year before that dance I was jilted four days out from my wedding.' She stared at Noah.

Don't you dare feel sorry for me, because I no longer do.

'We'd known each other pretty much all our lives, had been best friends and then fell in love and got engaged. When he ended it I was heartbroken, and couldn't seem to get on with my life. One of my friends suggested joining them at the dance and I reluctantly agreed. When I left home that night my father said to go out and enjoy myself, let my hair down—' She stopped when Noah's mouth twitched. 'Guess I did that.'

The twitch became a full-blown grin. 'You did. It was beautiful spread across the pillow.'

She gasped. 'Sure you should be saying things like that? We've only just got reacquainted.'

'It's been two days, far longer than last time.'

'Are you flirting with me?' That was a turnaround from last time.

'Should I be?'

Yes, please.

'Let's wait and see. I had a wonderful night with you, but it was three years ago and who knows if we're even on the same page with our lives any more.'

And there's something huge to tell you.

'At least you're being honest.' That couldn't be relief taking over his expression. He'd started this. 'Something else we have in common,' he added.

She didn't have to ask what else he was referring to. It was there in their easy way together. Funny, but she was completely relaxed, even knowing what lay ahead in the next few days. Stacey looked around the packed room, and then back to Noah. Lifting her flat white, she saluted him.

'I'm glad we've finally caught up. I've wondered where you were, even who you were. You were like a mystery. No one knew you when I asked around. I started thinking I'd made it all up.'

'You tried to find me?'

'I asked everyone from the General Hospital CEO to the janitors. Or close enough. You were a mystery, yet I hadn't imagined that night. Not a minute of it.'

'It was real.' He nodded. 'I asked my friend if he knew you, and I got the same result.'

'It seemed wrong to have such a good time and not follow up, though that might've spoiled the whole thing.' She grinned. 'I was a little tiddly by the time we left the dance.'

He held his thumb and forefinger out, almost touching. 'A little. But you seemed to know exactly what you wanted.'

'No regrets.' Not one. Right, they'd got that out of the way. 'Tell me about your time in New Zealand.'

He filled her in on where he'd lived and worked, and how well he'd got on with his cousin. 'Have you ever been there?'

'I've never left Britain.' Not enough money in the coffers for travelling overseas. 'I've been to Scotland to see where my grandparents came from. Loved all those mountains and lochs.'

'You're a stay-at-home girl? Or travelling not your thing?'

'Angus wasn't into holidays, preferred working on projects, and I guess it rubbed off. No point getting wound up about it when he'd never change his mind.' Though now she questioned her willingness to sacrifice her own dreams for his.

Noah was watching her closely again. 'I've been married.'

Her stomach lurched. 'You have?'

His nod was abrupt. 'Divorced two years before I met you.'

'What happened?'

His mouth flattened, and for a moment she thought she'd gone too far. But he wouldn't have raised the subject if he wasn't going to tell her more. Then he shrugged. 'Christine wasn't who I thought she was. Looking back, I don't think she ever loved me. She wanted the comfortable lifestyle I could provide and in return she offered to have two children in quick succession so we could move on with living the perfect, wealthy life.' Bitterness mingled with anger in his voice, and when Stacey looked into his eyes she saw the same emotions there. 'Like I wanted to have children in those circumstances, without any say in the matter.'

Did he mean he didn't want children, full stop? Or not with his ex? 'I'm sorry. That must've been hard on you.'

'It's fine. I'm over her. Just thought I needed to put it out there.'

Right. He was over his ex? He might not love her any more, but he hadn't got over what she'd done to him. He was where she'd been the night they'd met. Her hopes for tonight and sharing her news dropped. This wasn't looking good for her and Holly. He might not believe her when she said Holly was his. 'Thank you for telling me.'

What else could she say? *I'm here and I wouldn't do that to you. Give me a chance to prove it.*

Noah glanced at his watch. 'I'll have to go shortly.'

Already? 'No problem.' Glancing at the wall clock, she saw they'd spent nearly an hour here. The time had flown by, leaving her hyper and happy, and a little worried. Learning more about Noah was always going to come with pitfalls. Being with him hadn't. The way heat was tripping over her skin had her wishing they could find another hotel room for a few hours. She so wasn't ready to leave Noah, but she was a big girl. She'd get over her disappointment. She hadn't said what she'd come to say either.

'Can we do this again?' How would he take the news of Holly? Until he'd said that about his ex-wife planning on having children in quick succession and hadn't sounded too enthusiastic, she believed he'd accept being a father without too many problems. Now she wondered if she'd got that wrong, and what else wasn't as she thought.

'Absolutely.'

So he was still keen to see her. She exhaled slowly. That had to be good. 'Great.'

'I'll walk you to the station.' Noah stood up.

Brilliant. A few more minutes with him. Despite the children problem, she bounced beside him, like a kid who'd had too much sugar. 'Thanks.' Bundled up in thick jackets, they braved the cold air after the heat of the bar. 'I can't wait for winter to be over.'

'It's been a shock after leaving summer behind down under.' Noah strode out beside her.

Upping her pace to keep up, she shoved her hands deep in her pockets, for warmth and to stop herself from grabbing his hand and holding him until they reached the station. 'You wouldn't think of going back there?'

'It's tempting, but I own family property here that I would never sell. Other people used my house while I was away and I'm now stuck with a massive redecoration project.'

The Bloomsbury house spoke of other-world wealth. No one lived there on a budget. Noah must come from a very wealthy family. Lucky for him. Though nothing like that came without responsibilities, like not being able to live in a country he really liked. His life was nothing like hers, and never would be. It would be great to have a spare few thousand pounds in the bank, but she wasn't in need of a fortune.

From what she'd seen, money didn't necessarily make a person any happier either. With her, Holly would get a grounding in basics such as working for what she wanted. Unless Noah didn't have the same idea and gave her everything. Another thing to find out more about. These few precious minutes were hers to enjoy for herself. 'How handy are you with a paintbrush?'

'A what?' He grinned.

'That good? Fair enough.'

'I'm a doctor. There are qualified painters and decorators to fix my problems while I concentrate on what I am good at.' She waited. Was he going to reveal feelings about that night he wanted to follow up on?

Then he shook his head. 'Another time.'

Her heart sank. 'Okay.'

He touched her jaw, lifted her head. 'Don't worry, Anastasia. I'm not out to hurt you.' His mouth covered hers briefly. Then he took her hand and continued to the station.

At the entrance they stopped, turned to face each other. Stacey gazed at the man who'd changed her life so much without realising any of it and felt comfortable with him. As a thread of warmth wound through her, she had to admit to another feeling—desire. Nothing had changed in that respect. The softening of her stomach, the tightness at her centre, the thumping in her chest—all the same.

How could she feel like that about a man she'd made love with three years ago and not seen or heard from since? Easily, apparently, if the way he made her feel special was an indicator. Did this mean there was more to her feelings than was logical? But it seemed love wasn't logical, could come out of the blue and bang a person over the head like a thunderclap. Not that she *loved* him. But she certainly felt more for him than she'd have believed possible. He was under her skin now, and looked like he was staying there for a long time, if not for ever.

'Anastasia? There was something else you said to me that night.'

She stared at him, hope flickering behind her ribs, her tongue moistening her lips. Did he mean what she thought? What if she uttered those words and got it completely wrong? What was there to lose? Her pride could take a knock. 'Kiss me, please? Again.'

'It wasn't a question last time, it was a demand.' Noah's mouth touched her lips, gently at first, then more demanding, taking over, holding her close, his tongue pushing into her mouth. Kissing her, embracing her.

Weak-kneed, she leaned against him for strength, all the while kissing back with a fervour that brought need cascading throughout her starved body. This was what she'd remembered, and longed for, over and over during the years when only memories had been real. This was why she'd moved on from her past and started looking forward. It was also why she'd never given up trying to find him— for her and for Holly.

But at the moment she relished being with him for herself. She kissed him again and again. This had given her Holly. Their daughter. It could give her a whole lot more if Noah was as invested in her as she was becoming in him.

Stacey paused, and immediately Noah raised his head.

'Anastasia?' He was smiling, his eyes light and sparkling. 'We seem to connect the moment we're alone together, don't we?'

'Alone as in surrounded by others dancing, or people dashing to catch a train? We sure do,' she said with a grin. Leaning back, she stared up at him, and gathered her courage. 'Can I see you at the weekend?' The smile was diminishing, taking her heart with it. She rushed on.

'If it doesn't suit, that's all right.' She wanted to tell him now, but he was heading back to work, and to go with him so they could talk after he'd dealt with his patient didn't sit comfortably. Besides, Toby was looking after Holly while her parents were out, and he wanted to go to see a mate when she got home. Another day would have to do, which wasn't easy now that she'd made up her mind to get it over with.

Noah seemed to be considering his options, making her feel uncomfortable for asking in the first place.

'I know you're busy.'

He reached for her and dropped a kiss on her cheek. 'Stop it. You should come to my house and we'll have lunch.'

'Put like that, how can I refuse?' She smiled.

He answered, 'By saying no.'

'Are you already regretting inviting me? Because if you are, then please say so. But I do want to talk.'

Thump, thump.

She rubbed her chest. 'Spend some more time with you, catching up.'

Noah's eyes followed her movements. 'I am not regretting it. Not at all.'

She gripped his forearm, wished his jacket wasn't so thick she couldn't feel his warmth through it. 'I had a wonderful time with you three years ago, and I wonder what might've happened if we'd stayed in touch.'

'Have you always been so upfront?'

'I'm getting better at it.' Her smile felt strained. Putting in more effort, she looked directly at Noah. 'I'm a late learner about relationships, spending most of my years with one man. There were many signs I didn't see so didn't know to ask about. Learning the truth in such a blunt manner was hard, though probably for the best. I do not want to have that happen again, at least not unless I can say I did everything in my power to prevent it.' She was talking too much maybe, but this was who she'd become and, like she'd said, who she would always be from now on.

'I'm not presuming because we've had a coffee together that we're in a relationship. Not at all. I'd just like to spend some more time with you, and if it isn't what you want then I expect you to tell me.' Where had all that come from? It had nothing to do with Holly, and all to do with herself. Could be she wasn't the devoted mum she prided herself on being. No, not true. But she was entitled to look out for herself in all this as well as for Holly. Anyway, how could she deny the need growing inside her to get closer to Noah? Even while trying to keep on the straight and narrow until everything was sorted between them, she wanted him. Badly.

Noah was looking a little stunned. Then he chuckled. 'Let's have breakfast together in the morning before we start work. Meet at Connor's again. It's between the hospital and the private practice I'm at. Unless you're free in about forty-five minutes? When I've seen my patient?'

Temptation roared through her. There'd be nothing more wonderful than to spend time together, alone, kissing, hugging. Talking about Holly. On her toes, Stacey leaned in and kissed Noah. 'I'll see you tomorrow,' and she tried to step away.

'Not so fast.' His arms wrapped around her, held her hard against his strong frame, and his mouth devoured hers. His tongue tasted her, turning her knees to mush so that she'd have dropped to the pavement if Noah hadn't been holding her so tight. Breathing was impossible. Not that she cared.

If she had to die right now, then this was the only way to go. Why had she turned down his offer to go with him?

Noah watched Anastasia head down the escalator to the trains below ground, his finger touching where her last kiss had landed. 'I'm in trouble.' No matter how sensible he was, how he laid out the facts of his heart not wanting to be broken, or his trust trashed, he was falling for Anastasia Wainwright. He felt like a moth drawn to the light, in danger and unable to back away. It was scary. He hadn't learned enough about her yet.

Should he jump in and risk everything? Stop trying to overthink everything? But what if he'd got it all wrong, and she was another gold-digger? Yet when they were kissing his body was alight with need, and he wanted to rush her off to his bed and make love to her all night long. To enjoy her company, share some laughs and forget he could get hurt again.

When she'd asked to see him again there had been no way he could say no. Open, determined and so lovable, all in one. How could he not want her? Why wouldn't he just fall for her and be done with it?

He'd noticed she'd gone quiet for a brief moment when he'd mentioned yesterday where he lived, and then tonight when he'd told her the house needed redecorating there'd been another quiet moment, but he didn't think that meant she was calculating his worth, however little she knew. From what he'd seen and heard about her lifestyle with her family, he understood there wasn't a lot of money to spare, but he couldn't believe she would be someone to grab at him for what he had. Of course, he'd got that wrong once before.

Sighing, he turned in the direction of the hospital. A patient required his attention, and he required some work to silence the doubts and arguments cramming his head.

And in the morning they'd have breakfast together. It couldn't come fast enough and wouldn't be anywhere as much time with Anastasia as he'd like.

'Noah, wait.'

He spun around and caught Anastasia as she bounded up and threw her arms around him. 'I can't stay all night.'

Noah kissed her like his life depended on it. Then he drew back. 'Guess we'd better get a move on then.' The hospital visit wouldn't take long and then they'd grab a cab to his house. His blood was throbbing in his wrists and making his head light. Gripping her hand, he almost dragged her to the hospital and into the lift.

And finally, after making certain his patient was doing as well as expected, Noah took Anastasia out again onto the street to wave down a cab and take her home, kissing all the way.

Inside the front door, he leaned back to nudge it shut, Anastasia in his arms. 'Welcome to my house.'

She didn't stop to look around, just rose up on her toes and wound her arms around his neck. 'Run out of kisses?'

'Not likely.' And he lost himself in her arms, until he had to possess her. Swinging her up into his arms, he strode along the hall and into the sitting room to the sofa. When he laid her down, she remained holding him, keeping him close, her fingers working magic on his shoulders, reminding him of how she made him feel soft and hard, hot and strong whenever her fingers were on his skin. 'Anastasia, slow down.'

'Can't.'

Neither could he, unless she wanted him to, and it seemed she didn't. So he went with the passion rising throughout him, touching her soft, warm skin, caressing, sucking her nipples until she cried out. Somehow they were naked, though he couldn't recall removing any clothing, and he lay back with Anastasia on top of his pulsing body as she rolled a condom over his erection. Her legs were spread wide, her centre beckoning with heat and moisture, and then they joined. Anastasia's back arched under his hands, her head tipped back and that satiny hair skimming his thighs as they came.

Noah sank into a haze of release and satisfaction. This was what he'd been hoping for ever since Anastasia had walked out of his hotel room three years ago. Anastasia was his dream. With her, he lost all sense of everything but her. And it felt right. Good. Beyond good. Unreal.

Careful.

Sure, but not tonight.

His mind slipped back to when they'd met. He'd tried not to stare down at the petite woman beside him as they'd strolled into the hotel foyer to take a break from the loud music. She'd been impossible to ignore, having intrigued him when he'd seen her dancing on the perimeter of the dance floor. He'd never forgotten the way her hips had had his mouth drying faster than a puddle in the desert as she'd swayed in time. The colourful skirt had accentuated her delightfully curved butt, while her tiny waist gave way to breasts that had his hands itching to touch them. She had an urchin look. As for those brown hazel eyes, they'd snagged him every time she'd looked directly at him. And in every dream about her he'd had since.

Now here they were, sprawled across his sofa, exhausted from making love, and he was ready to do it again. His lips touched her forehead. 'Hey, you awake?'

Her mouth spread into a wide smile, lifting at the right corner, while her eyes filled with mischief. 'You're a lot better than that.'

He laughed. 'You say the nicest things.' He leaned in for another kiss. A simple yet intense kiss that rocked him on his firmly placed backside. A kiss that was rapidly heating his blood and banishing the lethargy following their lovemaking.

Her arms tightened around him, her breasts pressed closer, her thighs also.

On her face he saw a similar need to what was knocking at him, turning him into a pool of desire. He was a goner. 'Anastasia?'

She nodded slowly. 'Noah.' When she growled his name into his mouth he almost came before she did.

Anastasia.

It was over as fast as it started, and this time they sat up, leaning back against the sofa, until their breathing returned to normal. Then her phone pinged, and she stood up, taking his hopes with her as she began tugging on her clothes. As though she knew who'd messaged. 'Sorry, but I need to get home.'

'You can stay the night,' he said, trying not to sound needy. Or worried there was someone else in her life after all.

She shook her head. 'Not tonight.' The light was gone from her eyes, replaced by what? Disappointment? Regret? Yes, that was it. But why? Or someone else she'd just let down? She'd made love so acceptingly. Taking and giving. Completely involved.

'You are single, are you?' he demanded, suddenly on edge about her hurried departure.

Contrition blinked out at him. 'Yes, Noah, I promise I am. I would never play around on anyone.'

His lungs let out the air they'd been holding. He nodded. 'I believe you.' Without question, which only showed how involved he was getting.

'Thank you. I have to get home to cover for my brother.'

Bending down, she kissed his forehead. 'See you tomorrow for coffee?'

'Definitely.' He stood up. 'I'll walk you to the station.'

'That's not necessary.'

'Nevertheless, I'm doing it.' Taking her arm, he led her to the front door, and down to the street. At the station he kissed her gently. 'Until tomorrow.'

Anastasia smiled up at him, all trace of her previous rush to get away gone. 'I'm glad I've found you.' Then she whirled around and headed down the stairs to her train.

Noah followed her every step until she'd disappeared from sight, his heart pounding as longing for a full and happy life gripped him. 'I can't wait to see you again.' What was astonishing, he really meant it.

Friday morning in the staff cafeteria, Stacey fiddled with her mug of coffee, twisting it back and forth between shaky fingers. Those few snatched hours with Noah on Tuesday night had been wonderful and had proved she hadn't been exaggerating her memories. He made her feel special and happy being with him. If only she could've stayed all night. Leaving had been hard, but essential. Not so much Toby grizzling by text she was late, but the fact she and Noah hadn't talked about Holly, and hadn't been likely to if she'd stayed, had brought on a bout of guilt and had had her heading home where she'd lain awake most of the night, reliving their love making.

'Morning, Anastasia.' The man of her dreams slid onto the chair opposite her. 'How're you today?'

Tired, worried and... 'Happy to see you.'

His eyebrows rose, followed by a soft smile that did nothing to stop her wanting him. 'You're easily pleased.'

'I am.' That depended on the problem.

His brow knotted. 'Why? Don't you want a lot more in your life?'

Was he talking wealth? Of course he was used to it and probably had no idea how other people got by without bemoaning the world for their lot. So much for that smile turning her into jelly. He'd got serious very quickly. 'Like what, Noah? My family adores me, I have the job I've always wanted. I'm not incarcerated in the house when I'm not working. My parents aren't dragons and I can come and go as I please.' With her finger, she drew a circle on the table. 'What goes around comes around. Sure, one day I'd like a home of my own, and a man to share it with, but right now I have nothing to complain about.'

'What about a new car or a holiday?'

She dug up a smile and went with honesty. There was no other way to deal with his doubts and if he couldn't see the truth hitting him over the head then they weren't as suited as she was starting to think. Maybe she'd been blindsided by wishful thinking. They were poles apart in just about every facet of life, except for dancing, kissing, making love—and a child. 'I'd like those things, but I can live without them.'

'Without regrets.' He nodded.

'Totally.' Was he checking out her reaction to his house last night? She'd been so focused on Noah, she'd hardly taken any notice except it had felt large and spacious.

The girl from behind the counter appeared at their table with Noah's breakfast. 'Here you go.' She smiled coyly.

'Thank you,' he acknowledged the girl with a pleasant smile, nothing like the stomach-twisting ones he gave Stacey. Turning his attention back to her, he said, 'Your own house and man, huh?' Then he smiled and she relaxed a little.

'Naturally. And a family.' The words slipped out before

she knew she was going to say them. Testing the waters? Might as well go for broke. 'Do you ever think about having children? I know you said your wife wanted to have two, but you sounded as though you weren't interested.'

The smile slid off his face. 'Isn't this a bit soon to be talking about having children?'

'Says the man who just questioned how comfortable I am in my less than well off life.'

Putting down his knife and fork, Noah reached for her hand. 'I'm sorry. You're right, I did speak out of turn. So, yes, one day I would love to have a family, but not when I'm told to, and how many and what to name them before they're even conceived. Children should be a delight, not a duty.'

Stacey sat back, watching Noah as he returned to eating his bacon and eggs, her own scrambled eggs not looking so enticing any more. Which category did Holly fall into? Delight or duty? Only one way to find out and she wasn't about to tell him when they had to get to work shortly. He'd need time for reality to sink in, and then she'd have to answer a load of questions. Clock-watching wouldn't help. And since she couldn't change that, she ignored the gremlins holding her tight and said, 'What time shall I come into town tomorrow?'

'How about I pick you up at home and we go somewhere out of the city?'

The egg slid off her fork.

You can't come to the house with Holly there. Not until we've talked. Quick, think.

A phone rang quietly. Not hers. Saved.

Noah tugged his from his shirt pocket. 'Guess that's breakfast done.' He held it to his ear. 'Noah Kennedy.'

Despite her nerves, a thrill ran down her spine as she thought back to the day they'd first spoken on the phone.

That deep voice had got her wondering if she knew the
man on the other end and had made her skin tingle. Then
she'd met the man behind the voice and everything had
changed. Here was Noah, after all this time, and she had
to pinch herself every day to make sure she wasn't dreaming. He was as exciting and hot as she'd remembered. Tuesday night had only enhanced everything she adored about
him, and while they had a lot to talk about there was no
quietening the need for him that kept her filled with desire and hope.

'An elderly man fell down the stairs at an underground
station and needs surgery for a perforated lung. See you
tomorrow. I'll wait for you at the station near my house.'
He was stuffing the phone back in his pocket as he stood
up, his mind obviously on the patient ahead, and not her
and their date.

Without uttering a word, she'd got over that hurdle.
'Can't wait,' she said honestly.

Noah came towards her. 'Anastasia, you are special.
Not everyone appreciates what they have as much as you
do.' With that he was striding away, leaving his half-eaten
breakfast and her bewilderment behind.

So he hadn't been totally diverted by that phone call. Did
that mean he hadn't realised she was avoiding him going to
Harlow to pick her up? If so, she wouldn't get away with it
for long, but then she was going to reveal all in the morning anyway. Noah. The man who lifted her spirits just by
being himself.

He probably didn't realise she was keen on him, other
than to make love to. Or he did and was taking his time
revealing his own feelings. What *did* he feel about her?
Lust? Or more? She was being impatient. She still wasn't
totally certain how deeply she felt for him. All she knew
was that she wanted more of him, more with him, more,

more, more. His kisses spoke of need and desire, but was there something behind those that spoke of emotions that encompassed her?

CHAPTER FIVE

On Saturday Noah waited impatiently for Anastasia to arrive, scanning every face coming up the stairs. In his hand was a large black umbrella as outside the entrance rain bucketed down, filling the drains to overflowing. So much for a drive and lunch out in the countryside.

Anastasia had said she'd text him when she got to the station, but hanging around waiting at home had been impossible. Now he paced up and down, dodging other people almost as impatient for the train as he was. Bet they didn't have a gorgeous woman coming to see them, or dance music ready to play and mojito ingredients on the bench, or clean sheets on the bed. Did he have it bad, or what?

He wasn't going to rush her to the bedroom; he was being prepared, that was all. No denying he'd wanted her since the moment she'd turned to look at him in the ward on Monday, and making love the other night hadn't been nearly enough. Even better, Anastasia seemed to reciprocate his feelings. There were many doubts about their future, but he needed to see them through, to make sensible decisions, and to do that he had to get to know her better, and yet the moment he was with her he gave in to the clawing need only Anastasia brought on.

'Hi.' A soft hand slid into his, jerking him back to the

present. Then those soft lips he dreamed about brushed his mouth.

Noah groaned and pulled Anastasia into him, returned her kiss with vigour. This was what he'd been waiting for. 'Morning to you, too.'

Under his mouth, she laughed. 'We're crazy.' Then she moved back and looked at him intently, the smile dimming, concern in her eyes. 'I take it we're going to your place now that the weather's changed?'

'Yes, unless you don't want to.' Why wouldn't she? It was more relaxed and intimate than going to a café or bar. 'What's up?'

Anastasia straightened. 'Nothing. I'm pleased we're not going out in this, that's all.'

'Would you prefer to go to a restaurant or bar?'

Her smile returned. 'No, not at all.'

He could relax. Flicking the umbrella open and holding it above them, he took her hand in his free one. 'Let's go.'

Keeping in step with him—like their dancing—she leaned close, stayed close as they splashed through puddles along the footpath. Then she hesitated. 'That man under the shop overhang. He looks…'

'Very unwell, like—'

'He's having a medical—'

'Event. Heart attack?'

They ran, stopped in front of the man slumped against the wall, one hand gripping his upper left arm.

'Sir? I'm Noah Kennedy, a doctor, and Stacey here's a nurse. Are you all right?' The guy was grey and shaking.

'It's my arm. Pain.'

'He's sweating profusely,' Stacey noted. 'I'll call an ambulance.'

'Can you get us a chair from inside as well, please?'

Then to the man, 'We need to get you sitting down. What's your name?'

'Len.'

'Any history of heart disease?'

'No. The pain's in my arm, not my chest.'

Heart attacks often presented first as pain in the left arm. 'Any tightness in your chest? Difficulty breathing?'

'It feels strange, and sometimes I can't take a full breath. My jaw's hurting.'

'Here.' Stacey was back with someone from the shop carrying a chair. 'The ambulance is on its way.'

Noah helped Len onto the chair and knelt beside him. 'Take it easy.' It'd be better to be inside, but he wasn't having the man walking anywhere when his heart was playing up. That it was a heart attack wasn't in doubt, and all they could do was take obs and watch closely until the paramedics arrived, be prepared if Len's heart stopped.

Stacey had her phone on timer and was counting Len's pulse rate. 'One twenty.' Then she was onto the respiration rate. 'Abnormal.'

Noah nodded. 'Thanks.'

Her slight nod told him she was up with the diagnosis. They worked as a team, neither having to ask anything of the other. Could they work together as well in their private lives? So far they were in sync about most things, so why not? Was that what real love was about? Having each other's backs without being asked? Understanding where each was coming from and going with it? Sounded wonderful. If it was true. And so far it seemed to be. A wailing siren reached his ears, and relief took over. 'That was quick.'

Stacey was holding Len's hand, her finger on his pulse again. 'It's your lucky day, Len.'

'You think?' The man gave her a wry smile. 'Thanks for noticing me.'

'Not a problem,' they said in unison.

Noah laughed. How like them.

Within minutes they'd handed over to the paramedics and were on their way to his house.

'I'm so glad we noticed Len's distress. Most people wouldn't have thought he was in difficulty,' Stacey muttered.

'True, but we're trained to be medically observant.' At home, he took Stacey's sodden jacket to hang on the stand. She needed a decent leather one to keep dry and warm. 'You're shivering.'

She stepped up to him, warmth in her eyes at least. Winding her arms around his neck, she stretched up to kiss him. 'Then warm me up.'

'Cheeky.' Noah held her tight. This was becoming normal—the excitement, the being together, the enjoyment of each other. He could go with it, was starting to see they might have a future that didn't hold doubts and fears, that he might find the love he'd been looking for. And it had all started with a dance. 'Come on. We'll have some fun.'

Her eyes lit up. 'We're good at that.'

He couldn't help himself, he just had to kiss her again, and again, and hold her curvy backside in his palms, and kiss a trail down her neck to that alluring cleavage, and help her shrug out of her jeans, and pull her jersey over her head. And help her push his jeans down to his thighs and then to his knees and ankles so he could step out of them. Tugging his jersey and shirt off in one swoop, he scooped her into his arms and headed upstairs where he laid her on the bed and lay down with her.

Anastasia rolled onto her side and reached for him, the desire in her face heating him further and making his heart swell with need and care for this wonderful woman. Up on his arms, he covered her gently, and tasted her from top to toe and back again. Her frantic gasps and cries drove him to the edge, and then he was filling her, taking her, giving to her, and they were one.

Stacey's favourite dance tune cut through the blur in her head. She was dreaming. She and Noah were dancing. No, they weren't. She could feel his naked body lying the length of her languid leg, hip, arm.

'You going to turn that off?' Noah grunted beside her.

It was her phone. Not music playing in the background as they'd made love. Sitting up, she stared around the room, spied her bag on the floor. As she dug the phone out the music stopped. 'No need.' Dropping the phone on top of her bag, she lay down again, and splayed her hand over Noah's chest, absorbed his heat.

The music started up again. 'Go away, whoever you are.' Reaching for the phone to shut it down, she froze. 'Mum?' Her family knew she was with Noah and that today was the day to tell him about Holly so Mum wouldn't ring unless it was urgent.

'I have to get this.'

Noah sighed. Fair enough. This had spoiled a wonderful moment between them.

Hopefully he'd understand later. 'Mum? What's up?'

'It's Holly. She's had an accident and is on her way to hospital in an ambulance.'

'What? Holly's hurt?' Stacey shrieked. 'No, Mum, please, don't say that.' Her head spun so fast she had to lean back against the headboard. Not her girl. No, anything but that. 'What's happened? Is she going to be all right? Tell me. Who's with her?'

'Dad's with her. She ran into the road after her ball. The kids from next door brought us some eggs and left the gate open.' Her mother hesitated.

Stacey's fear cranked up harder. 'Mum? Please tell me she's all right.'

'A boy on a skateboard knocked her over. The ambulance crew think her arm is broken.' A deep breath and her mother raced on. 'She hit her head when she landed and lost consciousness for a while. There's a cut along her hairline above her forehead. Oh, darling, I'm so sorry this has happened. Those kids know to shut the gate, but I should've checked.'

'It's not your fault. I have to get to Holly. Which hospital? Noah can drive me there now. Did she regain consciousness?' Out for a while. What did that mean? Still out? Stacey scrambled to her feet, leaned against the wall to steady her wobbly legs, and swallowed hard. Her voice was rising uncontrollably. 'Tell me. Has she regained consciousness at any time? Is she in pain?'

'Anastasia? What's happened? You look terrible.' Noah stood before her, reaching for her arm.

'Mum?' she pleaded, grabbing Noah's hand, holding it tightly as she said to him, 'There's been an accident.'

'I think so. It was hard to tell but I saw her eyes open briefly and she was staring at her granddad for a moment.'

Was that consciousness or a reaction to a severe head injury? 'I'm on my way.'

'Anastasia, what's going on?' Noah demanded.

Pulling her hand free of Noah's, she started tugging on her clothes. 'I have to go to the hospital near home. Now. Holly's been in an accident.' Her voice was shrill. Fear clawed through her. Her baby was hurt and she wasn't with her, wasn't holding her, couldn't encourage her to be all right. 'Come on, Noah. Hurry.'

Noah shrugged into his clothes. 'Who's Holly?'

Not now. This wasn't how she was supposed to tell Noah he was a father. 'Mum, we're coming. Where are you?'

'Behind the ambulance. Toby's driving us. He raced out when he saw Holly head down the drive, but he was too late to stop her being hit.'

'He tried.' She shoved the phone in her bag. Toby would be gutted. He adored his niece—watch out anyone who hurt her.

'Anastasia, let's go.'

'Would the train be faster?' she cried as they ran down the stairs. Holly dominated her thoughts. Nothing, no one else mattered.

'Fifty-fifty, and we'd have to get to the hospital from the station.' It seemed like seconds and hours before she was belted inside Noah's four-wheel drive and he was pulling away from the kerb. 'Which hospital?' he asked.

Huddling down in the seat, she told him, and wished the trip to be fast and uneventful. 'Thank you for doing this.'

'Why wouldn't I take you to whoever has been injured when it's so obvious that person is very special to you? We can do lunch any time.'

Her tongue stuck to the roof of her mouth. Fear sat like a lead ball in her stomach. Sweat broke out on her brow. Clasping her hands tight, she stared at the road unfolding ahead of the car. Tense silence filled the air between them.

'Stacey?'

When he flicked to the shortened version of her name it put her off track. She didn't know the reason behind it, except it seemed he'd done it to get her full attention.

Here we go.

'Holly. My daughter.'

'You have a child?'

'Yes.'

'You've never mentioned her.'

'We haven't spent much time together.'

'I'd have thought a daughter would be the most important topic of discussion no matter where we were. In the café the other morning, on the ride up here, having a coffee and nibbles at the cafe. You mentioned your family. Surely family includes your daughter?' Noah sounded cross and confused, as he had every right to be.

In normal circumstances she'd have bored him silly, talking about Holly. Now she had to tell the truth, but while they were racing for the hospital? It was too much. Yet she needed his strength and support. What if he dropped her off at the hospital and she never saw him again, except at work? He wouldn't do that. He'd want to meet his daughter. No doubt about that.

'I'll ask once more. Is there someone else in your life? Someone important?'

'Only Holly.'

You can do better than that.

'I've been single for years, and not dated much. Being a mum takes most of my time when I'm not working.' Was Holly's accident payback for not being there? She shouldn't have come out today, should've been at home, playing with Holly, then this insane ride mightn't be happening. She should've talked to Noah the moment she'd arrived at his house, not got distracted making love. Holly, her beautiful, trusting little girl.

Your mother's stuffed up, sweetheart.

'Holly, hang in there. Mummy's coming.'

She didn't know she'd said that out loud until Noah placed a hand on her clenched fists. 'Easy. I'm getting you there as fast as I can.'

'I know, but it'll never be fast enough. I have to be with my girl.'

'Do you know what happened?' At least he was sounding friendly, though a bit cautious. And he was here for her, getting her to the hospital fast.

'The kids next door left our gate open. Holly chased her ball out onto the road and a boy on a skateboard collided with her.' Anguish gripped her, pain tightened her heart. 'I should've been there,' she cried, turning her hands, loosening her fingers to grab Noah's. 'What sort of mother am I to go out and leave her at home?'

'She was with your parents, wasn't she? No mother spends twenty-four seven with their child. It's not normal or good for them. You're allowed time out, Stacey.'

Stacey, huh? She wasn't getting her head around why he'd swapped between the versions of her name. 'You're right, but I can't accept it. She's on her way to hospital,' she cried.

Removing his hand, he said, 'Tell me about her.' He was concentrating on the road and the busy traffic ahead and swallowing hard.

Was he starting to wonder if Holly was his? He couldn't be. He didn't know how old she was.

I want to tell him. But not right now. Not when he's driving and I can't look into his eyes to show I am not lying.

Not when she was desperate to be with Holly, and nothing else mattered as much.

'Is she cute, and funny like her mother?' Noah seemed to have accepted she was a parent. Or was he just doing the right thing in trying to distract her from her pain on this *far too slow* journey?

'Holly's gorgeous. Her favourite stories are about fairies, and pink is the only colour she'd wear given half a chance. She doesn't have a dancing bone in her body, but that doesn't stop her trying. And wiping out the coffee table in her attempts.'

'Not entirely like her mother, then.' There was a hint of a smile in Noah's voice.

She still couldn't relax. 'Everything's an adventure, especially digging the veg garden with Granddad. He has a special patch where they plant carrots and radishes and peas that's Holly's garden.'

'Is she the reason you're living with your parents?' He was back to driving with two hands on the steering wheel, his knuckles white.

'Yes. Mostly.'

Holly.

'She's got to be all right.' She needed to explain, to tell Noah everything. Her heart was breaking, and her head aching. She just wanted to get to Holly and hold her—if she was able to. At least she'd hold her hand and be there for however long she was in hospital. She stared at the dark screen on her phone. Why wasn't Dad ringing? Did that mean bad news? Surely Mum had reached the hospital by now? She'd phone no matter what. Wouldn't she? 'Can we go any faster?'

'Not legally, no.' But the car lurched forward as the speed picked up.

Closing her eyes, Stacey leaned back and let Holly fill her mind. Laughing as she played with her favourite doll. Grinning when she ate ice cream in a cone and got more on her face than in her mouth. Crying when she'd had three stories at bedtime and wasn't allowed *one* more. Cuddling into her mum, thumb in her mouth, and watching TV.

'What are her injuries?'

'Suspected broken arm and head injury. She lost consciousness for a while.'

Noah was rummaging around in the side pocket of his door. 'Here.' He handed her a small packet of tissues.

Still being a gentleman after his idea of who she was had been tipped upside down. Couldn't ask for better than that. Not that she'd be asking for anything from him except understanding, and it was too soon for that. There was a lot

SUE MACKAY 97

for him to get his head around once he understood Holly
was also his daughter. It wouldn't be easy to take in. He'd
have lots of questions, and she'd do her utmost to answer
them. Stacey's heart ached for this man she'd placed so
much hope in.

'Th-thanks.' He might never understand or forgive.
Though she wasn't really guilty of anything. The pregnancy had been an accident. One she had been thrilled
about once she'd got over the shock.

Tapping her mother's speed-dial number on her phone,
she barely waited for her to answer before demanding,
'Have you heard anything from Dad?'

'Not a word, but he might not be allowed to phone while
in the ambulance.'

Highly unlikely, but she'd not say so. All she could do
was hope her father's silence was good news, that maybe
he was too busy holding Holly to call. 'How far from the
hospital are you?'

'Pulling in right now.'

'Give Holly a kiss from me if you see her before I get
there.'

'Will do. Travel safely.'

'We are.' She looked sideways at the man rushing her to
her daughter. He was a steady, capable driver, concentrating on getting them to hospital quickly and safely. Not bad
considering what must be going through his mind. Holly
could do worse for a father.

Noah whipped into the first available space in the staff
parking lot, put his surgeon's pass on the dash, and leapt
out of the car. Stacey wasn't going inside alone. He'd be
with her until she met up with her parents. Despite her stunning news about her daughter, he couldn't leave her alone.
She was distraught, and needed someone at her side. Even

him. Admittedly, he was angry she'd not mentioned she
had a child at any moment in their time together. It was as
though she'd been hiding Holly from him. But why? Having
a daughter didn't mean he'd stop seeing her.

So far he thought she'd always been honest about everything.
Unlike Christine who'd lied about loving him, about
just about everything. Anastasia might be just as adept.
Time for questions later. She was already half out of the
car as he strode around to join her. Putting on his best *don't
argue* voice, he said, 'I'm coming with you.'

'Thank you.' She reached for his hand and dragged him
along at a fast clip.

As easily as that Anastasia had accepted his presence.
Because she needed him especially? Or would she be grateful
for anyone to accompany her? That didn't add up considering
how close she seemed to be to her family. She
always talked about them with love in her voice, and that
touched a spot inside him that held envy and longing. She
had what he craved, and he wanted to share it with her. Yes,
with Stacey. He was willing to give it a try, to put the past
behind him, forget how he'd been lied to, and give this wonderful
woman every chance possible. He stretched out his
steps to keep up with her. They were on a mission. 'We'll
go straight to the emergency room.'

'Where else would I be headed?'

Noah realised he was out of his depth here. He wasn't a
parent rushing to his injured daughter. Squeezing Stacey's
hand, he said nothing more, but he didn't stop thinking
about Stacey and the pain she was going through. If only he
could take it away—or take it on himself. But all he could
do was be there for her, and in a few minutes she'd have
her family surrounding her and he'd become redundant.

I don't want that.

The idea of being left out in the cold already made him

shiver. Anastasia had got to him far more than he'd been prepared to admit. Today, seeing her agony, had woken him up, despite his misgivings about why she hadn't talked about Holly. Bottom line, he could no longer deny she was becoming important to him.

'Hurry up,' Stacey yelled at the slowly opening sliding doors at the entrance to the emergency room. She pushed through, still dragging him along, and headed to the reception desk. 'I'm Stacey Wainwright. My daughter, Holly, has been brought in by ambulance in the last twenty minutes,' she snapped.

Her hand was trembling in his. He stepped nearer. 'Steady.'

The woman behind the counter was looking at the screen in front of her. 'Holly Wainwright, date of birth?'

Noah listened as Stacey gave Holly's birth date. The door beside them clicked as the lock opened. 'Go through.'

Holly was two? That meant she'd been conceived after their night together. So there had been someone else, despite her denial. Not much dating, she'd said, but it only took once to get pregnant. His feet were leaden as he walked beside her. She'd become a mother since he'd first known her. That was hard to accept. As if he'd been abstaining throughout those years. There hadn't been cause to, but neither had he had many dates.

But— But he was being arrogant. She was entitled to live her life however she wanted, and he certainly couldn't complain. She'd said she was single, so he didn't have to walk away without seeing if they'd be a match. He just had to get over himself.

'Dad,' Stacey shrieked, pulling away from him and racing to the man standing by a cubicle. 'Where's Holly?'

The composed nurse he knew had flown out the window. Which warmed him. This was the Anastasia he'd al-

ways wanted to believe in. Nothing like his cold uncle and
aunt. He'd at first tried to deny Stacey's loving warmth
because that meant letting her in more than she'd already
managed to get.

Her father nodded to the bed beyond the curtains, and
Stacey disappeared out of sight.

Stepping up to the man, Noah put his hand out. 'I'm
Noah Kennedy. Anastasia was with me when her mother
phoned about the accident.'

The guy glanced at his daughter and then looked hard at
him, a question in his gaze. The question slipped away, replaced with welcome. Finally he shook Noah's hand. 'Yes,
we knew who she'd gone to see. Nice to meet you, Noah.
I'm Ian Wainwright, and this…' he turned slightly '…is my
wife, Stacey's mum, Judy. And our son, Toby.'

Judy was staring at him, caution couldn't be more direct on her face. Why were these two so wary about a man
their daughter had been out with that morning? Were they
overly protective? It wasn't his place to comment, and he
could be totally off track about this family. Anastasia never
spoke of them without love. Did she know how lucky she
was? Yes, she probably did. He held his hand out to Judy.
'Pleased to meet you, Mrs Wainwright.'

The woman before him blinked, also looked at her
daughter before coming back to him and taking his hand
in hers briefly. 'Hello, Noah. Thank you for getting Stacey here so quickly.'

Noah managed a small laugh. 'Anyone would have done
the same.' Then he turned to look at Stacey, and his heart
stuttered.

She was sprawled on the very edge of the bed, her hand
holding her daughter's and wearing a strained smile. 'Darling, it's Mummy. I'm here, baby.' She was blinking rapidly, trying to keep the tears at bay.

The girl was tiny in the large bed, her face abnormally pale with streaks of dried blood from her forehead staining her cheeks, and her eyes were closed, long, dark lashes black on that wan skin. She looked so fragile Noah felt his heart crack. For Stacey, and Holly.

Someone cleared his throat. 'Excuse me, I'm Dr Robinson. Harry Robinson. I've arranged for a CT scan of Holly's head,' he said directly to Anastasia. 'The paramedic said she was in and out of consciousness on the way here, and so far she's not responding to anything. I'll explain all the scenarios to you. She's also broken her arm, though an X-ray will confirm that.'

Judy said, 'Stacey's a nurse. She'll know what's going on.'

Stacey's head whipped up. 'Right now I'm a mother, not a nurse.' She nodded to Harry Robinson. 'Talk to Noah. He's a doctor. He can tell me what I need to know.' And she went back to gazing at her daughter, imploring silently for her to wake up.

Noah wanted to hug them both, hold them until this nightmare was over and they could all go home. Instead, he straightened his shoulders and faced the other doctor. 'Harry, tell me what you know.'

They stepped aside and instantly Stacey's parents moved up to the bed, where Judy began smoothing Stacey's hair with long strokes that spoke of love.

Noah watched them as he listened to Harry.

'Certainly concussion. I'm worried there might be swelling on the brain. The non-response has gone on too long.'

'Given she's only two, that might work in her favour, keep her still while everything settles down.' But the idea of brain trauma made him ill. This was Anastasia's daughter, she didn't need anything so awful happening to her girl. No parent did. But today, with the woman he was beginning to care too much for, it went beyond his normal horrified re-action for any parent whose child was suffering. He didn't want Holly injured. He didn't want Anastasia suffering for her daughter. They didn't deserve this.

Somehow he managed to listen to all the details Harry gave him. Stacey was right. It was different when the pa-tient was close to you, and though Holly wasn't his daugh-ter and he'd never met her, he felt a part of this family at the moment.

'I hope you're right,' Harry muttered. 'As soon as the scan's done she'll be admitted to the paediatric ward. Kath-ryn Cross has been alerted and is on her way in.'

Some relief filtered into the muddle in Noah's head. 'I hear she's good.'

'Better than good. Her reputation's stellar.'

'Glad she's on Holly's side then.' A bed was being rolled along towards them. 'This for Holly?'

Harry glanced around. 'Stacey, the porter's here to take Holly to Radiology. You go with her, and then on to the paediatric ward and a family room.'

The look Stacey gave the poor man said no one would've been able to stop her. 'My family will come, too.' No ques-tion about that either. Then she looked to him, a query in her face.

'You want me there?' Noah asked. He still had to tell her what Harry had said regarding Holly's injuries.

'Yes.' She looked away, and back at him, a stricken ex-pression on her face. 'Sorry. You do whatever suits you. I'm going with Holly. But…' She swallowed and nodded. 'I'd like you to stay around with us.'

'I'll be waiting outside Radiology.' He had no idea why this was important to him. He wasn't even going to start trying to figure it out. Chances were he'd be wrong. Sta-cey telling Harry to talk to him had made him a part of this family's problem, their fears, and he wanted to be there with them. Especially for Stacey.

Just like that he felt he belonged, if only for a few hours, and it gave him a deep sense of homecoming. Which was absurd. He didn't know these people, and one look at Stacey and Holly and deep inside there was a softening of the hopelessness he'd known most of his life, a sense of finally finding what he'd been looking for. From the moment he'd walked up to her on the dance floor there'd been a connection he'd never found before, a connection that simply wasn't going away.

One night had been all it had taken to mark him for ever. She'd been generous in her lovemaking, fun and open, and so damned special it was a constant ache in his heart.

Now she was on the other side of the door into Radiology with her heart breaking as she watched over her little girl fighting to regain consciousness. Anastasia was a mother. It didn't change how he felt about her. He only wished he'd known sooner.

What difference would that have made?

He would've still reacted the same way to seeing her that first morning on the ward. He'd still have smelt citrus perfume, been drawn in by her beautiful face, known how those curves felt on his palms.

Some things couldn't be changed. Best he accept it and get on with supporting Anastasia as much as she let him.

Had she got on with her life in the way she'd expected when she'd thanked him that night? Had she known she was pregnant and having sex with him, a complete stranger, as a way of accepting her condition and moving forward? Had he been a part of her decision over a man she had been about to commit to? She'd said she was single, and so far no one but her family had turned up here to be with Holly.

A lot of questions with no answers whirled around his

mind. If there ever was a time for that. There must be. Despite today's bombshell, she was becoming more important to him all the time, and they'd spent little of that together. It was that connection working between them. Inexplicable, yet it was there, distracting him from his long-held belief that love like his parents had had was rare, and probably not for him.

'Why don't you join Stacey?' Her father stood in front of him.

Noah got to his feet. 'I'll wait a bit, let you all spend time with Holly. It must've been a hell of a shock when she was hit by that skateboarder.' But he wanted to be with Stacey more than anything.

Ian studied him for a long moment. 'It was. She's so tiny and defenceless. Stacey adores her and nothing's going to come between them.' It sounded like a warning.

'From the little I know of Anastasia, I'm sure you're right.'

I know I care about her too much, and that I want to know more, want to further our relationship.

So why was her father looking at him as though summing him up? Wary of any man Anastasia might be interested in? Or just him? They were a tight family, but surely that didn't mean she was off limits? 'Make that, I know you're right. She's very straightforward in pursuing what she wants. It's one of the things I like about her.' Not that he could think of anything he didn't like.

Ian relaxed. 'It's what makes her such a good mother.'

Noah couldn't say why, but he felt he'd been accepted. Neither did he understand if that was important to him, or to Anastasia. But he'd run with it and see where it led. 'It's also why she's a superb nurse.'

'Come on.' Her father headed back into the small room, not looking to see if he followed.

Noah quietly followed and scoped the scene from the doorway. His heart went out to the little girl under the sheet, and to her mother holding her hand and watching over her with a look that said no one, nothing, was going to hurt Holly any more than she already had been. Stacey was tough and soft; loving beyond reason. Noah's heart swelled, filling with an emotion he was afraid to name.

CHAPTER SIX

STACEY SAT IN a chair at the bedside, her arm through the bars keeping Holly from rolling out if—when she woke up. Because she was going to come round. There was no alternative. Her baby would get through this. *They* would get through this. What had the radiology technician said? She looked around the room, locked eyes with Noah. 'Holly's going to be all right, isn't she?'

'Yes.'

He could've said a lot of medical stuff, talked in jargon that normally she'd understand but not today without having to put a lot of effort into thinking. Obviously he understood because all he'd said was, 'Yes.' She wanted to cry. Wanted, and very nearly did. But she wouldn't cry in front of Holly, not even when her girl wouldn't notice. She was the mother. The strong adult in this partnership. Holly was not going to see her wailing and carrying on. So she sniffed, and dug deep for a smile. 'Thanks for that.'

'You're welcome.'

'Noah?' Unbeknown to Noah, he was the strong person in their relationship, whatever that was. She had to tell him. This was not the time to be avoiding the truth. Wiping her eyes with a handful of tissues, she drew a breath. But not while her family were here.

'Yes?' he asked.

She thought about what to say, staring at him, believing in him, and yet worried. He might cry for their daughter and be pleased to know he was Holly's dad. He might swear and accuse her of fabricating his fatherhood for her gain. There were a hundred things he might do and say. She wasn't ready. She had to be. 'Nothing.'

'You sure?'

Not at all. 'I need to talk to you.' She pulled another tissue from the box and blew noisily.

Her mother was watching them from the other side of Holly's bed. 'Noah, we'll give you and Stacey time together, but first can you tell us what the scan means? Apart from Holly is going to be all right. How all right? No lasting damage? Or will there be ongoing problems?'

Her parents hadn't ignored Noah, had taken to him as she'd hoped. Almost. There was still a seed of doubt that would probably last until he'd been told about Holly and they all knew if he accepted her. 'Do you mind explaining, Noah?' Stacey asked, giving him permission to talk about her daughter to her family.

'Sure.' He gave a brief outline of what had shown up on the brain scan and the X-ray of Holly's arm. 'Basically it all comes down to a concussion that the doctors want to keep an eye on over the next twenty-four hours at least. Her arm's broken, hence the cast. I can tell you that with very young children it doesn't take long for a fracture to heal. Holly has been lucky.'

'Luckier still if it hadn't happened,' Stacey's father said.

Knowing how her father felt about the accident that had caused him to lose a foot, Stacey knew he was aching for Holly. Now that she'd calmed down and felt some relief at what Noah told them, she quietly admonished her father. 'Dad, you never wanted Toby or me to grow up not living life to the full and getting the odd knock. I feel the same

about Holly, though I admit I wasn't going as far as thinking a run-in with a skateboard would make her tougher.'

Toby grinned. 'Like me falling out of the tree in the
back garden and breaking both my arms when you said I
shouldn't climb it.' Dad had cried that day, and Toby had
survived, no less adventurous afterwards when it came to
having fun. 'Or that time Stacey got up on the roof to get
the tennis ball out of the gutter.' He looked at Noah. 'Our
house is three storeys high.'

'I'm not surprised. She likes pushing the boundaries.'

Suddenly her mother looked at Stacey, her eyes full of
meaning. 'We'll go and get something to eat, leave you for
a while.' She was saying spend time alone with *Noah* and
Holly. No pressure. But if she didn't tell him now, when
did she? Was there such a thing as the perfect opportunity?
What if something worse had happened to Holly and he
hadn't known? Gulp. Now the threatening tears were too
close for comfort.

'Okay.'

Bending over the bed, her mother kissed Holly on both
cheeks. 'See you later, sweet pea. Get better for Grannie,
for all of us.'

The tears were filling Stacey's eyes and she had to look
away, still holding Holly's hand. They'd been so lucky, but
it was hard to accept when her girl wasn't opening her eyes
or giggling and asking for an ice cream. 'Thanks, Mum.'

'You need time without all of us hanging around.' Her
meaning was so clear it was a wonder Noah didn't get the
message. Talk to Noah. Tell him the truth. Did that mean
Mum approved of him? Or just wanted the obstacle gone
from the room?

Gulp. 'Can you get me some basic toiletries from the
supermarket? I'm staying overnight.'

'Already on my list.' Mum came around to hug her. 'Tell her we love her the moment she opens her eyes.' Sniff.

'You bet.' Sniff. She hugged back. 'Love you, too.' Her family was always there for each other. When Dad had been injured they'd made sure he didn't get down or let the loss of a foot change him for ever. She'd been the one to harangue him into walking on crutches every day, more times than he thought he should. She'd been the person to get him outside for the first time on his prosthetic foot to visit his friends at the pub for a pint and try to get back to normal. Her parents had always supported her from the moment she'd told them she was pregnant. For her, this was what family meant. Not everyone was so lucky.

Her father gave her a special dad hug that always warmed her, no matter how upset she might be. 'Take care. Watch over her for all of us.'

They wouldn't be able to stay away that long. 'I will.' Then she turned to Toby and wound her arms around him. 'Don't beat yourself up. It wasn't your fault.'

'Bossy boots.' But he gave her a small smile.

'Someone has to be.' She smiled, then returned to sit with her girl. 'Hey, Holly, it's Mummy. How're you doing, little one? Can you wake up now?' It didn't matter what the doctors said, she needed Holly to open her eyes before she'd feel totally at ease. Her cheeks were colourless, and never had she been so still. Or quiet. Usually hyperactive, this was unreal. She was a right little giggler so to be silent came out of left field. 'Talk to Mummy, sweetheart.'

'Here, get this into you.' Noah held out a paper cup of coffee. 'Not the best, but it's something.' He pulled up the other chair and sat down beside her, another full cup in his hand. 'How are you doing? Feel any better now that you know there's no brain damage?'

'Definitely.' She soaked in the sight of Holly, barely able

to breathe. 'She's so little and breakable, I can't believe how lucky we've been. But concussion's no fun, and she's only two. I've seen other children suffering from it, and thought how awful it was, but this is my daughter. I can't quite comprehend it, and yet I can. I know the details, the whys and what-ifs. A part of me is terrified that they've got it wrong and she's not going to recover quickly.'

'She will.'

'How can you be so positive?' She *was* overreacting, but that was the mother in her.

'The scan's normal. Besides, it's what I want. Not a very medical answer, I know, but it's how I feel.'

Stacey stared at him. Had he guessed the truth? Nothing showed in his expression to suggest so. Did she know what she was looking for? He'd hide it, wouldn't he? He could be waiting for her to fess up.

'For both you and Holly,' he added.

'Oh, Noah.' If only he knew. Well, he would, if she found the courage to tell him.

A murmur came from the bed.

Stacey spun around and leapt up to lean over the sidebar. 'Holly? It's Mummy, sweetheart.'

'Mmm.'

Reaching out, Stacey touched her cheek with the backs of her fingers. 'Holly. I'm here.'

'Mummy.' Her eyes fluttered open, then closed again.

Relief poured into Stacey and the tears flowed freely. So much for not letting Holly see. 'Holly, you're in bed and Mummy's with you.' Now she was talking gibberish.

Holly was looking at her, confusion filling her beautiful grey eyes. Her father's eyes.

Handing her cup to Noah, Stacey dropped the bar and sat on the bed, reaching for her girl, carefully slipping under her and holding her against her breast. 'There, sweetheart. Mummy's got you.'

'She looks like you,' Noah said quietly.

'So people tell me.'

Don't look at her eyes.

'You don't agree?'

'Yes, I can see quite a few Wainwright genes in there.' She'd spent most of Holly's life looking for signs of Noah, and so far only her eyes came close. 'She's a happy wee soul, always giggling and having fun.'

'Like her mum.'

Deep breath. 'Noah. I need to tell you something.' She couldn't put it off for another moment. This was eating her up. Now or never. Never wasn't an option. She didn't want to do that to Holly or Noah. They were bonded through Holly, and watch out anyone or anything that threatened to come between them.

Heavy grey eyes locked onto her, not moving, not looking at the girl who was his daughter. 'This sounds serious.'

'It is.'

Please, still like me when I've finished.

'Holly's a little over two years old.'

'I heard you tell the woman her date of birth when we arrived here.' The words were spoken in a monotone, as though he was holding back an emotion she wouldn't like. Or he was afraid of? His mouth flattened. His shoulders were tightening, and his eyes boring into her. Getting the idea?

'That's right. Nine months give a day or three after the dance.' Her chest rose, then she spilled the facts before she could overthink this. 'Holly was conceived the night we were together.'

He didn't blink. Didn't move at all. His mouth was still flat, as though he'd been expecting news he didn't want to hear. The grey stare darkened, not giving away anything her words might've wrought on him, but coffee spilled onto the floor between his feet from the squashed cardboard mug in his hand.

She was his focus, a long, breath-defying stare. Her stomach curled into a tight little ball, her heart slowed while her lungs struggled to do their job. 'It's true, Noah. Holly is your daughter.'

At last his gaze moved slowly down to the precious bundle tucked against her, focusing on his daughter. Stacey held Holly tighter, closer. She preferred it when he looked at her with all those blistering questions and not at Holly. Holly was innocent. So was she. She hadn't planned on getting pregnant. It had just happened.

This beautiful child was her daughter. Noah's daughter, too, but hers no matter what. He had a choice—accept or deny. She'd never had a choice, and had never wanted one. From the moment she'd learned she was pregnant there hadn't been a single doubt she'd love her baby and was to raise him or her no matter what the world threw at them. Noah would accept eventually. He would. But then what? Would he want to know his daughter, love her, support her? Or deposit money into a bank account every month and leave it at that?

No, she could not believe Noah would do that. He was honourable. But this was about more than that. It was about responsibility, about caring and sharing, about wanting to be a father, about love. Her heart banged. Love. Was Noah ready for that? She'd often wondered if he would ever love her. Now she needed to know, more than anything, would he love Holly?

'I used protection,' he intoned in that same voice.

'I know.' Condoms every time. But Holly was real.

'You're saying they didn't all work?' A scathing tone.

'It's the only answer I've been able to come up with throughout the years since.' Okay, so she could do scathing, too.

Silence took over, only interrupted by voices as people passed the open door. Stacey glanced down at Holly, and felt her heart drop. Was she asleep now? Or had she fallen unconscious again? Her fingers found a pulse in Holly's neck. Using her phone, she timed it and sighed with relief. All good. Brushing a kiss on her daughter's forehead, she glanced up at Noah.

He was watching them both intently.

'Noah?'

He said nothing, letting the silence expand. This time a little chilly.

She opted for quiet, letting Noah absorb what she'd told him. No doubt he'd be doing the sums to make sure she hadn't lied. Her back stiffened. Lying wasn't one of her habits. But, then, how often had he been told he was the father of a two-year-old girl?

'Is it true you weren't in a relationship when we got together at the dance? That you hadn't had an argument with your partner?'

'I was single and had been for a year. There was no one else. Holly is yours, Noah. You are her father.' Her mouth dried. She'd known there'd be questions, lots of them. But how to cope with them without sounding needy and pathetic?

He locked his steady gaze on her, watched her for a long, long moment.

Her breath stuck in her chest as she waited.

His knuckles were white against his hips, his body rigid, chin thrust forward. Then he slumped. 'I believe you.'

The air exhaled from Stacey's lungs in a rush. 'Thank you,' she whispered.

'Who'd have thought? I used protection.' He shook his head. 'Each time.'

'I remember.' Tears poured down her cheeks and she did nothing to stop them. 'I tried to find you, but I had little to go on. Noah—that was it. I didn't even know you were a doctor.' She hadn't told anyone why she wanted to find the man she'd danced with. Certainly hadn't mentioned spending the rest of the night in his hotel room having sex. And how she'd been reluctant to leave next morning but knowing she had to. They hadn't had a future.

Noah had been heading away somewhere unknown, and she had been getting on with a new job at London Riverside while trying to get over a broken heart. 'I wanted you to know about Holly. I really did.' Her heart was cracking for them all. Now Noah finally knew, she understood she never wanted to lose him. She felt deeply for him and wanted a future with him.

He was watching her, his chest rising and falling as he breathed deep and often. Then his eyes drifted down to Holly in her arms. His chest rose, stalled. His eyes softened while his hands gripped his hips tighter. His tongue slid over his lip from left to right. 'You've had to cope on your own. That must've been hard.'

'My family supports me. But, yes, there have been times when I've longed for you to be around, to be in Holly's life.'

If not mine.

'It would've changed so many things. She needs you as much as she needs me.'

'So why didn't you tell me the day we bumped into each other?' Wariness was creeping into his face.

'On the ward, surrounded with patients and staff? In the tearoom when at any moment we'd get interrupted?'

'Come on, Stacey. You can do better than that.' It was a comment, not an accusation.

But he was right. 'True. I'm sorry. After looking for you so long, when the moment arrived I was stunned. Suddenly Holly wasn't just mine for real. Then when we had coffee that night it was too noisy, and then, well, we kissed and went to your house and you know what happened.'

His gaze fell onto Holly, almost though he was sucking in the sight of *his* girl. When he spoke it was quietly, as though afraid to disturb his daughter. 'I sort of understand, but there was afterwards, and the morning over breakfast, and any number of times.'

'I felt guilty for getting distracted. I planned on telling you today. I really did.' Thud, thud went her heart.

Lifting his head slowly, dragging his eyes around to her, he stared at her again. 'I guess it must've been difficult, not really knowing me that well. But now I do know, there's a lot to absorb.' Then he turned away and strode out of the room without another word.

Leaving her feeling bereft. And fully aware that she was very close to being in love with him.

When that had happened, she wasn't sure. It wasn't as though there'd been much time for falling in love. Maybe it didn't take long when it was the real deal. It could've happened three years ago when he'd danced with her. Or held her in his arms as they'd made love that same night. Or on Monday when he'd turned and she'd seen him for the first time since that wonderful time. Or today when he'd leapt to help when she'd received the dreadful news about Holly's accident. Or could be that now she'd finally been able to get the truth out to him she'd let other emotions to the fore.

Holly. This had to be about her more than her own feelings for Noah. Loving him, rightly or wrongly, could not dominate the coming days when they sorted out where they went from here.

Give Noah time to think it all through. Don't hassle him.

Nothing to be gained by doing that. Concentrate on see-ing Holly through her injuries and getting back on her little feet.

That was her role. Be her mother first and second. Noth-ing else mattered.

Tell that to her newly awakened heart. And Noah. She gazed down at the greatest gift she'd ever received.

Thank you for believing me, Noah. Now, please, come back and talk to me.

It had hurt beyond imagination when Angus had walked away from her after a lifetime together as friends then lov-ers. His betrayal had undermined her capacity to love with-out question. Not that she'd tried.

Then along had come Noah, followed by Holly. She wanted to give the same back. Share the gift of their daughter. She'd never stop doing the absolute best for their daughter either, surrounding her with love and care and encouragement. She also wanted to love Noah openly, be loved in return.

Her heart lurched. That was unlikely. Noah had been friendly, even aware of her as more than a nurse or friend, but for him to love her seemed a long way off, if ever pos-sible. He'd not said as much, but he'd been hurt by his ex, and that would carry over to any relationship he had. Which only said there wasn't much opportunity for her to win his heart.

Noah strode along the side of the road, head down, hands jammed in his pockets. The air was chilly, more rain due any minute. People were walking past him in all directions, intent on getting inside before the weather dumped on them.

'I'm a father.'

If Anastasia was being honest with him. Why wouldn't she be? There was nothing for her to gain, because he knew those tricks, though not even Christine had been cold enough to throw a baby into the mix, only her plans for two. Was Anastasia that calculating? Had seeing his home been the catalyst? It didn't seem right. She'd asked to see him today, and now he thought maybe it had been to tell him about Holly.

Hearing she had a daughter had slammed into him. Why, when he hadn't been a part of her life except for one night, had it knocked him sideways? She was entitled to a life of her own. He had no claims on her. Even if Holly wasn't his, Stacey didn't owe it to him to mention the child unless they got into a relationship.

To be told the child was his had taken the ground out from under him. It was a game-changer. He didn't know what to think. What should he do? What did he want to do? Accept Holly as his, accept Stacey had told the truth without checking it out? Huh, a part of him already did, or wanted to at least.

Holly was gorgeous, even unconscious and as pale as whitewash. Biased already? She was so tiny, as two-year-olds were. When her eyes had fluttered open he'd felt a tap on his heart, and that had been before he'd known who she'd inherited those from.

Sounds like you're truly believing she's yours.

Could he be? Did he want to be a father? He'd always thought he would have children one day. But he'd expected to be there from the beginning, not come in a couple of years on. Stacey said she'd done all she could to find him, and thinking back he really had to believe that. There was no way she could've found him in Auckland. He'd never worked at London General so no one at the dance had known him except for the friend who'd dragged him along to keep him company until he got up the courage to ask the light of his life for a dance.

He shivered as rain got under the collar of his jacket and trickled down his back. What did Anastasia expect of him now? Did she want a permanent relationship? Or financial gain? Or—and this was what he'd want if he was going to accept Holly as his own—did she just hope he'd be a father to their daughter? That would suit him. He could love Holly unconditionally. He wouldn't be looking for love, he'd be giving it wholeheartedly with no expectations of what he'd get back.

Wasn't that how all love was meant to be? Wasn't that how his parents had loved him, and he them in return? And each other. So why wasn't he listening to his heart and giving everything to Anastasia? Because he was afraid she'd be another Christine.

Come on, she's not.

Stacey was strong, independent despite living with her family, and open to others. Her family supported her, and no doubt did a lot for Holly, but she gave it back just as much, if not more. The little she'd told him about her father's accident and how she'd stepped up showed that. Holly wouldn't miss out on what was important in life. But *he* might. It was him who could blow this tentative relationship apart by not trusting Anastasia fully, by letting the past get in the way of the present and future. Stacey and Holly were his future, if he'd let them.

Noah stumbled. A new shock registered in his beleaguered mind. He was accepting Holly was his? Already? Without thinking about everything involved? Without proof? Couldn't be. Sure, he was coming close to falling deeply for Anastasia, but that didn't mean stepping up and taking responsibility for her daughter, no questions asked.

Her father had agreed she was straightforward about everything. Her father. So this was why Ian had been eyeing him so intently. Her family knew he was their granddaughter's father. Were they expecting him to find out today? It made sense when he thought about it, explained a lot of things. If he chose to believe Anastasia. Why shouldn't he? Not everyone was out to get what they could from him.

'Look out.' Someone grabbed his arm as he was about to step off the footpath and cross the road, right in the path of an oncoming car. 'Thanks,' he muttered, and waited impatiently for the lights to change. Getting taken out by a car wouldn't help anyone, especially Anastasia when she was already distressed about Holly, and waiting for his next move.

Holly. What a cute little girl. She had her mother's looks and her thick hair might be curly but it was the same dark blonde. Was he really her father? And if so, what was he going to do about it?

As the first spots of rain touched down on his face, Noah ducked into a pub and ordered a whisky. 'A large one.' He headed to a table by a window and sat, rolling the glass back and forth between his hands.

Only that morning he'd been impatient to see Anastasia, arriving at the tube station early. The moment she'd stepped into his view he'd felt deep happiness. His stomach had softened, his heart had thumped.

The happiness was still there, if only he'd let it grow and stop trying to push it away. He'd always wanted to fall in love and experience the wonder of having someone who loved him back and supported him. But he'd also always been afraid of screwing up again. He hadn't fallen deeply enough in love with Christine, but enough to believe they could make a go of it, and hopefully get to where his parents had been. He'd been wrong. Unfair to Christine even. While she'd been out for everything she could get from him, a clinical relationship like his aunt and uncle had, he'd been blind in his bid to get what he'd wanted.

How he'd not recognised that from the outset had always bothered him and made him even more cautious. He had made a big mistake in thinking that love could grow if both people involved put the effort in.

Love happened. From what he'd seen with friends it seemed to be there from the get-go, like a light switch being flicked on, and not necessarily with the kind of person anyone expected. Then he'd met Anastasia and within hours—or had it been minutes on the dance floor?—every idea of the perfect partner had gone in a puff of need.

Could be Anastasia was the perfect woman for him. Might not be either. How did a man decide? He could go with his heart. Or let his brain choose.

Or he could just go back to the hospital and sit with Anastasia and his daughter, and absorb the sense of them, their loving natures and generous hearts.

A bitter laugh huffed from his mouth. How could he think that about Holly when he'd only seen her unconscious? What about that small smile and the word 'Mummy' whispering across her lips? Not so out of it then. And that's why he felt she was just like her mother. How could she not be?

Sipping his whisky, he stared out the window into the night lit by streetlamps. Rain slapped the pavement, glistening in the light. It was cosy in here, yet he shivered. He was teetering on a cliff edge. He wanted to grab Anastasia and Holly, hold them to him for ever and make the most of everything. He wanted to go back to early that morning when he had been climbing out of bed and heading to the bathroom for a shave, and when he hadn't known about this child who'd turned the world as he knew it upside down.

Hell, he didn't know what he wanted—except not to make a bigger mess of everything than it already was.

It's only a mess because you're overthinking everything.

He wanted to get this right. For Holly. For Anastasia and, yes, for himself. Then 'how' was the next big question. That had to be decided by talking to Anastasia, not just to himself.

There was a warmth in his gut and touching his heart. If it was true and Holly was his, he'd become a father in the time it had taken Anastasia to say, 'Holly was conceived the night we were together. It's true, Noah. Holly is your daughter.' No planning, no nine months to get used to the idea, no agreeing it was a good thing to start a family when he wasn't in a relationship. A matter of seconds and he'd become a father. Whether he'd wanted to or not.

He could walk away. Except he'd never do that. He knew the pain of losing parents, the pain of not being taken in by other family to share their love and camaraderie. It wasn't something he'd ever impose on his daughter. Holly would be well cared for and loved by the Wainwright family and have everything important to grow up into a wonderful woman.

Could he do any better? Did he want to? Yes, damn it, he did. She would be loved by him as well, with all that entailed. But to trust Anastasia completely was a big ask. Despite her reassurances about being happy with her lot, she might change when she fully understood his background and all that was on offer.

Another sip of his drink and he thought about Christine. His wife had hurt him, but she hadn't wrecked him. She'd let him down by not meeting his love with hers. He'd wanted a family, like the one he'd known for the first ten years of his life. She'd never had that herself so didn't believe in it.

Anastasia came from a loving environment and gave love out without thought. Love was a part of her. Did she have any for him?

His head was going round and round, and getting nowhere. Shoving the almost full glass aside, he straightened
up and headed for the door and the wet weather. He was
not making any decisions about any damned thing tonight.
He was going back to the hospital to sit with Anastasia and
Holly, watching over them as they waited out the time it
took for Holly to get well enough to go home.

CHAPTER SEVEN

STACEY OPENED HER eyes slowly and looked around the darkened room from the bed she was sprawled over. Shock rippled through her at the man standing at the end of Holly's bed, hands in pockets, a poignant look on his face as he gazed down at his daughter. 'Noah?' she whispered.

Slowly he turned to face her, sadness radiating out at her. 'How hard *did* you try to find me?'

He was regretting missing out on the early years of Holly's life. 'On the train heading home that morning I wished I'd taken a moment to ask when you were coming back from wherever it was you were headed. I didn't know if you were going on holiday or off to a permanent job in Britain or another country.

'You mentioned staying at the hotel since you'd packed up your house so your move seemed long term. I wanted to see you again.' She paused, hoping for a response, got none. 'At work on Monday I asked my friends to check around at London General to see if anyone knew you and they came up blank. Most people didn't even know me, let alone who I was dancing with.'

Another pause while she thought back to those frantic days when she'd almost begged people to give her a name for the man no one had known. 'Now I know you'd never worked at London General it makes sense.'

'And that was it?'

'No. A few weeks later I found I was pregnant. At first it was scary. I was single, still getting over my broken relationship.' Tell him how he'd made Angus start sliding into the background? Maybe not. Noah didn't look as though he'd want to hear that. 'But as the days turned to weeks I began to get excited. I was going to be a mother, and even if I had to raise my child on my own, it was wonderful.'

'So you gave up looking for me?'

Her chest ached for him. And her. She'd told him this already. He was looking for reasons to be angry with her while he accepted the truth in front of him. 'No, Noah, I didn't. I began a methodical search of the hospital, checking out all the medical staff, and then anyone else working there who might've known you. You didn't exist. That was the only blight on my pregnancy. Like I said before, I never stopped looking for you.'

Lifting her hands and turning them palms upwards, she asked, 'What else was I supposed to do? There's more than one Noah out there, believe me.' And none that she'd seen were a patch on this one.

To give him his due, he was trying to deal with the situation in a cautious but non-aggressive way. No surprise really. She'd shocked the living daylights out of him, and that would take time to absorb and decide how he'd deal with Holly. And her. He'd probably never felt more for her than like and care, which wasn't enough. He wouldn't've been stupid enough to fall for her in a few hours when they'd been making love. For him that had probably been sex, not making love, and he'd got as much as he could. Sex that they'd repeated already this week. Sex that to her was making love and made her feel happy. 'You said you only tried once to find me.'

'I don't think that's important right now, Anastasia.'

Sudden anger burst from her. 'Anastasia. What's with not using Stacey like everyone else, huh?' She'd liked how he'd used her full name, but tonight it made her feel he was putting her in a bubble, to be looked at and thought about without the hindrance of others who knew and loved her.

'Stacey it is, then. Not that it changes a thing. We have a problem, and I'm trying to understand it all. Starting with the fact that three years have gone by when I didn't know you'd become pregnant. *Allegedly* with *my* child.' Noah glared at her, then sighed. 'Sorry, that doesn't help. I owe you better than that.'

Swallowing her own anger, she nodded. 'It's okay. Really. I expected denial in the beginning.' And withdrawal. Even disinterest. Though, no, not that. She'd watched Noah gazing at Holly earlier with something like hope and a tentative love growing in his eyes. Maybe he wasn't aware of those emotions, but they'd been there, she'd swear. 'I'm not going to make a scene, Noah. Holly's yours. There was no one else in my life at the time. Not even another one-night stand,' she added with unexpected bitterness. So much for not making a scene.

Getting off the chair, she crossed to her girl, and reached over the guard rail to touch her. To make sure she was real. To feel that soft skin and the warmth that was Holly inside and out. 'Love you, baby,' she whispered.

Your father is the only man I ever slept with for one night.

He was still the only man other than Angus, and he'd made a greater impact in one night than Angus had in a lifetime. She'd loved Angus, but after Noah she'd realised how much of her relationship with Angus had been about friendship. She'd loved him, totally, with all she had to offer. It just hadn't held the passion she'd found with Noah. Passion that still woke her, that had begun twisting her heart every time she saw him, whether at work, in the street, or here when he was struggling to trust her honesty.

Standing at the end of the bed, Noah said nothing, but she could feel his eyes boring into her. Looking for what? Warning signs that said she was a liar? That she was looking for any man to be her daughter's father? That she'd use him to get what she wanted?

The anger was back, increasing as though it had been waiting for months, if not years, for this moment to express itself. Anger over not being able to find Noah. Over not having told him who she was apart from Anastasia, which no one would have recognised as her name. Over having a child and not being able to tell her who her father was and why he wasn't around. Whipping around, she snapped in a low voice, 'Go away. Leave us alone. I don't want toxic vibes to disturb Holly. She doesn't need anything but love at the moment.'

Steely grey eyes locked on her.

She waited, cool on the outside, seething internally. He didn't believe anything she said. He was going to walk away. From his daughter. Maybe for the time it took to get his head around the fact he was a parent, like it or not. He hadn't had enough time to think it all through, yet he was going to leave. She sensed it in his stance, in those eyes and the grim tightness of his usually kind mouth. Not knowing what to say to change his mind, she waited, and waited.

'Mummy.'

Stacey's shoulders drooped forward, her knees softened, and her heart rate increased. Gripping the rail, she turned to her daughter. 'Hey, baby, Mummy's here.' She dropped the rail and sank onto the bed to lift Holly into her arms, and lay her chin on her head, breathed deeply to absorb her girl's smell. Noah could go do whatever he liked. So long as he didn't upset Holly.

* * *

'That went well,' Noah muttered as he stood in the lift taking him to the bottom level and his car outside after talking to a nurse about Holly's condition since Anastasia hadn't taken back her permission for him to ask the staff.

He'd been going to sit with An—with Stacey and Holly while he thought about his new life. It *was* new. If nothing else, he was now a father. He wouldn't be a remote dad, only turning up for birthdays and Christmas, adding to Stacey's bank account to make sure Holly never went without.

So he did believe the child was his? Actually… He sighed. He did. Holly's eyes were replicas of those he saw in the mirror every morning while shaving. The truth was in her mother's voice, face, stance. Stacey hadn't lied. Holly was his daughter. Hadn't he admitted that to himself already? He should've told Stacey. Instead, he'd pushed her hard about how she hadn't found him when he'd known the odds had been stacked against them from the beginning. He tipped his head back to stare at the lift ceiling. He wasn't playing fair. Being blindsided was not an excuse. He was human?

So is Anastasia. Stacey.

He'd been looking for hidden meanings behind her reactions, and had got an earful of disappointment in him instead. Which only showed she was the woman he hoped, and not one who lied to get what she wanted.

The lift jerked to a halt and the doors slid open. Two women in nurses' uniforms joined him, one pressing the button for the third floor.

He made a decision. Reaching around the nurse, he pressed four—Paediatrics. And Stacey.

In the ward he found a nurse to ask if he could use their kitchen to make a coffee for Stacey and was told yes, and to take her a piece of the fruit cake on the bench.

'Here, thought you might want something to drink.' He placed the mug and plate with cake on the table beside her. 'You haven't eaten at all.'

'Mum brought me some sandwiches earlier, but I'm not hungry.' She was sitting with her knees under her chin and her arms wound tightly around her legs.

'Try something.' When he'd walked in she'd been watching Holly with such tenderness it had torn his heart in two. He knew that look from his childhood. It meant everything to him, then and now. Holly didn't know how lucky she was. He pulled up the chair and sat down. 'I'm sorry for being a prat.' He wasn't going to come out with things like he was still in shock, no matter how true they were. Excuses didn't solve any of what lay between them.

Her gaze still on Holly, she shrugged. 'It's all right.'

It wasn't. There was hurt in her voice, put there by him. 'She's doing fine, Stacey.' Noah sat back quietly and watched the two females dominating his life as though he was guarding them, which he was in a way, though what from was another question with no answer.

'Sure.' Finally Stacey stretched her legs out, and reached for the mug. 'Thanks for this. I wanted a coffee but couldn't bear to leave Holly even for a few minutes. She might wake and panic if I'm not here.'

'Your parents have gone home?'

'Yes. They didn't want to, but I insisted.'

'You're all so close.'

Finally she looked at him. 'Yes, we are. Always have been.'

And I'd be a fool to forget that.

'Feel free to ask me anything you need to know to make this real,' she added, then she went back to watching over her daughter.

And he went back to watching over them both, with a lot of questions making themselves known in his head.

Stacey yawned and leaned back, closing her eyes.

Noah fought the urge to go across and kiss her cheek. Instead, he stood to gaze down at the beautiful girl lying in the bed attached to the monitor on the stand behind her. A weight settled over his heart. Not a painful one but sadness for the two years of her life he'd missed. He hadn't been there to hold her when she'd arrived in the world, hadn't kissed her or promised to love and care for her for the rest of his life. Hadn't heard her first word or seen her first steps. Her giggles didn't ring in his skull. He didn't know what her favourite food was, if she slept all night or woke on and off.

'Her favourite toy is Goggy, a well-worn teddy bear that has to go to bed with her every night or there's hell to pay. Mum's bringing Goggy in with her tomorrow.'

Noah smiled. 'Goggy, eh?'

'There's a doll named Jack after her best friend at day care.'

He laughed. 'Does Jack know that?'

'Yes, but I don't think he realises what it means or their friendship might be off.' Stacey sat up straighter.

Noah turned to look at Stacey. For the first time since they'd caught up no reminiscing smile came his way. But at least she continued giving him snippets about their girl. 'Holly loves butterflies and frogs, hates cornflakes and eggs.'

Returning to his chair, he waited for more as the heaviness inside him lightened.

'I can push her on the swing for half an hour and it's nowhere near long enough. Brushing her hair is an ordeal for everyone. Though a couple of months ago she found the kitchen scissors and cut off large hunks.' Stacey's mouth

twisted into a cute smile filled with reverence for Holly.
'She's a little minx. Uncle Toby is fair game for having his
clothes hidden in the same place behind the couch every
day, while Granddad is a sucker for cuddles and sweets
whenever I'm not looking. Grandma is the kiss-it-better
go-to when I'm not around.'

'It must be hard going off to work every day, not knowing what you might miss.'

'It is.'

'Is Holly the reason you asked to spend time with me
today?'

Her eyes met his. 'Yes. I was going to tell you about her.'

Convenient. Or truthful. Judging by that steady look she
was giving him, definitely truthful. 'I see.'

'I don't think you do, Noah. When I saw you on Monday
for the first time since all this started, I've known what I
had to do, and that there was no reason to wait. As it wasn't
something to say at work or in a noisy café I thought meeting up at the weekend would be best.'

'True. But—'

Her hand was up. 'Stop right there. I always intended
telling you. I don't have the right to decide if Holly knows
her father or not.' She breathed in. 'I was nervous, to say the
least.' Shaking her head, her lips curved into a small wry
smile. 'Here, with Holly injured and floating in and out of
consciousness, I wanted you to learn your relationship to
her so you could be here for her.' Stray tears slipped down
her cheeks and she brushed them away angrily.

It would be too easy to go to her, lift her into his arms
and kiss away the distress darkening those beautiful eyes.
He wanted to make her smile, and be happy again, and
take away all her fears—especially those concerning him
and what he wanted for the future with Holly. He wasn't
ready for that.

There was a lot to consider. Especially Anastasia and his feelings for her. He had to get everything right, not make half-baked decisions they might all regret later. Putting the past away for ever was proving difficult now he was faced with taking a giant step forward without any guarantees it would work out.

'Tell me about your family.' Her words cut through his turmoil.

'Which one? My devoted, loving parents I still miss? Or my aunt and uncle who believe life is about being aloof and proper, and not falling head over heels in love, like my father did? According to Robert, if Dad hadn't married Mum he'd still be here. It was her love of life and friends and family that had them on that road the night they were killed.'

He sounded bitter, because he still was whenever he saw friends falling in love and being so happy. Now Anastasia wound him up with hope, something he wasn't certain if she reciprocated even in the smallest way. Yet whenever they touched, they fell together, no hesitation on her part.

'You have a cousin in Auckland?'

'His mother is my mother's sister. Another happy soul.'

Stacey was watching him, a small smile lightening her face for the first time in hours.

'What?'

'You've got it in you to be like that too.'

Surprise hit. 'You think?' She was right, only he'd thought he had to find the right person to help him bring it out. Could it be he should've got on with being happy with his lot and let his relatives get on with theirs? Then he said something stupid. 'I'll take you to meet Robert and Alice next weekend. I have to sign some documents for them.' That would certainly test Stacey. Hard to be cheerful around those two, and she'd get to see the mansion he'd spent time in growing up. That'd tell if she suddenly thought being rich might be a good idea.

Noah groaned. How horrid could he be? Stacey would no doubt think of all the windows that'd need cleaning and the floors to vacuum, rather than want to live in such a huge house. 'Stacey, I'm being a prat again. Say no if you want to.'

She shook her head, still smiling. 'I want to know more about you, Noah. I'll come.'

Stacey slapped at her face, wiping the moisture away and probably smearing mascara over her cheeks. If there was any left after her crying jag when Holly had woken again and said, 'Mummy.' Her body ached, her heart ached more. There was a set of drums in her skull doing their best to give her a headache, and succeeding. She wanted to curl up on the bed, holding Holly close, and cuddle her all night long. Equally, she'd be afraid of holding her too tight and hurting her.

Eyes closed, Noah was sprawled in the chair. Was he asleep? Or was he going over and over the fact he was a father? He hadn't said outright she couldn't be his. Instead, he'd said he believed her, even though the doubts had crept back in since then. He had also been more willing to listen than she'd have believed. But he hadn't said a word about accepting he was a father, about what he'd want for his daughter's future, and how much time he'd want to spend with Holly. As in have her for nights, or weeks.

She'd feel bereft, not having Holly at home. A chill crept into her stomach, spread throughout her body. Could she trust Noah not to hurt her? To understand her feelings and the sense of loss just sharing Holly time between them might bring on? Of course, she was being selfish, and had known this might happen, but she couldn't help herself.

She didn't know a life without Holly in it all the time. She spoke aloud, hoping he heard.

'I put Holly before all else. I have to go to work, but she's well cared for by my family and the nursery she attends two mornings a week.' The neighbour left the gate open and that's why they were here. Would he hold that against her?

Those eyes she'd first fallen for opened and locked onto her. 'Relax, Stacey. I give you my word I will not take her away from you. You're a devoted mum and love her to bits. I've seen that already.'

She couldn't relax but some of the chill warmed. 'Thank you.' When his gaze returned to Holly she realised he hadn't made a move to hold her, or even touch her. Standing up, she crossed to the bed and lowered the rail. 'Come and sit by your daughter.'

At first she didn't think he was going to, but after a couple of laden minutes he crossed to the bed and did as instructed. Slowly he reached out and ran his finger down Holly's arm, avoiding the needle and tube feeding her pain relief. The look of wonder in his eyes stole Stacey's breath away. Noah was accepting his daughter. Step one passed. Mind you, who couldn't fall for her little girl? She was so sweet and cute and downright wonderful.

A shiver ran down Stacey's spine. 'What if she'd been injured even worse than she was?'

'Don't go there. She wasn't. Be grateful for that. She's still got a little way to go before she'll be back dancing and singing, so you need to stay strong.'

He was right. The nurse in her was returning and bringing along a load of common sense. 'I wonder when she'll be able to go home.'

Noah glanced up. 'Don't rush it. Keep her here as long as possible. It's best for her.'

'I know.' Bending down, she carefully lifted Holly off

the bed and placed her in her father's arms. She didn't need to tell him to be careful. 'There you go.'

As he gazed down at Holly, she moved away to sit on the chair and watch Noah falling in love. He had the right instincts, and Holly was going to be the winner. And Noah. She was glad he knew about his daughter. He'd already missed out on too much. Whatever unfolded between Noah and herself, this was the right thing to have done.

If only he could fall for her as he had for Holly. Watching his fascination with his girl, the love for Noah that'd been growing day by day came to the fore, filling her heart, making her wish she could kiss him, and hold him. Do that now and he'd think she was trying to win him over about Holly. There'd been moments between them all week whenever they had been close that had made her wonder if he felt something for her, or if he was only thinking of the sex they'd shared.

On Monday she'd wondered if she might come to love him. Today, even before this moment, she'd known deep down she was close, if not there. Only time would tell. And Noah's thoughts on the future involving the three of them.

Watching him, the tension holding her tight since the phone call to say Holly had been hurt began softening. Her neck moved without pain, her hands weren't opening and shutting into balls any more, and her toes had stopped tapping a rhythm. Her eyelids dropped, cutting off the picture mesmerising her, but it was still there inside her head as she relaxed against the back of the chair. She wasn't alone here. She had her daughter's father to share this. Very different from her parents' support. Not that she could relax entirely. They had a long way to go.

Noah's mouth dried as he gazed down at the little girl in his arms. His girl, his daughter. Holly. Holly Wainwright.

Holly Kennedy. Wham. Holly Kennedy. That was her name. No, that wasn't fair to Anastasia. But he wanted his child to carry his name. Taking a peek at Stacey, he let out a long breath. She was asleep. He could avoid that problem for now.

But it wouldn't go away unless he gave in. Like a lot of the issues they'd have to face and sit down for a full and frank discussion about. Not tonight. It was after eleven, and Stacey was shattered. She needed sleep. He'd remain here until she woke up, whatever time that was. And continue holding Holly. Unless she woke up. If she did she'd get a fright to find it wasn't Mummy holding her.

Damn, she was gorgeous, he repeated to himself. Biased, by any chance? Naturally, he smiled, and again looked at Stacey. Another gorgeous female in his life—if he was careful and didn't let her get away. She'd given him something he'd only ever dreamed of. He owed her big time. She could've kept quiet and he'd have been none the wiser, unless they'd started getting serious about each other, and he had been wishing for that—when he wasn't looking for excuses to run before he got too involved. Which proved yet again how genuine she was.

Stacey wasn't someone to ignore truth. Deep down, he accepted that. It was what he'd been looking for, for so long.

'Hello, someone looks comfortable.' The night nurse assigned to Holly appeared at the bedside.

'Holly or Stacey?'

'Both. I'm glad Stacey's sleeping. She was exhausted.' The nurse talked in a low voice, obviously not wanting to wake anyone. 'And this little one needs all the sleep she can get.'

'It's the best cure for concussion,' Noah agreed.

'I'm going to take Holly's temperature.'

Noah remained still, holding Holly a little tighter in case she felt the ear thermometer and woke with a start.

'Temperature's normal,' the nurse commented as she read the thermometer. Then she straightened the sheets. 'I think we should put her back into bed now—so she can move her legs and good arm in her sleep,' she added as Noah tried to come up with a reason to keep holding her.

Standing, he laid his precious bundle on the bed and tucked the top sheet up to her chin. Then he leaned over and kissed her forehead. Tears filled his eyes immediately.

A box of tissues appeared in his blurred vision, and he snatched a handful. 'Thanks,' he said gruffly.

'It always gets to you, doesn't it? They're so vulnerable and you're supposed to be able to protect them from this sort of thing, but the real world's different from our hopes and dreams.'

Noah gasped as he realised this woman was presuming he was Holly's father, and had been there for her whole, short life. About to put her right, he hesitated. Why would he do that? She was a nurse on this shift and had nothing else to do with them. He was still getting his head around the fact his life had changed so completely in such a short time. Talking about it to a stranger didn't seem like a great idea. If he talked to anyone it would be to the other woman in the room. When she woke up.

CHAPTER EIGHT

'BECAUSE YOU'RE A nurse I'm letting you take Holly home later this afternoon as long as the nurses don't find a reason not to,' the paediatrician told Stacey when she did her round on Monday morning. 'She's through the worst, but you need to keep an eye on her concussion. Any sign of change and I want her back here immediately.'

'Believe me, I'll have her here fast. Can you run through everything with me one more time?' Stacey asked. 'I can't quite relax yet.'

'Medical staff make the worst caregivers of their nearest and dearest.'

'Don't they ever,' Stacey agreed. She hadn't expected to get quite so stressed when it came to Holly, though. 'I'll give you both a lift home,' came the deep voice of the man she'd been waiting to see all morning.

How long had he been standing there? Not long or she'd have noticed. Her skin would've tingled, and her stomach tightened.

Got it bad, girl.

'Hi, Noah. You've heard the good news, then?'

Holly was staring him with a little smile. Oh, hell, now what?

Holly, meet your dad. Holly—

Stacey froze, staring at her girl, whose world was about

to change radically. Not that Holly would understand much past 'This is Daddy'. If she understood that. Neither could she bring up the subject in front of the paediatrician and her entourage of nurses and registrar.

'You're okay with that? Last night you were happy for her to stay in as long as possible.'

'I hadn't expected her to improve so much. She's restless and being at home might be better for her, or for everyone else around here anyway.' Rubbing Holly's arm softly, she grinned. 'My girl's got some of her noise back.'

The paediatrician spoke to Noah. 'I'm very happy with the concussion, and Stacey's fully aware of what to look out for. As she says, little children do better at home surrounded by those who love them than in here, with strangers coming and going all the time.'

'I guess.' Noah sounded doubtful. The father in him coming out? Not the doctor?

Stacey laughed for the first time in days. 'She'll be fine, promise.'

'Mummy, I want a story.'

'What's the magic word?'

'Please.'

'Noah, can you stay with Holly while I get a book?' Deep breath. 'Holly, this is Noah, Mummy's friend.' Talk about a cliché.

Noah stepped forward. 'Hello, Holly. I see you banged your head.'

She raised her arm in front of him and knocked on the cast. 'It's broken.'

'That's not your head, silly billy.' Stacey tickled her under the chin. A giggle erupted from her girl, and Stacey relaxed some more. 'That's a very normal sound.'

Holly rubbed her forehead. 'Hurts, Mummy.'

'That's because you banged it. You've got to be careful.'

She turned to Noah. 'Thanks for the offer of a lift but you don't have a car seat suitable for Holly.'

He pulled out his phone and brought up a picture of a car seat. 'There's this one or…' he flicked the screen '…this one. Both seem suitable but you need to make sure for me.'

She took the phone and studied the top-of-the-range seats. 'Either one will be ideal.'

'Good. I'll order it now and pick it up shortly. I'd like to meet your parents again now that this is out in the open.'

'No problem. They want to talk to you, too.' She didn't like his controlled tone. Now he'd had more time to think about everything, had he come up with things not to his satisfaction?

'Do they? Good.' He sounded as though he expected them to give him a set of rules to follow, and that he already had his own ground rules to put in place.

'They want to clear the air and start over as they mean to go on.' She'd never seen him in this mood before and should've expected it. He'd had hours to go through everything, would've been churning things over and over. Now she needed to brace herself for the battle, for more questions fuelled by his doubts.

'Tell me about your previous relationship.'

Hadn't she already done that? *Stay calm.* They were in a ward with staff, patients and parents. This was not going to be the entertainment. Reaching the bed, she sat beside Holly and opened a book.

'Har-ree.' Holly pointed at the picture of the hairy monster.

'Sure is, sweetheart.' She began reading, ignoring Noah pacing over the small space between her and the window. Once the story was finished she handed over the book to Holly to run her fingers over the pictures. It would take a few minutes, giving her time to deal with Noah's question.

'Angus and I grew up two houses apart. We were play-mates, then teenage friends, then we fell in love and finally got engaged. Then he met someone else.'

'How did you feel about that?'

'I was gutted. I loved him. I believed we were meant for each other.'

'And now?'

Her chest rose and fell. 'I'm over him. In a way he was right when he said we'd been friends too long before we became lovers and there was something missing from our relationship. It took me a while to see that.' It had taken Noah, and even then she wasn't trusting herself to believe she'd fallen for a man she'd only known for a few hours. 'Why's this important?'

His guard didn't slip. 'I know very little about you.'

About the mother of his child. She got it. He wasn't in-terested in her as a woman, and she'd best keep that in the forefront of her mind. Pain knocked her. So much for think-ing they might have a future together. It wasn't happening. She had to be realistic. Rubbing her chest, she snapped, 'I could say the same about you, but I trust you to be con-siderate to me and Holly throughout what lies ahead,' and was pleased to see him jerk his head back.

'I've landed you with a child and no lead-in time.' At least she wasn't expecting marriage and a full-time relation-ship. Her heart ached for what could've been if only he felt the same. But she obviously hadn't done any more than turn him on for as long as it took to make love. Often. Watch-ing Noah, the same tingling was going on in her palms, a familiar heat unfurling deep down, a longing she'd only known for him.

'So it would seem,' he said.

'You're still having doubts about Holly's paternity?' she demanded. 'We can have a DNA test done.' Her heart throbbed painfully at the thought of not still being believed over something so crucial.

Again Noah jerked his head and stared at her, his teeth digging into his bottom lip. After a long, leaden moment he shook his head. 'That won't be necessary, but thank you for understanding and offering.'

She didn't feel any relief. If anything, she was more uncomfortable. He was right about one thing. They didn't know each other, were mostly going on gut instinct. Which sometimes was safer than knowledge. Less overthinking.

'No, story.' Holly was holding out the book Stacey had just read, this time towards Noah. 'No?'

'Noah, his name's Noah.' Or Daddy. Stacey gulped as she glanced at him. And was struck by the awe shining from him at his daughter. She could relax on Holly's behalf. This was going to work out for her, one way or another. But for *her*, she'd be waiting in the wings for any snippet of acknowledgement. No kisses, or passionate lovemaking. He wasn't interested in her.

Except there'd be a child's car seat ready by the end of the day so he could give them a lift. He had a way about him that brooked no argument when he was adamant about getting something. Another thing to watch out for when it came to discussing parenting with him.

At ten past five he appeared on the paediatric ward. 'Ready to go home?' he asked. 'I've got everything sorted.'

'She's been given the all clear as long as I stay at home with her tomorrow. I'd already arranged to take the day off. We'll see where we go after that. Dad's already put his hand up if I have to come in. There is a shortage of nurses due to the flu.'

'It's the same in Theatre,' Noah acknowledged. Then he

turned to her and gave one of his heart-wrenching smiles. 'How're you feeling?'

Surprised. 'Happier now we're leaving here.' Deep breath.

Tell him what you think.

'Thanks for this. I'm glad you haven't walked away.'

Now who looked surprised? 'Anastasia…' Noah hesitated. Started again. 'I meant it when I said I won't do that. As you can imagine, I was awake most of the night, going over what you've told me, and I completely accept it's the truth.'

'Just like that?'

'Not quite. After my previous relationship I'm a little short on trust, but every argument I put up during the night crumbled away when I went through the little I know about you.'

Did that mean what it sounded like?

'I don't know where you and I are headed. I do know that from the moment we bumped into each other last Monday I've wanted to spend more time with you.'

Hope flared. She deliberately squashed it. 'Isn't it a bit soon to be telling me this? Shouldn't you wait until you've totally accepted your daughter into your life?'

Stepping closer, he continued. 'Maybe but when I think of Holly I always end up thinking about you instead. And, yes, I do question what you expect of me, and what you'll give back in return.'

Which was why he wanted more time. The hope disappeared. She couldn't blame him for that. It was a big ask to be accepted so easily. 'Guess you'll have to wait and see.' She lifted her girl into her arms. 'But first…' Deep breath. 'Holly, this is Daddy. Say, "Hello, Daddy."'

Holly grinned and stared at him. 'Hello, No.'

Noah laughed, not appearing at all disappointed. 'Does

this mean "No" is going to be your favourite word, my girl, instead of yes? If so, we're in for some arguments.'

'No. No.' Holly banged her hand on Stacey's arms, and grinned some more.

The Wainwright house was a three-storey, semi-detached in neat condition with a tidy front lawn. Despite Holly having been in hospital, the gate onto the road was firmly shut. Noah shuddered at the thought of her running out and being hit by the kid on a skateboard. Turning back to his vehicle, he opened the rear door, unclipped Holly from her seat and handed her to Stacey. 'I'll grab the bag.'

Stacey handed Holly back. 'You carry her. I'll get that.'

His heart softened as he reached for his daughter. It was hard to get enough of her now he'd accepted parenthood. 'Thanks.' He leaned over and kissed Stacey's cheek, tried to ignore the jolt of longing that caught him. Backing off, he waited to follow her to the house.

She'd looked stunned then pleased at the kiss. Damn, he should've kept his emotions to himself. Now she'd be thinking he was ready for more with her. Not that he wouldn't enjoy making love again. His body was wired for hers, rarely quietened when around her. But to take Anastasia to bed now would be wrong, and unkind. It would suggest nothing had changed, that they were still seeing each other as two people without a child between them, and before both of them had worked out what they wanted for the future. He was presuming Stacey hadn't too many expectations of him and her position in his life.

The front door opened before they reached the steps. 'Holly, sweetheart, you're home. She's looking better, Stacey.' Ian Wainwright stood there, looking relaxed and pleased to see them all. Even him. 'Hello, Noah.'

Noah stuck his hand out. 'Ian, I hope I'm not inconveniencing you.'

'Of course not. You're welcome to visit anytime.' He wasn't saying who he should be visiting. Holly or Stacey? 'Come in out of the cold.' His welcome was genuine, like his daughter.

It was like stepping into the past. Laughter came from another room, music was playing in the background, the smell of dinner cooking reached his nostrils and warmed him. Noah closed his eyes and breathed deeply, drew up memories of when he'd been a little boy. 'Wonderful.'

'It is, isn't it?' Caution laced Stacey's question.

'You're lucky.'

'I know, though sometimes I take it all for granted.'

Judy appeared in the kitchen doorway and crossed to lift her granddaughter out of his arms. 'Hello, sweetheart. Grandma's happy to see you.' Kiss, kiss, kiss on Holly's cheeks. Then she smiled at Noah. 'You'll stay for dinner.'

Did he have a choice? He chuckled. 'I'd love to.'

'I'll heat up some baked beans for Holly and you can sit with her while she eats.' Stacey grinned. Which was the first easy grin he'd had from her in days.

It warmed his heart and relaxed some of the tension that had built up on the short drive from the hospital. 'Is my shirt going to survive?'

Stacey's spread hand flipped back and forth. 'Maybe.'

Only one red splotch marred the front of his white shirt by the time Holly decided she'd had enough and shoved the plate aside. 'Read me a story, No.'

'What's the magic word?' her mother asked from the kitchen, where she was helping her mother.

'Please, No.'

'Please, Daddy.' Stacey had come to stand in the doorway. 'Noah is your daddy.'

'No Daddy?' Those beautiful eyes were huge in the tiny face.

'Yes, Daddy,' he growled around a blockage in his throat.

'No, Daddy.' The little minx giggled.

Reaching for her, Noah wrapped his daughter in his arms and kissed the top of her head. His heart was pounding, his throat still blocked, and when he glanced across to Stacey she was wiping her eyes with the back of her hand. Anastasia was full of love for so many people. She was happy for him to be a part of Holly's life, had offered to have a DNA test for his peace of mind.

In his arms, Holly began wriggling to get down. 'Careful or you'll hurt your arm,' he cautioned in a croaky voice. Setting her carefully on her feet, he watched her dash across to Granddad and scramble up onto his knees.

'It's bedtime, missy,' Ian said as he hugged her.

'No.'

No as in Noah, or, no, I don't want to go to bed?

Noah grinned. This was family, right here in this old-fashioned sweet house that was so different from the modern sterile place he lived in. This was what he remembered from his childhood—not the house and its fixtures but the genuine love and kindness, the acceptance of each other. It was perfect. Happiness crept under his ribs. Unbelievable. Everything he wanted was right here. If he dared take a chance.

Another glance at Stacey had his heart dancing again, this time for her. And them. Could it be as easy as saying, 'Come with me and make magic, bring up our daughter together and be happy?' Could he trust himself to make that decision?

'Stacey, it's Noah. You wanted me?' Wednesday and she was back at work. They might get to steal a few minutes together throughout the day. According to the nurses, she'd been trying to get hold of him for the last hour while he'd been in surgery.

'Jonathon Black's got another problem, more pain in the abdomen. It's severe. The registrar's seen him and thinks you should take a look.'

'Can you put him on?' He'd get the details and suggest what would be necessary until he finished in Theatre.

Then he recalled what she'd said the first time she'd phoned him to see Jonathon. She'd rightly suspected appendicitis. 'Forget it. I'm on my way.' He was going to be unpopular either way he did this, and if Black was seriously ill again then that was more important than delaying an operation.

The lift doors swished open, reminding him what he should be focused on. Heading directly to the room where Jonathon had spent the last couple of weeks, he hesitated at the door when he saw Stacey talking to his patient. His heart did a little dance. No hesitation there. It was his mind that kept throwing up reasons not to get too involved. And frankly he was over what his mind was trying to do to his hopes.

He hadn't been cautious the first time round, but he was being so this time, and it was getting uncomfortable. If he wasn't careful, Stacey and Holly would bear the brunt of his past. As if Stacey would deliberately hurt him. What he saw and knew would be what he got and more, and that was good—kind, loving and fun. Heart and mind were getting mixed up now. Time to take a break.

But it wasn't that simple. The Wainwrights were friendly and caring, open and sharing. Which was Stacey through and through. That's what he remembered and had longed for since that fatal night when Robert had come to tell him his parents had died. After his blunder with Christine he'd thought he'd never find it. Now he might have it with Anastasia. Might, but he was not totally convinced his heart was right.

There was no denying his attraction for her physically. It was strong and kept him awake most nights. So why not find out if he could live without Stacey in his life? There was doubt there already: it just needed looking into further. There was only one way to find out and that was by shoving caution aside to spend more time with her, starting with asking her out for a meal one night this week.

Decision made, he walked over to his patient. 'I hear you're in pain again, Jonathon. Whereabouts?'

Stacey helped Jonathon lift the sheet and pull his hospital gown up to expose his belly.

'All around here.' With his palm, Jonathon touched most of his abdomen. 'It's not like the last twice. It's more a widespread ache, worse when I cough or go to the bathroom.'

'Any nausea?' Noah gently probed the abdomen.

'Every time I eat or drink. And the pain gets worse about half an hour after eating.'

'Can I see the notes?' he asked Stacey, and took the proffered board.

Flicking through Jonathon's history, he could find nothing to raise alarm bells. But the blood tests showed not everything was settling down as quickly from the appendicitis as he'd hoped. An underlying cause? Another problem they hadn't known about?

'We need more blood tests done. When did you last eat?'

'Breakfast.'

'Four hours ago,' Stacey informed him.

'The pain was excruciating then.'

Diverticulitis? 'Right, no more food by mouth. Stacey'll set you up with intravenous nutrition via fluids. I'm prescribing stronger antibiotics and arranging a CT scan of your bowel.' Turning to Stacey, he added, 'Liver functions, urine and stool samples, please.'

When they were well away from Jonathon's room, Stacey asked, 'What are you thinking?'

'Diverticulitis.'

'Another severe infection. What's going on?' She was on to it straight away.

'I'm going to arrange further screening to see if there's an underlying cause that we haven't found yet. The cancer could be in other organs, though symptoms haven't presented.' Though that didn't feel right.

Stacey's face fell. 'He doesn't deserve that. He's so sweet and nice to everyone, even when we're doing awful procedures on him.'

No one deserved cancer, but he agreed with her. 'Fingers crossed I'm wrong. Let me know as soon as you get the lab results.' He turned for the lift, paused, and returned to Stacey, his heart hammering. She might think he wanted to soften any blow he might have for the future. But he hadn't decided completely on what he had to offer yet, was afraid of getting it wrong and losing any chance of working this out so that all three of them were happy. 'I thought we might go out for dinner on Friday night if that suits you.'

'I usually spend the nights with Holly. If you'd like—'

The emergency buzzer screamed throughout the ward.

Stacey leapt around the counter to read the number flashing from the screen. 'Bed eleven. Cardiac arrest. Jason, resus cart.' And she was gone, Jason right beside her with the cart.

Noah was on her heels. 'Who is it?'

'Fifty-five-year-old female, post gastro surgery, history of cardiac arrest, last time six months ago.' She raced into the room. 'Keep doing compressions, Ada. Jason, prepare the defib.' She tore the woman's gown open and pressed the patches onto the woman's skin before attaching the leads and reading the monitor.

Noah took the electric pads from Jason. The screen showed the heart had stopped. 'Stand back.'

Everyone else put space between themselves and the bed.

Stacey watched the screen.

Noah tapped the button on the defib.

Melissa's body jerked upwards.

Stacey watched the line on the screen, said calmly, 'Prepare for another shock.'

Noah primed the defibrillator. 'Stand back.'

The flat line rose and fell, trailing a pattern matching life. Then it stopped.

'Prepare for another shock,' Stacey ordered.

Shock. Jerk. The line rose, fell, rose, fell.

Noah was holding his breath, and when he looked around he saw everyone was doing the same. Except Stacey. She had a stethoscope to her ears and was listening to the woman's chest. Not satisfied with the monitor? Not taking anything for granted? That was Stacey. Finally she straightened. 'Well done, everyone. Jason, stay with Melissa. She's your sole charge for the rest of the day. I'll phone her surgeon and let him know what's happened, though I doubt he's going to be surprised.' Then she turned to him. 'Noah, do you think you could examine our patient so I can report back to her surgeon?'

'Of course. Where are her notes?'

'Here.' Jason extended a file.

After a quick appraisal of the woman's history of heart surgeries and the recent gastro op, her temperature, heart rate before and after the arrest, her blood flow before checking the wound for sepsis, Noah said, 'All clean. She hasn't complained of pain any time today?'

Ada shook her head. 'No. In fact, she was saying she hadn't felt so good for months.'

Hadn't he heard that often enough to almost take it as a warning something was about to happen? After a thorough examination, he told Stacey and Jason, 'I can't find anything that might've triggered that attack other than her history of cardiac failures. But her surgeon should see her ASAP.'

'He's on his way,' Stacey informed him.

'Then I'll get back to Theatre.' He'd nearly reached the lift when he heard Stacey call out.

'Noah.' She approached with what he thought was apprehension. 'About Friday night? We're spending time together seeing your relatives on Saturday. Can we leave it at that for now?'

'If that's what you want.' Disappointment at not having time alone with her touched him. But, then, he didn't want to rush anything, did he?

'I'll bring Holly, too.'

That would cause a stir with the relatives for sure. But they had to find out sooner or later as he didn't intend hiding his daughter from anyone. 'Good idea.'

Relief poured into her face. 'Glad you think so.' She gave him such a sad smile he found himself wanting to banish it by saying they'd get through this okay and to haul her into his arms, hug her hard, but the lift doors opened behind him and Melissa's surgeon, Connor Harrison, charged out.

'Stacey, is Melissa conscious?'

'Yes,' she answered, still looking at him. 'Noah checked Melissa over.'

'Noah, thanks for that. Talk later. I need to see her.' Connor headed down the ward.

'I'd better join him,' Stacey said, but she didn't move.

'I'd better get on with surgery. Talk to you later about Saturday.'

'Looking forward to it.' She gave him a wave over her shoulder as she chased after Connor.

She wouldn't be looking forward to meeting Robert and Alice if she knew how cold they were. Not even Stacey's friendly disposition would warm their hearts. Noah watched until she disappeared into Melissa's room. She certainly did things to his heart that he wasn't used to. Was this what he'd been looking for? The feeling of coming home when he'd walked into her parents' house yesterday said so. How did he know for certain? By taking time to find out more, and waiting to see if he did love her, or if this was a passing fancy.

Time to get back to work. Phoning downstairs, he told them he was on his way.

CHAPTER NINE

STACEY'S STOMACH WAS tied in knots when Noah arrived to pick them up on Saturday. They weren't going to stay long at his relatives' house as Holly might get grumpy, as she did sometimes when she couldn't do something because of the cast, and Noah said it wouldn't work to put her down for a nap there. He wouldn't explain why, just said that afterwards they'd go to his place for a while so he'd have more time with Holly.

As he opened the back door to his four-wheel drive, he leaned in and kissed Holly on the cheek. 'Hello, Holly.'

'Hello, No Daddy.'

Stacey's heart wobbled. At least these two were getting along. If only she and Noah could make headway. They got on fine at work, where nothing personal came up, but away from the hospital there was an undercurrent of uncertainty running between them that had started when she'd told him he was Holly's father, and so far nothing had seemed to change it.

Then he surprised her with a kiss on her cheek. Chaste and still making her heart beat harder than normal. 'Noah?'

He breathed deeply. 'Citrus. That tangy, sweet smell always reminds me of you.'

'Are you trying to butter me up?' she asked, a little too abruptly.

'Not at all. Just stating a fact.' His smile was skewwhiff.

Trying for relaxed, she smiled. 'Lemons and oranges, my lasting impression, huh?'

'One of them.'

She wasn't asking what the others were. She had enough of her own about Noah to make her blush if he knew what she was thinking. She handed Holly over to him to put in the car seat. 'I've brought a colouring-in book and pencils to keep her occupied at the house. Do I need to grab some paper to protect any surfaces?'

Noah shook his head. 'I'm sure Jackson will rustle up something.'

'Who's Jackson?'

'The butler.'

Her stomach dropped. The butler. Just where were they going? Here she'd been worrying if Noah's aunt and uncle would accept her and Holly, and now there was a butler in the picture. That spoke volumes, told her she had no idea what the morning would bring. She wasn't against butlers as such, but a sense of being out of her depth was creeping in and they hadn't left Harlow yet.

She climbed into the vehicle, laid the flowers she'd bought on the floor by her feet, and strapped herself in tight, then looked at her outfit. Black leggings under a short red skirt, a fitted floral blouse and a tight corduroy jacket. She'd splashed out in the winter sales for those items, and then had really blown the budget with new—no nicks and scratches—black, knee-high boots, so she was dressed up for the occasion, and now she felt cheap.

Noah wore navy trousers and jacket, offset with a cream shirt and blue tie. Classy without going over the top. Not that she knew a lot about classy, but he looked good enough to eat. Now, there was a thought.

The back door closed, then the vehicle rocked as Noah got into the driver's seat. 'Ready?'

As she'd ever be, which was never. 'Yes.' Then, 'Why are you taking me to meet your relatives when you don't seem to like them much?'

Good point. Noah still couldn't get his head around the fact he'd invited Anastasia to Robert and Alice's. It was a step forward, introducing her to his family in case they got together permanently. And also to finally lay his doubts to rest when Stacey saw the property. She'd be amazed, and stoic, and get on with being polite and keeping Holly amused. Not like his aunt. Alice had been her usual frosty self when he'd said he was bringing a friend and her daughter to meet them.

'I hope she's got class, Noah.'

Oh, Anastasia was classy all right, just not aloof and a boorish snob. 'She's a wonderful woman.' Anastasia was no mug, and certainly could hold her own, but so could Alice. He didn't want Anastasia feeling hurt or upset over anything that might be said today. He shouldn't be taking her there. He straightened his back. He'd support her, no matter what, show Robert and Alice who was important in his life.

'Are flowers all right for your aunt?' Anastasia asked tightly.

'Of course they are. You didn't have to do that.' Though Alice would be miffed if she hadn't.

'I think I do.' Her smile was brief.

Fingers crossed for a smile of any sort during the next couple of hours. 'I hope you're comfortable with this visit,' he reiterated.

'Noah, hush. You've already warned me it might be a little cool, and I'm prepared. I can be well mannered if required. Which usually means saying very little.' Her attempt at laughing at herself fell flat when she started staring out the window.

'I'm going to tell them Holly's my daughter.'

Her head spun round. 'You're sure about that?'

'Absolutely.' Introducing Holly into the mix would raise more questions, but he was prepared for those. She was his daughter, and that, Robert and Alice, was that.

'Good.' Her fingers on her free hand were clenched, not exactly backing up that comment. Then she added, 'Thanks. It means a lot that you're accepting Holly completely.'

Time for some light relief. 'Did you bring some music for our girl to break the boredom of travelling?'

Relief filled her face. 'Sure did.'

Soon the sound of squeaky voices that kids apparently liked filled the interior and Holly was joining in. Noah began to relax.

Finally when he pulled through the gate and started up the long sweeping drive lined with old oak trees, his breath caught in the back of his throat and he was afraid to look at his companion in case he saw an expression that would tell him he'd got it all wrong, that she did want a lifestyle unknown to her and attainable only by fooling him.

Anastasia said nothing until he pulled up outside the wide stairs leading to the front door and she turned to him. 'What a beautiful home.' There was nothing but genuine honesty in her face. No avarice or hope or envy.

Noah exhaled. 'You're right. It is.'

'Has it always been in your family?'

'About two hundred and twenty years. Robert was the oldest brother so it was passed down to him, and my cousin is next in line to own it.' He was still looking for a reaction that would scream a warning. When none came, he expanded. 'Thank goodness. I don't want to live here. It was bad enough in the times I had to come back during holidays. Large, cold rooms that go on for ever. No small, comfortable spaces to be happy in.'

'Oh, Noah.' Her hand enveloped his, squeezed tight. 'That's hideous.'

One word for it. 'Yes. Shall we go in?' Of course neither Alice nor Robert had come to the door to greet them, but Jackson was waiting. Thank goodness some delightful things never changed. Out of the car, he went to get Holly but Anastasia had beaten him to it, clinging to her like a shield.

She looked around once and then at him, her shoulders suddenly tense. 'Do I look all right?'

Wrapping an arm around her, he tucked her in against him and shut the car door. 'You're beautiful.' He wasn't lying. Her gleaming dark blonde hair spilled down her back and her funky red earrings bobbed whenever she turned her head. 'You're not on display.' But Alice would take note of every piece of clothing and the hairstyle and those earrings. Damn the woman. Not everyone lived like her, and she'd never accepted that because it was her right to lord it over people about how she was married to a Kennedy.

Tempting as it was to drive away for a relaxed lunch somewhere else, it couldn't happen. He'd told Robert he'd come, and that meant he had to. And sometime soon he had to let his relatives know he was a father anyway. May as well get that over with.

Taking a quick look around at the familiar land sprawled out beyond the mansion, he thought about those relaxed years in Auckland that already seemed a lifetime ago. Stacey had hit the nail on the head when she'd asked why he'd left there when he was happy. If only he could've stayed on down under and ignored the family for good. But irresponsibility wasn't one of his flaws.

He'd never intended to stay away quite as long as he had, but the months had got away from him as he'd worked with some amazing and friendly plastic surgeons, constantly perfecting his skill level. In reality, he had missed London and his friends, and the gnawing need to find Anastasia just to put his mind at rest that she wasn't the right one for him had also played a part in buying a ticket home.

He breathed deeply. His mouth dried. His gut churned. Goosebumps rose on his arms. Citrus. Anastasia's scent. Her mark on him. A scent he couldn't forget, or their time together that one night. Drawing in another huge lungful of air, the tang of lemons and oranges teased his senses, and set his blood humming. No getting away from that smell that had haunted him for so long. 'Come on. Let's get inside where hopefully there's a fire roaring in some room.'

Stacey shivered, and not from the cold. She shouldn't have come. The house was formidable. From another world, and made her feel inferior, which she shouldn't. She was no different from Noah. Their emotions were the same, they ate meals and worked in a hospital, they were parents to Holly. She shivered again. And he was wealthy beyond her comprehension. This was a timely wake-up call. They couldn't be together. She didn't belong. The night she'd gone to his house in the city she hadn't taken a lot of notice, having been too interested in Noah himself, and where their kisses had been leading. This place was intimidating and she hadn't gone inside yet. Though that was only a few steps from becoming real.

'Good morning, Noah.' The older man in a black suit standing erect at the door smiled happily. 'It's good to see you.'

'Jackson, great to see you, too.' Noah hugged him. 'How have you been?'

'Can't complain. Nobody listens.' The man laughed.

'Jackson, this is Anastasia Wainwright, a friend and colleague of mine. And our daughter, Holly.'

Stacey gasped. Noah had told the butler Holly was his daughter? Just like that? Wow. She could love him for that alone. And the fact he obviously treated everyone with respect and genuine friendliness. Some of her concerns backed off. He would always be caring for her and Holly. How was she going to sort this conundrum out? She loved Noah but did she love him enough to accept all that came with him? When he stood up for her by speaking out about Holly then, yes, she could. She held her hand out to shake Jackson's. 'Glad to meet you,' she said with a smile.

'You, too, Anastasia. I hope this young man is looking after you.'

Putting a finger to her lips, she pondered the question, and finally said, 'Can't say I have any complaints.'

'Phew. I was waiting with bated breath.' Noah smiled as though he'd truly been worried. Maybe he had, though not likely about any complaints she might come up with, but more along the lines of regretting bringing her here.

'Let's go inside.' Noah took her elbow.

'Your aunt and uncle are in the conservatory,' Jackson informed Noah as he closed the door after them.

Stacey felt Noah flinch. He wasn't happy about which room they were going to?

'Thank you, Jackson.' Then to Stacey he said with an annoyed smile, 'It's all right. The conservatory will be very warm.'

But the occupants mightn't be? Was that the cause of that tight expression? She leaned closer briefly. 'Everything's fine.'

'Yes, of course.'

She'd never heard Noah speak so sharply. She didn't

feel this was about her and Holly, but more about his family. Talking to Jackson, he'd relaxed a little, but that had changed in an instant. Interesting, and worrying. She didn't want Noah unhappy. It didn't bode well for the coming hour.

Noah strode into the conservatory. With his hand still on her elbow, Stacey struggled to keep up with him, so her entrance was less than gracious. Gracious? What sort of word was that in her life? A quick glance around at the perfectly potted plants and polished leather chairs and she instantly felt out of place. Then her eyes spied two people sitting very straight in large, uncomfortable-looking seats, watching her and Noah, and Holly. Yes, the woman's eyes widened as they landed on Holly.

'Robert, Aunt Alice.' Noah bobbed his head. His mouth lifted into a facsimile of a smile, nothing like the ones he usually gave her that turned her to mush.

She moved as close to him as possible without looking like she was his pet.

Robert stood up, crossed to give Noah a perfunctory slap on the back. 'Glad you could come.'

Noah nodded. 'This is Anastasia Wainwright, a friend of mine. Stacey, my Aunt Alice and Uncle Robert.'

Stacey stepped forward, holding her hand out. 'Pleased to meet you, Robert.'

The handshake was short and sharp. 'And I you, Anastasia.'

She stepped around him and approached Noah's aunt, who was appraising her. And coming up with not a lot for recommendation if that blank expression meant anything. 'I'm Stacey and I work in the same hospital as Noah. These are for you.' She presented the bouquet of flowers she'd been gripping while holding Holly. They looked battered and bruised.

'You're a doctor?' Surprise brought some animation to the woman's face as she took the proffered flowers and immediately handed them to Jackson.

'Not at all. I'm a nurse and love it.'

'A very good one, too,' Noah added from directly behind her.

She hadn't heard him move, or sensed his proximity, which showed how this woman was unnerving her.

Well, I might not be rich or have the dress sense of the famous, but I am genuine and love my family and life.

'Thank you.' She smiled at Noah.

Noah straightened his already straight back. 'And this is our daughter, Holly.'

'Right.' Robert stepped nearer. 'Take a seat. Jackson, would you please bring Noah and Anastasia something to drink.' He totally ignored Holly.

Stacey glanced at Alice, saw incredulity on her face. Why? Noah was capable of fathering a child. Even with her. No wonder he wasn't overly happy with these people. They were cold, and aloof. What had that done to a grieving ten-year-old boy needing someone to love him? She sank onto the nearest chair, cuddling Holly closer. Holly seemed to sense the atmosphere because she was unusually quiet, too.

'A glass of wine, Anastasia?' Jackson asked with a friendly smile.

Was Jackson his first or last name? She hoped it was his first name. Calling someone by their surname didn't sit comfortably. 'Yes, please, Jackson. A pinot noir, if that's possible?' A very large one, please.

'Of course. What would Holly like? An orange juice, perhaps?'

'She'd love that.'

'No problem.' He was still smiling when he turned to Noah. 'A chardonnay for you?'

'A very small one, thanks.' Noah sat in the chair next to her. 'Where are the others?' he asked Robert.

'Unfortunately your cousins have had to cancel,' Robert answered. 'Perhaps you and I could go to my study before Jackson brings the wine. There are a couple of issues I need to discuss with you.'

'Good idea.'

Stacey saw Noah's slight shrug as he stood up again. Who was this Noah? No one she'd met before. There wasn't any love going round as there would be at her home. Not that her family made an issue of it. It was just there in the way they spoke to each other.

'I won't be long, Anastasia. If Holly gets restless, sit her at that low table where she can colour her pictures.'

'Will do.' And she'd try to ignore that glare from Alice.

'Mummy, down.'

Great. 'Shall we do some colouring in?'

'What happened to her arm?' Alice asked.

'She was knocked over by a kid on a skateboard.'

'Should she be on the road at her age?'

'Someone left the gate open.' Placing pencils and the colouring book in front of Holly, Stacey sat back on her ankles and looked around the room. 'You've got some wonderful paintings in here.'

'Yes, I'm a bit of a collector. Do you like art yourself?'

'I know very little about it. Just like what I like without understanding the nuances.'

'At least you're honest.' For a moment Alice seemed to relax with her. She stared at a painting in front of her. 'I used to dabble in art myself, but unfortunately I wasn't very good.'

'That's a shame.'

'Oh, well, can't be helped. Ah, here are our drinks.'

Stacey almost felt sorry for this woman, stuck in this

massive house and not doing the things she got enjoyment from. Though she seemed to enjoy being the hostess, even to Stacey, someone they clearly wouldn't have expected Noah to bring home.

Then Noah was back, and she could relax more. Concentrating on keeping Holly happy, she let most of the conversation go over her head, until Noah stood up. 'Right, we'd better be heading back to the city before Holly gets too tired. She's recovering from an accident and needs special attention at the moment.'

Then Stacey got a shock as she lifted Holly into her arms.

Alice came across and lightly ran a finger down Holly's cheek. 'Thank you for visiting us, Holly.' It was the first real acknowledgement there'd been that Holly even existed.

Stacey looked at Noah, and saw him swallowing hard, shock registering on his face. She hugged her daughter. She'd done what no one else seemed to have. She'd got through to Alice.

Noah gulped. Alice had gone to Holly and touched her cheek. Like she cared for his daughter. Hell, she'd never once been so kind to him. Not even when his heart had been broken and he'd been missing his parents desperately.

He stared at this stranger. Alice? Seriously? He didn't know whether to laugh or cry. The young boy who'd wanted only to be loved had not known this woman to have a gentle side.

And now she was talking to Holly.

And Holly was smiling back, as she always did, believing everyone was as kind and loving as her mother's family.

Noah shook his head. Unbelievable. But it didn't alter a thing when it came to sorting out the future. That belonged entirely to Anastasia and himself.

* * *

On Monday Stacey was getting up to speed with patients that had been admitted over the weekend when Noah showed up on the ward.

'How was the rest of your weekend?' he asked, without checking if anyone was within hearing.

'Quiet. Holly still gets tired quickly.'

'Can the three of us spend some time together at my house next weekend?' He looked tired too.

Guess this was part of settling everything into place. 'Sure. I'd like that,' she added, because it was true. She'd spent most of yesterday thinking about Noah and his relatives and just what he might want to do about their future.

'You're being generous with your time and daughter.' He smiled.

Which stirred her from head to toe. 'Only way to go,' she said truthfully. No point in worrying if she was doing the wrong thing. Holly deserved her father in her life, and this way her mother would be there too, assessing everything for the time a decision had to be made.

Damn it, she couldn't be blushing. But something was turning her skin red hot. Thank goodness no other staff were at their desks. 'We do seem to connect, don't we?'

'Very well.' Another smile to tighten her stomach. 'I'd better get a wriggle on with seeing my patients. The surgical list is long today.'

Stacey picked up the pile of files she'd already prepared and followed him in to see Jonathon, who was getting fed up with being stuck in hospital and showing it.

'The infection in your bowel has lessened off enough that you should be able to go home on Wednesday,' Noah told him. Turning to Stacey, he added, 'I'll fill out a lab form for more blood tests before I head downstairs.'

On the way to the next patient, he said quietly, 'See you

for breakfast one morning? I'm on call all week so won't get away at other times easily.'

'I'll be in the cafeteria every morning,' she said with a grin.

'I'm discharging Ben Ibbotson today. He needs to have weekly physio appointments and a follow-up with me in two weeks,' Noah told her.

'All sorted,' Stacey replied.

'Good. Now, Linda Garrick.' He turned into the opposite room. 'Morning, Linda. How're you today?'

'Fine, Doctor. I've been walking up and down the ward for thirty minutes and while the wound is painful I got along quite well.'

'Very well, from what I saw,' Stacey added.

'Don't get too carried away,' Noah told his patient. 'After such a deep tear, that calf muscle is going to take time to fully heal.'

It was a typical ward round, and afterwards Noah stayed a few minutes, talking about his patients, dropping in a few smiles for her when he thought no one was looking.

Though Liz seemed to notice everything. 'You sure you haven't got something going with our hot surgeon?' she asked as Stacey tried not to watch Noah striding along to the lift, his shoulders back and his head high.

Stacey wasn't sure about anything except she was falling deeper in love with Noah, and still didn't know where they were headed. 'It's great catching up with him again.'

Liz snorted. 'I might not be the brightest lightbulb in the room but I ain't blind.'

She laughed. What else could she do? If she said anything Liz would put her own interpretation on it and probably be closer to the truth than Stacey wanted anyone to get.

* * *

They managed two shared breakfasts over the week, her parents enthusiastically pushing her out the door with promises of getting Holly up and fed before taking her to the nursery or settling down for the day at home with Granddad. Stacey skipped onto the train and off at the other end, racing to the hospital cafeteria for toast and coffee, and time with Noah, deliberately forgetting the issues between them. It was great just to have time alone with him. And in the evenings, after dinner was over, the dishes were stacked in the dishwasher, and she'd read the requisite stories to Holly, she'd phone Noah. 'How was your day, apart from a perforated lung and an appendectomy?'

'You missed out the three hernias.'

'They didn't come to our ward. Holly said goodnight to Daddy tonight.'

'She did? Cool.' Noah sighed. For the first time in days he sounded irritated.

'Something wrong?' she asked, apprehension tightening her throat.

'What do you want? How do you see this working out? Why haven't you said anything about this, Anastasia?'

Anastasia, but not the having-fun one. Pounding set up behind her ribs. This discussion had been lurking in the background even during the fun moments, no matter how hard she'd tried to deny it. 'I've been giving you time to come to terms with being a dad.'

'Right. I'm there. Tell me what you want.'

'It's hard. I've been Holly's mother all her short life, been there for her all the time other than when I've gone to work. I can't imagine any other way to raise my child.' She certainly didn't want to divide the time with her father.

'She has two parents now.'

'I know what that entails. I really do.' She could hardly say she wanted to be with him as his partner or wife. He'd gag on that.

There was a silence that seemed to get heavier by the second. Then, 'We'll talk over the weekend.'

'Okay.' She could let it go for now and enjoy the relief of not coming to a final decision just yet. More time to enjoy as a solo parent.

Noah found a bottle of headache pills and swallowed two. His head had been pounding all morning. The week had been long and tedious. All he'd wanted was to spend time with Anastasia; to make love, to talk and laugh and share everything. Okay, he'd fallen for her fast. Too fast? Or had this been three years in the making and now he'd caught up with her he wanted to make up for lost time? That was more likely the answer, and the deeper in love he became, the more the warning bells tolled. What if he was wrong? Well, today he was about to find out, as Anastasia and Holly would be here soon.

Anastasia had been completely honest with him about Holly. She seemed to enjoy his company, giving him a sense that she had feelings for him beyond a friend who had a child with her. She didn't appear to be out for all she could get. She hadn't gone all simpering or gushing when he'd shown her around the house, hadn't made overtures about how Holly would be happy here and how she'd have to accompany her daughter if she was to spend time with him.

Yet the past kept waving at him, reminding him how easily he'd been duped before. But Anastasia didn't know coldness of the heart. It wasn't in her. What if they married? Would she make demands on him as his ex had? Would she always be wanting more and more, never satisfied with what she had? Given how she was happy with the little she did have, he couldn't see her changing radically. On the other hand, suddenly finding herself well off might be a catalyst to going overboard and needing to spend large and become fixated with the whole lifestyle he was desperate to avoid.

Ding-dong. The doorbell rang out.

His heart lifted. Anastasia and his daughter were here. *Their* daughter. He had to let go of the past if he wanted to find true happiness, something he suspected was on his doorstep right now if only he found the courage to follow his heart. He would be the one to lose out if he got this wrong. And the last thing he wanted to lose was Anastasia. She was his other half, if only she recognised that. She had to. He finally had. Deep breath. Yes, damn it. He did. He loved Stacey and Holly.

Pulling the door wide, he gazed at the two females who had his head in a spin. It wasn't hard to smile wide and deep. 'Hey, come in. I'm glad you're here.' He really was. All the doubts had taken a back seat the moment his gaze came to rest on Anastasia. Leaning in, he kissed her briefly.

Her return kiss was quieter than he'd become used to, and he'd have thought she'd changed her mind about being with him if he hadn't seen the flicker of need in her eyes. Closing the door, he led them down to the kitchen and the alcove on the side where he'd set out an array of toys he'd bought during the week.

Holly made a beeline for them and plopped down on her backside, reaching for the doll dressed in pink.

'That's a hit.' Anastasia smiled, the visible tightness in her shoulders loosening as she sat on a stool at the counter.

'Coffee?'

'You're a lifesaver. There wasn't any at home. Someone stuffed up the shopping yesterday.'

'Whose job is it usually?' From what he'd seen, the Wainwrights seemed to share all the chores around the house.

'Anyone who has an hour to spare. Which wasn't me, what with taking Holly to see the paediatrician after I finished my shift.'

'She got a good report.' Anastasia had filled him in last night. 'Hard to keep her down, isn't it?'

'Sure is. I hope you haven't got anything precious lying around at her level.' She scoped the room.

'I spent time putting things out of reach this morning.'

When Holly became bored with the toys, they took her into the sitting room with the piano and she created noise that only doting parents could cope with. After lunch they strolled along the streets and when Holly grizzled Noah piggy-backed her the rest of the way.

'She needs to have a sleep,' Anastasia said as they returned to the house.

'I've set up the room next to my office as a bedroom for now.' Breath held, he waited to see what her reaction would be.

'Lovely, thank you.'

She lifted Holly down from his back. 'Hey, darling, how was that?'

'Good. Daddy horse.'

He laughed. 'I've got my uses. I'll fetch your bag. I presume you need it to change Holly.'

'Thanks.' Anastasia was totally focused on her girl.

He felt almost redundant but then she was used to doing all this herself. Even when her parents were at home she did most of it, she'd told him. *I am her mum.*

It would be different if they were together, living under the same roof, sharing the responsibilities. He'd definitely do his share of whatever was required. Damn it, he wanted to be doing it now.

'Here.' He walked into Holly's room and handed Anastasia the bag, the questions churning in his head. He knew what he wanted, he didn't know if he could ask for it. 'How long will Holly sleep?'

'About two hours, if I'm lucky.'

We, not I. Noah kept that to himself. No point in aggravating her. There were more important things to say once they were out in the warm conservatory.

Within minutes Holly had fallen asleep and Anastasia led him out and closed the door quietly, leaving behind a monitor so she'd know if Holly cried.

'Would you like a glass of wine?' he asked.

'That'd be nice.' She still wasn't as relaxed with him as she'd been other times. Because Holly was here? Or something else?

When they were sitting, glasses in hand, he asked, 'What made you want to be a nurse?'

As they chatted about everyday subjects the tension left Anastasia and she became animated in the way he adored. Listening to her talking about her need to be the best in her nursing class, why she loved dancing so much, how her dad had taught her to be strong through his own traumas, reinforced why he loved her.

And then she asked, 'Are you settling back into London life?'

There'd been too many shocks for that. First the extent of Robert's debts and what Noah was expected to do about them, then learning he was a father. And especially his feelings for Anastasia. They had blown him out of the water. 'I've had too many other things on my mind to think about it.'

'I guess you have a lot on your plate.' Her hands were tightening.

'I've finalised everything with Robert and got him out

of the jam he was in.' May as well let her know a little of
his family's problems. 'He got into debt and needed me to
save his butt. It's what our family does. Up to a point anyway. I've now locked things up legally so he can't go off
the edge again.'

'Fair enough.'

'That was the main reason I came home, and once here
I saw that if I didn't stay to keep an eye on things, Robert
would only make other mistakes.'

'Then you bought into a private practice and took up the
job at London Riverside.' There was a sharpness creeping
into her voice.

What was that about? 'I *am* a surgeon. I'm not going to
sit around not using my skills. What's this about, Stacey?
You seem upset.'

She locked her eyes on him. 'I understand you're busy,
and life as you saw it has changed drastically with the ad-
vent of Holly. How do you see her and I fitting in with you?'

He sat up straighter, his chin lifting. 'Actually, that's one
problem I have put some thought into.'

'Problem? I see.' Anger flashed across her face, gone
as quickly as it rose. 'I understand this has been a shock,
but if we're being designated to the problem basket then
please don't give it another thought. We'll be on our way
home and out of your way for good.'

Damn. He'd gone and blown it. He needed to approach
this slowly, carefully. 'Anastasia.' She winced. 'Stacey, I
didn't mean it like that. You're not a problem. It's just that
there are no simple answers. I'm getting comfortable with
being a father and want to have a bigger part in Holly's life.'

She continued to watch him without saying a word.
Waiting for what?

'And I want to be a part of your life. I would like to share
raising Holly as a family, not take turns. I've longed for a

family to love and cherish, and I could have that with you and Holly.' Deep breath. 'Would you marry me?' So much for slow and careful. But why procrastinate? He knew what he wanted. He'd admitted to himself he loved Anastasia, so there was no reason to hold back.

'Why should I do that?' Her words were sharp, like small pebbles slapping into mud.

'We connect whenever we're together.' Except right now. 'We could raise Holly together, living here so we both can be a part of her life every day.'

So I can see you, love you, share everything I've got with you.

'You could become a full-time mum if you want to.' Her expression was wary. He still wasn't getting through. 'You can have anything you want to make life easier. Think about it. Being married could work for all of us.'

'I see.'

'Do you?' She wasn't reacting how he'd hoped.

'We'd live here?'

'Of course.' He waited, his fingers tapping the counter. Then when he couldn't bear the silence any longer, 'You're not saying much.' Not what he'd expected from someone who was usually talkative and cheerful.

She stood up abruptly. 'I think you're testing me to see what I really want from you. You're wondering if I'm going to be like your ex. Well, news flash. I'm not. By the way, you left out any mention of a pre-nup, which I'm sure is part of the deal.'

What could he say? Behind his need to have Anastasia in his life lay the nagging worry he'd screwed up by not believing in her. He wanted to believe he'd laid that to rest, but here it was again, swinging in front of him.

'As far as proposals go, yours needs a lot of practice. I'm not marrying you just to share Holly. If I'm ever to

marry, it will be for one reason only. Love.' She faltered
and looked away.

'Anastasia—'

'My name is Stacey,' she hissed. 'Now, if you don't
mind, I'll take Holly home. It's been a long day for her.

'And for me,' he thought she muttered as she pushed
past him.

Noah watched as she stormed out of the room. He'd
turned the day cold in the last few minutes. He'd got it all
wrong. His heart ached for the missed chance of happiness. Instead of telling her his feelings, he'd gone about
his offer like a business proposal and not a loving marriage
one, not a declaration of love. Stacey would not give him
an opportunity to redeem himself. Now that he'd blown it,
he understood how much he wanted her in his life, at his
side, as his wife. Because he did love her so much it was
impossible to breathe properly any more.

'Here, have this seat.' A man stood up as Stacey entered
the train carriage holding onto Holly and the stroller, with
her heavy bag slung over her shoulder.

'Thank you so much.' She couldn't find the strength to
argue, neither did she have enough energy to stand for the
ride home. She didn't think she'd ever feel strong again after
Noah had decimated her hopes so quickly and sharply. Sure,
she could have said yes and married him. For what? There
was no mention of love, and that's all she ever wanted from
a relationship and marriage.

Love came with understanding, caring, sharing, support.
Not a cool hope that they could live under the same roof
while seeing their daughter had the life she deserved. Because there was no chance of that when Noah didn't love
her. Holly was different. He genuinely loved her already.
Like it had been for her when Holly was born, he'd fallen

for his daughter quickly. But that wasn't a reason for her to accept his proposal.

Stacey hugged Holly. The last thing she was interested in was his money. It hurt that he might have thought so for one minute. She loved him beyond reason. Living with him, sharing a bed with him as his wife, would be unbearable since he obviously didn't have the same feelings for her. At least she knew where she stood. On the outside. Alone with her love.

She gave a cynical huff. When it came to men she never got it right. She'd loved Angus and look where that had got her. Now she loved another man who only wanted her to stay around for all the wrong reasons. Angus had been right about one thing: their love did lack the passion he'd found with his new partner, and which she'd discovered with Noah. Noah was wrong to think they could be together long term with only passion and not love to live by.

Holding Holly tight, she watched the passing roads and buildings without seeing them. Now what? She worked with Noah, had to face him every day. Had to figure out how to share their daughter without becoming angry or hurt every time she handed Holly over.

Her stop came far too quickly. She wasn't ready to go home. One look and her parents would know what had happened. With Holly in the stroller she headed out of the station and down the road in the opposite direction of home.

'Damn you, Noah Kennedy. Why couldn't you be an ordinary guy who didn't make me feel vulnerable? Didn't steal my heart? Why did you have to return to London, and the hospital where I work? What was wrong with any of the other hospitals in the city? Or even staying in Auckland?'

She bumped into a woman and received a glare.

'Sorry,' Stacey muttered, aware she hadn't been looking where she was going. She was outside a café buzzing with people. An open fire tempted her in out of the chilly air, and she found an empty table at the back of the café. After ordering herself coffee and a biscuit for Holly, she sat down and stared at her clasped hands. This was her fault for thinking Noah might return her feelings. Once again she'd been naïve. They'd had great sex one night three years ago, and had then repeated it since finding each other again. Not a lot to go falling in love on. But people did fall quickly. She'd read about it often. Seen it with her close friends.

Noah's life was the polar opposite of hers. He was wealthy, she barely made ends meet. They both cared about people and looked after them. She had a close family, he didn't. His aunt and uncle were cold, and from what he'd told her nothing like his parents had been. Obviously he still missed them a lot. His wife had hurt him, hadn't delivered on what he'd required from a marriage.

She could. She would. But she wasn't marrying him if he didn't love her.

Deep in her bag the phone rang. Not wanting to talk to anyone, Stacey ignored it.

But she couldn't keep Holly out for ever. Finally she trudged home, pushing the stroller and wishing she hadn't got out of bed that morning.

CHAPTER TEN

THE NEXT MORNING Noah parked outside the Wainwright house and drew a deep breath. Then he climbed out of his four-wheel drive and headed up the path to the front door to knock loudly.

When the door swung open, it took all his willpower not to pull Stacey into his arms and never let go. To beg her for another chance. She looked sad, and dark shadows under her eyes suggested she'd had as little sleep as he had. He'd done that to her. 'I'm really sorry.'

She blinked. Then nodded. 'Okay.'

When she made to shut the door, he stepped forward. 'Wait. I need to talk to you.'

The door stopped moving. 'I think you said it all yesterday, Noah. Quite bluntly, in fact.'

'I haven't come here to make demands.'

'I'm sure you haven't. But you will anyway.' Again the door was being pushed closed.

'Stacey, give me five minutes and if, after that, you tell me to go, I will.' Five hours wouldn't be anywhere long enough to say what was in his head. In his heart. But how else could he get her to listen to him? Going down on bended knee might work, but Stacey would more likely laugh at him.

'Why, Noah? We are so different it'd be funny if not for Holly.'

'No, we're not. We laugh at the same things. We have the same values. And, yes, we have Holly.'

'Holly can't be used to get me back on side.'

Stacey was strong and self-contained. She fought for what she believed in. He'd found the woman he'd been searching for most of his life. She was absolutely nothing like Christine in any way, shape or form. Now he had to convince her to give him a chance. The way she was looking at him with impatience in her expression said it wasn't going to be easy.

'You're right. And I had no intention of using her to get you to listen to me.' He waited, aware that anything else he said might close the door firmly in his face.

Finally Stacey stepped back and held the door wide.

He stepped inside before she could change her mind.

When the latch on the door snapped shut the air around them felt a little warmer, and the tension in his body eased a little. He was nowhere near reaching what he'd set out for when he'd driven off from home, but Stacey was prepared to hear him out. All in five minutes.

With Toby present. His stomach clenched when he saw Stacey's brother seated at the table with Holly on his knee as they ate breakfast. No sign of her parents. Then he recalled Stacey saying something about them being away for the weekend. Of course he'd known the chances of being alone with Stacey were still remote, but he'd hoped for a miracle, and it hadn't been forthcoming.

'Morning, Toby. Hello, Holly.' Noah brushed a hand over her sweet head and felt his heart lurch. She was gorgeous. She was his and Stacey's. More Stacey's than his. So far she'd done all the parenting. Done it well, and with love.

'Hi, Noah. You're out early. I hope you've come to put a smile on Sis's face. She's been in a grump for ever.'

'Shut up, Toby,' Stacey snapped as she filled the kettle.

Her brother merely shrugged. 'See what I mean?'

'Haven't you got somewhere to be?' Stacey glared at him.

Toby grinned. 'Yep. Holly and I are going to the park to play football, aren't we, Hols?'

'Yes, football!'

Stacey looked flustered. 'No, leave Holly here.'

Did she need to have her girl by her side while he was here? Noah wondered.

'I want football,' Holly demanded.

Getting more like her mother every day. 'I won't be long,' Noah said. Though he hoped that wasn't the case. 'I'm sure Holly will love getting outside.'

'Yeah, sis, we'll be back soon. We need to make the most of the fine day.'

Stacey's shoulders slumped. 'Go on, then. I'll join you shortly.' Then she looked directly at Noah. 'This had better be good.'

Noah waited while Toby got Holly into a thick jacket and slipped her tiny feet into pink shoes and tied the laces firmly, all the while watching his daughter and loving her, and trying not to glance at Stacey for fear of seeing anguish in those beautiful eyes. For she'd think he was here to lay down the rules on how they raised Holly. Little did she know what he really wanted to tell her.

Finally they were gone and silence fell, broken only by the sound of coffee being poured from the plunger into mismatched mugs.

Stacey placed them on the table and sat down, then waited.

Five minutes. Would she really hold him to that? Then

again, this was Stacey and he couldn't rely on her to be kind to him. Slowly he sank onto a chair opposite her. Where to start? During the long night he'd worked out how to approach her, and now it had all gone out the door with Holly and Toby. He hadn't a clue where to start. There was a lot to explain. But only one thing was really important. He gulped.

Sipped the steaming coffee. Looked at Stacey. His Anastasia. Her hands were gripping her mug, her gaze fixed on the table. Could he do this? He had to or lose out for ever. His heart thumped, his belly was in a knot. 'Stacey...' He paused, waiting for her to lift her head. When she didn't, he said, 'Please look at me.'

Slowly she obliged, wariness in her expression.

'Stacey, I love you.'

Her eyes widened, but the wariness remained.

Noah reached for her shaking hands and removed the mug before enfolding her fingers in his. 'I love you, everything about you. Your bravery, laughter, sense of worth and consideration for others, even the way you stand up to me. Your love for our daughter.'

Her fingers tightened under his, loosened. 'Is that what this is about? Holly?'

Her question didn't surprise him, and yet it still hurt. 'Not at all. I'm not making this up. I've probably loved you from the night we first met, only I tried to deny it, especially when we met up again a couple of weeks back. You gave me hope that I'd actually find someone I could be happy with, and love and be loved.'

Her hands turned over and she gripped him. 'Noah, are you sure? I don't want to hurt you. Neither do I want to find that you've changed your mind, and think you've got it all wrong.' She was looking at him with such longing the lump of fear that she might reject him out of self-preservation melted. 'I don't wish to be hurt by you either.'

Standing up, he rounded the table and pulled her up into his arms. 'I am more certain of my love for you than I am about anything else. I would never willingly hurt you. Will you marry me? As in a real marriage filled with love?'

Noah was asking her to marry him again. Twice in two days. Should she believe him? Or was this another way to get her to compromise on her own needs? Stacey's heart stopped as she gazed into his eyes. This time there was love in his gaze, his face, in the hands holding her. No hesitation at all. He'd said he loved her before anything else.

She wanted to believe him with everything she had.

'Stacey, I made a mistake when I married last time. I thought I could change love, make it fit to suit. This time I know I've found love, and I don't want to alter anything. It's you who's stolen my heart. You're all I've been hoping for. I love you, Anastasia Stacey Wainwright.'

Relief and love bubbled up as her heart kick-started and sent warmth racing through her chilled body. She clasped his hands. 'I've always loved you, Noah. Right from the moment you took my hand to lead me further onto the dance floor. Don't ask me how it happened so quickly, or so truly. I have no idea, except it's right. I love you, too.' Locking her eyes on his, she drew a breath and said in as firm a voice as the love bubbling through her allowed, 'Yes, I will marry you.'

Then she was being spun around in his arms as he yelled, 'I'm getting married.'

'So am I.' Stacey laughed, leaning closer to kiss him. It was a kiss that went on for ever and left her breathless—and so happy she had to pinch herself.

The coffee was cold when they finally sat down, this time side by side, her hand in Noah's.

'Who needs coffee anyway?' Noah grinned. 'I've got you.'

He loved her. He really did. It had been so easy to tell him she loved him. After a night of tears and anger and frustration over his blunt proposal yesterday, she'd accepted his love and offered hers in return. No questions, no doubts. She stared at this man who'd changed her life in so many ways. This would never have happened if he hadn't returned from Auckland.

'Stop overthinking it, Stacey. We will work through everything—together.' He paused and looked away, then back at her. 'I've spent my life looking for the kind of love my parents shared. I was always a part of that and to lose them meant I lost love as well. Then I met you. We danced and made love, then I went away. That night I felt a tingle of anticipation I'd not known before. Throughout those years I dreamt that you were with me, making love or dancing as we'd done that night.

'When we met again those feelings returned, stronger than ever. Yet I hesitated, wary of being hurt again, of being used for what I had and not who I am. Yesterday when I asked you to marry me I meant it, but I admit my doubts were exposing themselves, causing me to voice things I'd never intended to. I'm so sorry.'

Squeezing his hand, Stacey leaned in to brush a kiss over his mouth. 'It's all right. We got there in the end.' She took her time with what she had to say. 'About your wealth. It isn't something I'm after. If anything, it frightens me a little. But I'm sure I'll manage.' She smiled. 'Seriously, it's more important that we're happy, and that Holly's happy and grows up knowing she's loved by her parents. And that we love each other.'

'We do. She will.' His look was fierce, and protective.

Stacey sighed with happiness. All was good, very good, and she'd found her man was on the same page as her. 'I love you, Noah Kennedy.' And she kissed him like they had all the time in the world. Which they did because they had found each other and would be together for ever.

* * * * *

COMING SOON!

WE'RE LOOKING FOR NEW AUTHORS FOR THE MILLS & BOON MEDICAL SERIES!

Whether you're a published author or an aspiring one, our editors would love to read your story.

You can submit the synopsis and first three chapters of your novel online, and find out more about the series, at **harlequin.submittable.com/submit**

We read all submissions and you do not need to have an agent to submit.

IF YOU'RE INTERESTED, WHY NOT HAVE A GO?

Submit your story at:
harlequin.submittable.com/submit

MILLS & BOON